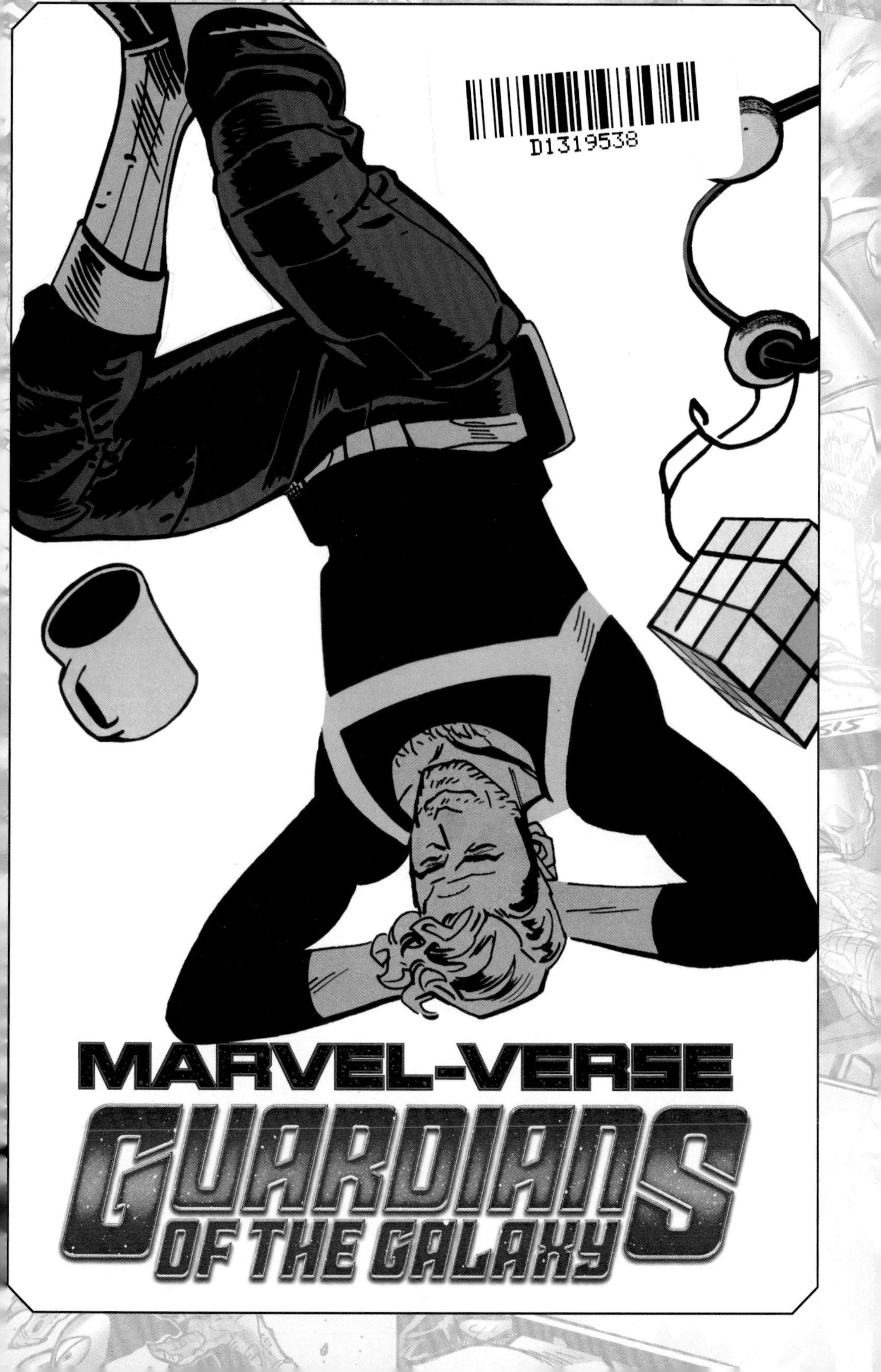

MARVEL-VERSE
GUARDIANS OF THE GALAXY

MA VEL-VERS
GUARDIANS OF THE GALAXY

GUARDIANS TEAM-UP #1

WRITER: **BRIAN MICHAEL BENDIS**
PENCILER: **ARTHUR ADAMS**
COLORIST: **PAUL MOUNTS**
LETTERER: **VC's CORY PETIT**
COVER ART: **ARTHUR ADAMS**
& **IAN HERRING**
EDITOR: **KATIE KUBERT**
GROUP EDITOR: **MIKE MARTS**

SPECIAL THANKS TO JOYCE CHIN

GUARDIANS TEAM-UP #2

WRITER: **BRIAN MICHAEL BENDIS**
PENCILER: **STÉPHANE ROUX**
INKER: **JAY LEISTEN**
COLORIST: **BRETT SMITH**
LETTERER: **VC's CORY PETIT**
COVER ART: **STÉPHANE ROUX**
ASSISTANT EDITOR: **XANDER JAROWEY**
EDITOR: **KATIE KUBERT**
GROUP EDITOR: **MIKE MARTS**

MARVEL-VERSE: GUARDIANS OF THE GALAXY. Contains material originally published in magazine form as GUARDIANS TEAM-UP (2015) #1-2, GUARDIANS OF THE GALAXY: DREAM ON (2017) #1, GUARDIANS OF THE GALAXY: GALAXY'S MOST WANTED (2017) #1 and ALL-NEW GUARDIANS OF THE GALAXY (2017) #5. First printing 2023. ISBN 978-1-302-95070-5. Published by MARVEL WORLDWIDE, INC., a subsidiary of MARVEL ENTERTAINMENT, LLC. OFFICE OF PUBLICATION: 1290 Avenue of the Americas, New York, NY 10104. © 2023 MARVEL No similarity between any of the names, characters, persons, and/or institutions in this book with those of any living or dead person or institution is intended, and any such similarity which may exist is purely coincidental. **Printed in Canada.** KEVIN FEIGE, Chief Creative Officer; DAN BUCKLEY, President, Marvel Entertainment; DAVID BOGART, Associate Publisher & SVP of Talent Affairs; TOM BREVOORT, VP, Executive Editor; NICK LOWE, Executive Editor, VP of Content, Digital Publishing; DAVID GABRIEL, VP of Print & Digital Publishing; SVEN LARSEN, VP of Licensed Publishing; JEFF YOUNGQUIST, VP of Production & Special Projects; JENNIFER GRÜNWALD, Director of Production & Special Projects; SUSAN CRESPI, Production Manager; STAN LEE, Chairman Emeritus. For information regarding advertising in Marvel Comics or on Marvel.com, please contact Vit DeBellis, Custom Solutions & Integrated Advertising Manager, at vdebellis@marvel.com. For Marvel subscription inquiries, please call 888-511-5480. **Manufactured between 1/20/2023 and 2/21/2023 by SOLISCO PRINTERS, SCOTT, QC, CANADA.**

10 9 8 7 6 5 4 3 2 1

GUARDIANS OF THE GALAXY: DREAM ON

WRITER: **MARC SUMERAK**

ARTIST: **ANDREA DI VITO**

COLORIST: **LAURA VILLARI**

LETTERER: VC's **TRAVIS LANHAM**

COVER ART: **MICHAEL RYAN & JAVIER MENA GUERRERO**

EDITOR: **MARK BASSO**

GUARDIANS OF THE GALAXY: GALAXY'S MOST WANTED

WRITER: **WILL CORONA PILGRIM**

ARTIST: **ANDREA DI VITO**

COLORIST: **LAURA VILLARI**

LETTERER: VC's **CLAYTON COWLES**

COVER ART: **JEEHYUNG LEE**

ASSISTANT EDITOR: **MARK BASSO**

EDITOR: **BILL ROSEMANN**

MARVEL STUDIOS:
VP PRODUCTION & DEVELOPMENT: **JONATHAN SCHWARTZ**

SVP PRODUCTION & DEVELOPMENT: **JEREMY LATCHAM**

PRESIDENT: **KEVIN FEIGE**

ALL-NEW GUARDIANS OF THE GALAXY #5

WRITER: **GERRY DUGGAN**

ARTIST: **CHRIS SAMNEE**

COLORIST: **MATTHEW WILSON**

LETTERER: VC's **CORY PETIT**

COVER ART: **AARON KUDER**

ASSISTANT EDITOR: **KATHLEEN WISNESKI**

ASSOCIATE EDITOR: **DARREN SHAN**

EDITOR: **JORDAN D. WHITE**

COLLECTION EDITOR: **JENNIFER GRÜNWALD** ASSISTANT EDITOR: **DANIEL KIRCHHOFFER**
ASSISTANT MANAGING EDITOR: **MAIA LOY** ASSOCIATE MANAGER, TALENT RELATIONS: **LISA MONTALBANO**
ASSOCIATE MANAGER, DIGITAL ASSETS: **JOE HOCHSTEIN** MASTERWORKS EDITOR: **CORY SEDLMEIER**
VP PRODUCTION & SPECIAL PROJECTS: **JEFF YOUNGQUIST** RESEARCH: **JESS HARROLD**
BOOK DESIGNER: **SARAH SPADACCINI** SENIOR DESIGNER: **JAY BOWEN**
SVP PRINT, SALES & MARKETING: **DAVID GABRIEL** EDITOR IN CHIEF: **C.B. CEBULSKI**

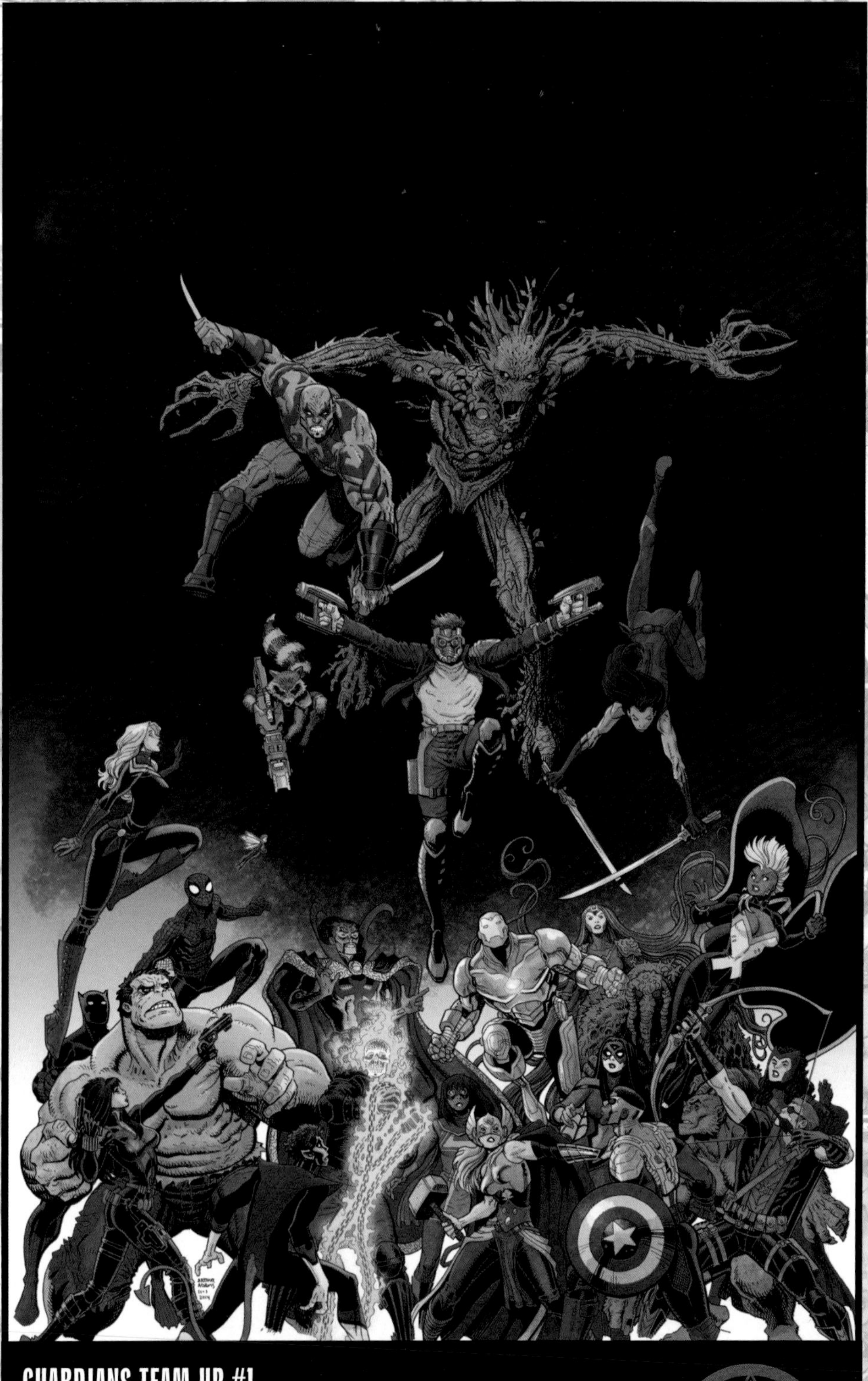

GUARDIANS TEAM-UP #1

TWO TITANIC TEAMS UNITE AS THE GUARDIANS OF THE GALAXY ASSEMBLE WITH THE AVENGERS TO FACE A COSMIC THREAT!

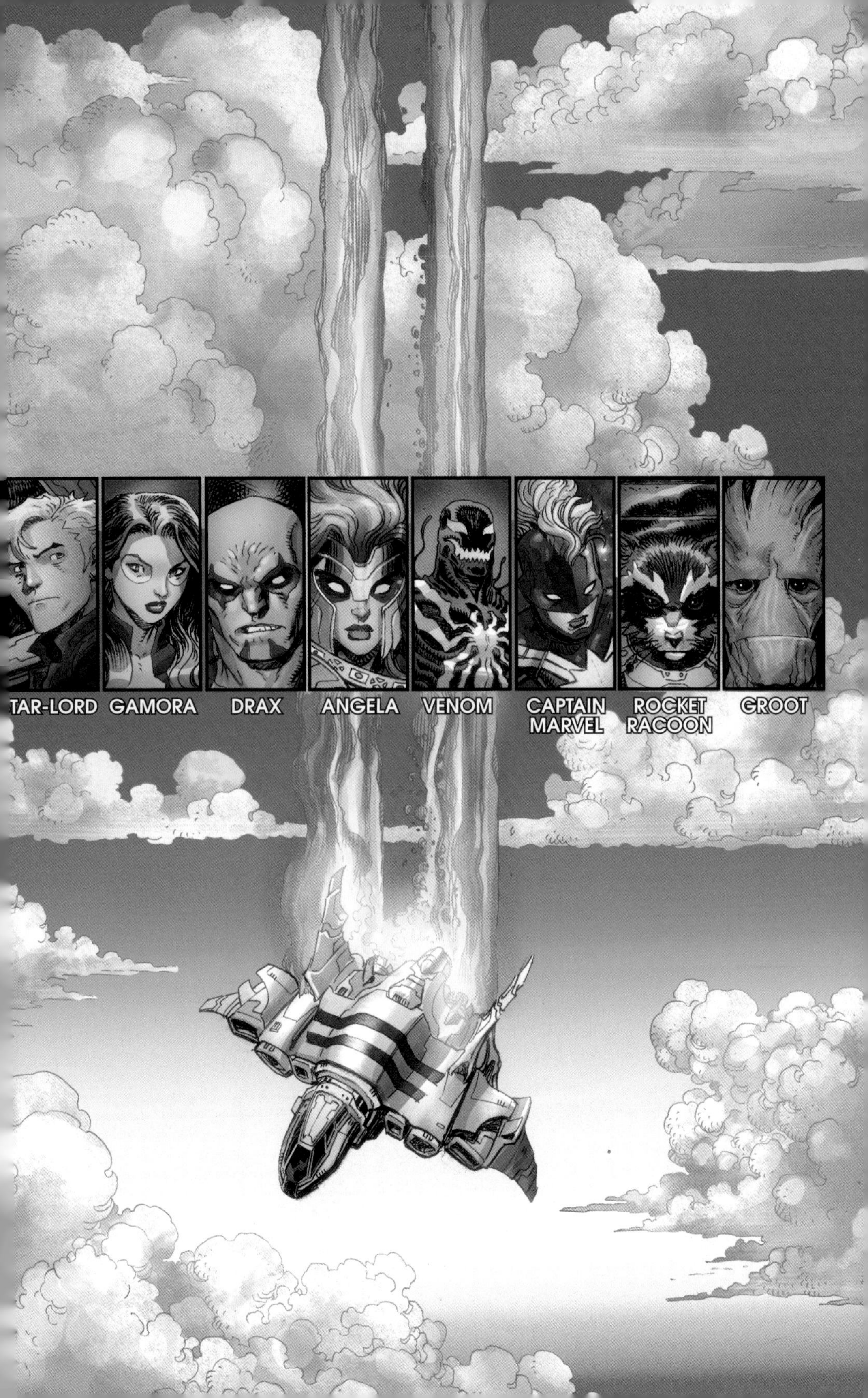
TAR-LORD
GAMORA
DRAX
ANGELA
VENOM
CAPTAIN MARVEL
ROCKET RACOON
GROOT

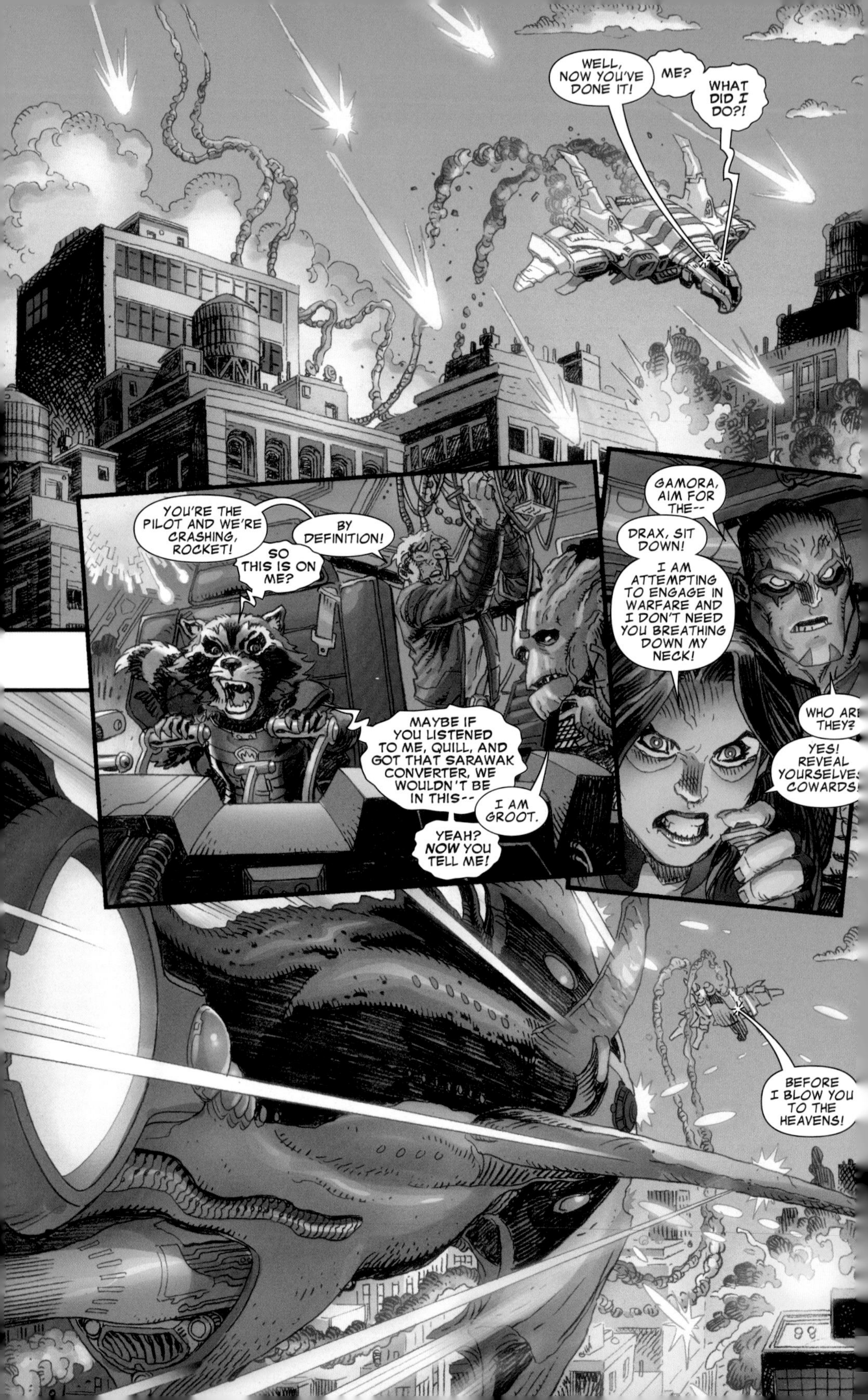
WELL, NOW YOU'VE DONE IT!
ME?
WHAT DID I DO?!
YOU'RE THE PILOT AND WE'RE CRASHING, ROCKET!
BY DEFINITION!
SO THIS IS ON ME?
MAYBE IF YOU LISTENED TO ME, QUILL, AND GOT THAT SARAWAK CONVERTER, WE WOULDN'T BE IN THIS--
I AM GROOT.
YEAH? NOW YOU TELL ME!
GAMORA, AIM FOR THE--
DRAX, SIT DOWN!
I AM ATTEMPTING TO ENGAGE IN WARFARE AND I DON'T NEED YOU BREATHING DOWN MY NECK!
YES! REVEAL YOURSELVES, COWARDS!
BEFORE I BLOW YOU TO THE HEAVENS!

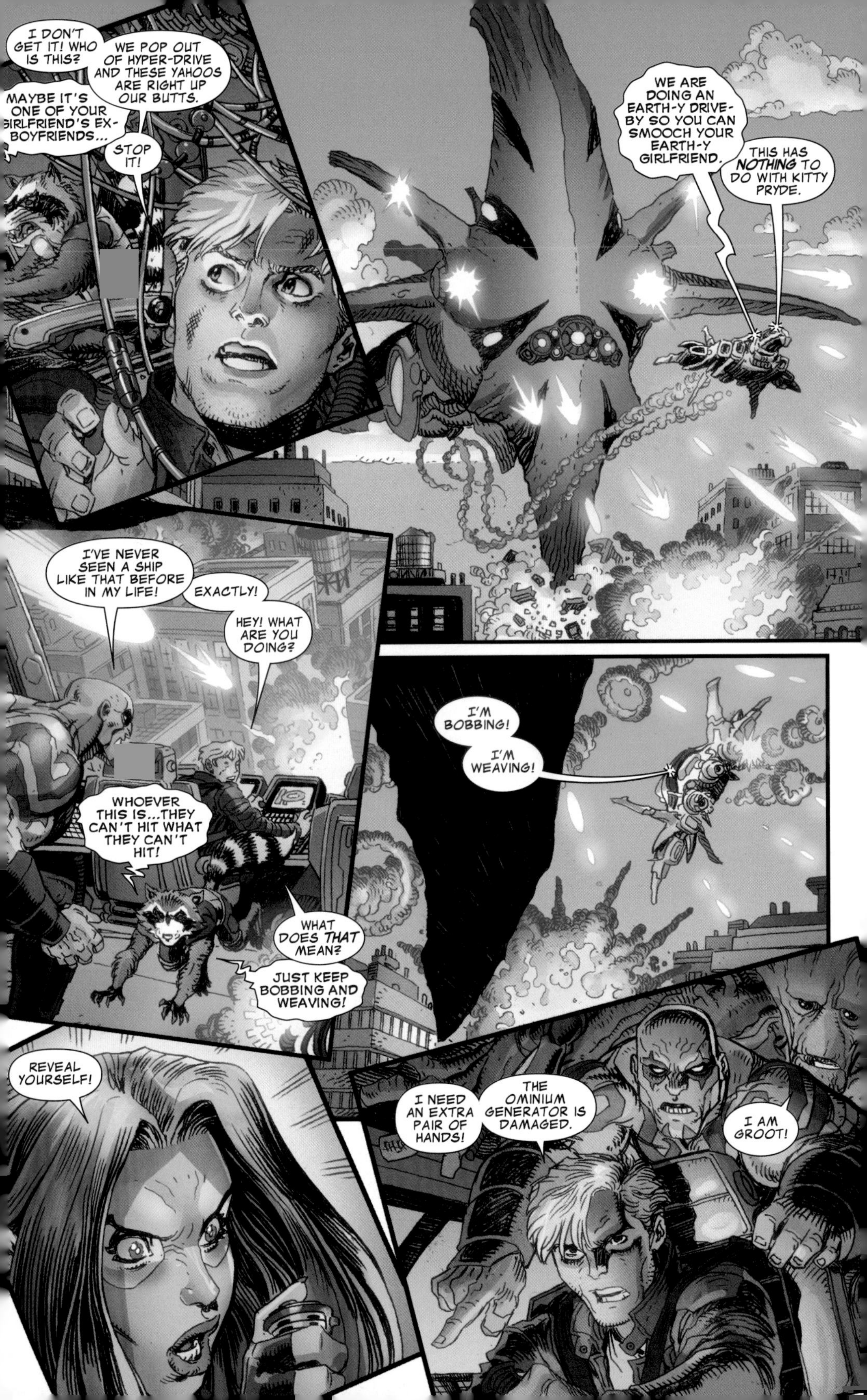
I DON'T GET IT! WHO IS THIS?
WE POP OUT OF HYPER-DRIVE AND THESE YAHOOS ARE RIGHT UP OUR BUTTS.
MAYBE IT'S ONE OF YOUR GIRLFRIEND'S EX-BOYFRIENDS...
STOP IT!
WE ARE DOING AN EARTH-Y DRIVE-BY SO YOU CAN SMOOCH YOUR EARTH-Y GIRLFRIEND.
THIS HAS NOTHING TO DO WITH KITTY PRYDE.
I'VE NEVER SEEN A SHIP LIKE THAT BEFORE IN MY LIFE!
EXACTLY!
HEY! WHAT ARE YOU DOING?
WHOEVER THIS IS...THEY CAN'T HIT WHAT THEY CAN'T HIT!
WHAT DOES THAT MEAN?
JUST KEEP BOBBING AND WEAVING!
I'M BOBBING!
I'M WEAVING!
REVEAL YOURSELF!
I NEED AN EXTRA PAIR OF HANDS!
THE OMINIUM GENERATOR IS DAMAGED.
I AM GROOT!

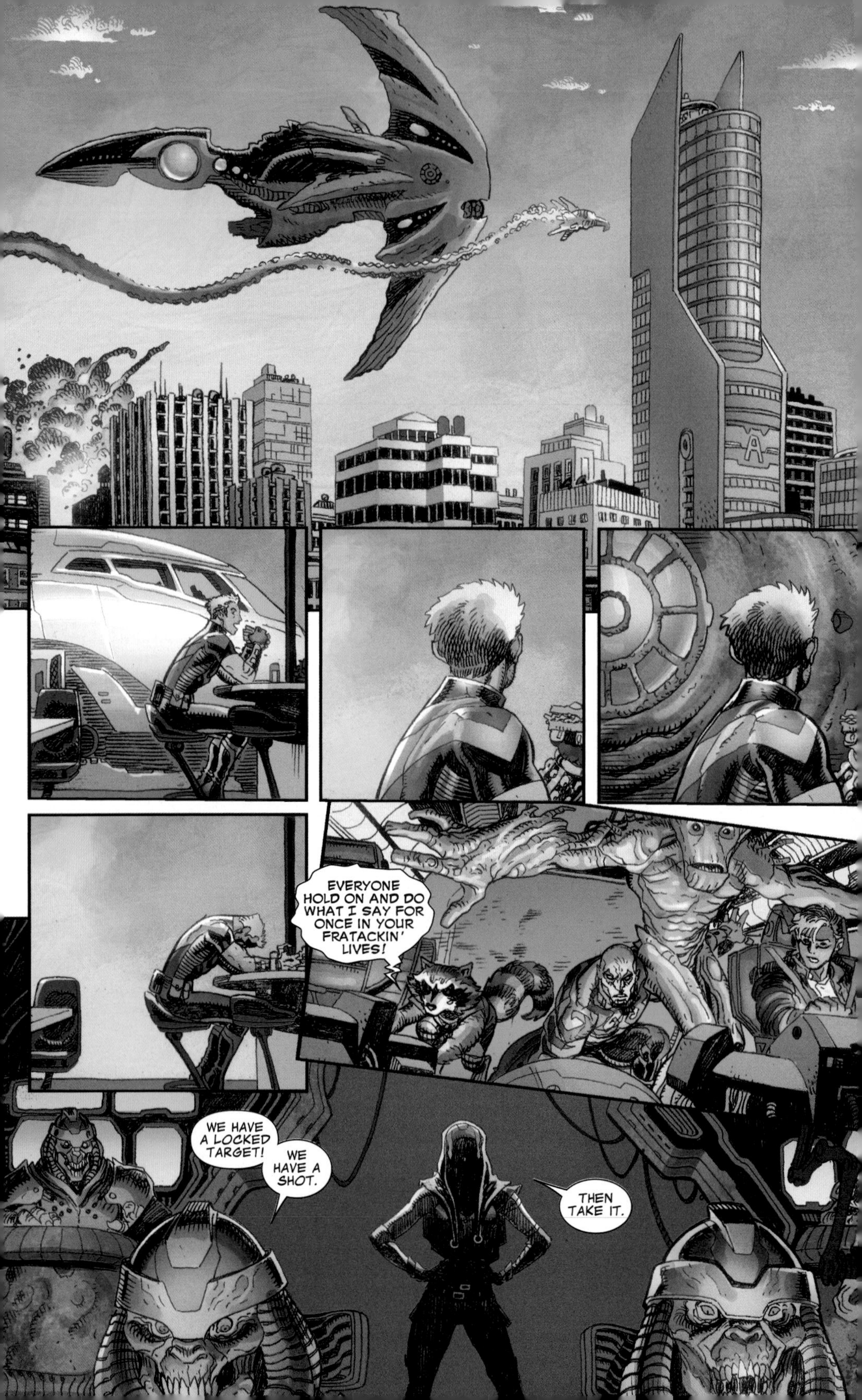
EVERYONE HOLD ON AND DO WHAT I SAY FOR ONCE IN YOUR FRATACKIN' LIVES!
WE HAVE A LOCKED TARGET!
WE HAVE A SHOT.
THEN TAKE IT.

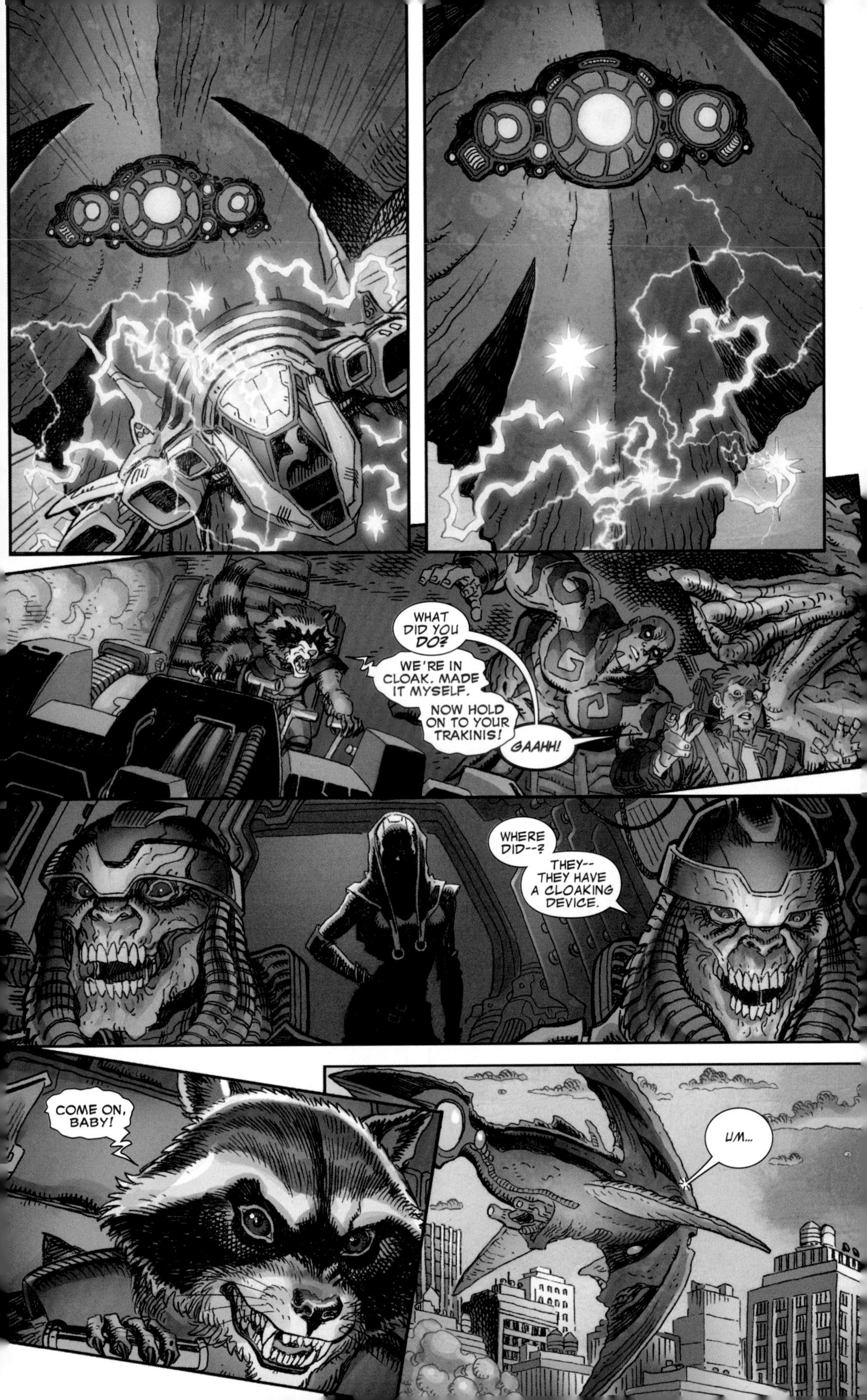
WHAT DID YOU DO?
WE'RE IN CLOAK. MADE IT MYSELF.
NOW HOLD ON TO YOUR TRAKINIS!
GAAHH!
WHERE DID--?
THEY-- THEY HAVE A CLOAKING DEVICE.
COME ON, BABY!
UM...

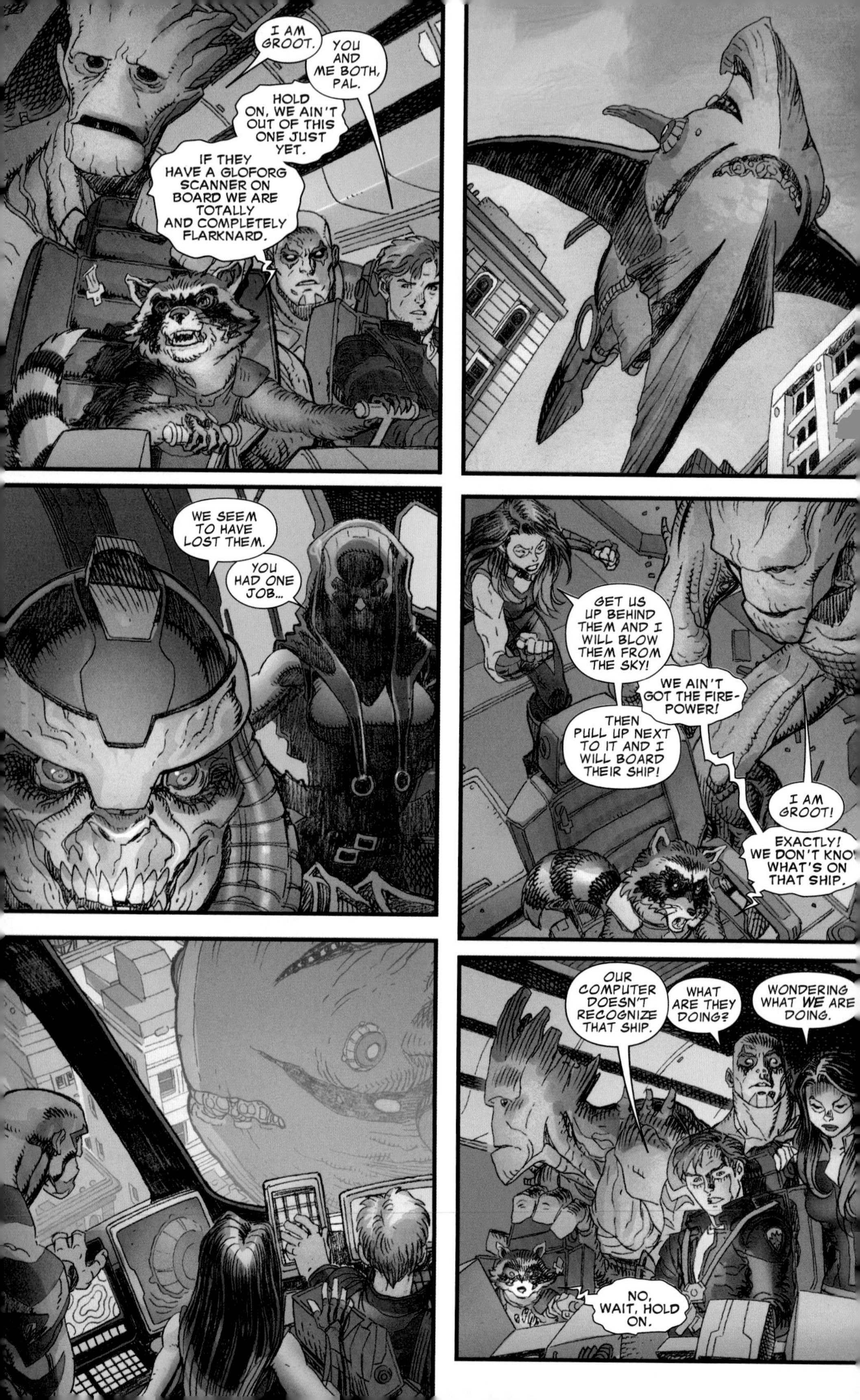
I AM GROOT.
YOU AND ME BOTH, PAL.
HOLD ON, WE AIN'T OUT OF THIS ONE JUST YET.
IF THEY HAVE A GLOFORG SCANNER ON BOARD WE ARE TOTALLY AND COMPLETELY FLARKNARD.
WE SEEM TO HAVE LOST THEM.
YOU HAD ONE JOB...
GET US UP BEHIND THEM AND I WILL BLOW THEM FROM THE SKY!
WE AIN'T GOT THE FIRE-POWER!
THEN PULL UP NEXT TO IT AND I WILL BOARD THEIR SHIP!
I AM GROOT!
EXACTLY! WE DON'T KNO WHAT'S ON THAT SHIP.
OUR COMPUTER DOESN'T RECOGNIZE THAT SHIP.
WHAT ARE THEY DOING?
WONDERING WHAT WE ARE DOING.
NO, WAIT, HOLD ON.

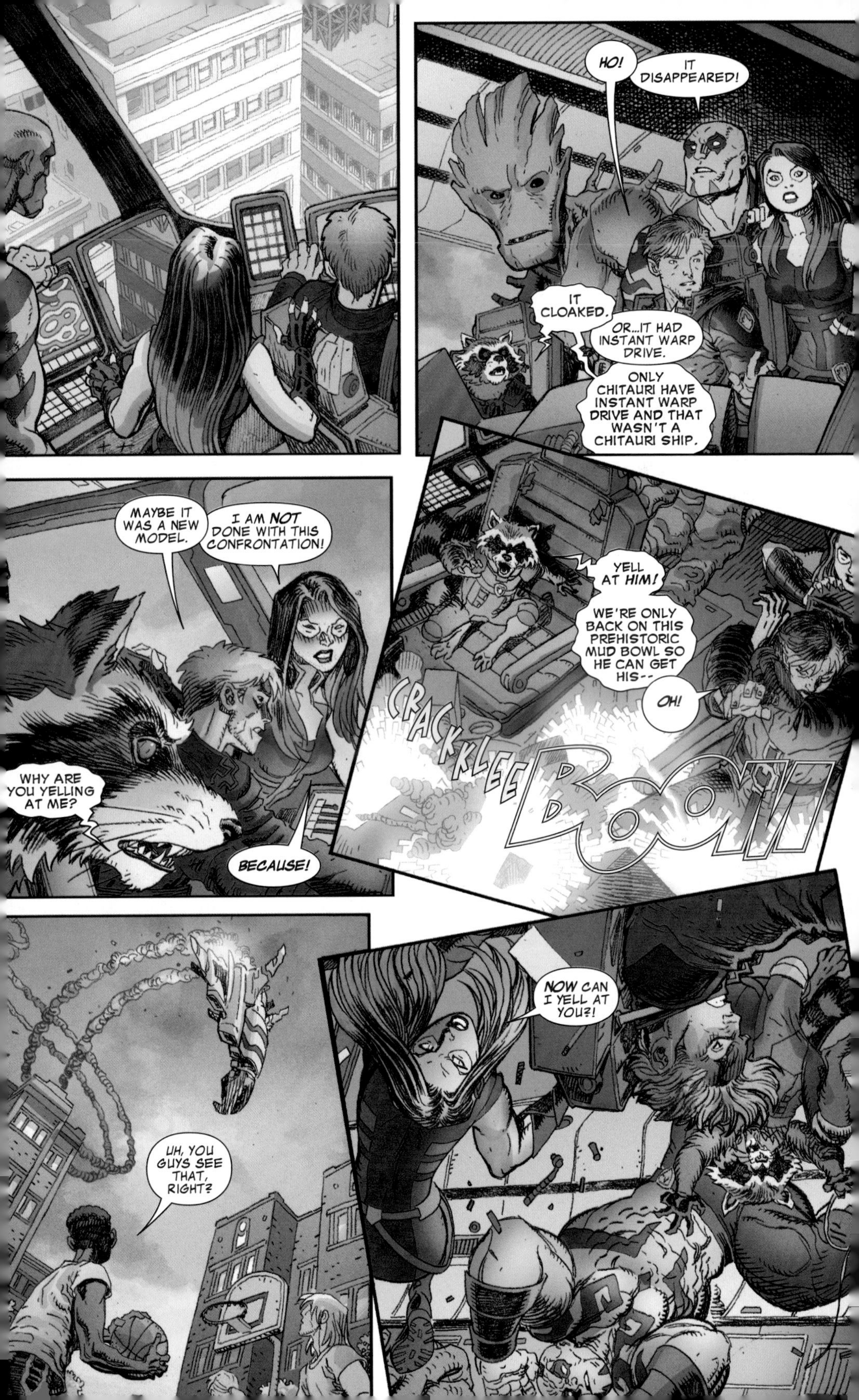
HO!
IT DISAPPEARED!
IT CLOAKED.
OR...IT HAD INSTANT WARP DRIVE.
ONLY CHITAURI HAVE INSTANT WARP DRIVE AND THAT WASN'T A CHITAURI SHIP.
MAYBE IT WAS A NEW MODEL.
I AM NOT DONE WITH THIS CONFRONTATION!
WHY ARE YOU YELLING AT ME?
BECAUSE!
YELL AT HIM!
WE'RE ONLY BACK ON THIS PREHISTORIC MUD BOWL SO HE CAN GET HIS--
OH!
CRACKKLEEBOOM!!
UH, YOU GUYS SEE THAT, RIGHT?
NOW CAN I YELL AT YOU?!

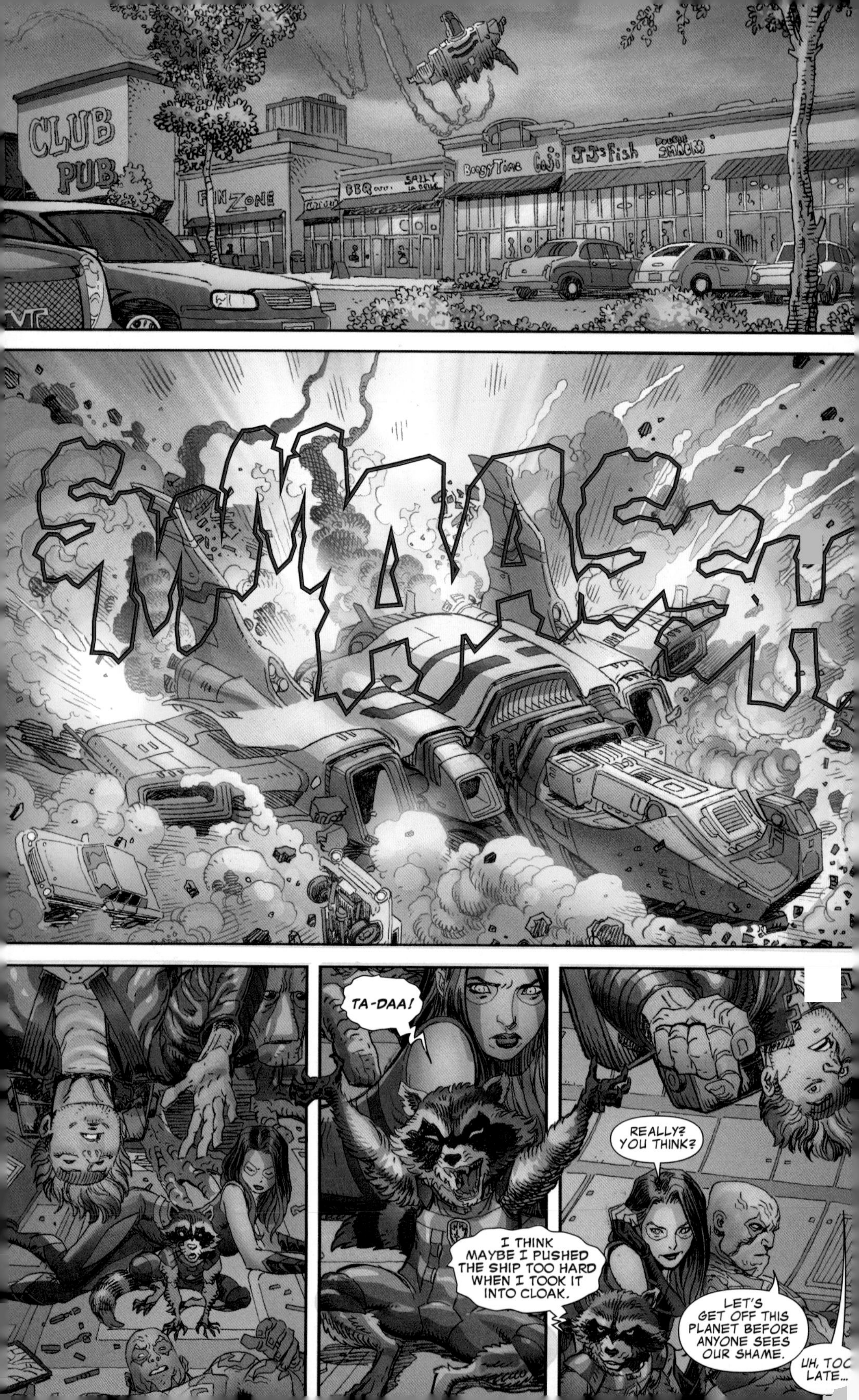
CLUB PUB
FUN ZONE
JJ's Fish
SMMASH
TA-DAA!
I THINK MAYBE I PUSHED THE SHIP TOO HARD WHEN I TOOK IT INTO CLOAK.
REALLY? YOU THINK?
LET'S GET OFF THIS PLANET BEFORE ANYONE SEES OUR SHAME.
UH, TOO LATE...

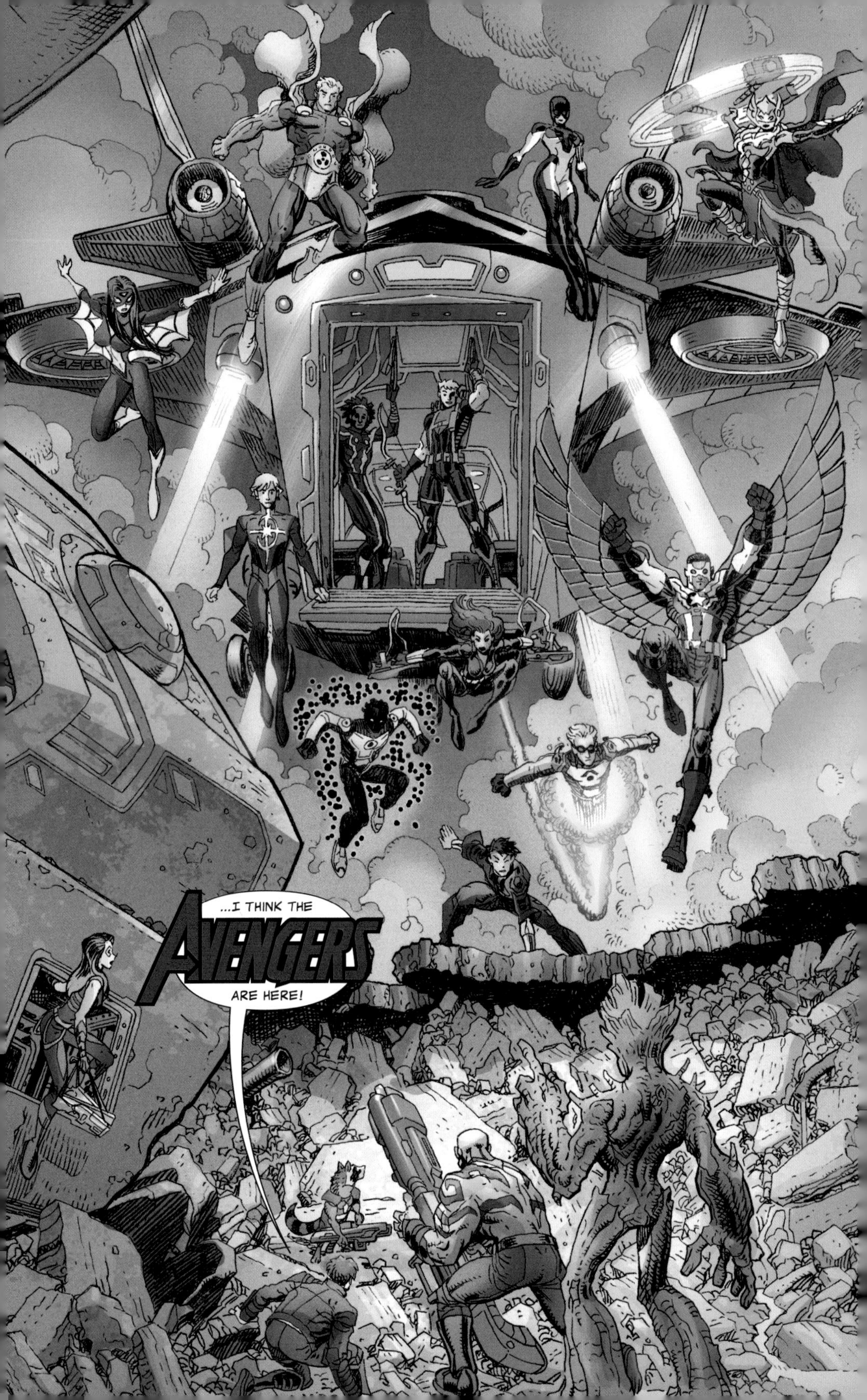
...I THINK THE
AVENGERS
ARE HERE!

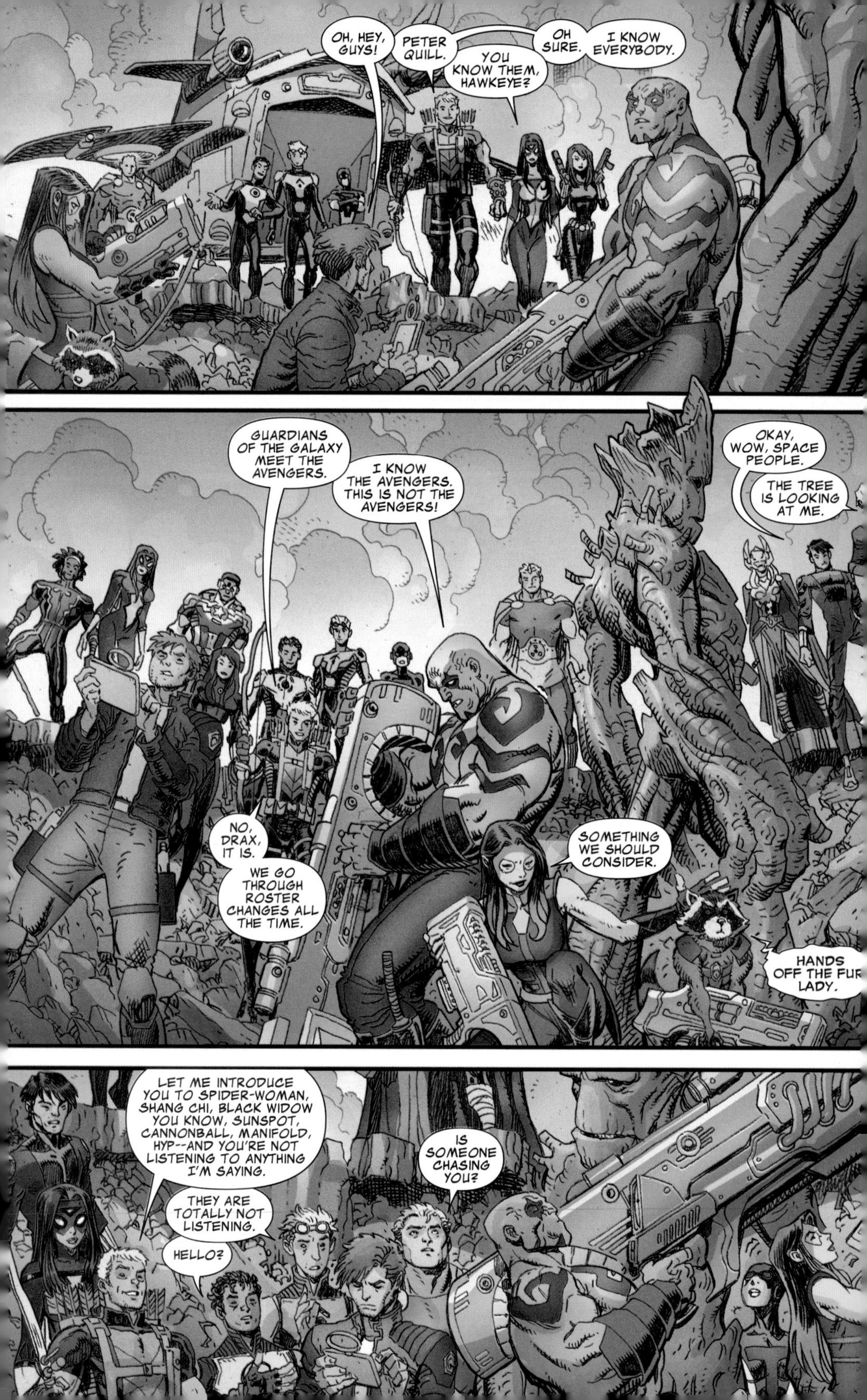
OH, HEY, GUYS!
PETER QUILL.
YOU KNOW THEM, HAWKEYE?
OH SURE.
I KNOW EVERYBODY.
GUARDIANS OF THE GALAXY MEET THE AVENGERS.
I KNOW THE AVENGERS. THIS IS NOT THE AVENGERS!
OKAY, WOW, SPACE PEOPLE.
THE TREE IS LOOKING AT ME.
NO, DRAX, IT IS.
WE GO THROUGH ROSTER CHANGES ALL THE TIME.
SOMETHING WE SHOULD CONSIDER.
HANDS OFF THE FUR LADY.
LET ME INTRODUCE YOU TO SPIDER-WOMAN, SHANG CHI, BLACK WIDOW YOU KNOW, SUNSPOT, CANNONBALL, MANIFOLD, HYP--AND YOU'RE NOT LISTENING TO ANYTHING I'M SAYING.
IS SOMEONE CHASING YOU?
THEY ARE TOTALLY NOT LISTENING.
HELLO?

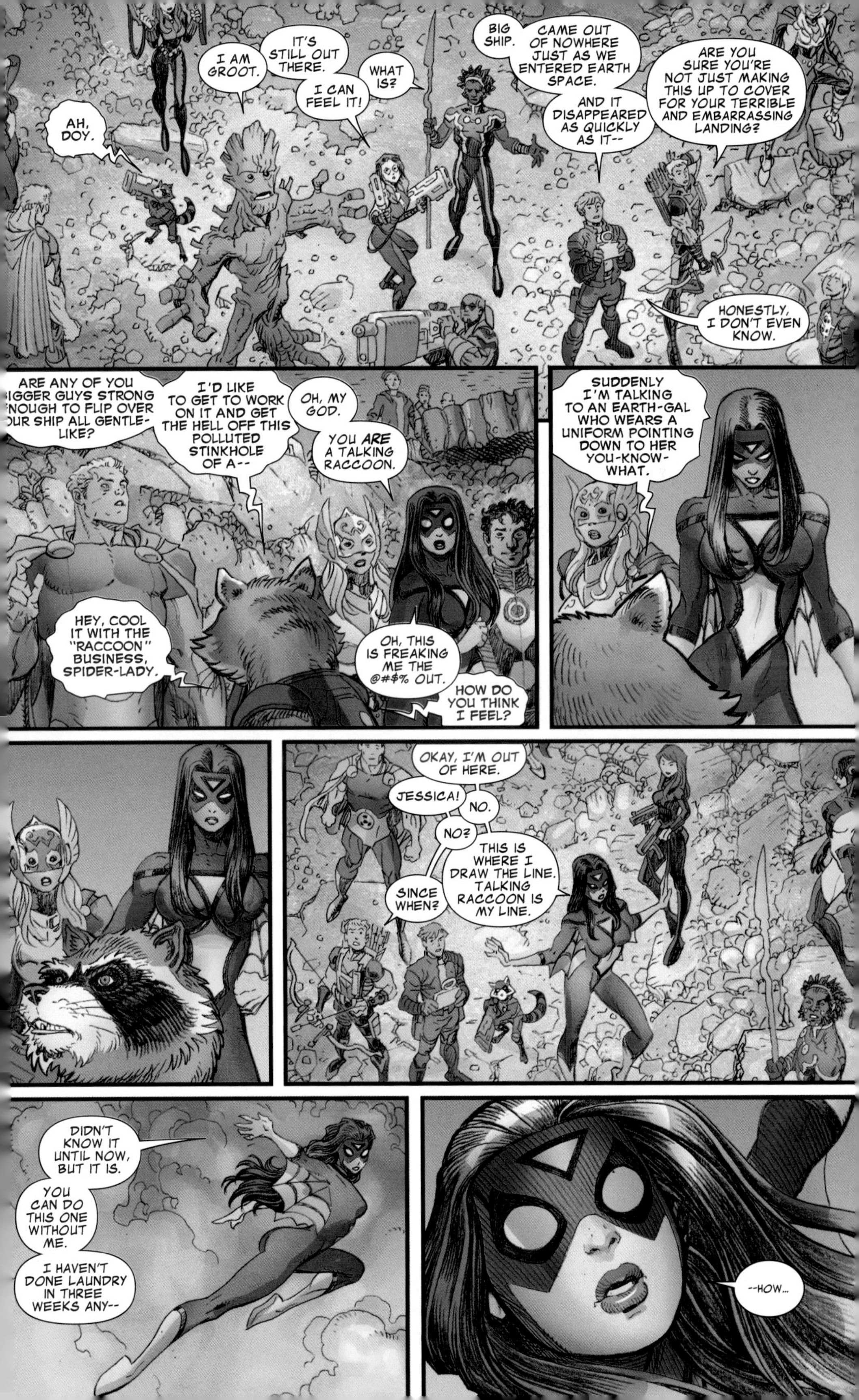
AH, DOY.
I AM GROOT.
IT'S STILL OUT THERE.
I CAN FEEL IT!
WHAT IS?
BIG SHIP.
CAME OUT OF NOWHERE JUST AS WE ENTERED EARTH SPACE.
AND IT DISAPPEARED AS QUICKLY AS IT--
ARE YOU SURE YOU'RE NOT JUST MAKING THIS UP TO COVER FOR YOUR TERRIBLE AND EMBARRASSING LANDING?
HONESTLY, I DON'T EVEN KNOW.
ARE ANY OF YOU IGGER GUYS STRONG NOUGH TO FLIP OVER UR SHIP ALL GENTLE-LIKE?
I'D LIKE TO GET TO WORK ON IT AND GET THE HELL OFF THIS POLLUTED STINKHOLE OF A--
OH, MY GOD.
YOU ARE A TALKING RACCOON.
HEY, COOL IT WITH THE "RACCOON" BUSINESS, SPIDER-LADY.
OH, THIS IS FREAKING ME THE @#$% OUT.
HOW DO YOU THINK I FEEL?
SUDDENLY I'M TALKING TO AN EARTH-GAL WHO WEARS A UNIFORM POINTING DOWN TO HER YOU-KNOW-WHAT.
OKAY, I'M OUT OF HERE.
JESSICA!
NO.
NO?
THIS IS WHERE I DRAW THE LINE. TALKING RACCOON IS MY LINE.
SINCE WHEN?
DIDN'T KNOW IT UNTIL NOW, BUT IT IS.
YOU CAN DO THIS ONE WITHOUT ME.
I HAVEN'T DONE LAUNDRY IN THREE WEEKS ANY--
--HOW...

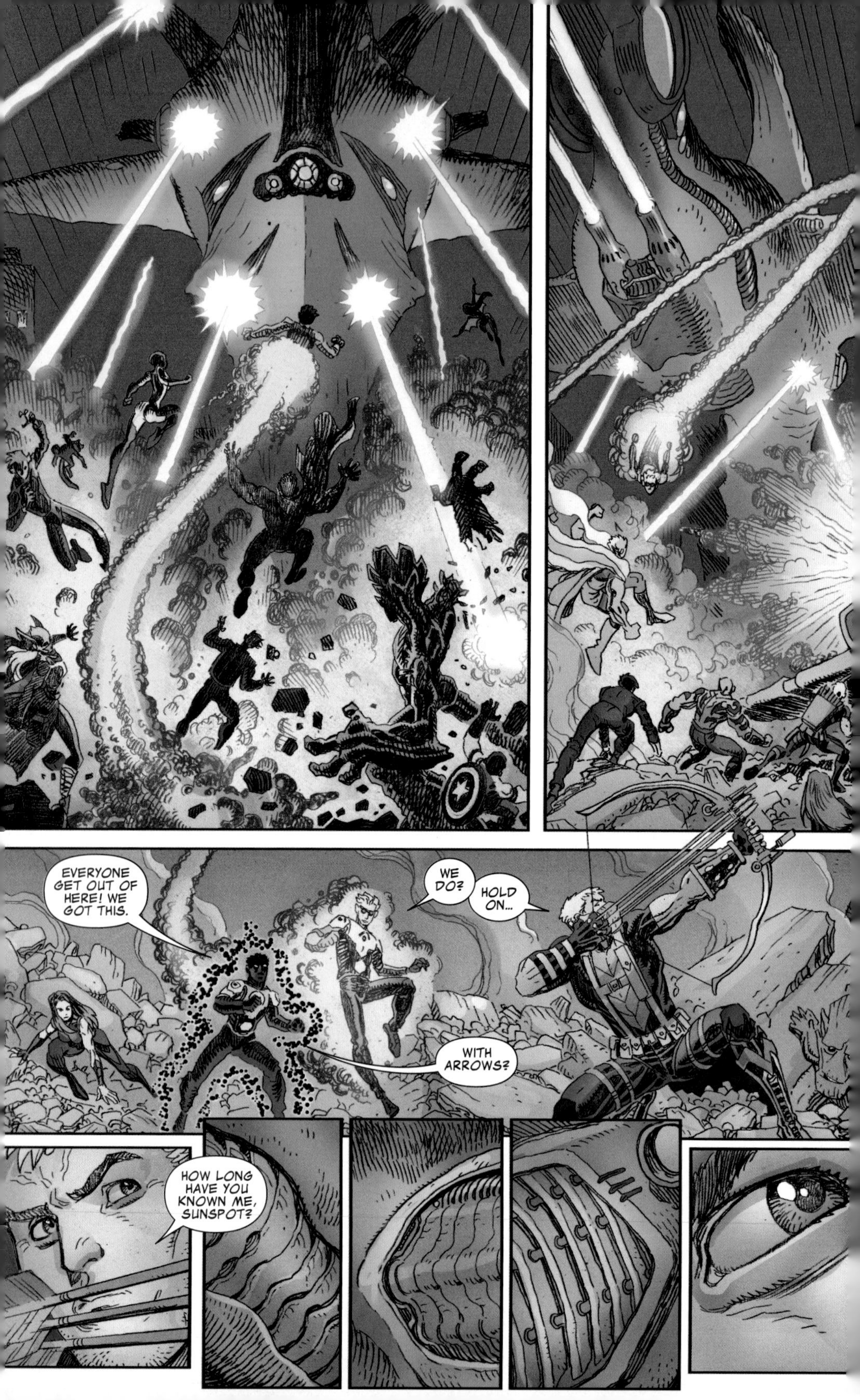
EVERYONE GET OUT OF HERE! WE GOT THIS.
WE DO?
HOLD ON...
WITH ARROWS?
HOW LONG HAVE YOU KNOWN ME, SUNSPOT?

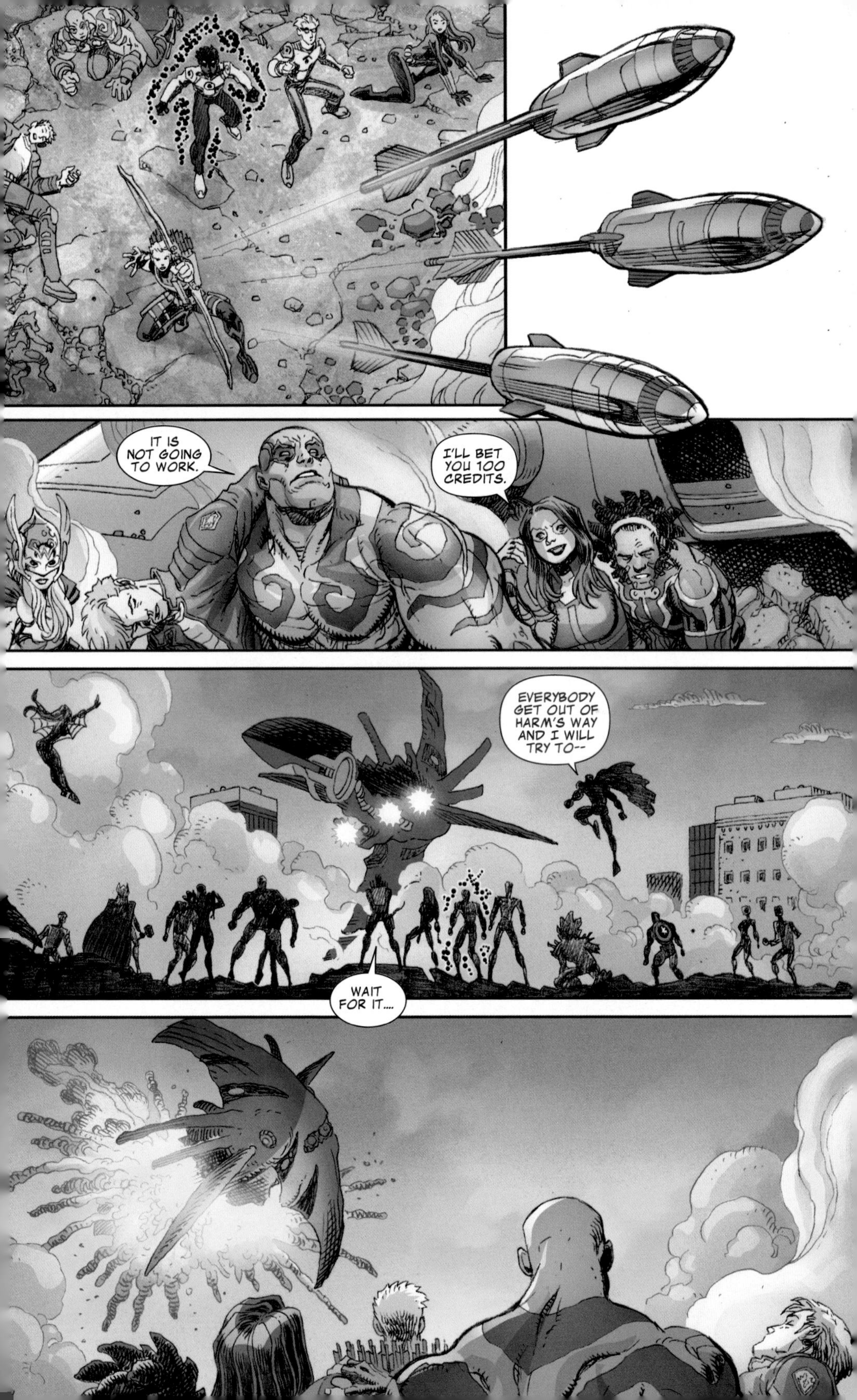
IT IS NOT GOING TO WORK.
I'LL BET YOU 100 CREDITS.
EVERYBODY GET OUT OF HARM'S WAY AND I WILL TRY TO--
WAIT FOR IT....

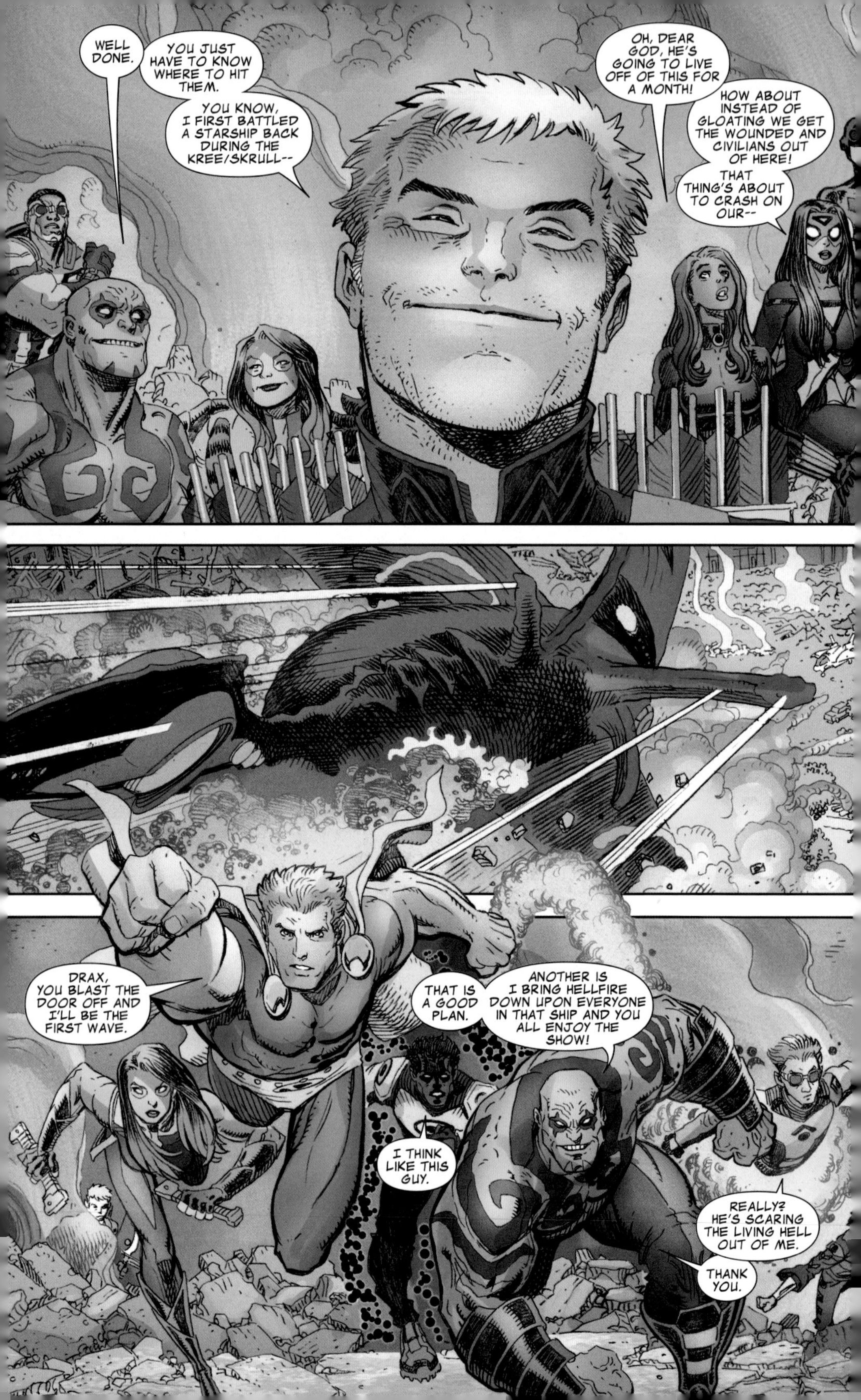
WELL DONE.
YOU JUST HAVE TO KNOW WHERE TO HIT THEM.
YOU KNOW, I FIRST BATTLED A STARSHIP BACK DURING THE KREE/SKRULL--
OH, DEAR GOD, HE'S GOING TO LIVE OFF OF THIS FOR A MONTH!
HOW ABOUT INSTEAD OF GLOATING WE GET THE WOUNDED AND CIVILIANS OUT OF HERE!
THAT THING'S ABOUT TO CRASH ON OUR--
DRAX, YOU BLAST THE DOOR OFF AND I'LL BE THE FIRST WAVE.
THAT IS A GOOD PLAN.
ANOTHER IS I BRING HELLFIRE DOWN UPON EVERYONE IN THAT SHIP AND YOU ALL ENJOY THE SHOW!
I THINK LIKE THIS GUY.
REALLY? HE'S SCARING THE LIVING HELL OUT OF ME.
THANK YOU.

CHITAURI!!

GESUNDHEIT!

HQVEX XQVAX SQX GXEGHX QYXQX

AXTEQY IE HEIXH XE QX HXXX

UGH!

WHASGOINON?

ALIEN BATTLE IN A STRIP MALL.

YOU KNOW, SAME OL'.

NO, FOOLISH EARTHER-BABY! CHITAURI!! THAT IS WHO CHALLENGES US.

OKAY, GEEZ, YOU DON'T HAVE TO BE A JERK ABOUT IT.

XCH

THIS ESCALATED QUICKLY.

I WAS JUST THINKING THAT.

WHO LEADS YOU DEMONS?

WHO IS YOUR MASTER?!

YOO-HOO!

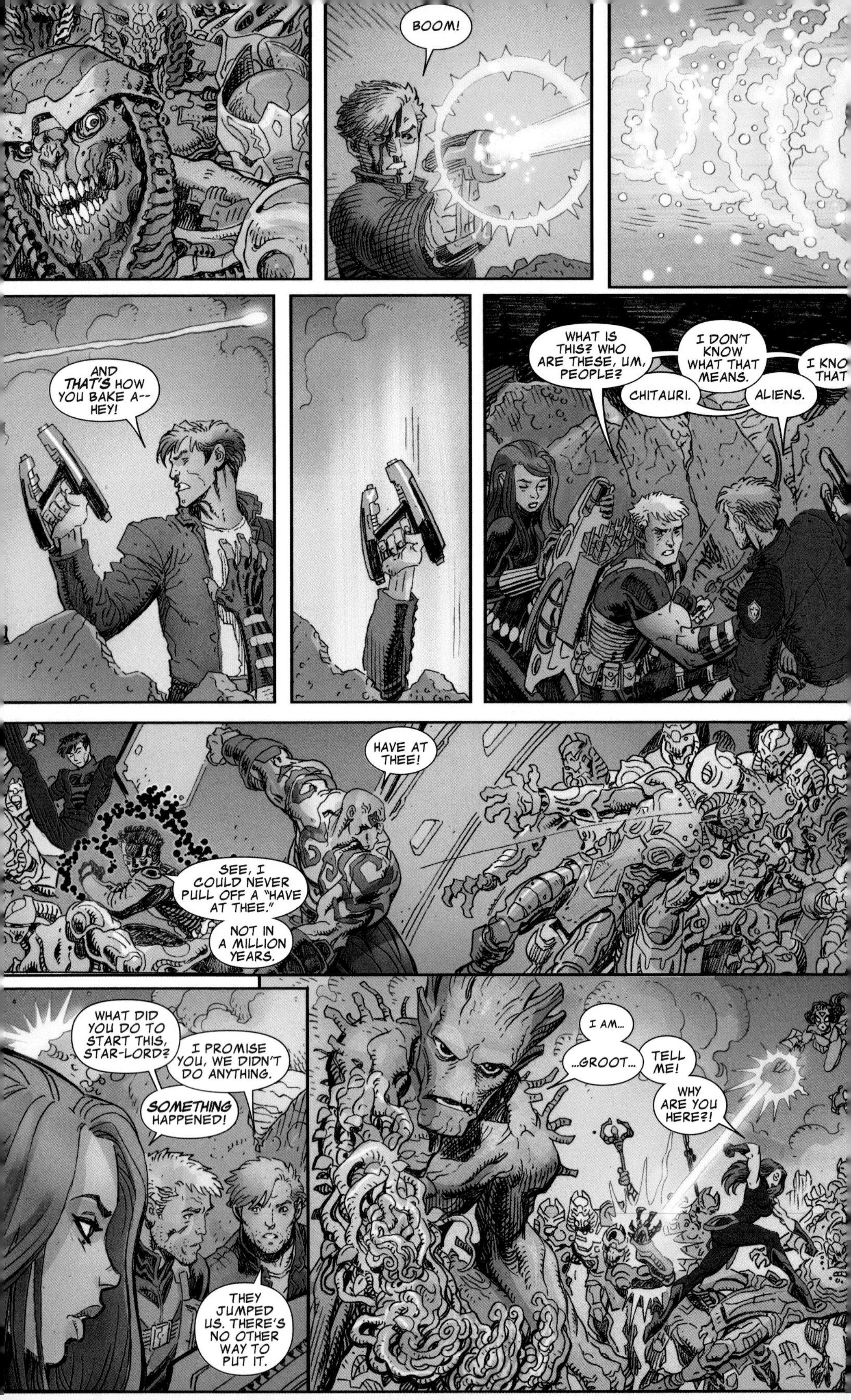
BOOM!
AND THAT'S HOW YOU BAKE A-- HEY!
WHAT IS THIS? WHO ARE THESE, UM, PEOPLE?
CHITAURI.
I DON'T KNOW WHAT THAT MEANS.
ALIENS.
I KNO THAT
HAVE AT THEE!
SEE, I COULD NEVER PULL OFF A "HAVE AT THEE."
NOT IN A MILLION YEARS.
WHAT DID YOU DO TO START THIS, STAR-LORD?
I PROMISE YOU, WE DIDN'T DO ANYTHING.
SOMETHING HAPPENED!
THEY JUMPED US. THERE'S NO OTHER WAY TO PUT IT.
I AM...
...GROOT...
TELL ME!
WHY ARE YOU HERE?!

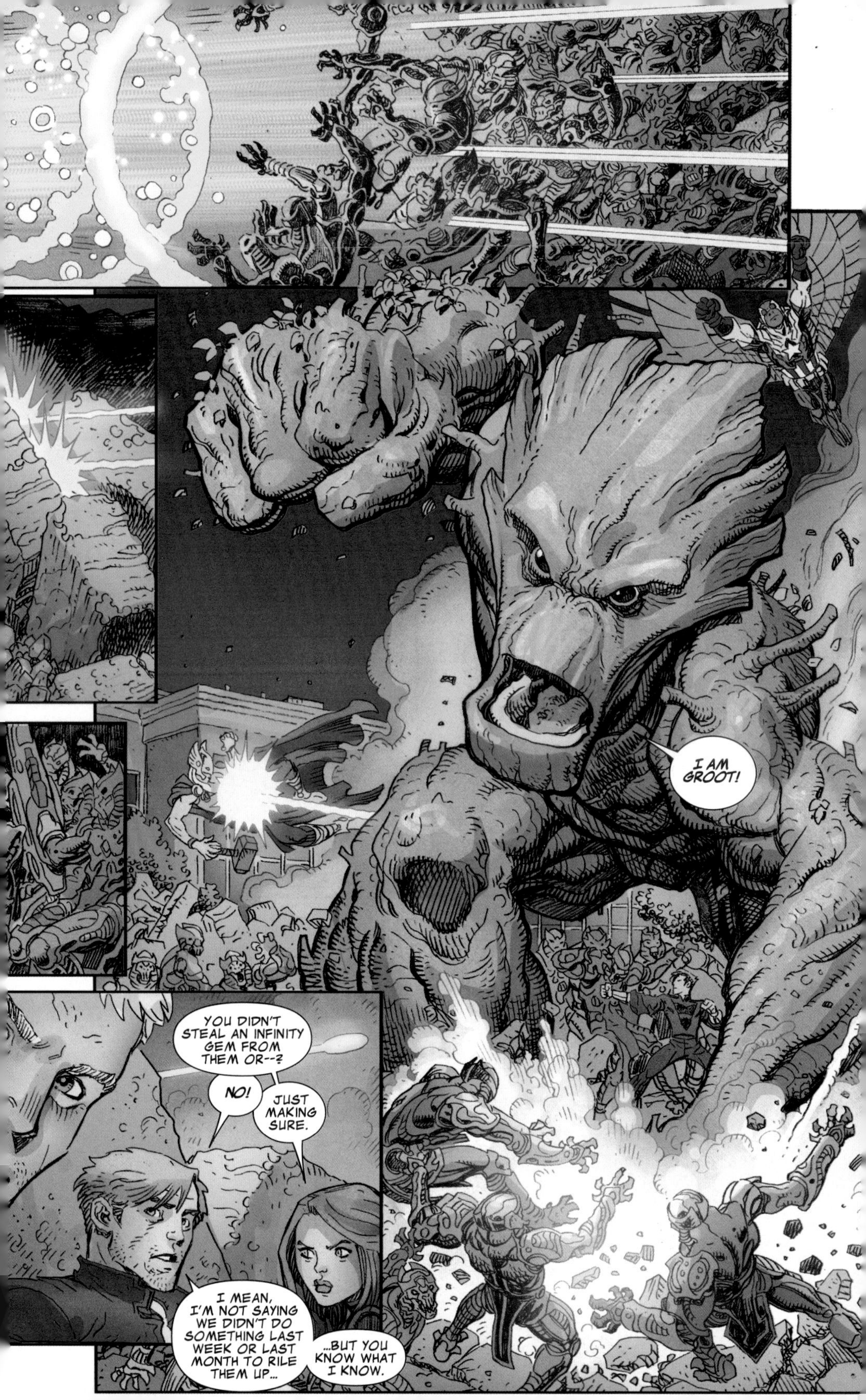
I AM GROOT!
YOU DIDN'T STEAL AN INFINITY GEM FROM THEM OR--?
NO!
JUST MAKING SURE.
I MEAN, I'M NOT SAYING WE DIDN'T DO SOMETHING LAST WEEK OR LAST MONTH TO RILE THEM UP...
...BUT YOU KNOW WHAT I KNOW.

WATCH IT, STARBRAND!

SORRY.

I AM GROOT!

WHY IS EVERYTHING A TEST? I THOUGHT YOU CHITAURI WERE BETTER THAN THIS.

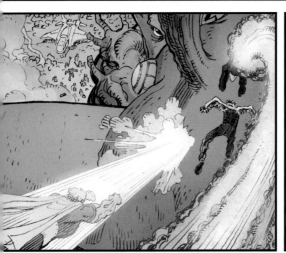

IS IT READY?

WELL, WHAT ARE YOU WAITING FOR?

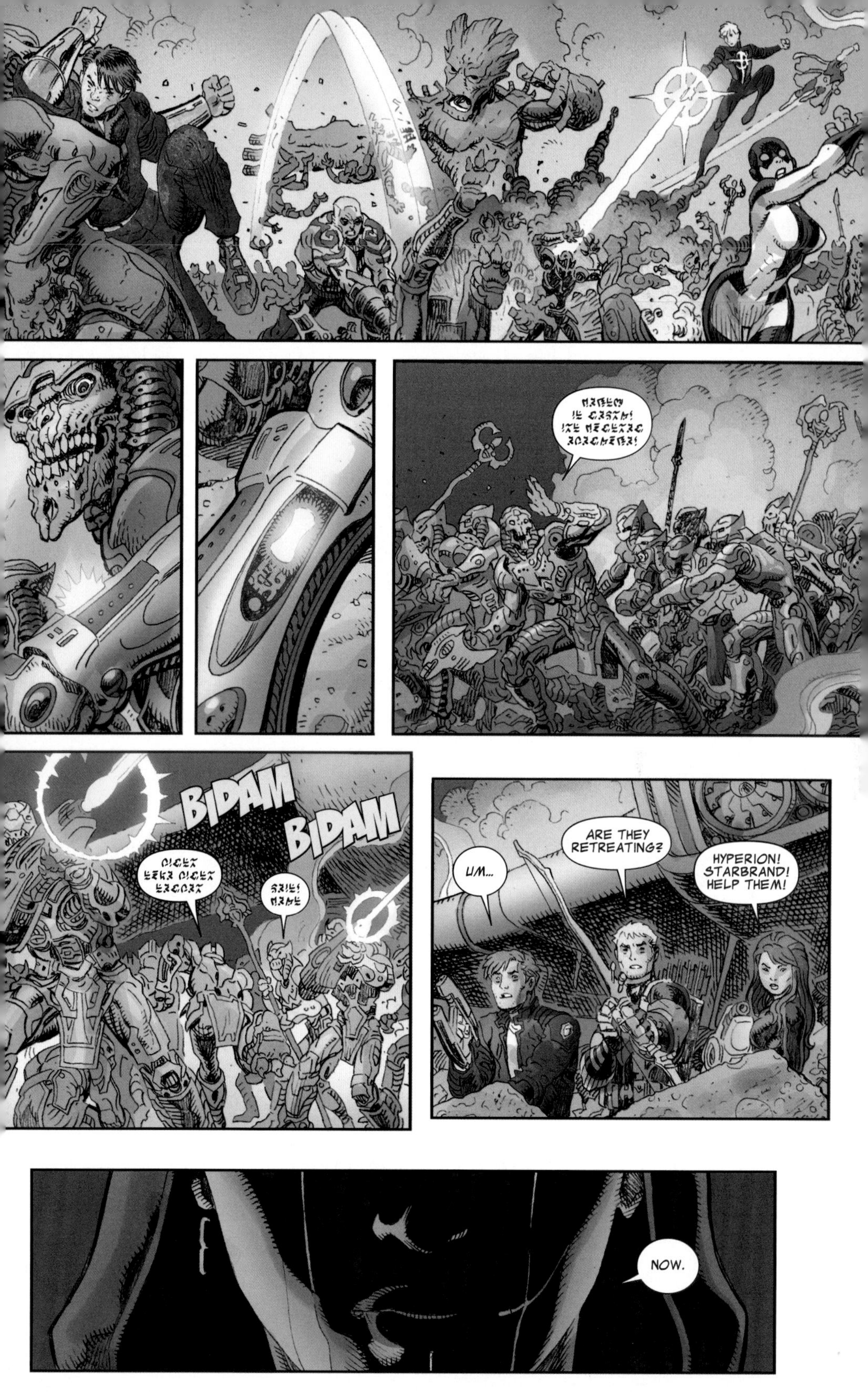
BIDAM
BIDAM
UM...
ARE THEY RETREATING?
HYPERION! STARBRAND! HELP THEM!
NOW.

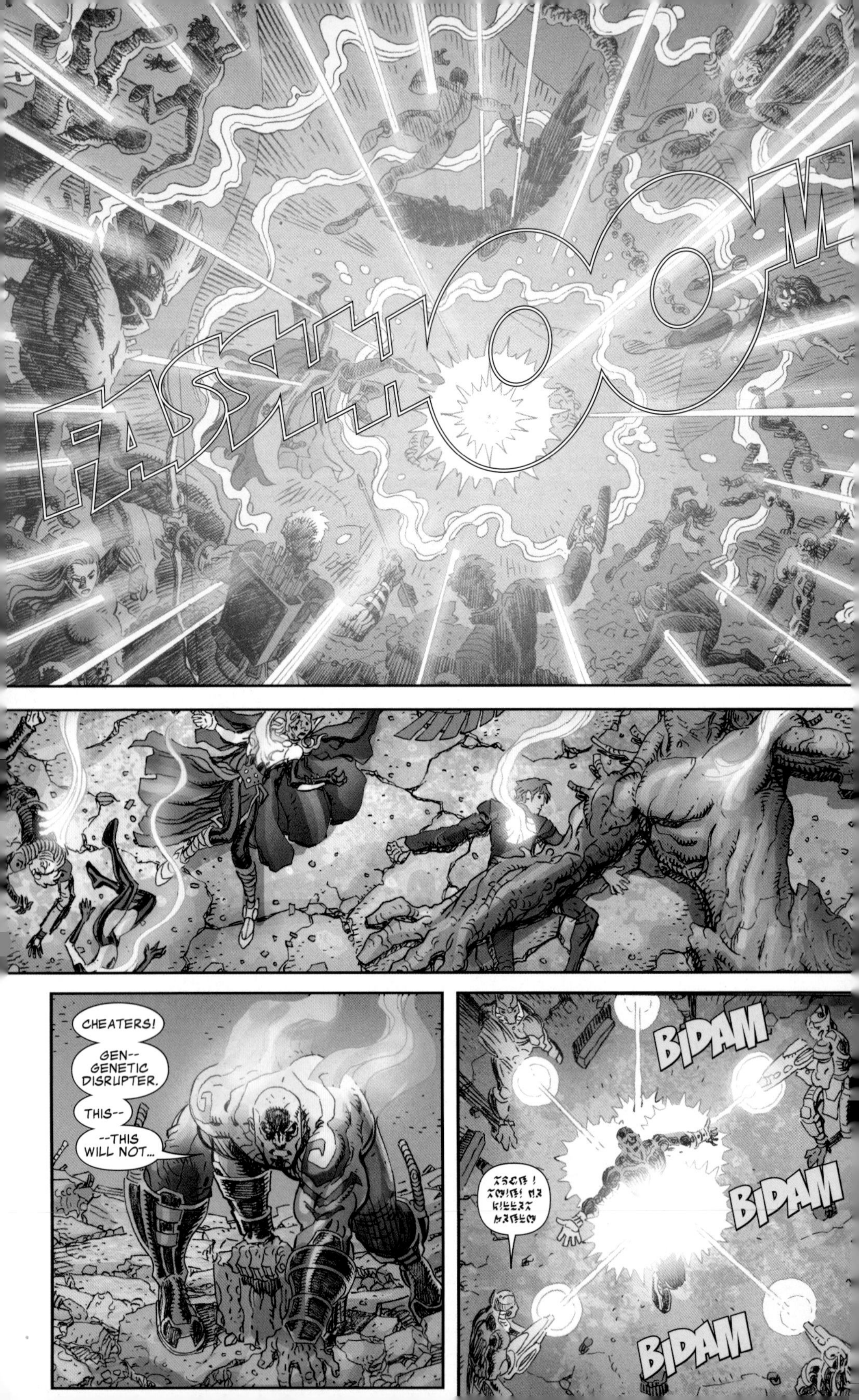
FASSHHOOM
CHEATERS!
GEN-- GENETIC DISRUPTER.
THIS--
--THIS WILL NOT...
BIDAM
BIDAM
BIDAM

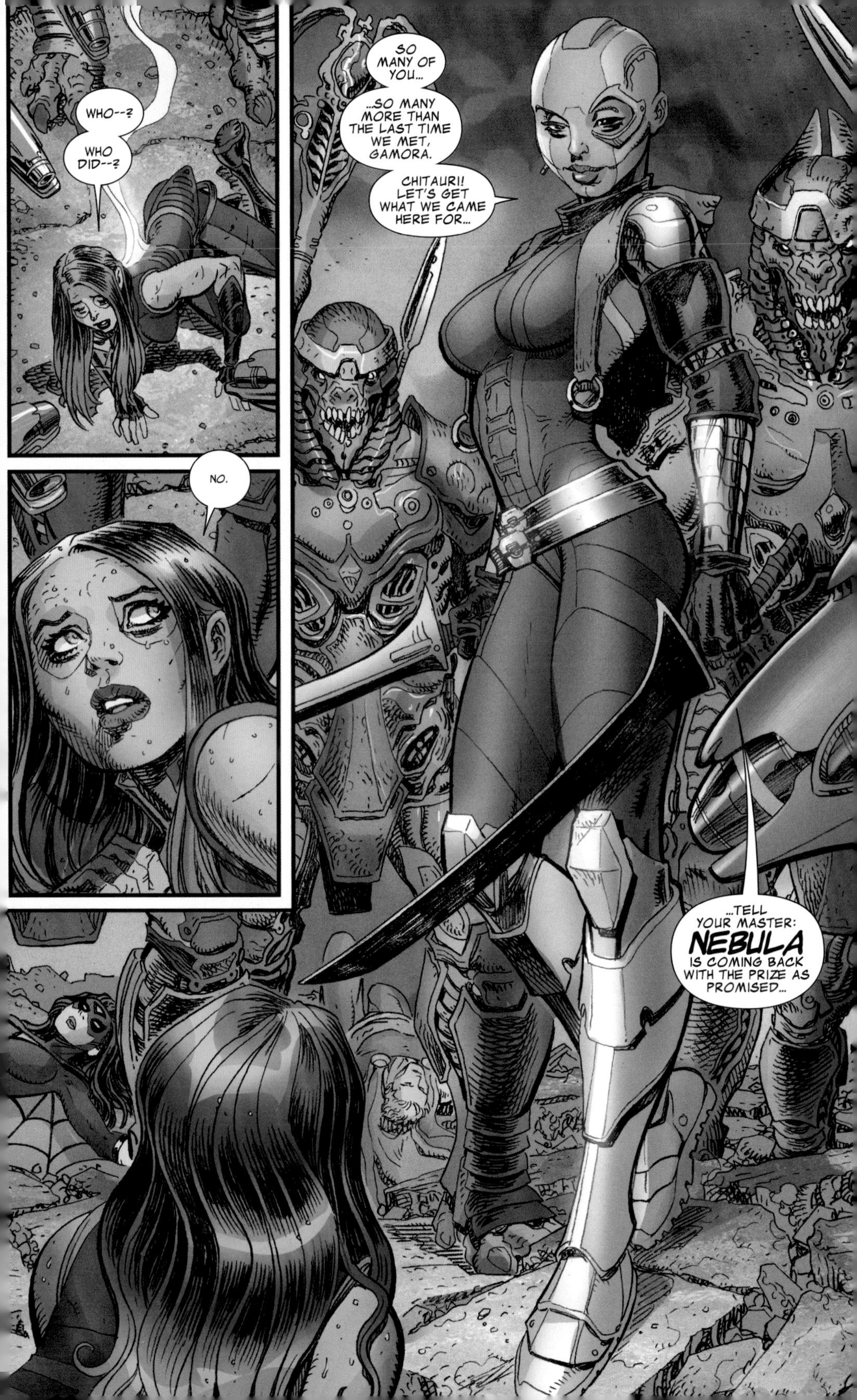
WHO--?
WHO DID--?
SO MANY OF YOU...
...SO MANY MORE THAN THE LAST TIME WE MET, GAMORA.
CHITAURI! LET'S GET WHAT WE CAME HERE FOR...
NO.
...TELL YOUR MASTER: NEBULA IS COMING BACK WITH THE PRIZE AS PROMISED...

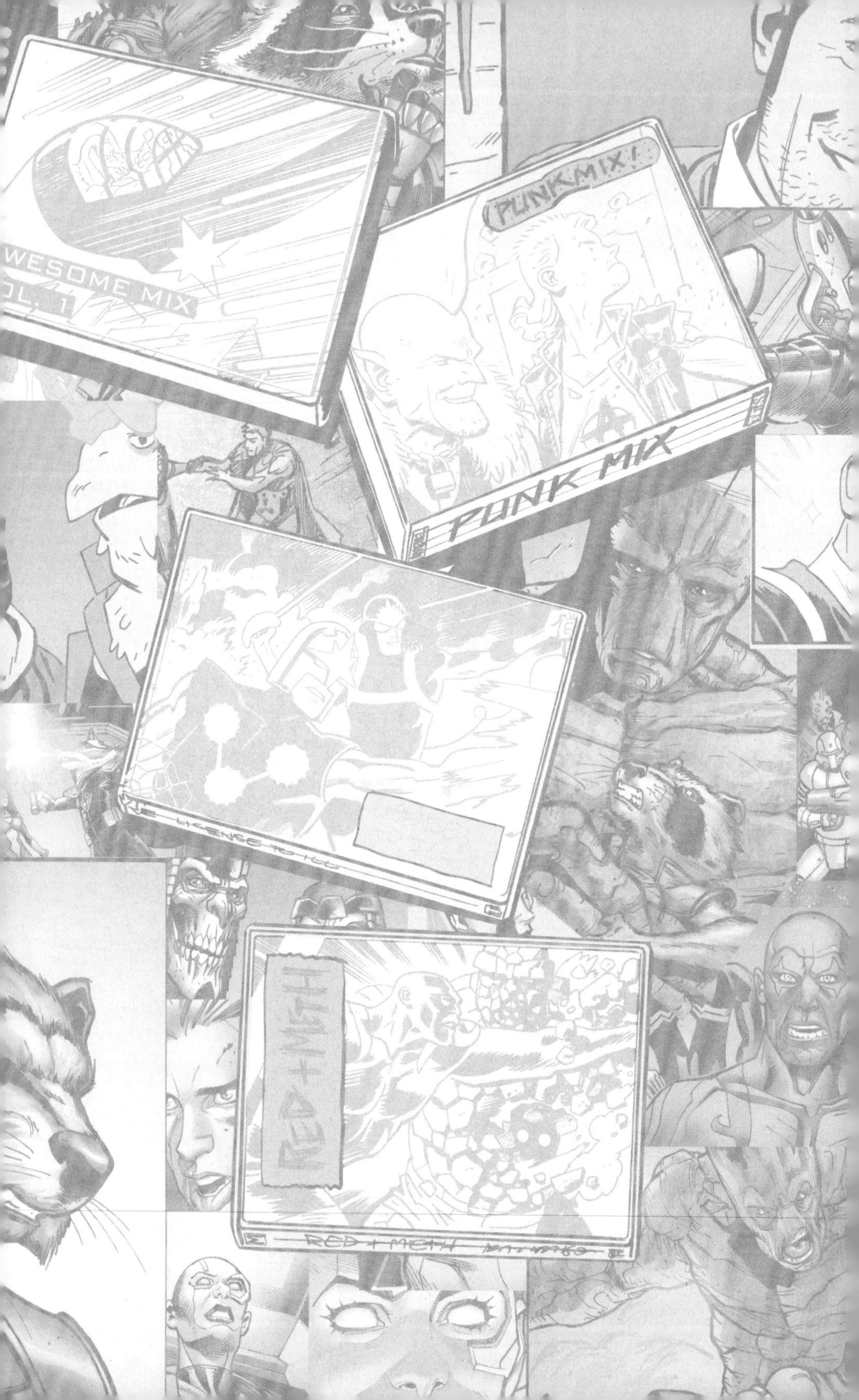
WESOME MIX
OL. 1
PUNK MIX!
PUNK MIX
LICENSE TO ILL
RED + METH
RED + METH

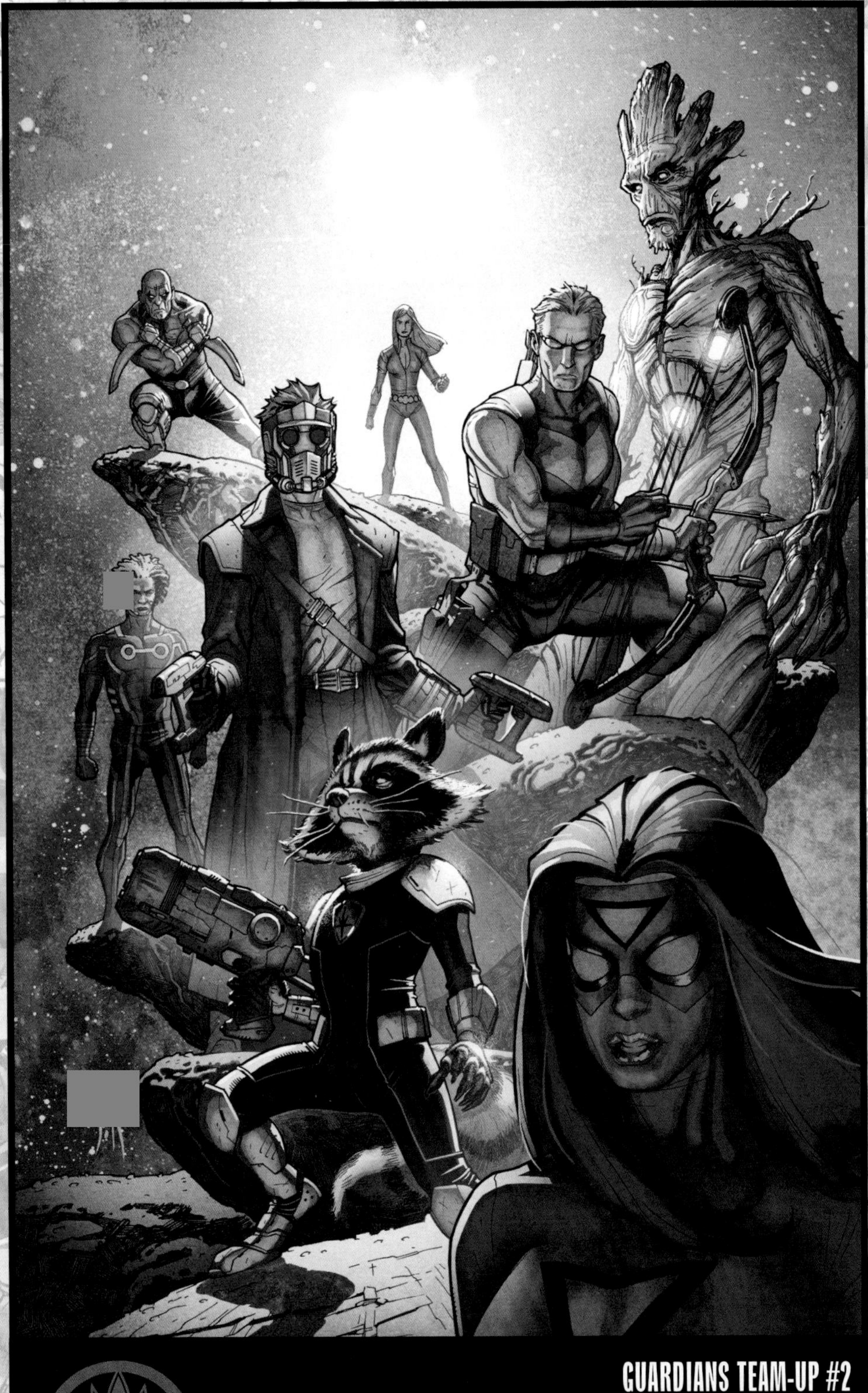

GUARDIANS TEAM-UP #2

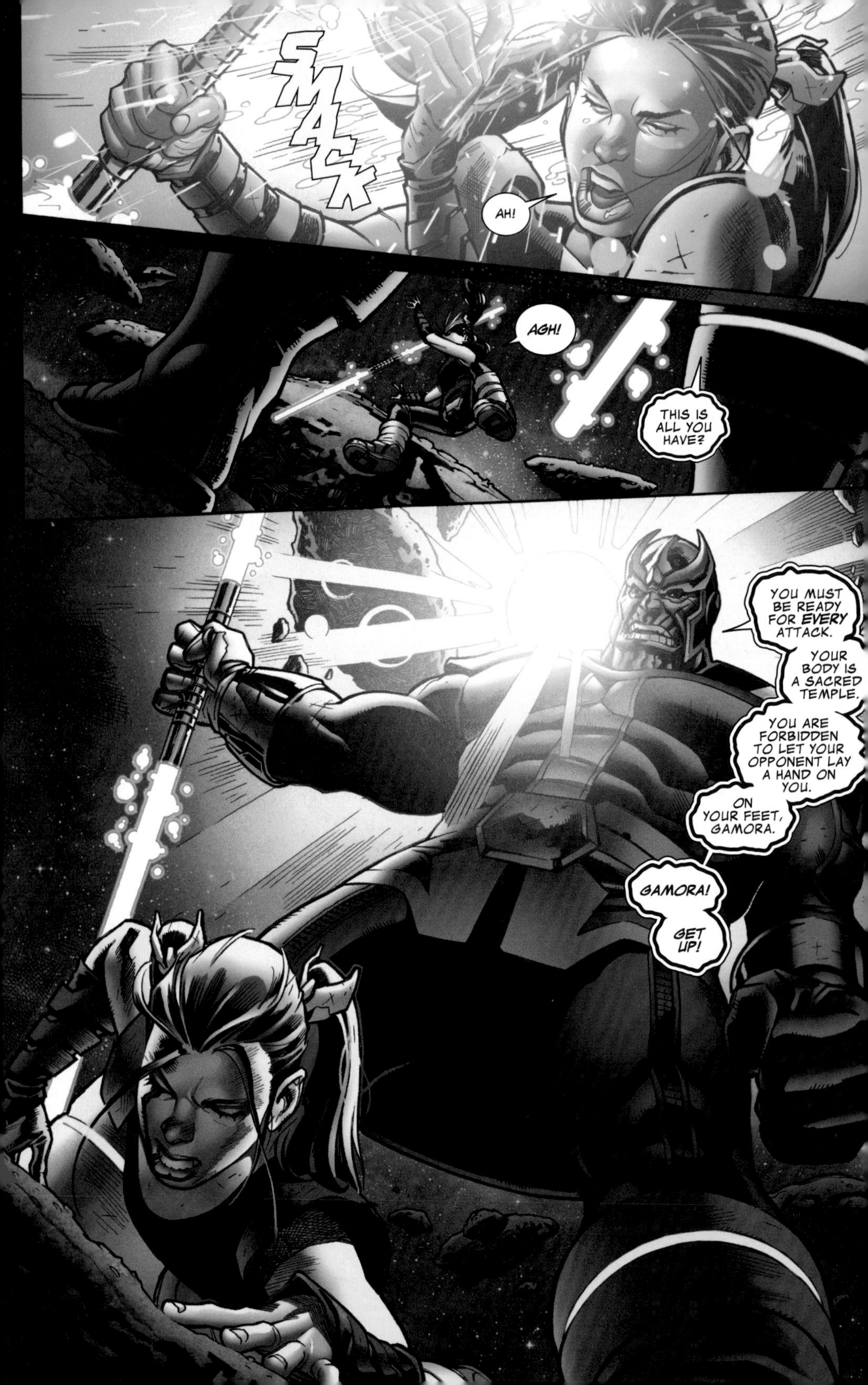
SMACK
AH!
AGH!
THIS IS ALL YOU HAVE?
YOU MUST BE READY FOR EVERY ATTACK.
YOUR BODY IS A SACRED TEMPLE.
YOU ARE FORBIDDEN TO LET YOUR OPPONENT LAY A HAND ON YOU.
ON YOUR FEET, GAMORA.
GAMORA!
GET UP!

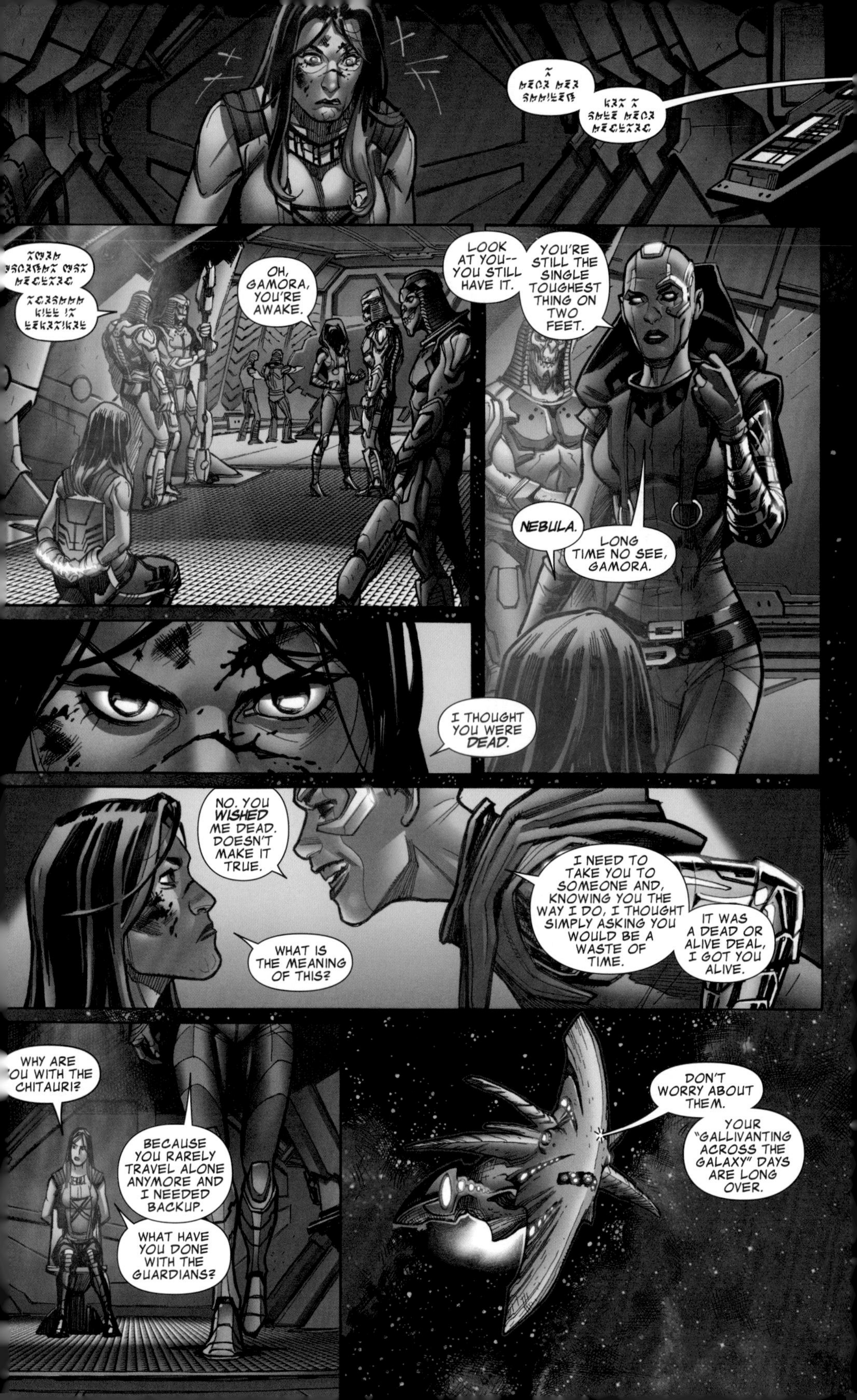

OH, GAMORA, YOU'RE AWAKE.
LOOK AT YOU-- YOU STILL HAVE IT.
YOU'RE STILL THE SINGLE TOUGHEST THING ON TWO FEET.
NEBULA.
LONG TIME NO SEE, GAMORA.
I THOUGHT YOU WERE DEAD.
NO. YOU WISHED ME DEAD. DOESN'T MAKE IT TRUE.
WHAT IS THE MEANING OF THIS?
I NEED TO TAKE YOU TO SOMEONE AND, KNOWING YOU THE WAY I DO, I THOUGHT SIMPLY ASKING YOU WOULD BE A WASTE OF TIME.
IT WAS A DEAD OR ALIVE DEAL, I GOT YOU ALIVE.
WHY ARE YOU WITH THE CHITAURI?
BECAUSE YOU RARELY TRAVEL ALONE ANYMORE AND I NEEDED BACKUP.
WHAT HAVE YOU DONE WITH THE GUARDIANS?
DON'T WORRY ABOUT THEM.
YOUR "GALLIVANTING ACROSS THE GALAXY" DAYS ARE LONG OVER.

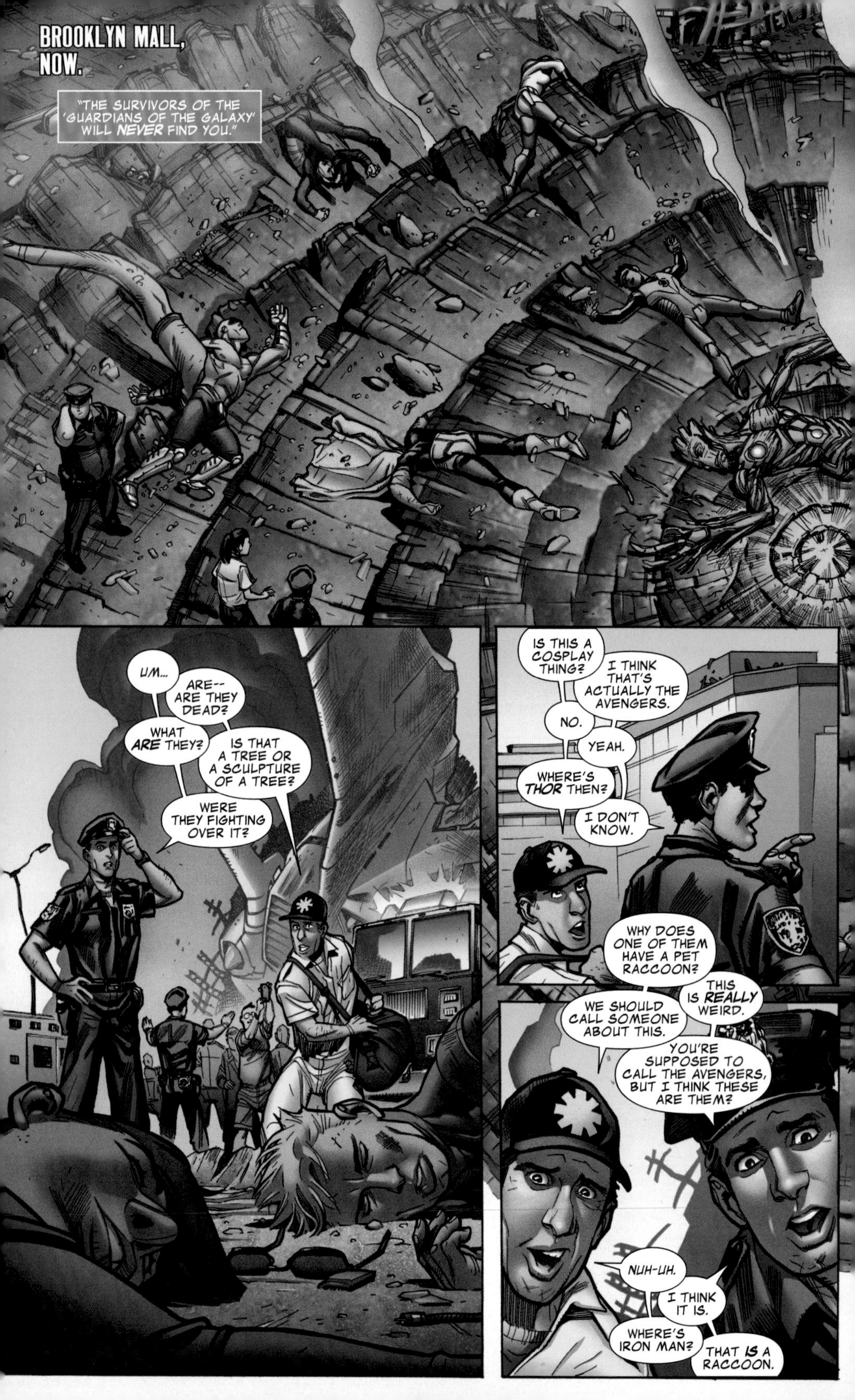
BROOKLYN MALL, NOW.
"THE SURVIVORS OF THE 'GUARDIANS OF THE GALAXY' WILL NEVER FIND YOU."
UM...
ARE-- ARE THEY DEAD?
WHAT ARE THEY?
IS THAT A TREE OR A SCULPTURE OF A TREE?
WERE THEY FIGHTING OVER IT?
IS THIS A COSPLAY THING?
I THINK THAT'S ACTUALLY THE AVENGERS.
NO.
YEAH.
WHERE'S THOR THEN?
I DON'T KNOW.
WHY DOES ONE OF THEM HAVE A PET RACCOON?
WE SHOULD CALL SOMEONE ABOUT THIS.
THIS IS REALLY WEIRD.
YOU'RE SUPPOSED TO CALL THE AVENGERS, BUT I THINK THESE ARE THEM?
NUH-UH.
I THINK IT IS.
WHERE'S IRON MAN?
THAT IS A RACCOON.

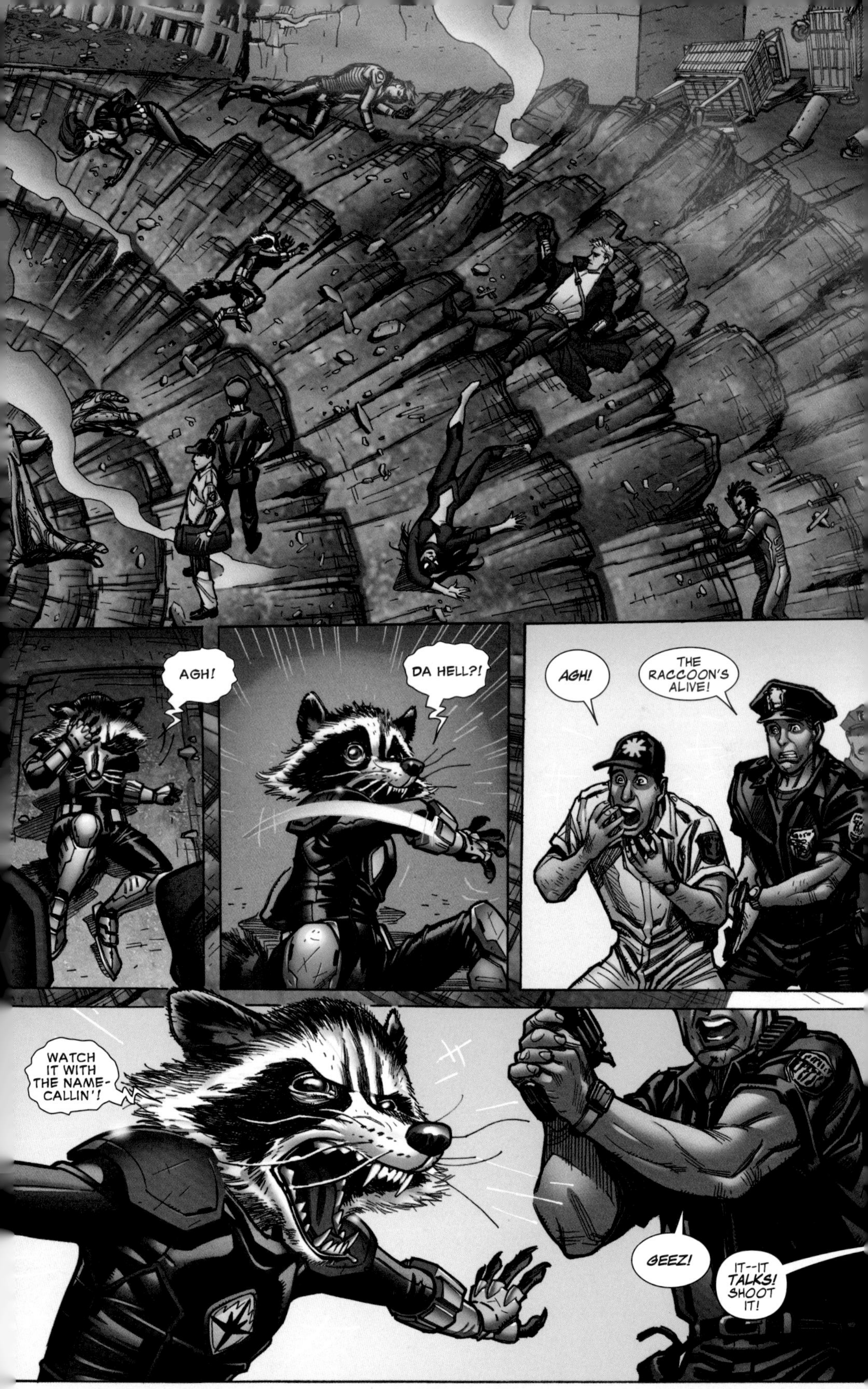
AGH!
DA HELL?!
AGH!
THE RACCOON'S ALIVE!
WATCH IT WITH THE NAME-CALLIN'!
GEEZ!
IT--IT *TALKS!* SHOOT IT!

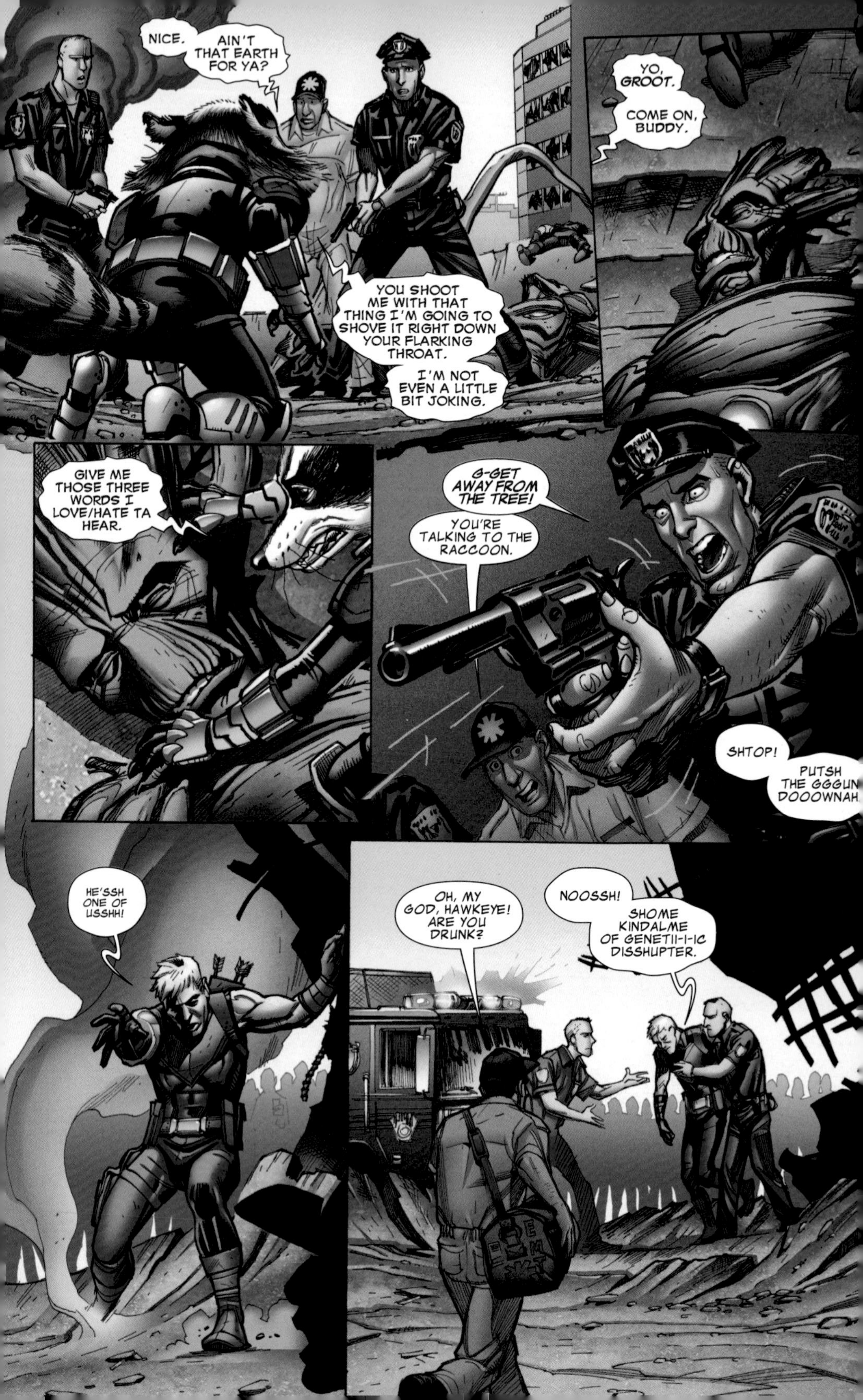
NICE.
AIN'T THAT EARTH FOR YA?
YOU SHOOT ME WITH THAT THING I'M GOING TO SHOVE IT RIGHT DOWN YOUR FLARKING THROAT.
I'M NOT EVEN A LITTLE BIT JOKING.
YO, GROOT.
COME ON, BUDDY.
GIVE ME THOSE THREE WORDS I LOVE/HATE TA HEAR.
G-GET AWAY FROM THE TREE!
YOU'RE TALKING TO THE RACCOON.
SHTOP!
PUTSH THE GGGUN DOOOWNAH.
HE'SSH ONE OF USSHH!
OH, MY GOD, HAWKEYE! ARE YOU DRUNK?
NOOSSH!
SHOME KINDALME OF GENETII-I-IC DISSHUPTER.

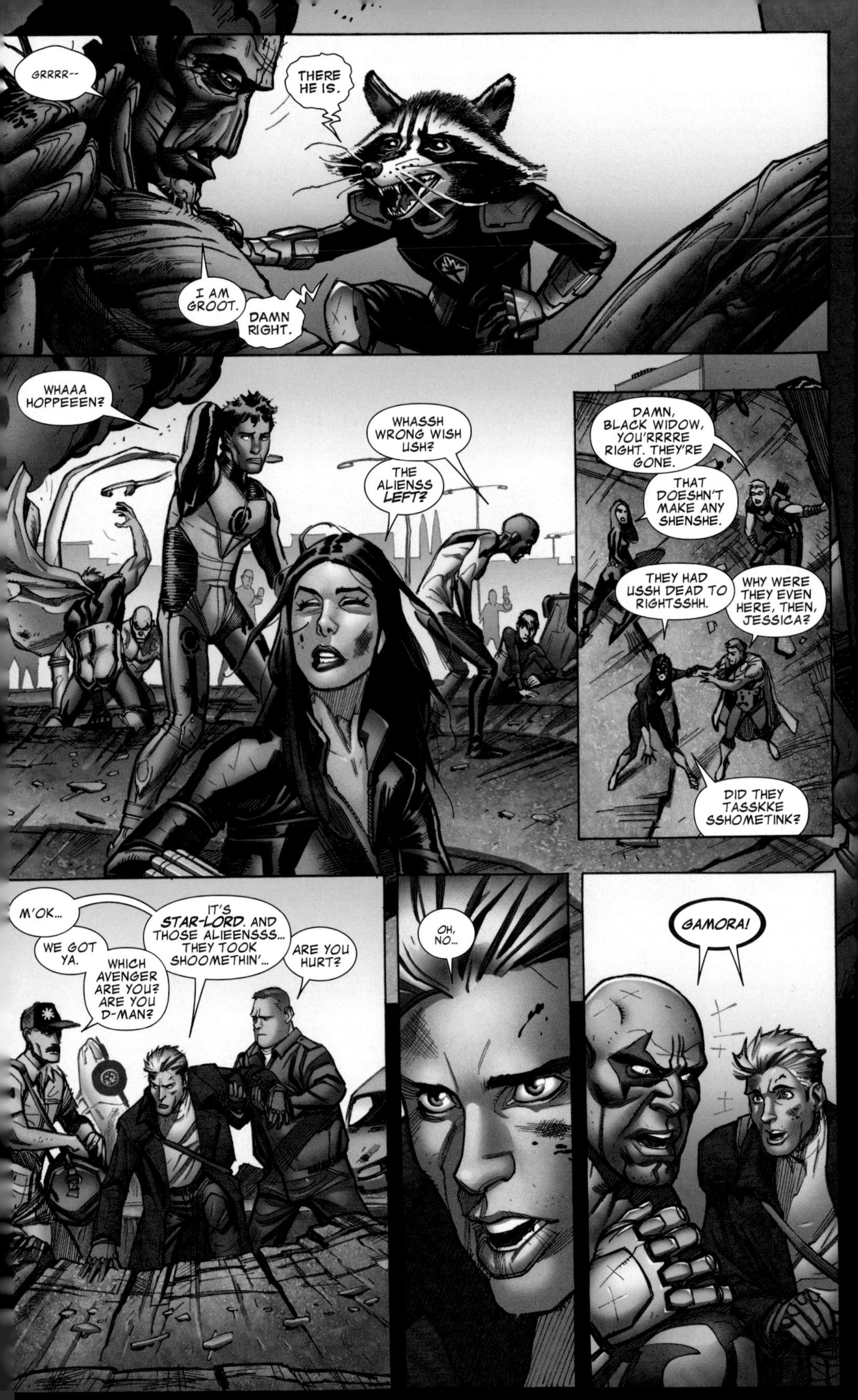
GRRRR--
THERE HE IS.
I AM GROOT.
DAMN RIGHT.
WHAAA HOPPEEEN?
WHASSH WRONG WISH USH?
THE ALIENSS LEFT?
DAMN, BLACK WIDOW, YOU'RRRRE RIGHT. THEY'RE GONE.
THAT DOESHN'T MAKE ANY SHENSHE.
THEY HAD USSH DEAD TO RIGHTSSHH.
WHY WERE THEY EVEN HERE, THEN, JESSICA?
DID THEY TASSKKE SSHOMETINK?
M'OK...
WE GOT YA.
WHICH AVENGER ARE YOU? ARE YOU D-MAN?
IT'S STAR-LORD. AND THOSE ALIEENSSS... THEY TOOK SHOOMETHIN'...
ARE YOU HURT?
OH, NO...
GAMORA!

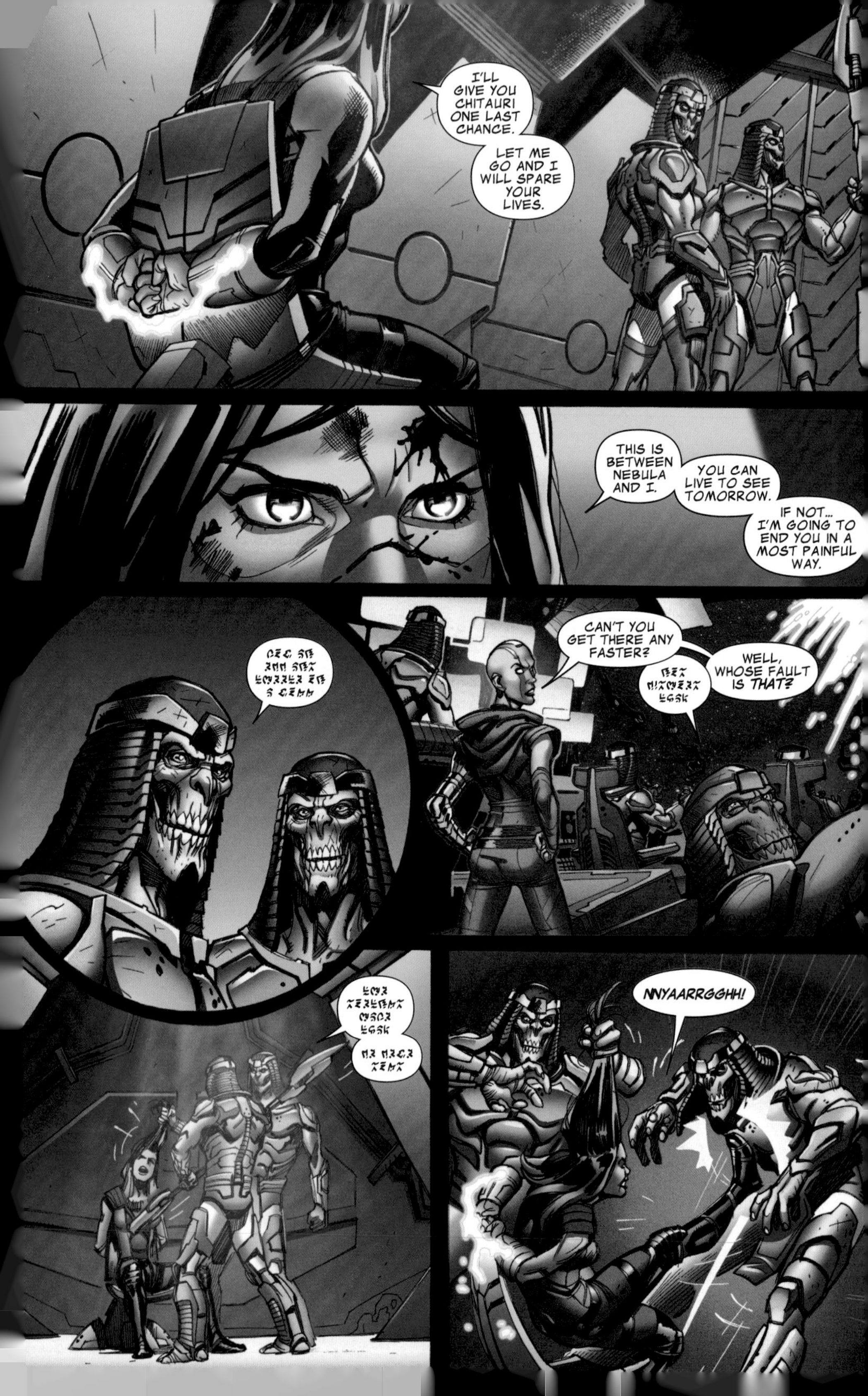
I'LL GIVE YOU CHITAURI ONE LAST CHANCE.
LET ME GO AND I WILL SPARE YOUR LIVES.
THIS IS BETWEEN NEBULA AND I.
YOU CAN LIVE TO SEE TOMORROW.
IF NOT... I'M GOING TO END YOU IN A MOST PAINFUL WAY.
CAN'T YOU GET THERE ANY FASTER?
WELL, WHOSE FAULT IS *THAT?*
NNYAARRGGHH!

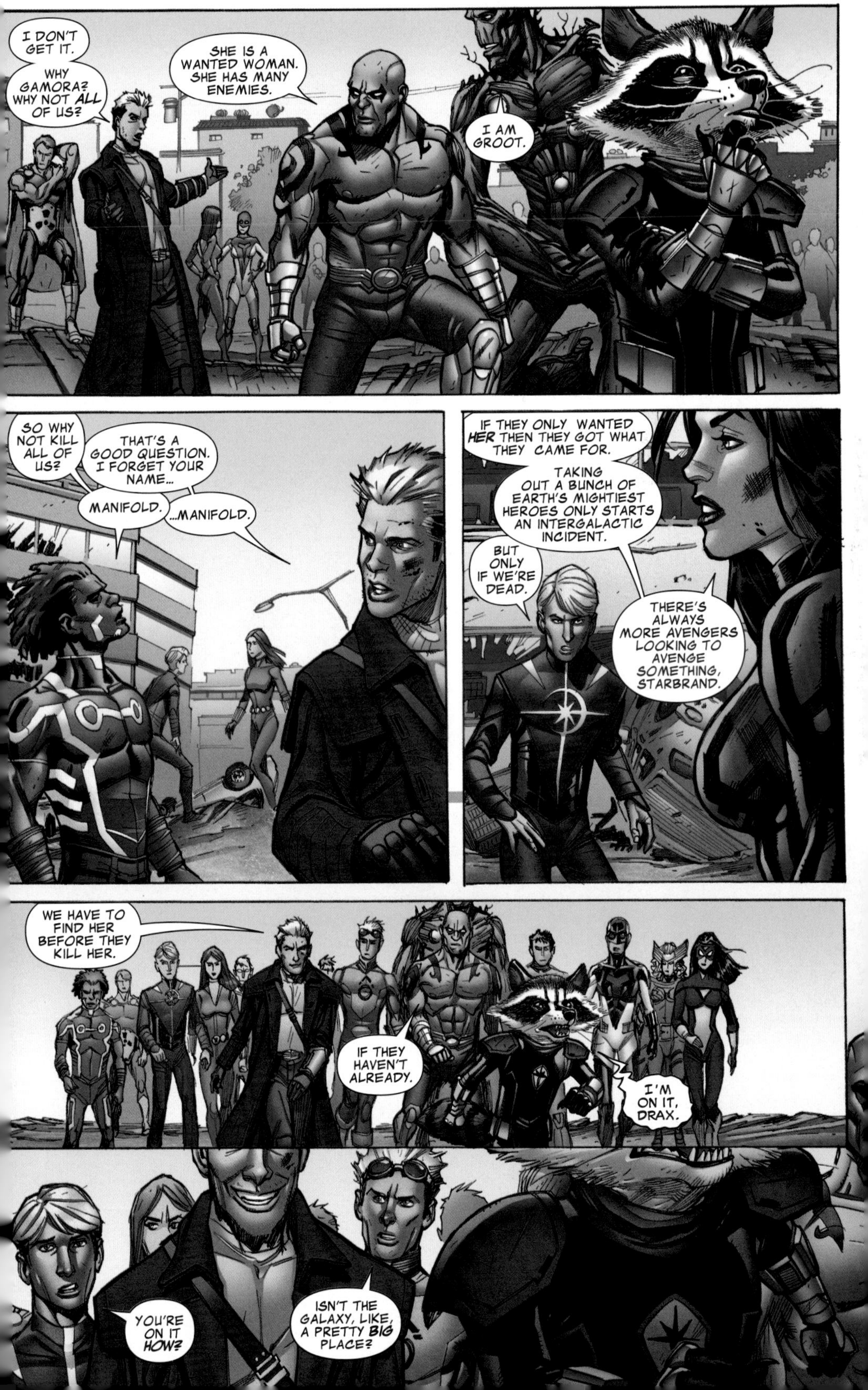

I DON'T GET IT.
WHY GAMORA? WHY NOT ALL OF US?
SHE IS A WANTED WOMAN. SHE HAS MANY ENEMIES.
I AM GROOT.
SO WHY NOT KILL ALL OF US?
THAT'S A GOOD QUESTION. I FORGET YOUR NAME...
MANIFOLD.
...MANIFOLD.
IF THEY ONLY WANTED HER THEN THEY GOT WHAT THEY CAME FOR.
TAKING OUT A BUNCH OF EARTH'S MIGHTIEST HEROES ONLY STARTS AN INTERGALACTIC INCIDENT.
BUT ONLY IF WE'RE DEAD.
THERE'S ALWAYS MORE AVENGERS LOOKING TO AVENGE SOMETHING, STARBRAND.
WE HAVE TO FIND HER BEFORE THEY KILL HER.
IF THEY HAVEN'T ALREADY.
I'M ON IT, DRAX.
YOU'RE ON IT HOW?
ISN'T THE GALAXY, LIKE, A PRETTY BIG PLACE?

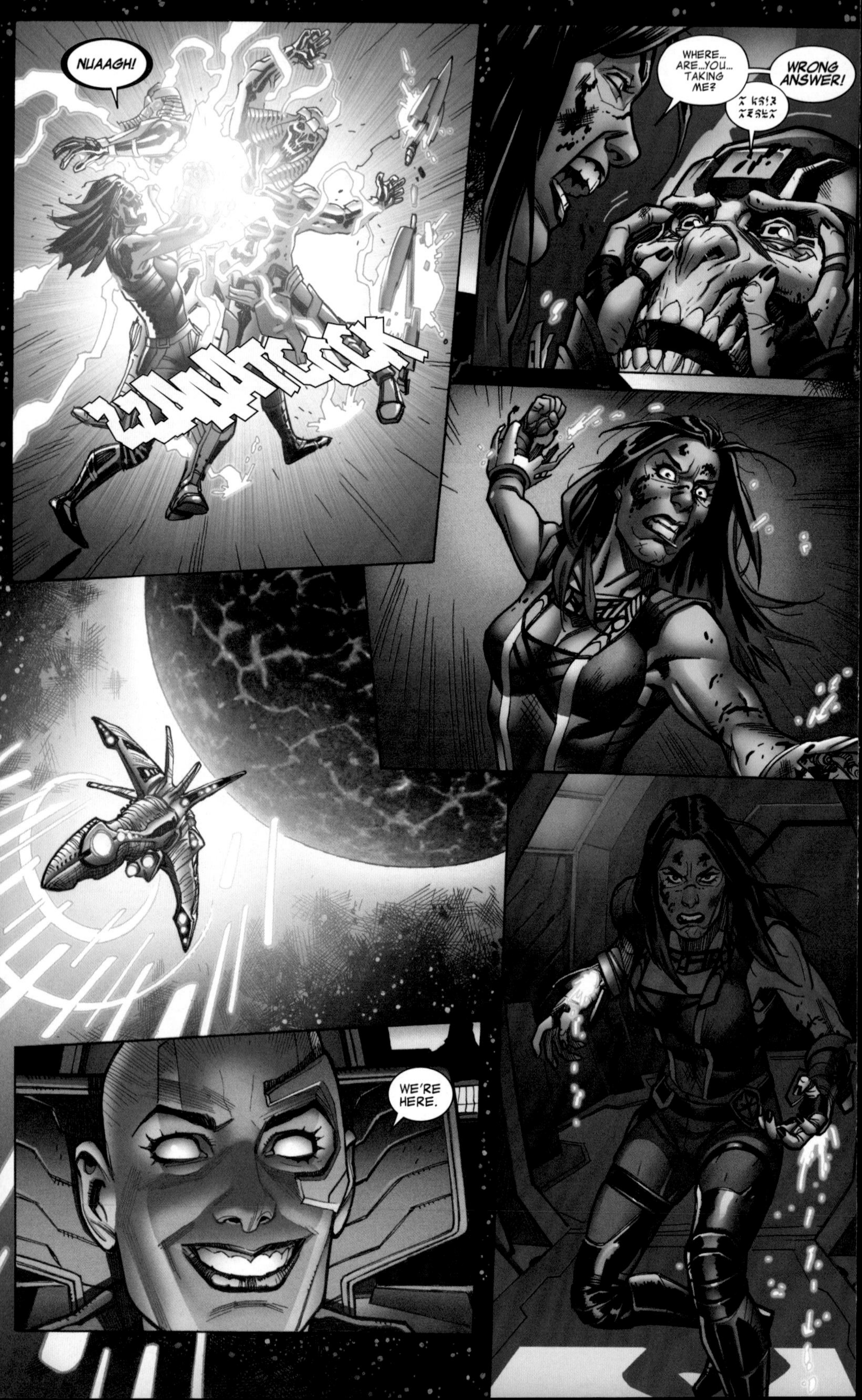

NUAAGH!
ZZAKTCCK
WHERE... ARE...YOU... TAKING ME?
WRONG ANSWER!
WE'RE HERE.

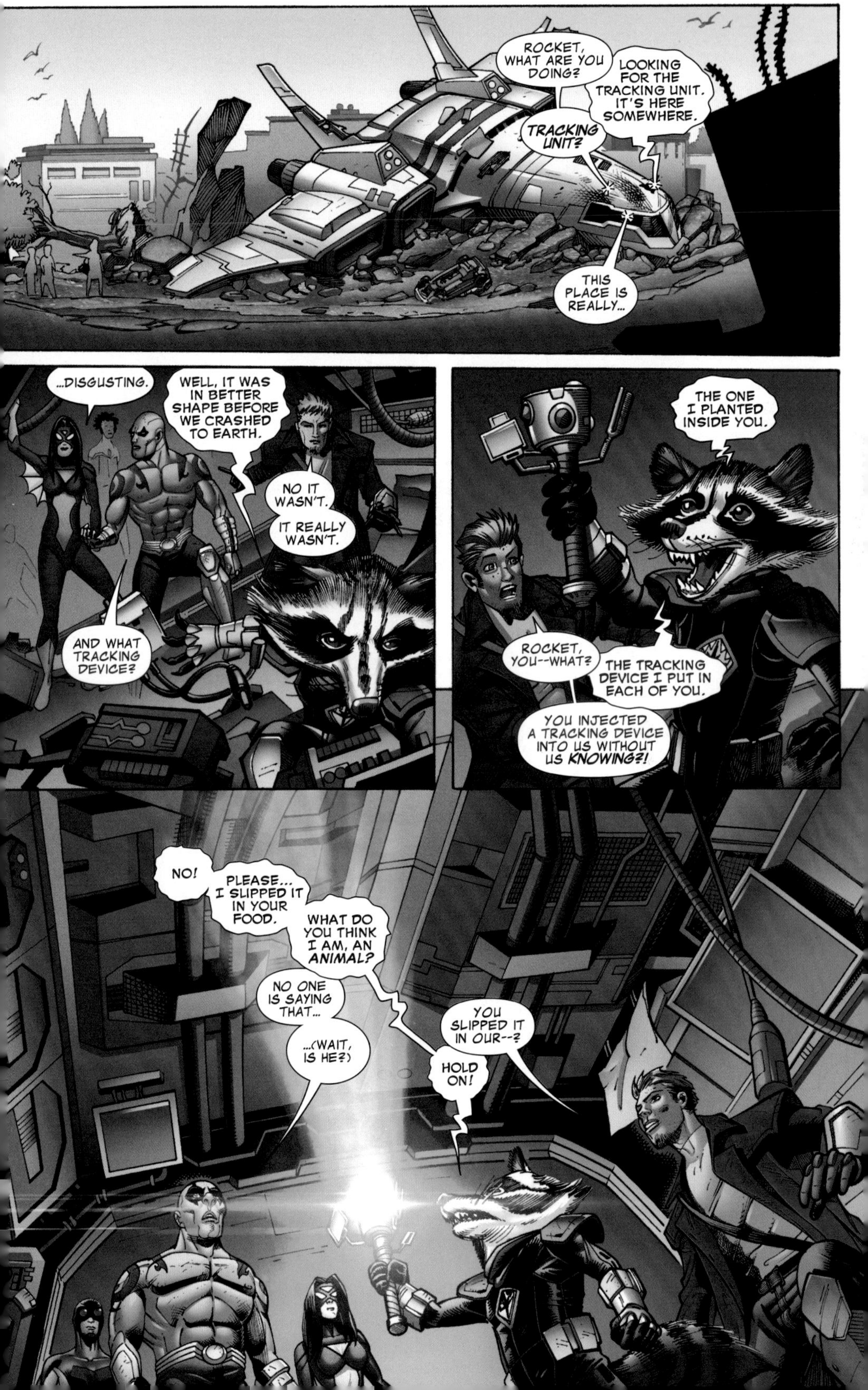

ROCKET, WHAT ARE YOU DOING?
LOOKING FOR THE TRACKING UNIT. IT'S HERE SOMEWHERE.
TRACKING UNIT?
THIS PLACE IS REALLY...
...DISGUSTING.
WELL, IT WAS IN BETTER SHAPE BEFORE WE CRASHED TO EARTH.
NO IT WASN'T.
IT REALLY WASN'T.
AND WHAT TRACKING DEVICE?
THE ONE I PLANTED INSIDE YOU.
ROCKET, YOU--WHAT?
THE TRACKING DEVICE I PUT IN EACH OF YOU.
YOU INJECTED A TRACKING DEVICE INTO US WITHOUT US *KNOWING?!*
NO!
PLEASE... I SLIPPED IT IN YOUR FOOD.
WHAT DO YOU THINK I AM, AN *ANIMAL?*
NO ONE IS SAYING THAT...
...(WAIT, IS HE?)
YOU SLIPPED IT IN OUR--?
HOLD ON!

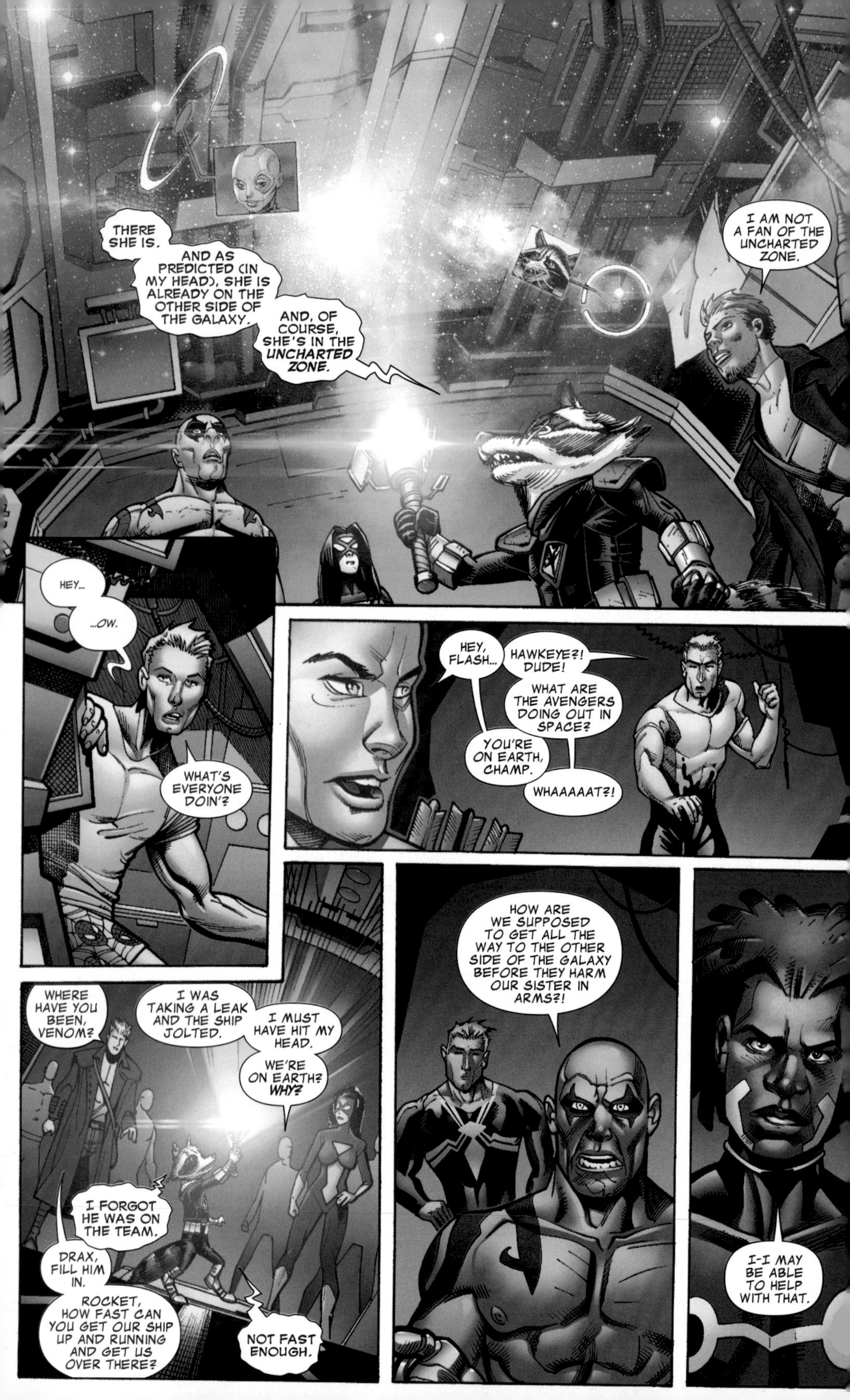
THERE SHE IS.
AND AS PREDICTED (IN MY HEAD), SHE IS ALREADY ON THE OTHER SIDE OF THE GALAXY.
AND, OF COURSE, SHE'S IN THE UNCHARTED ZONE.
I AM NOT A FAN OF THE UNCHARTED ZONE.
HEY...
...OW.
WHAT'S EVERYONE DOIN'?
HEY, FLASH...
HAWKEYE?! DUDE!
WHAT ARE THE AVENGERS DOING OUT IN SPACE?
YOU'RE ON EARTH, CHAMP.
WHAAAAAT?!
WHERE HAVE YOU BEEN, VENOM?
I WAS TAKING A LEAK AND THE SHIP JOLTED.
I MUST HAVE HIT MY HEAD.
WE'RE ON EARTH? WHY?
I FORGOT HE WAS ON THE TEAM.
DRAX, FILL HIM IN.
ROCKET, HOW FAST CAN YOU GET OUR SHIP UP AND RUNNING AND GET US OVER THERE?
NOT FAST ENOUGH.
HOW ARE WE SUPPOSED TO GET ALL THE WAY TO THE OTHER SIDE OF THE GALAXY BEFORE THEY HARM OUR SISTER IN ARMS?!
I-I MAY BE ABLE TO HELP WITH THAT.

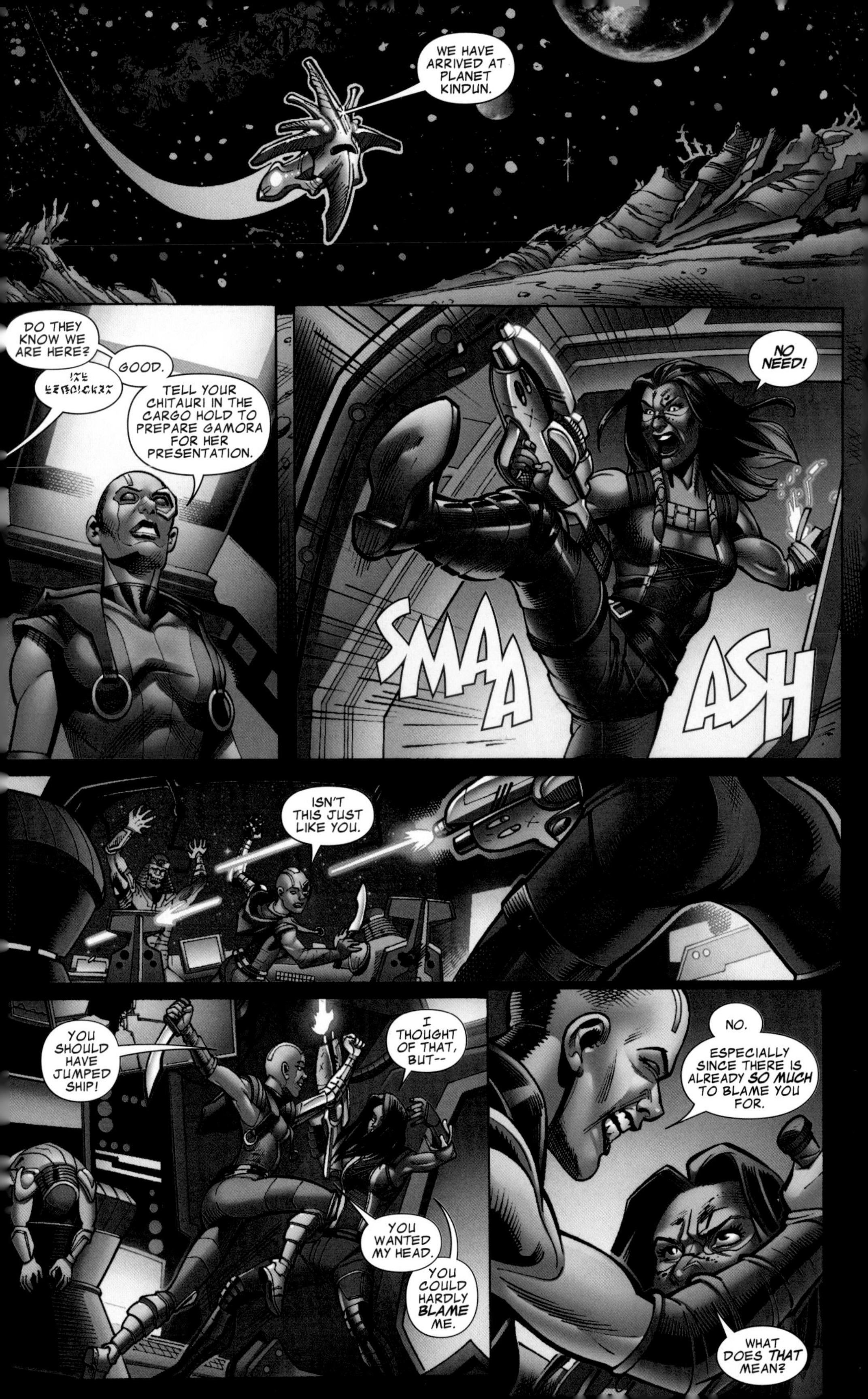
WE HAVE ARRIVED AT PLANET KINDUN.
DO THEY KNOW WE ARE HERE?
GOOD.
TELL YOUR CHITAURI IN THE CARGO HOLD TO PREPARE GAMORA FOR HER PRESENTATION.
NO NEED!
SMAAASH
ISN'T THIS JUST LIKE YOU.
YOU SHOULD HAVE JUMPED SHIP!
I THOUGHT OF THAT, BUT--
YOU WANTED MY HEAD.
YOU COULD HARDLY BLAME ME.
NO.
ESPECIALLY SINCE THERE IS ALREADY SO MUCH TO BLAME YOU FOR.
WHAT DOES THAT MEAN?

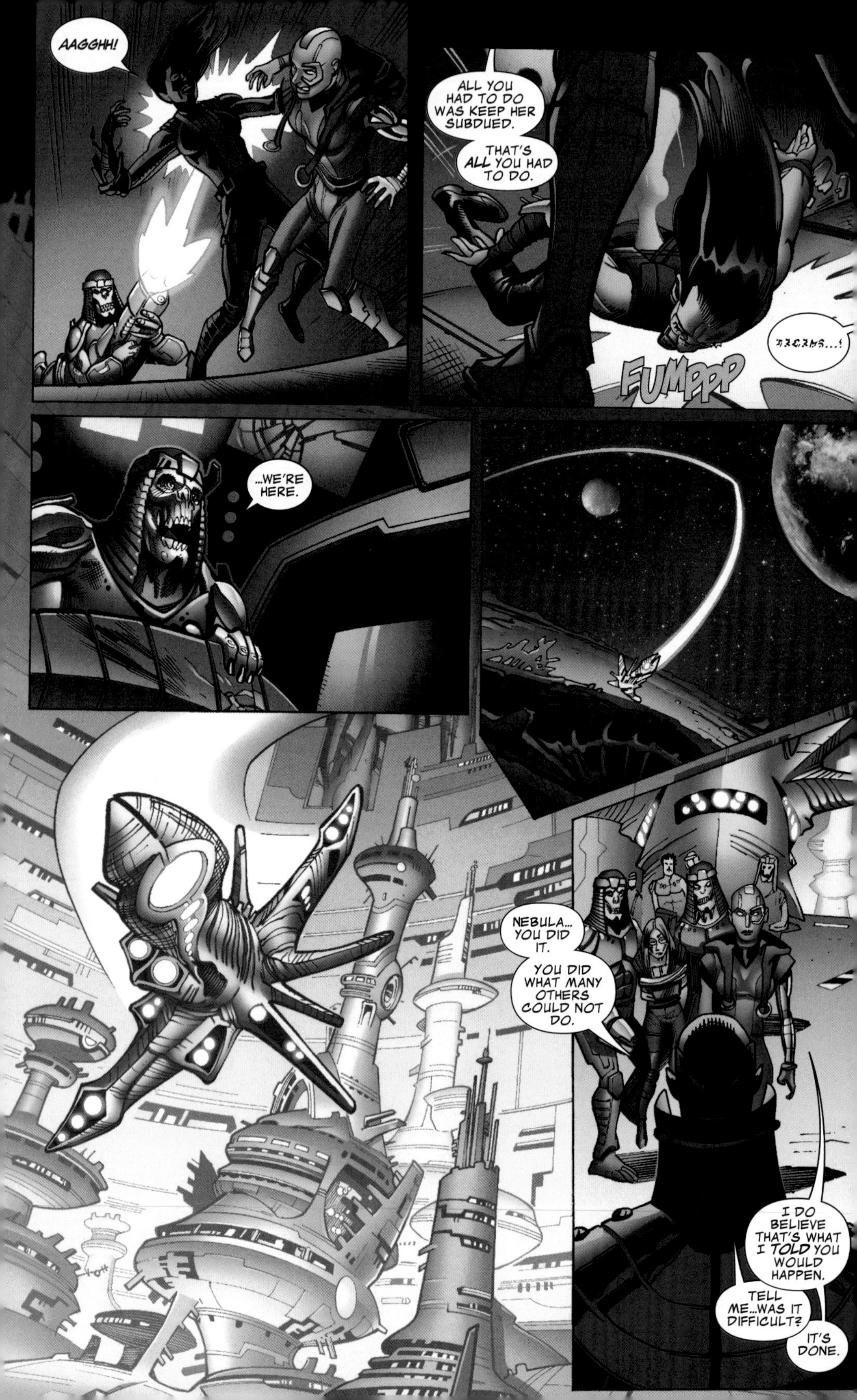
AAGGHH!
ALL YOU HAD TO DO WAS KEEP HER SUBDUED.
THAT'S *ALL* YOU HAD TO DO.
FUMPPP
...WE'RE HERE.
NEBULA... YOU DID IT.
YOU DID WHAT MANY OTHERS COULD NOT DO.
I DO BELIEVE THAT'S WHAT I *TOLD* YOU WOULD HAPPEN.
TELL ME...WAS IT DIFFICULT?
IT'S DONE.

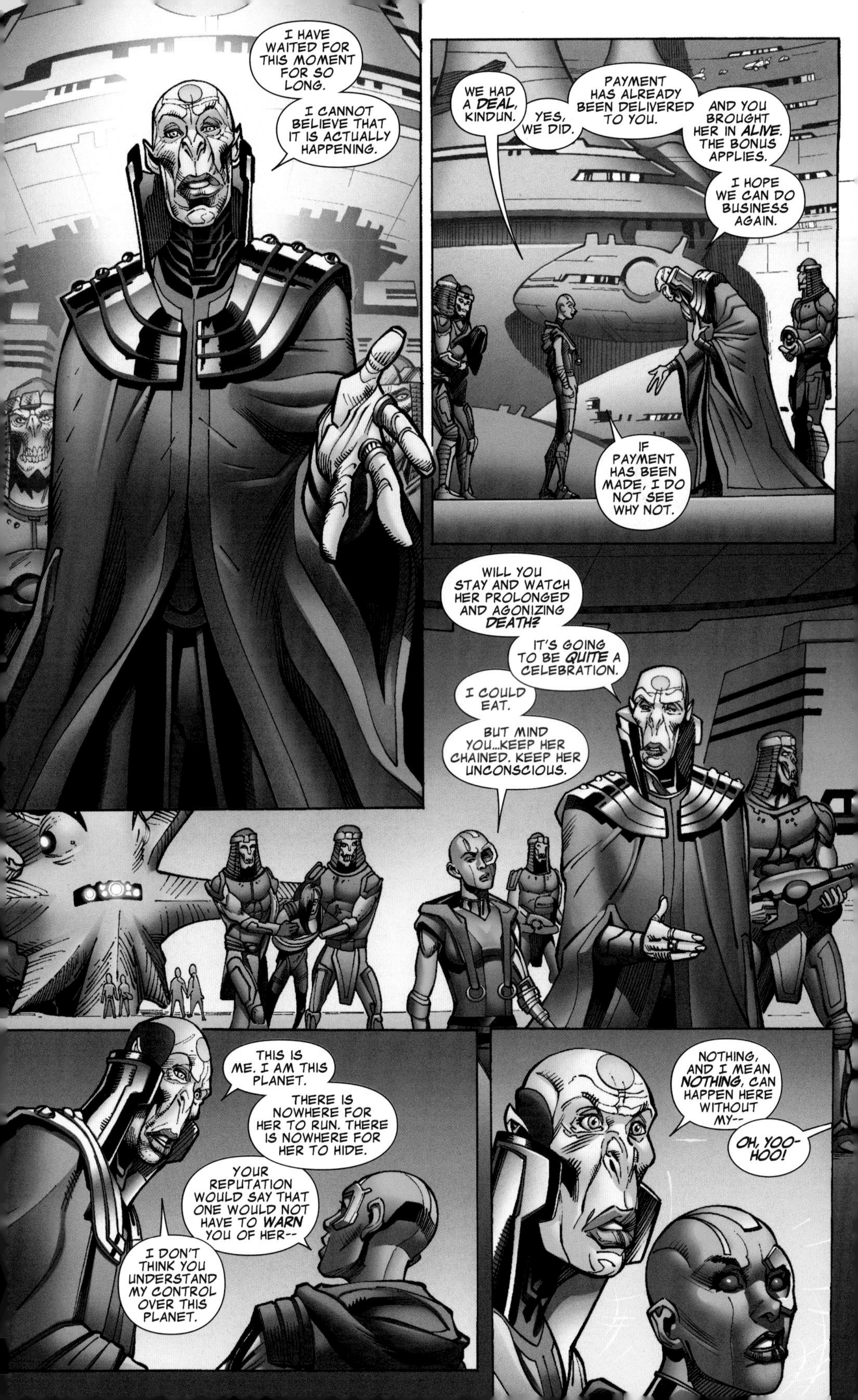
I HAVE WAITED FOR THIS MOMENT FOR SO LONG.
I CANNOT BELIEVE THAT IT IS ACTUALLY HAPPENING.
WE HAD A DEAL, KINDUN.
YES, WE DID.
PAYMENT HAS ALREADY BEEN DELIVERED TO YOU.
AND YOU BROUGHT HER IN ALIVE. THE BONUS APPLIES.
I HOPE WE CAN DO BUSINESS AGAIN.
IF PAYMENT HAS BEEN MADE, I DO NOT SEE WHY NOT.
WILL YOU STAY AND WATCH HER PROLONGED AND AGONIZING DEATH?
IT'S GOING TO BE QUITE A CELEBRATION.
I COULD EAT.
BUT MIND YOU...KEEP HER CHAINED. KEEP HER UNCONSCIOUS.
THIS IS ME. I AM THIS PLANET.
THERE IS NOWHERE FOR HER TO RUN. THERE IS NOWHERE FOR HER TO HIDE.
YOUR REPUTATION WOULD SAY THAT ONE WOULD NOT HAVE TO WARN YOU OF HER--
I DON'T THINK YOU UNDERSTAND MY CONTROL OVER THIS PLANET.
NOTHING, AND I MEAN NOTHING, CAN HAPPEN HERE WITHOUT MY--
OH, YOO-HOO!

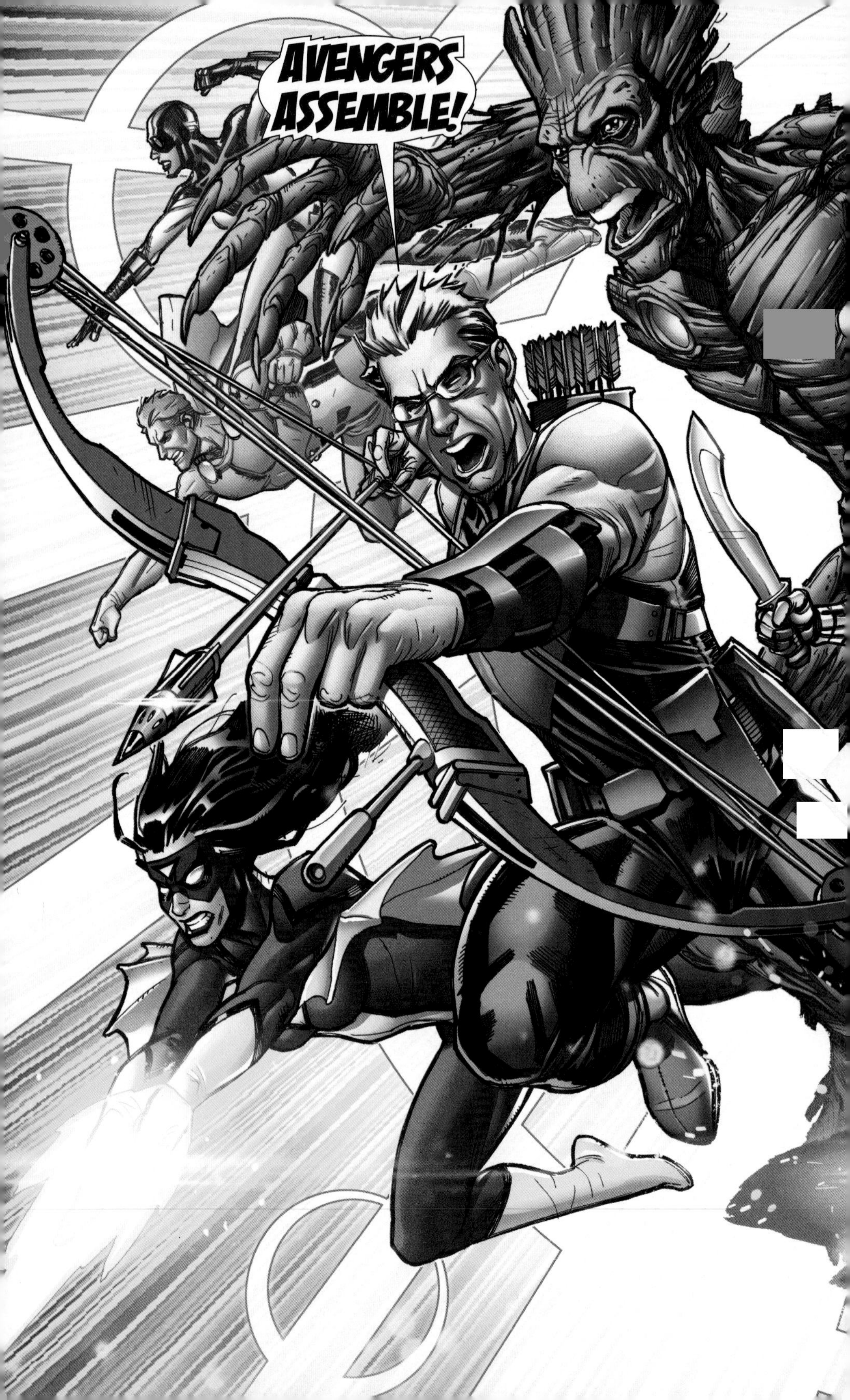
AVENGERS ASSEMBLE!

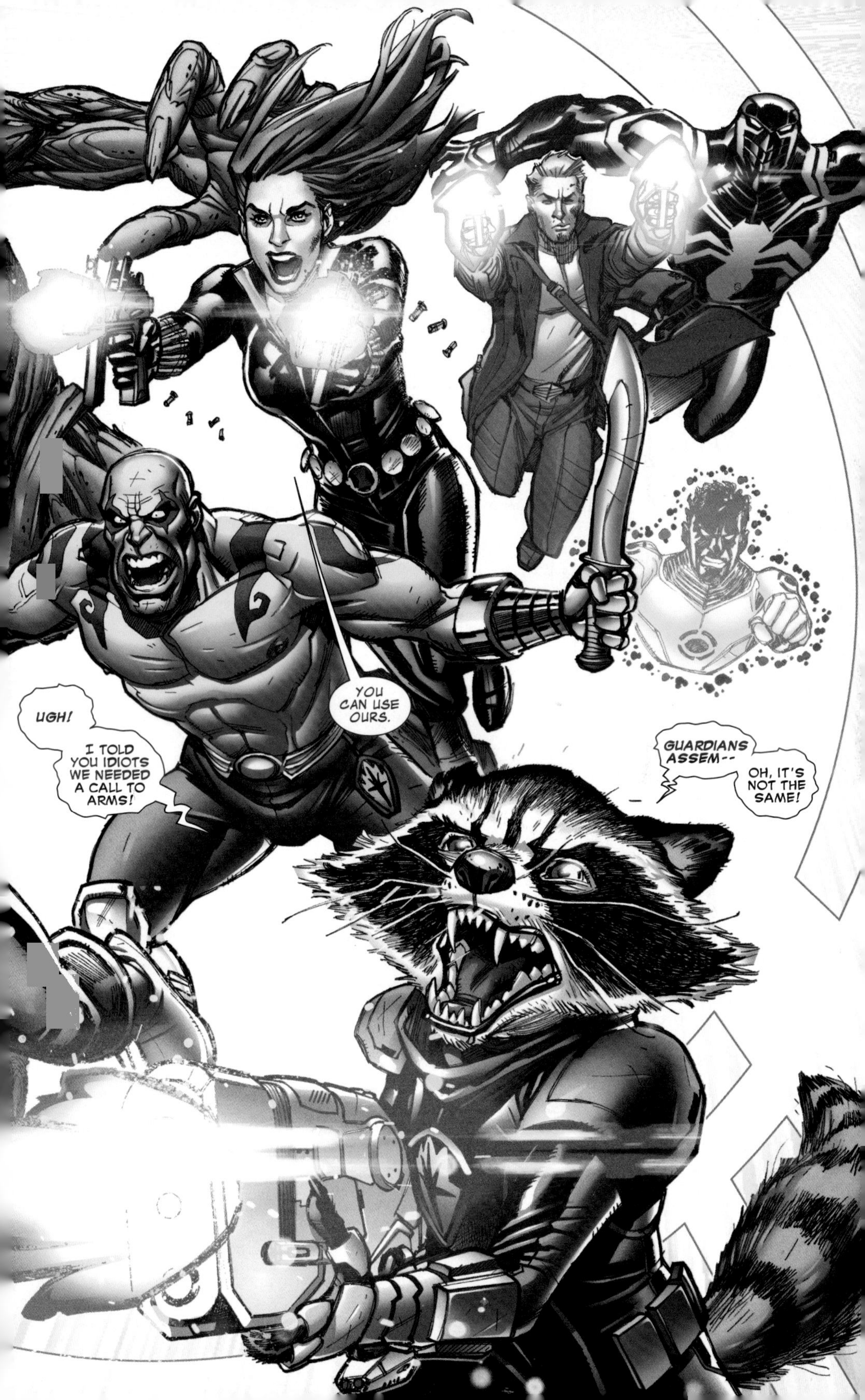

YOU CAN USE OURS.
UGH!
I TOLD YOU IDIOTS WE NEEDED A CALL TO ARMS!
GUARDIANS ASSEM--
OH, IT'S NOT THE SAME!

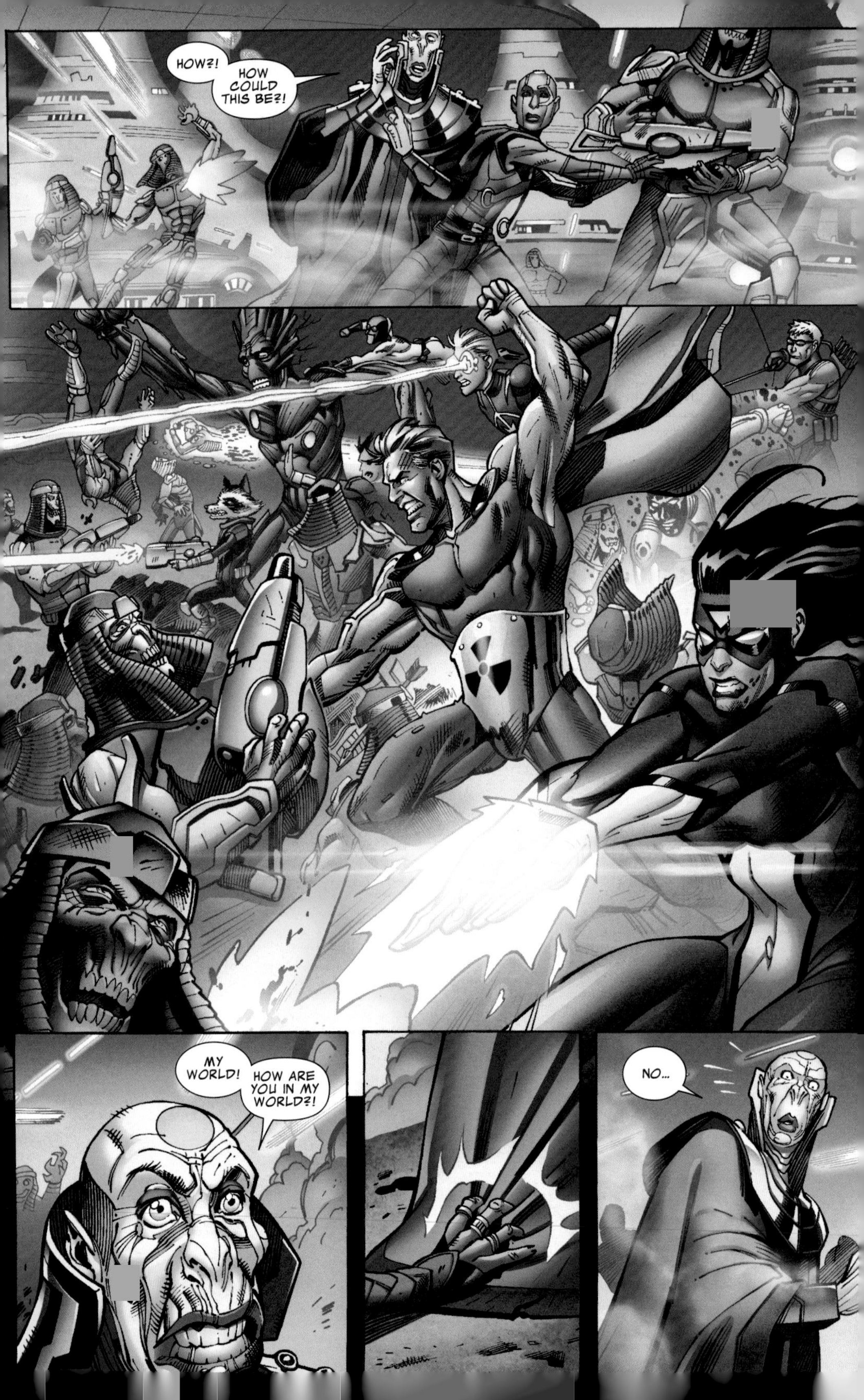
HOW?!
HOW COULD THIS BE?!
MY WORLD!
HOW ARE YOU IN MY WORLD?!
NO...

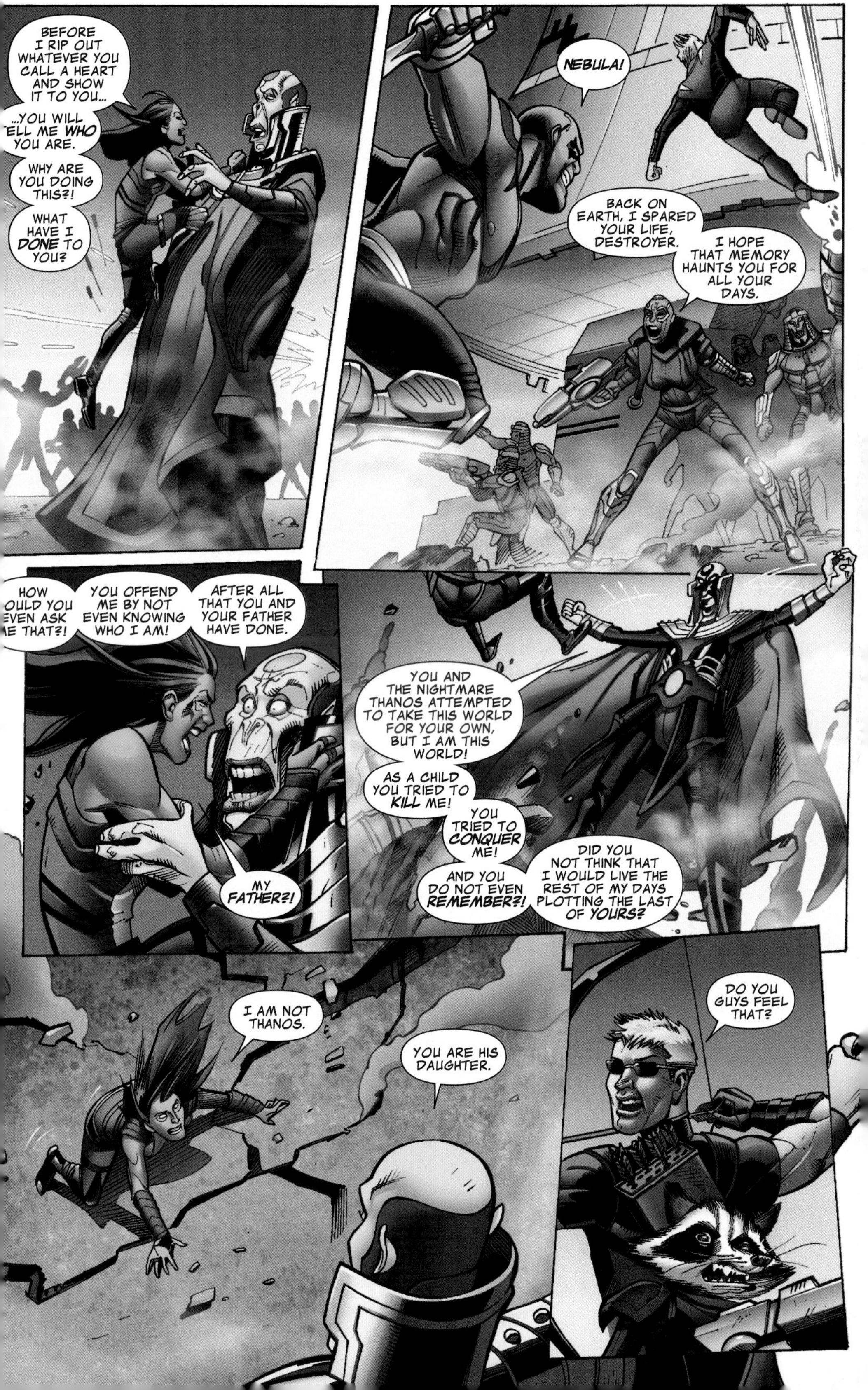
BEFORE I RIP OUT WHATEVER YOU CALL A HEART AND SHOW IT TO YOU...
...YOU WILL TELL ME WHO YOU ARE.
WHY ARE YOU DOING THIS?!
WHAT HAVE I DONE TO YOU?
NEBULA!
BACK ON EARTH, I SPARED YOUR LIFE, DESTROYER.
I HOPE THAT MEMORY HAUNTS YOU FOR ALL YOUR DAYS.
HOW COULD YOU EVEN ASK ME THAT?!
YOU OFFEND ME BY NOT EVEN KNOWING WHO I AM!
AFTER ALL THAT YOU AND YOUR FATHER HAVE DONE.
MY FATHER?!
YOU AND THE NIGHTMARE THANOS ATTEMPTED TO TAKE THIS WORLD FOR YOUR OWN, BUT I AM THIS WORLD!
AS A CHILD YOU TRIED TO KILL ME!
YOU TRIED TO CONQUER ME!
AND YOU DO NOT EVEN REMEMBER?!
DID YOU NOT THINK THAT I WOULD LIVE THE REST OF MY DAYS PLOTTING THE LAST OF YOURS?
I AM NOT THANOS.
YOU ARE HIS DAUGHTER.
DO YOU GUYS FEEL THAT?

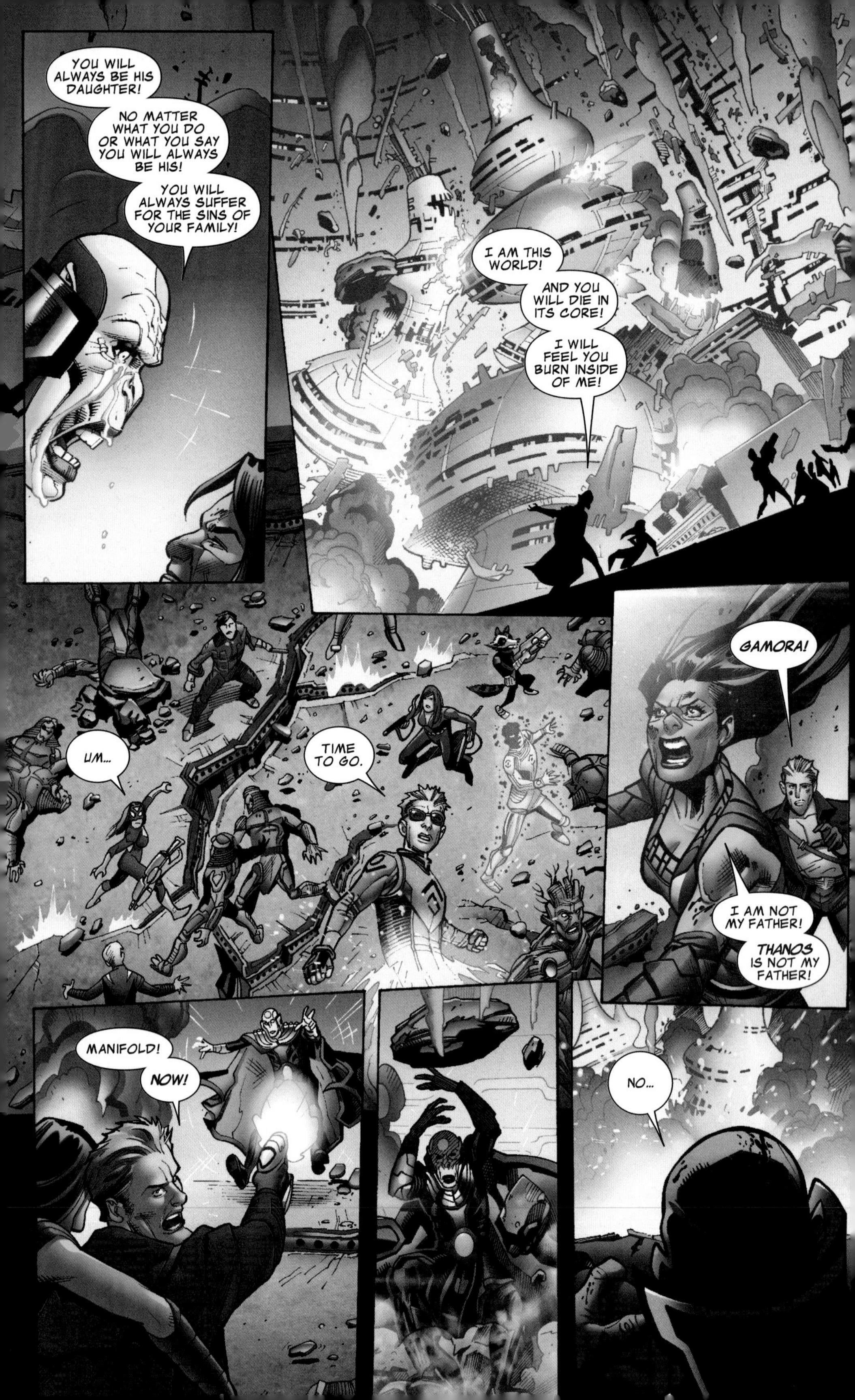
YOU WILL ALWAYS BE HIS DAUGHTER!
NO MATTER WHAT YOU DO OR WHAT YOU SAY YOU WILL ALWAYS BE HIS!
YOU WILL ALWAYS SUFFER FOR THE SINS OF YOUR FAMILY!
I AM THIS WORLD!
AND YOU WILL DIE IN ITS CORE!
I WILL FEEL YOU BURN INSIDE OF ME!
UM...
TIME TO GO.
GAMORA!
I AM NOT MY FATHER!
THANOS IS NOT MY FATHER!
MANIFOLD!
NOW!
NO...

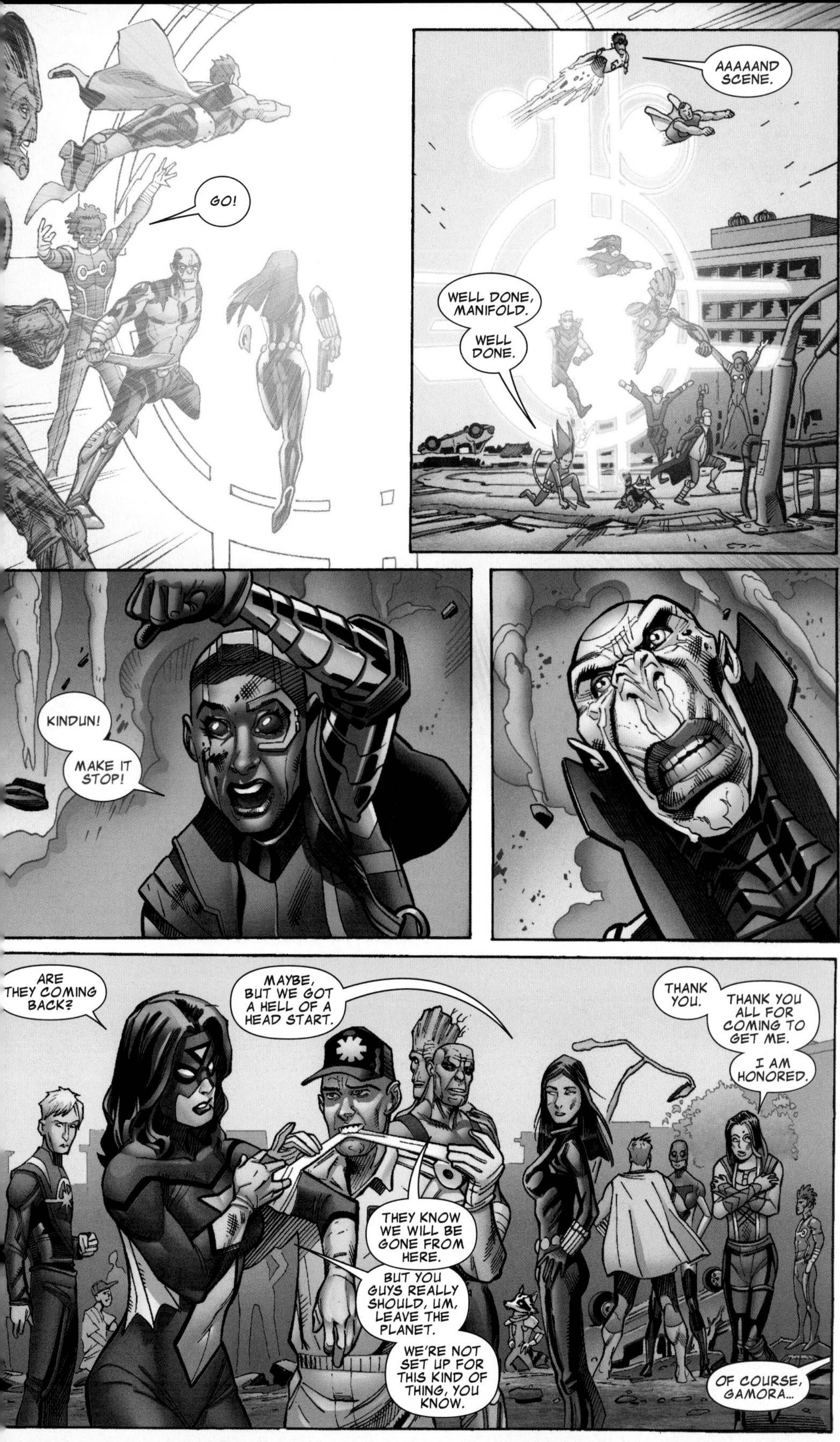
GO!
AAAAAND SCENE.
WELL DONE, MANIFOLD.
WELL DONE.
KINDUN!
MAKE IT STOP!
ARE THEY COMING BACK?
MAYBE, BUT WE GOT A HELL OF A HEAD START.
THANK YOU.
THANK YOU ALL FOR COMING TO GET ME.
I AM HONORED.
THEY KNOW WE WILL BE GONE FROM HERE.
BUT YOU GUYS REALLY SHOULD, UM, LEAVE THE PLANET.
WE'RE NOT SET UP FOR THIS KIND OF THING, YOU KNOW.
OF COURSE, GAMORA...

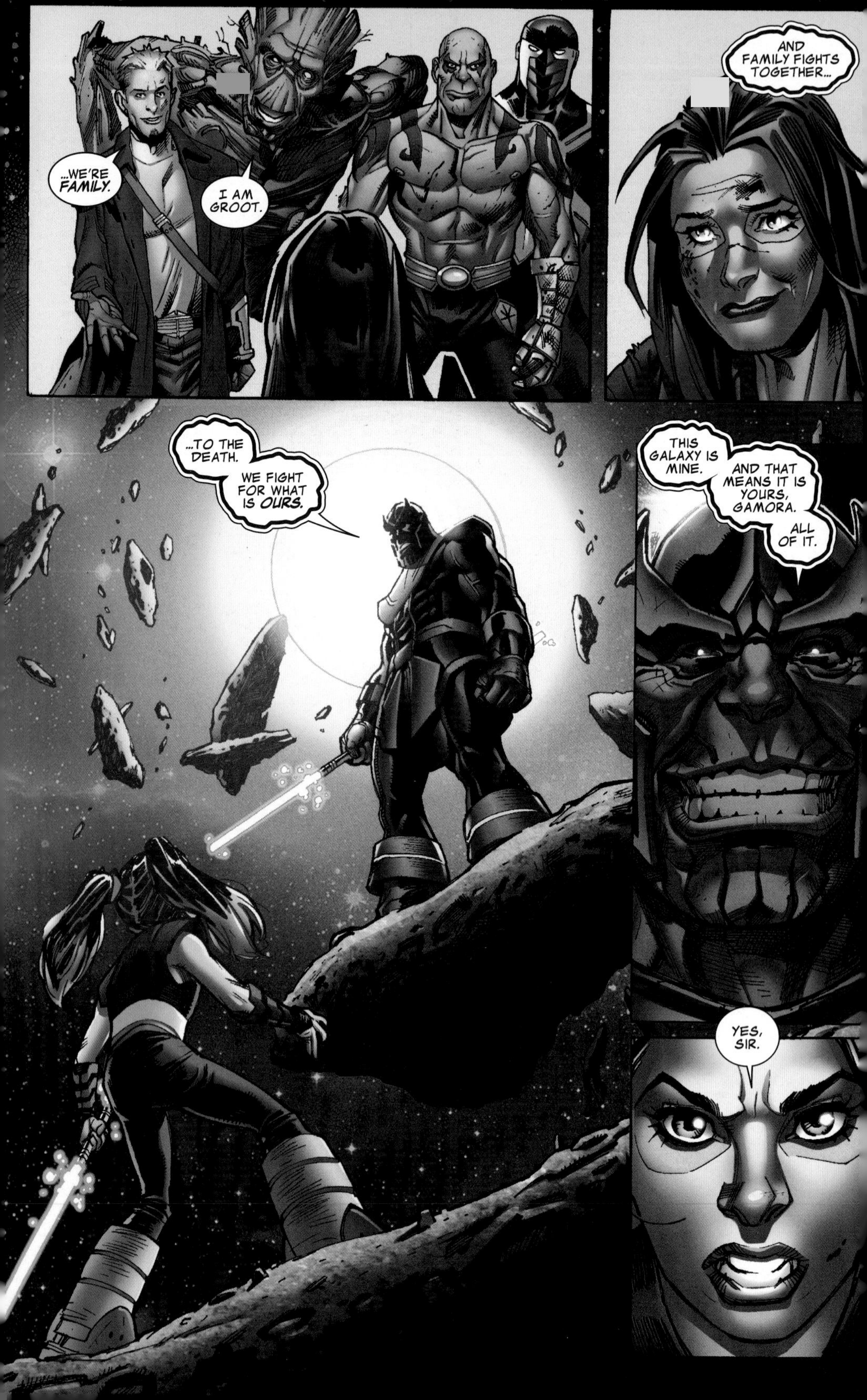
...WE'RE *FAMILY.*
I AM GROOT.
AND FAMILY FIGHTS TOGETHER...
...TO THE DEATH.
WE FIGHT FOR WHAT IS *OURS.*
THIS GALAXY IS MINE.
AND THAT MEANS IT IS YOURS, GAMORA.
ALL OF IT.
YES, SIR.

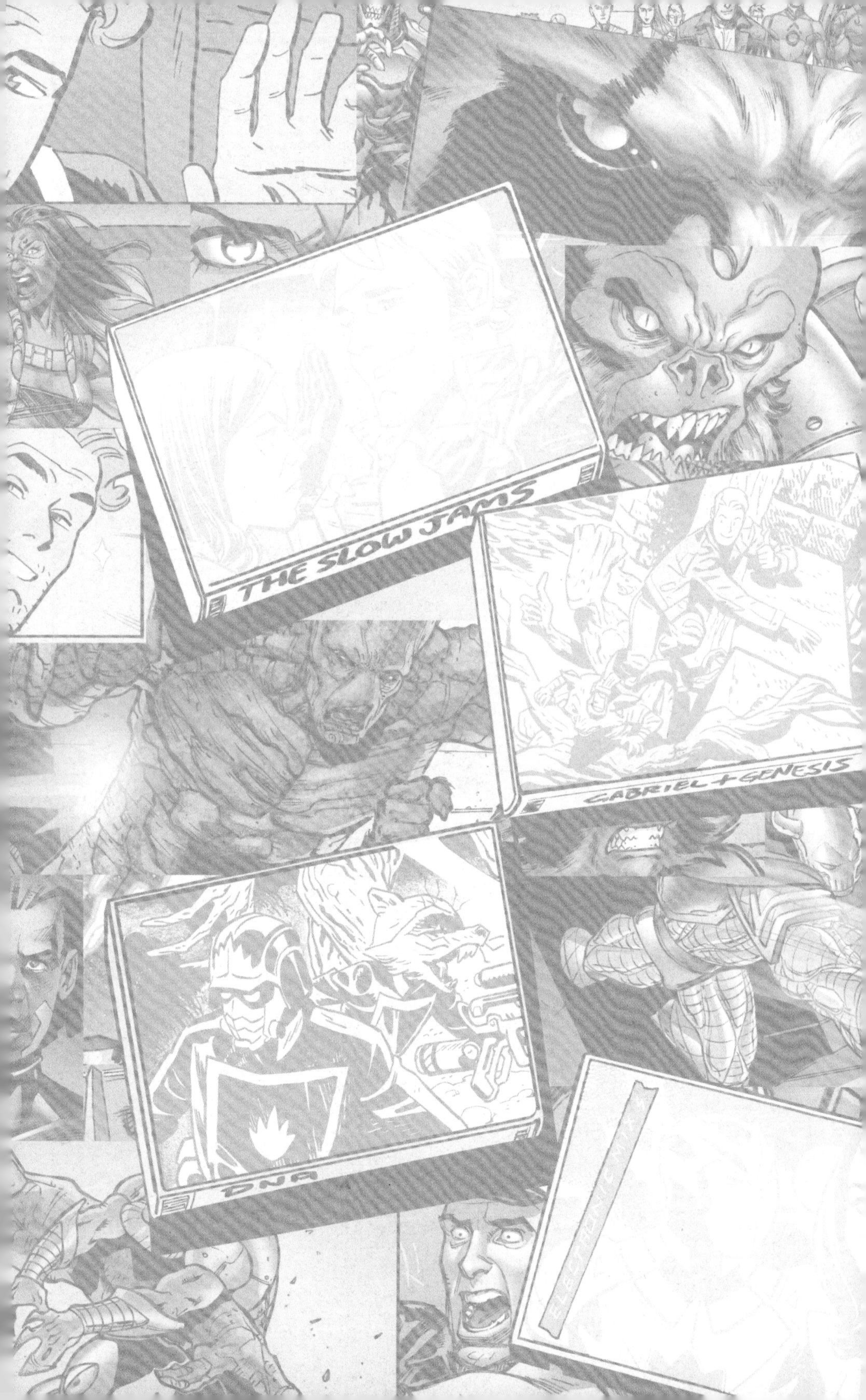
THE SLOW JAMS
GABRIEL + GENESIS
DNA

GUARDIANS OF THE GALAXY: DREAM ON

ONE OF THE GALAXY'S GREATEST BOUNTY HUNTERS IS AFTER THE GUARDIANS! CAN THE TEAM ESCAPE WHEN THEY FIND THEMSELVES LIVING OUT THEIR WILDEST DREAMS?

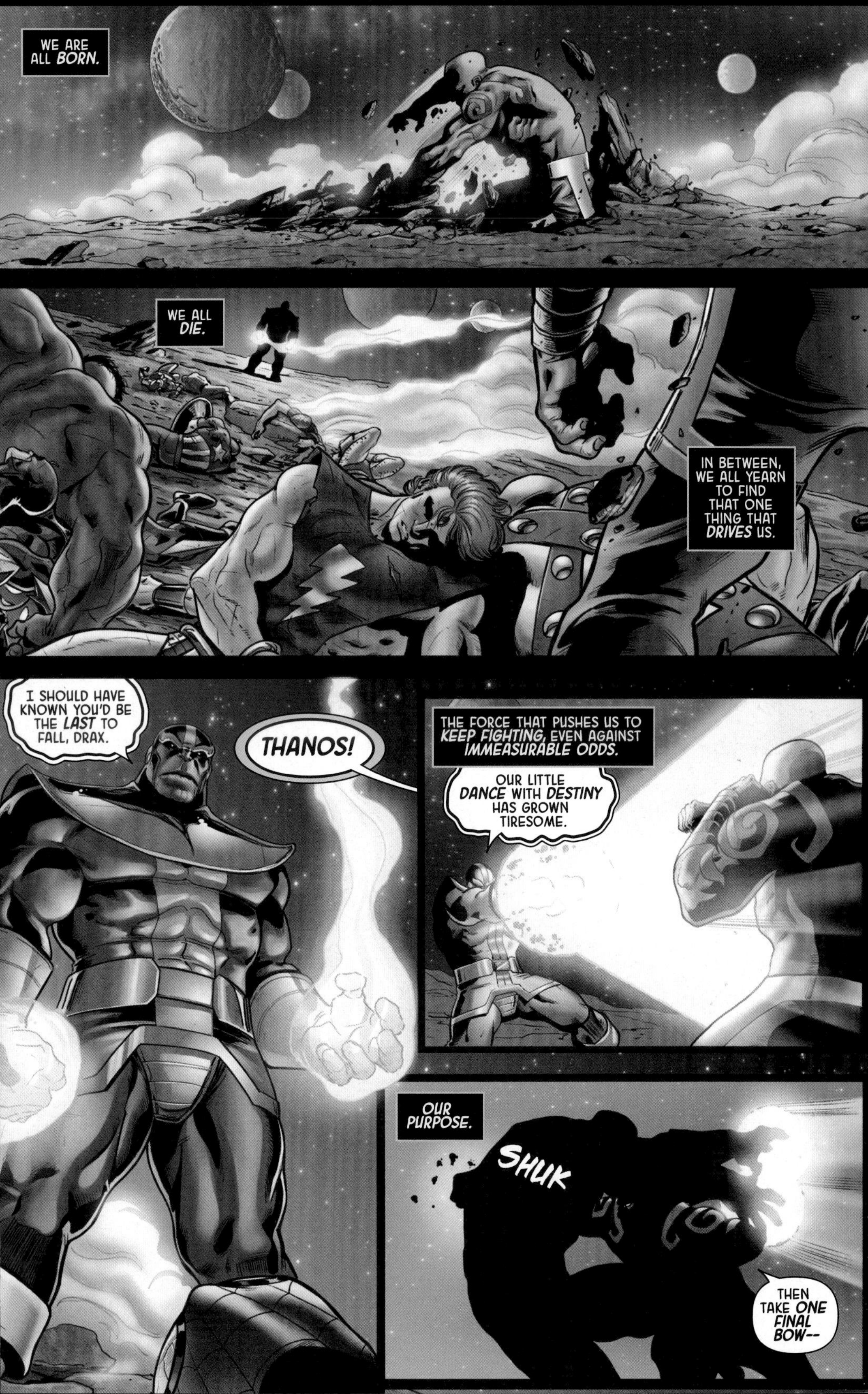
WE ARE ALL BORN.
WE ALL DIE.
IN BETWEEN, WE ALL YEARN TO FIND THAT ONE THING THAT DRIVES US.
I SHOULD HAVE KNOWN YOU'D BE THE LAST TO FALL, DRAX.
THANOS!
THE FORCE THAT PUSHES US TO KEEP FIGHTING, EVEN AGAINST IMMEASURABLE ODDS.
OUR LITTLE DANCE WITH DESTINY HAS GROWN TIRESOME.
OUR PURPOSE.
SHUK
THEN TAKE ONE FINAL BOW--

ONLY ONCE WE HAVE ACHIEVED THAT WHICH WE WERE BORN TO DO CAN WE FINALLY BEGIN TO ANSWER LIFE'S GREATEST QUESTION:
DREAM ON
--FOR TONIGHT, THANOS, YOU ARE DESTINED TO DIE!
HRRRK!
WHAT COMES NEXT?

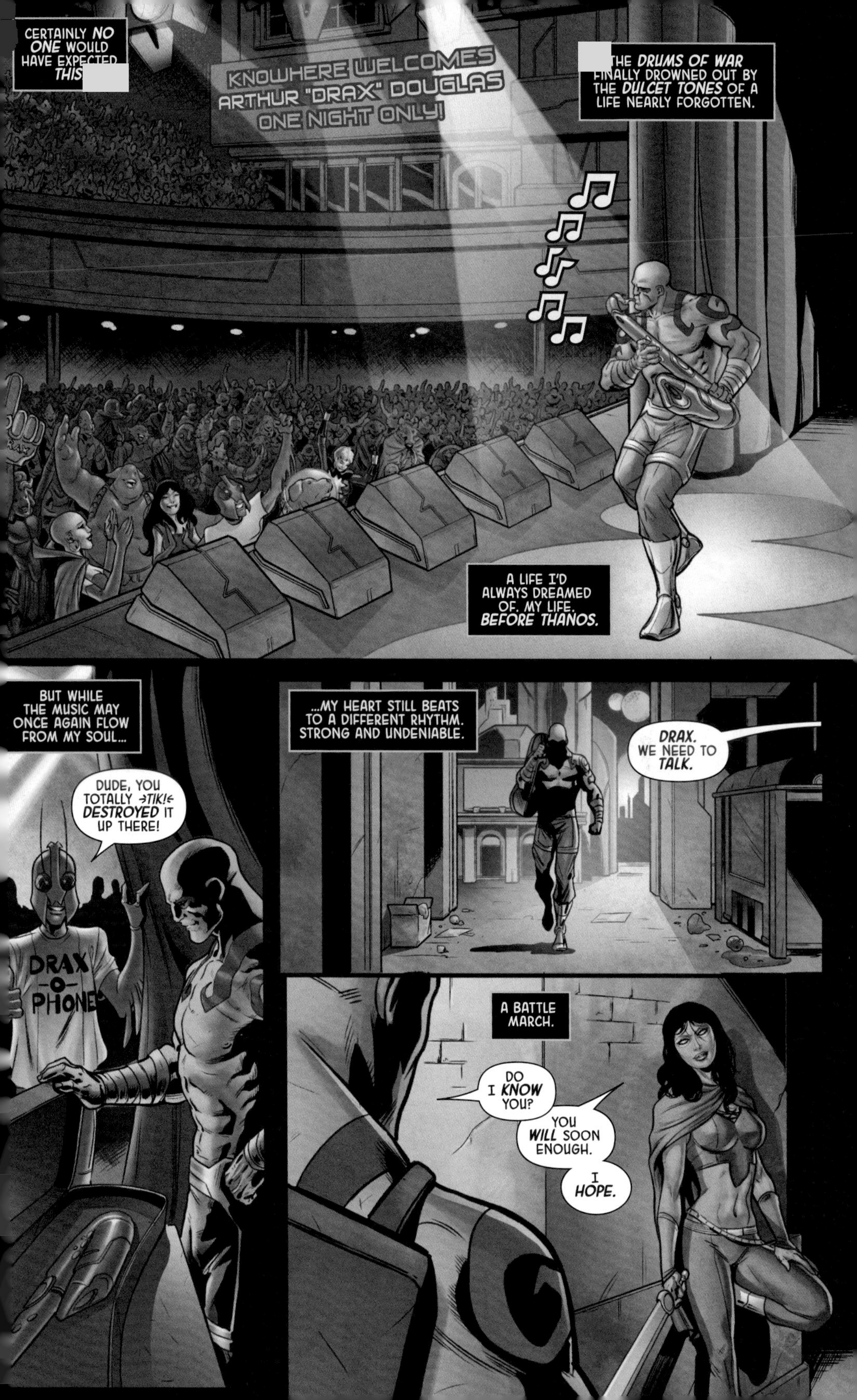
CERTAINLY NO ONE WOULD HAVE EXPECTED THIS
KNOWHERE WELCOMES ARTHUR "DRAX" DOUGLAS ONE NIGHT ONLY!
THE DRUMS OF WAR FINALLY DROWNED OUT BY THE DULCET TONES OF A LIFE NEARLY FORGOTTEN.
A LIFE I'D ALWAYS DREAMED OF. MY LIFE. BEFORE THANOS.
BUT WHILE THE MUSIC MAY ONCE AGAIN FLOW FROM MY SOUL...
DUDE, YOU TOTALLY →TIK!← DESTROYED IT UP THERE!
DRAX -O- PHONE
...MY HEART STILL BEATS TO A DIFFERENT RHYTHM. STRONG AND UNDENIABLE.
DRAX. WE NEED TO TALK.
A BATTLE MARCH.
DO I KNOW YOU?
YOU WILL SOON ENOUGH.
I HOPE.

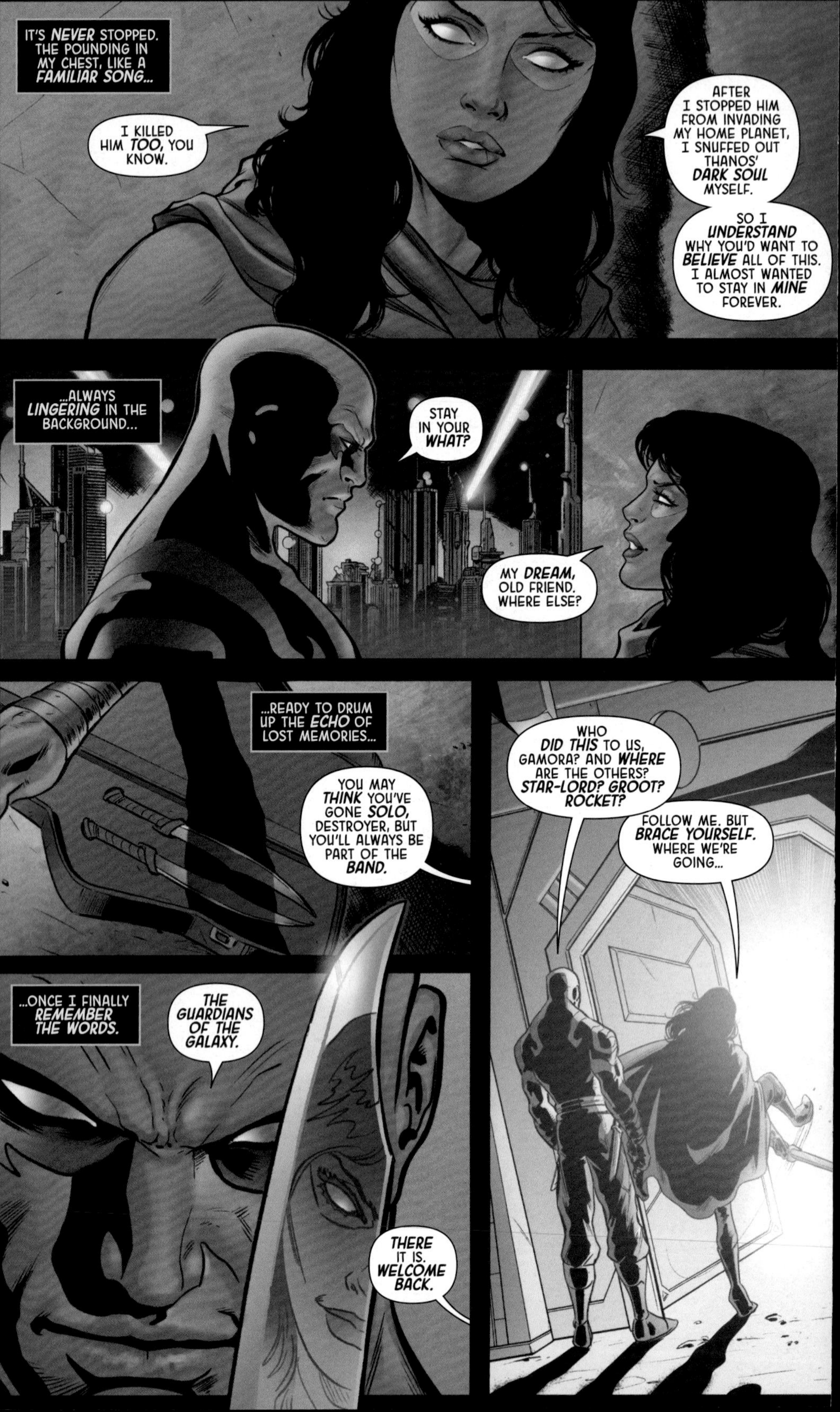
IT'S NEVER STOPPED. THE POUNDING IN MY CHEST, LIKE A FAMILIAR SONG...
I KILLED HIM TOO, YOU KNOW.
AFTER I STOPPED HIM FROM INVADING MY HOME PLANET, I SNUFFED OUT THANOS' DARK SOUL MYSELF.
SO I UNDERSTAND WHY YOU'D WANT TO BELIEVE ALL OF THIS. I ALMOST WANTED TO STAY IN MINE FOREVER.
...ALWAYS LINGERING IN THE BACKGROUND...
STAY IN YOUR WHAT?
MY DREAM, OLD FRIEND. WHERE ELSE?
...READY TO DRUM UP THE ECHO OF LOST MEMORIES...
YOU MAY THINK YOU'VE GONE SOLO, DESTROYER, BUT YOU'LL ALWAYS BE PART OF THE BAND.
...ONCE I FINALLY REMEMBER THE WORDS.
THE GUARDIANS OF THE GALAXY.
THERE IT IS. WELCOME BACK.
WHO DID THIS TO US, GAMORA? AND WHERE ARE THE OTHERS? STAR-LORD? GROOT? ROCKET?
FOLLOW ME. BUT BRACE YOURSELF. WHERE WE'RE GOING...

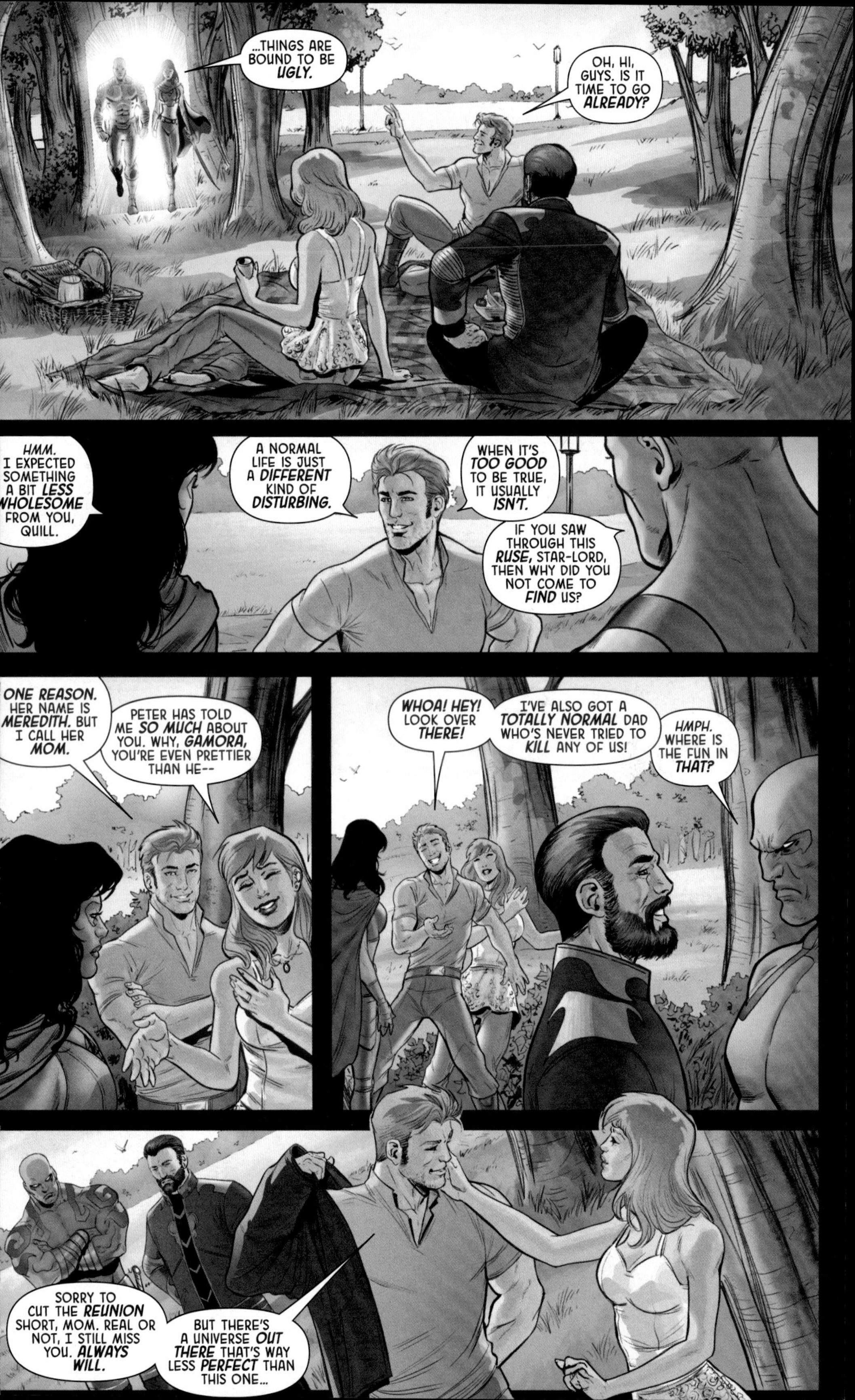
...THINGS ARE BOUND TO BE UGLY.
OH, HI, GUYS. IS IT TIME TO GO ALREADY?
HMM. I EXPECTED SOMETHING A BIT LESS WHOLESOME FROM YOU, QUILL.
A NORMAL LIFE IS JUST A DIFFERENT KIND OF DISTURBING.
WHEN IT'S TOO GOOD TO BE TRUE, IT USUALLY ISN'T.
IF YOU SAW THROUGH THIS RUSE, STAR-LORD, THEN WHY DID YOU NOT COME TO FIND US?
ONE REASON. HER NAME IS MEREDITH. BUT I CALL HER MOM.
PETER HAS TOLD ME SO MUCH ABOUT YOU. WHY, GAMORA, YOU'RE EVEN PRETTIER THAN HE--
WHOA! HEY! LOOK OVER THERE!
I'VE ALSO GOT A TOTALLY NORMAL DAD WHO'S NEVER TRIED TO KILL ANY OF US!
HMPH. WHERE IS THE FUN IN THAT?
SORRY TO CUT THE REUNION SHORT, MOM. REAL OR NOT, I STILL MISS YOU. ALWAYS WILL.
BUT THERE'S A UNIVERSE OUT THERE THAT'S WAY LESS PERFECT THAN THIS ONE...

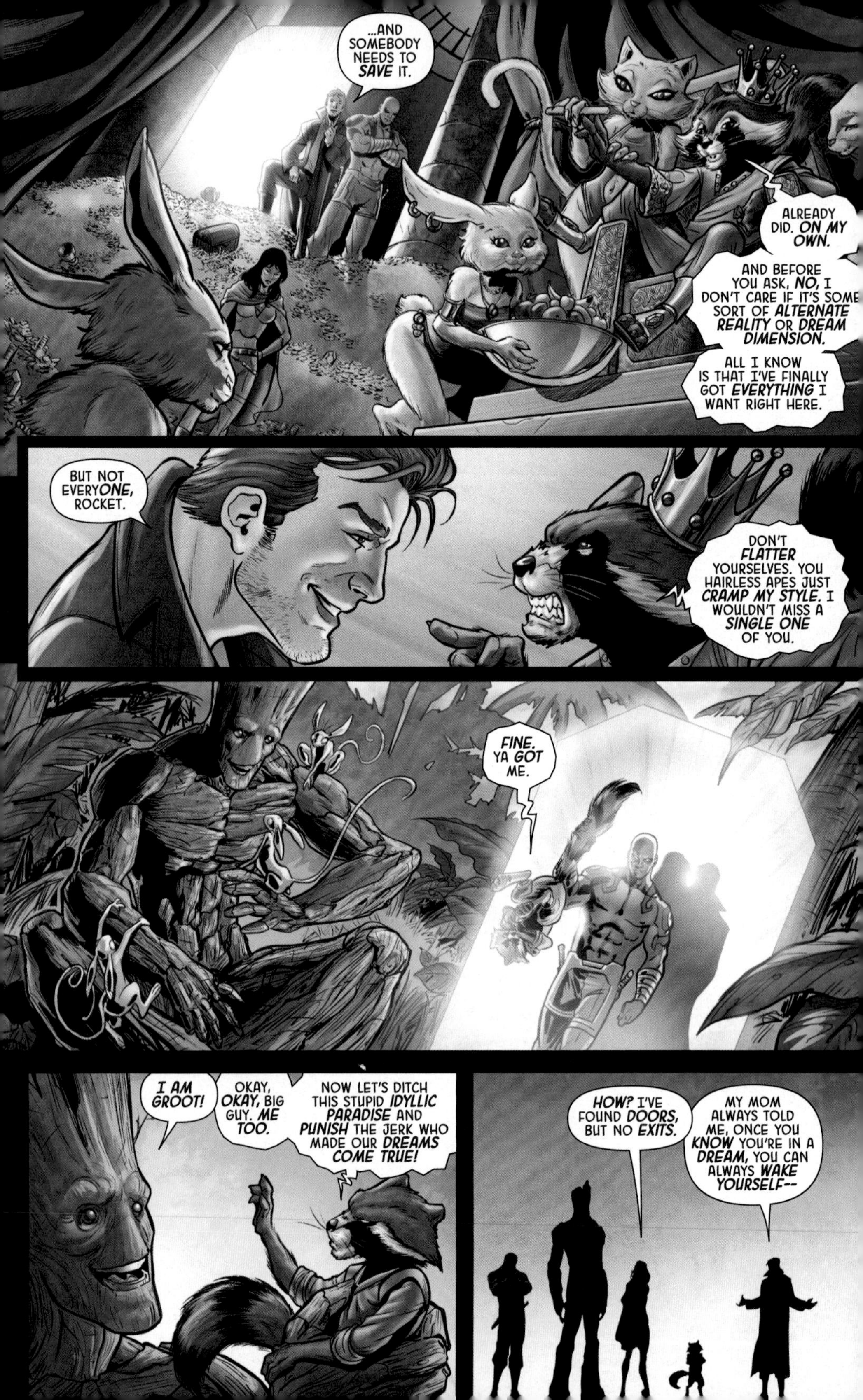

...AND SOMEBODY NEEDS TO SAVE IT.
ALREADY DID. ON MY OWN.
AND BEFORE YOU ASK, NO, I DON'T CARE IF IT'S SOME SORT OF ALTERNATE REALITY OR DREAM DIMENSION.
ALL I KNOW IS THAT I'VE FINALLY GOT EVERYTHING I WANT RIGHT HERE.
BUT NOT EVERYONE, ROCKET.
DON'T FLATTER YOURSELVES. YOU HAIRLESS APES JUST CRAMP MY STYLE. I WOULDN'T MISS A SINGLE ONE OF YOU.
FINE. YA GOT ME.
I AM GROOT!
OKAY, OKAY, BIG GUY. ME TOO.
NOW LET'S DITCH THIS STUPID IDYLLIC PARADISE AND PUNISH THE JERK WHO MADE OUR DREAMS COME TRUE!
HOW? I'VE FOUND DOORS, BUT NO EXITS.
MY MOM ALWAYS TOLD ME, ONCE YOU KNOW YOU'RE IN A DREAM, YOU CAN ALWAYS WAKE YOURSELF--

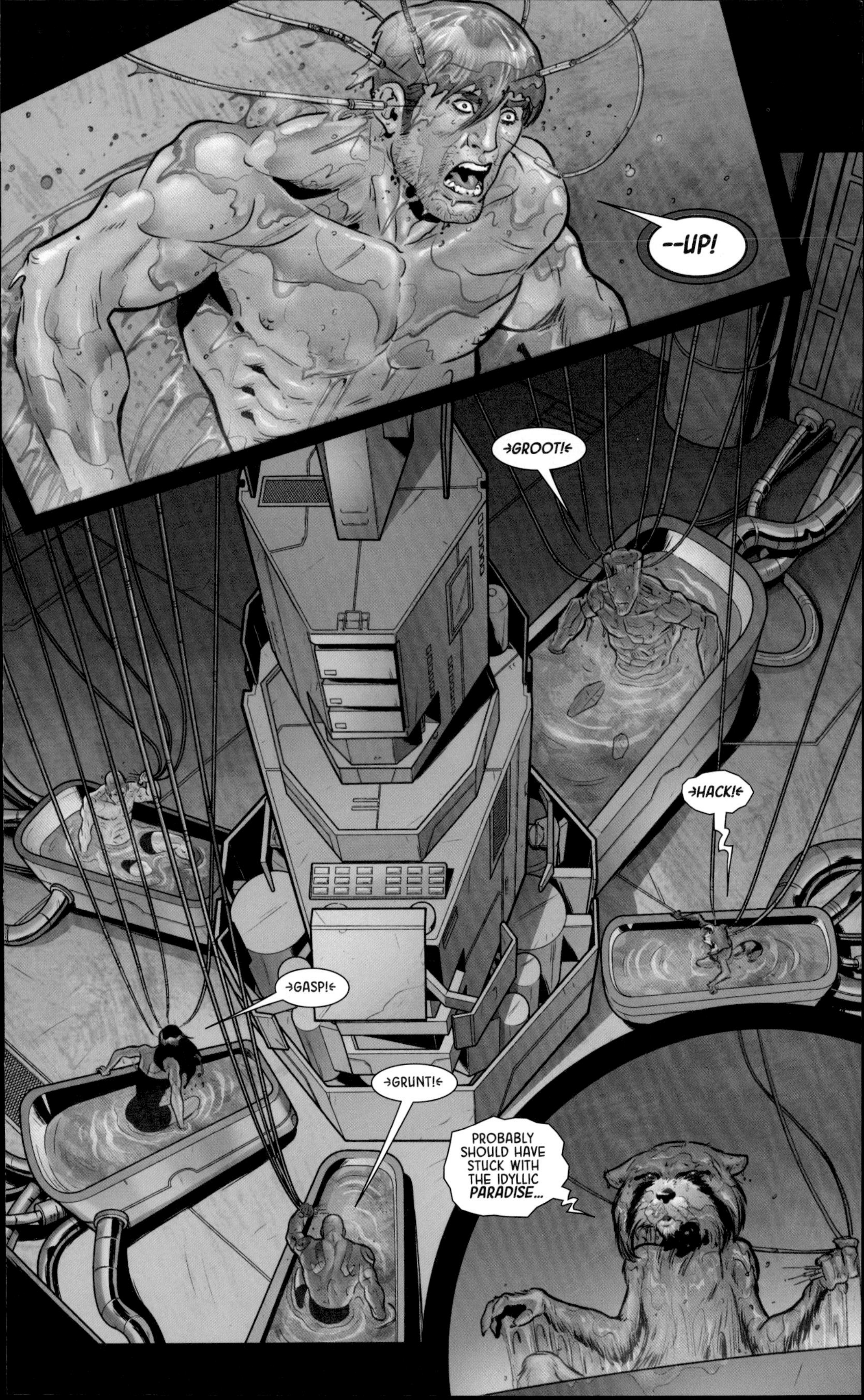
--UP!
GROOT!
HACK!
GASP!
GRUNT!
PROBABLY SHOULD HAVE STUCK WITH THE IDYLLIC *PARADISE*...

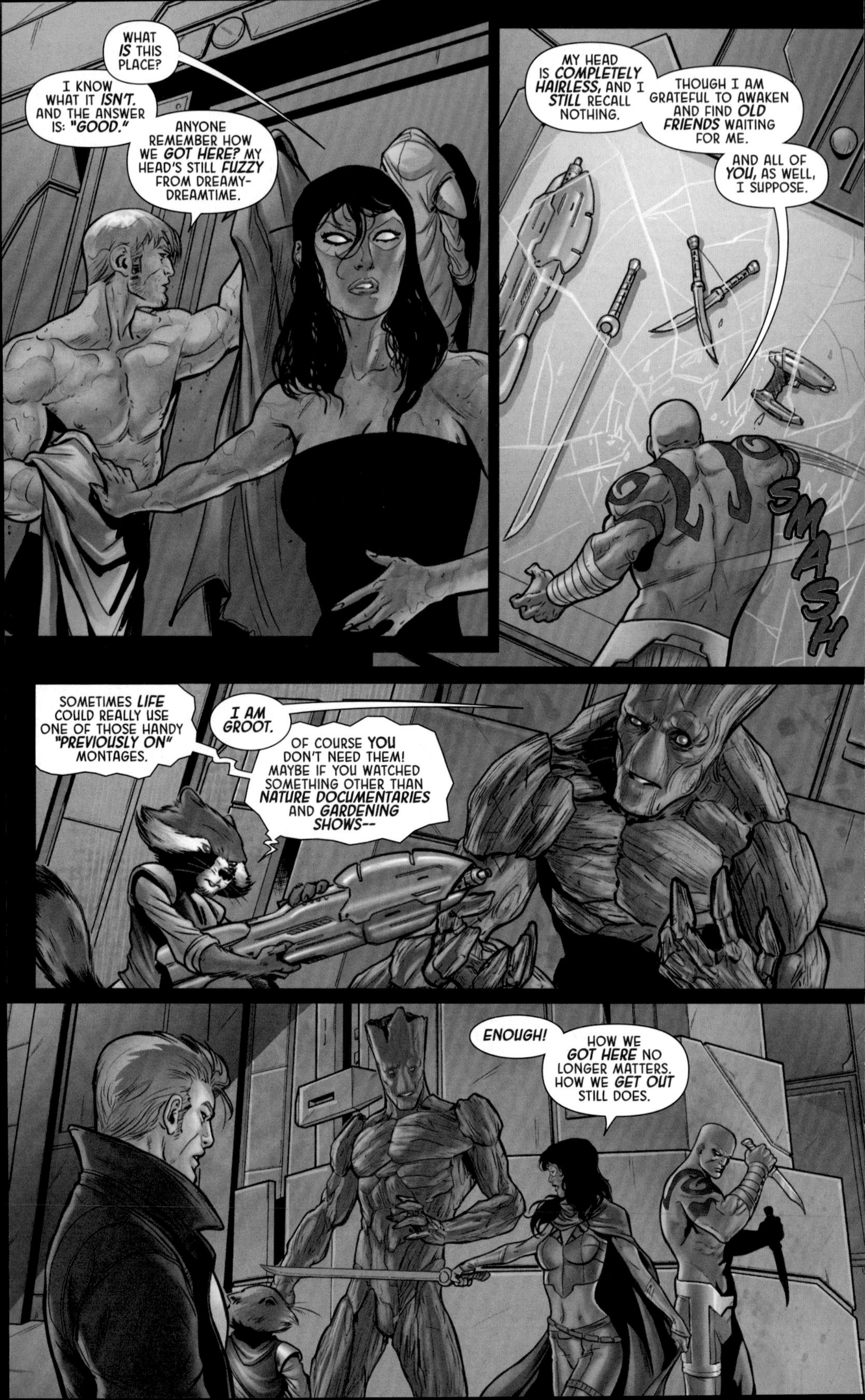
WHAT IS THIS PLACE?
I KNOW WHAT IT ISN'T. AND THE ANSWER IS: "GOOD."
ANYONE REMEMBER HOW WE GOT HERE? MY HEAD'S STILL FUZZY FROM DREAMY-DREAMTIME.
MY HEAD IS COMPLETELY HAIRLESS, AND I STILL RECALL NOTHING.
THOUGH I AM GRATEFUL TO AWAKEN AND FIND OLD FRIENDS WAITING FOR ME.
AND ALL OF YOU, AS WELL, I SUPPOSE.
SMASH
SOMETIMES LIFE COULD REALLY USE ONE OF THOSE HANDY "PREVIOUSLY ON" MONTAGES.
I AM GROOT.
OF COURSE YOU DON'T NEED THEM! MAYBE IF YOU WATCHED SOMETHING OTHER THAN NATURE DOCUMENTARIES AND GARDENING SHOWS--
ENOUGH!
HOW WE GOT HERE NO LONGER MATTERS. HOW WE GET OUT STILL DOES.

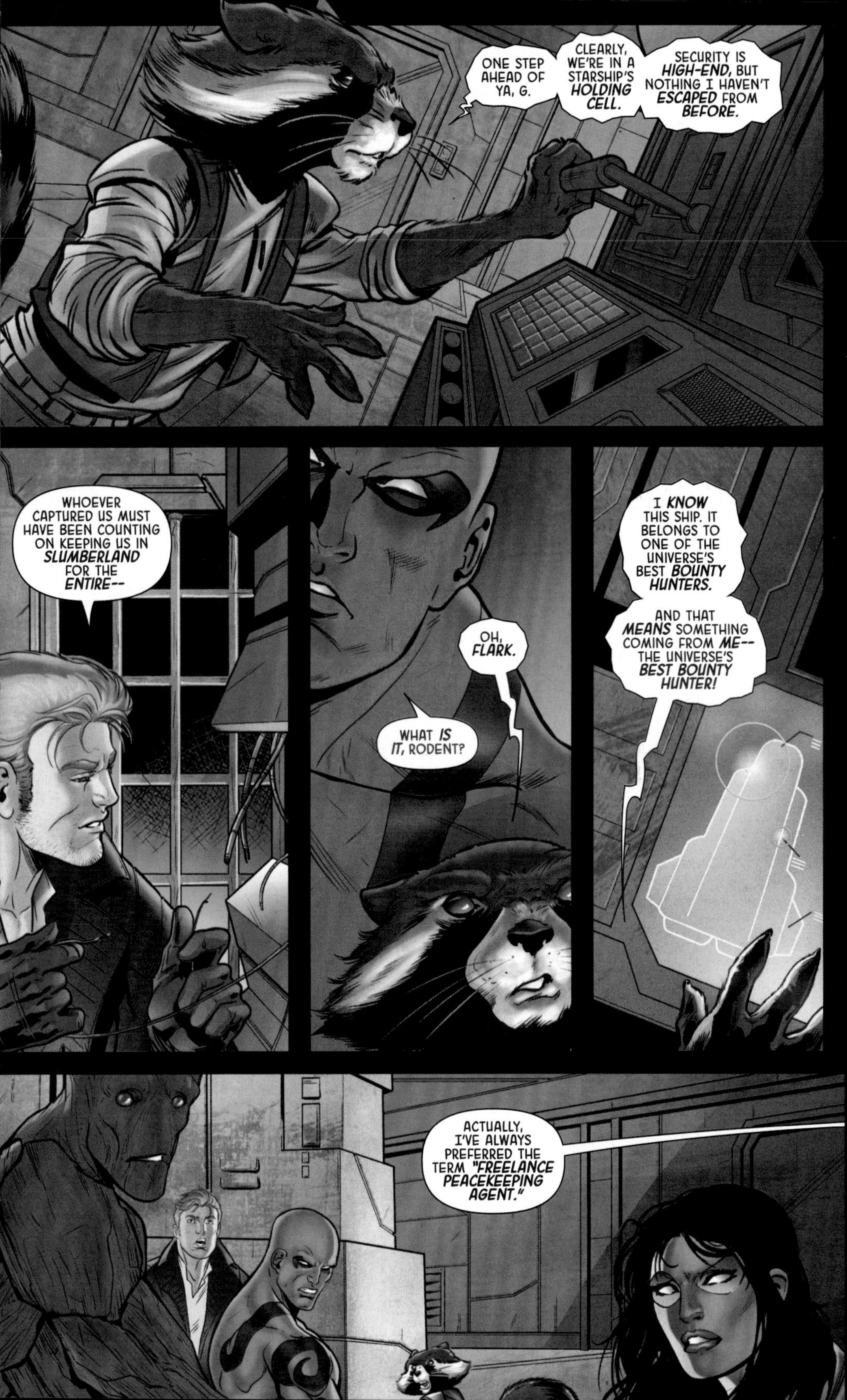
ONE STEP AHEAD OF YA, G.
CLEARLY, WE'RE IN A STARSHIP'S HOLDING CELL.
SECURITY IS HIGH-END, BUT NOTHING I HAVEN'T ESCAPED FROM BEFORE.
WHOEVER CAPTURED US MUST HAVE BEEN COUNTING ON KEEPING US IN SLUMBERLAND FOR THE ENTIRE--
OH, FLARK.
WHAT IS IT, RODENT?
I KNOW THIS SHIP. IT BELONGS TO ONE OF THE UNIVERSE'S BEST BOUNTY HUNTERS.
AND THAT MEANS SOMETHING COMING FROM ME-- THE UNIVERSE'S BEST BOUNTY HUNTER!
ACTUALLY, I'VE ALWAYS PREFERRED THE TERM "FREELANCE PEACEKEEPING AGENT."

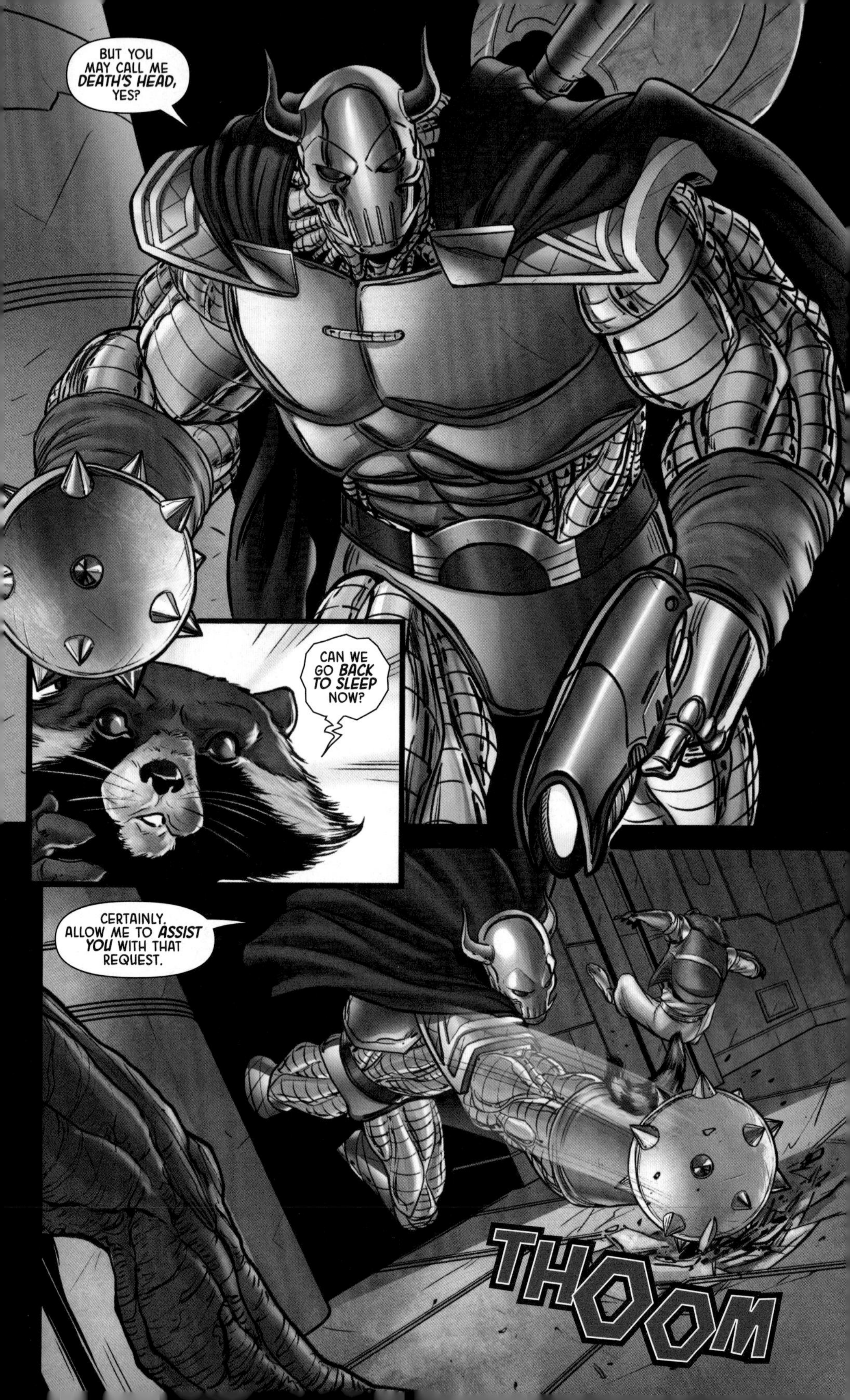
BUT YOU MAY CALL ME DEATH'S HEAD, YES?
CAN WE GO BACK TO SLEEP NOW?
CERTAINLY. ALLOW ME TO ASSIST YOU WITH THAT REQUEST.
THOOM

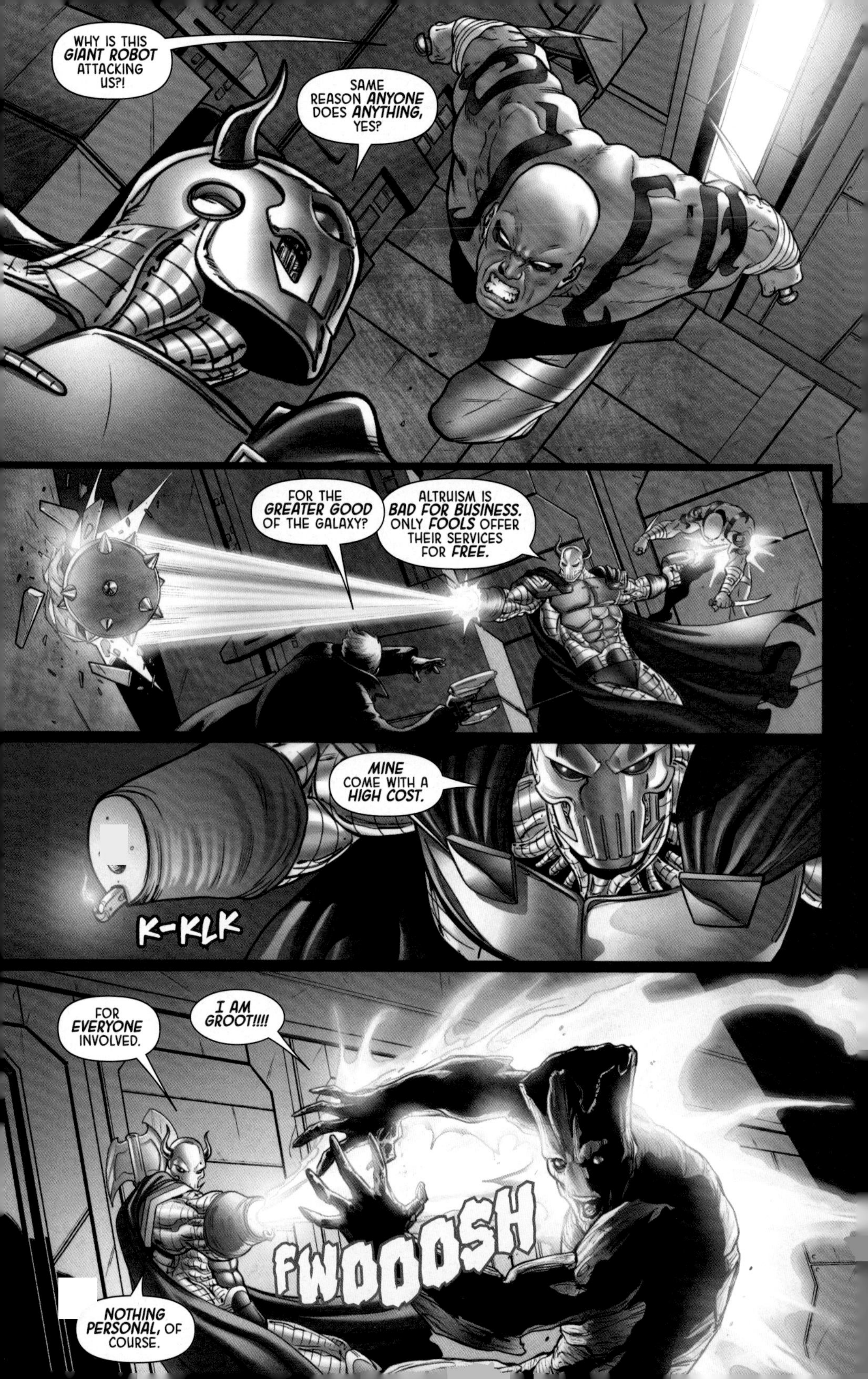
WHY IS THIS GIANT ROBOT ATTACKING US?!
SAME REASON ANYONE DOES ANYTHING, YES?
FOR THE GREATER GOOD OF THE GALAXY?
ALTRUISM IS BAD FOR BUSINESS. ONLY FOOLS OFFER THEIR SERVICES FOR FREE.
MINE COME WITH A HIGH COST.
K-KLK
FOR EVERYONE INVOLVED.
I AM GROOT!!!!
FWOOOSH
NOTHING PERSONAL, OF COURSE.

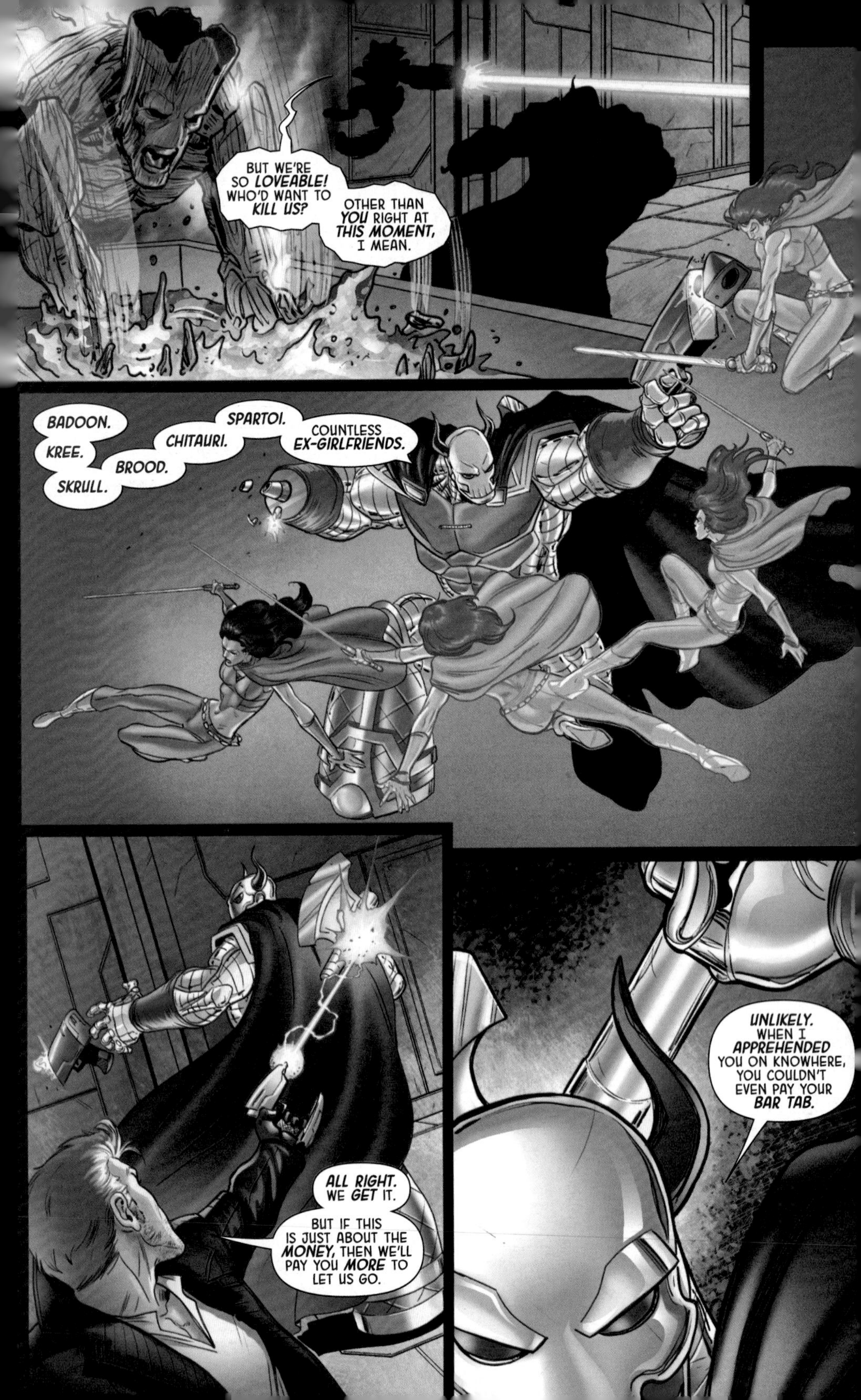
BUT WE'RE SO LOVEABLE! WHO'D WANT TO KILL US?
OTHER THAN YOU RIGHT AT THIS MOMENT, I MEAN.
BADOON.
KREE.
SKRULL.
BROOD.
CHITAURI.
SPARTOI.
COUNTLESS EX-GIRLFRIENDS.
ALL RIGHT. WE GET IT.
BUT IF THIS IS JUST ABOUT THE MONEY, THEN WE'LL PAY YOU MORE TO LET US GO.
UNLIKELY. WHEN I APPREHENDED YOU ON KNOWHERE, YOU COULDN'T EVEN PAY YOUR BAR TAB.

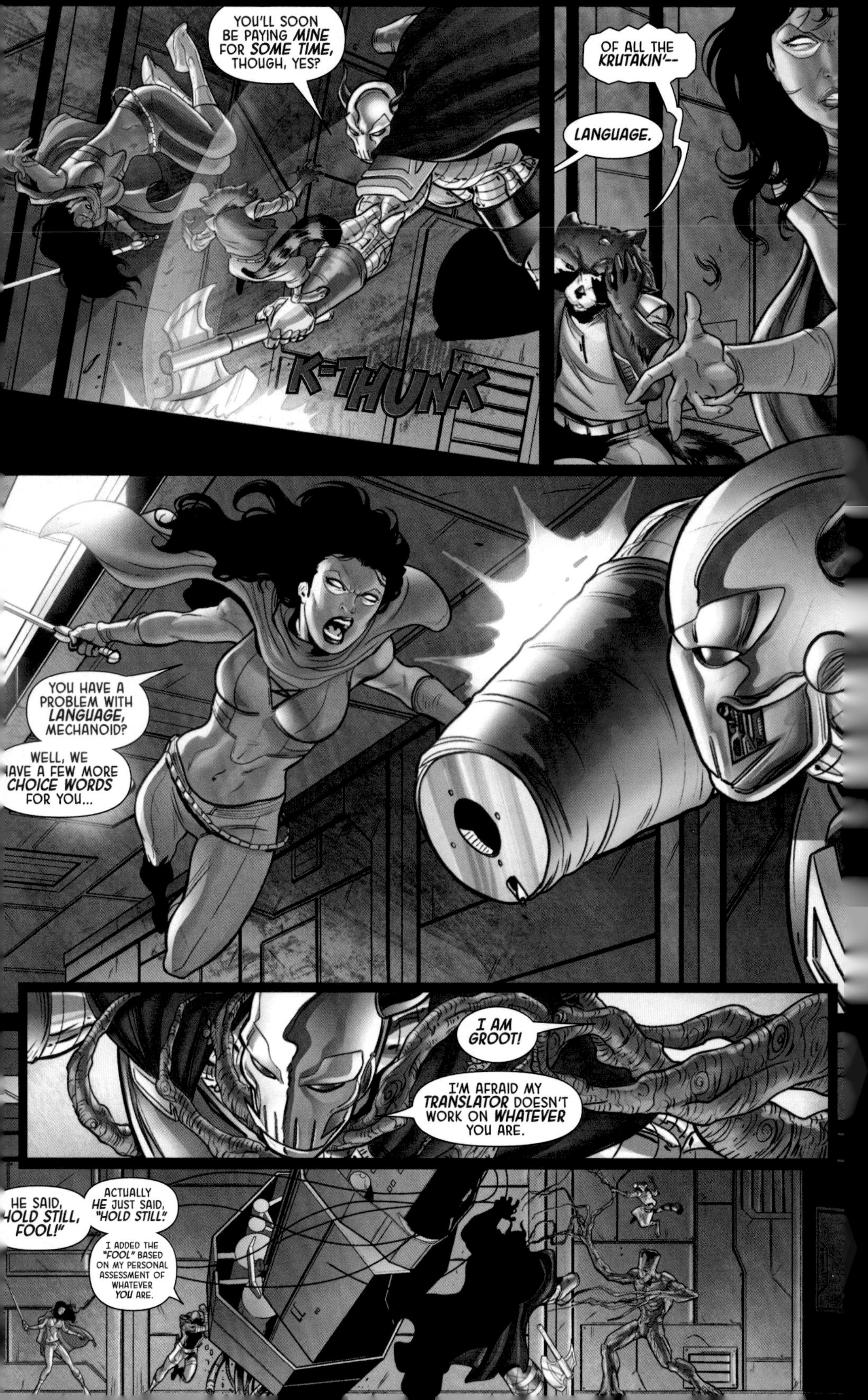
YOU'LL SOON BE PAYING MINE FOR SOME TIME, THOUGH, YES?
K-THUNK
OF ALL THE KRUTAKIN'--
LANGUAGE.
YOU HAVE A PROBLEM WITH LANGUAGE, MECHANOID?
WELL, WE AVE A FEW MORE CHOICE WORDS FOR YOU...
I AM GROOT!
I'M AFRAID MY TRANSLATOR DOESN'T WORK ON WHATEVER YOU ARE.
HE SAID, OLD STILL, FOOL!"
ACTUALLY HE JUST SAID, "HOLD STILL."
I ADDED THE "FOOL" BASED ON MY PERSONAL ASSESSMENT OF WHATEVER YOU ARE.

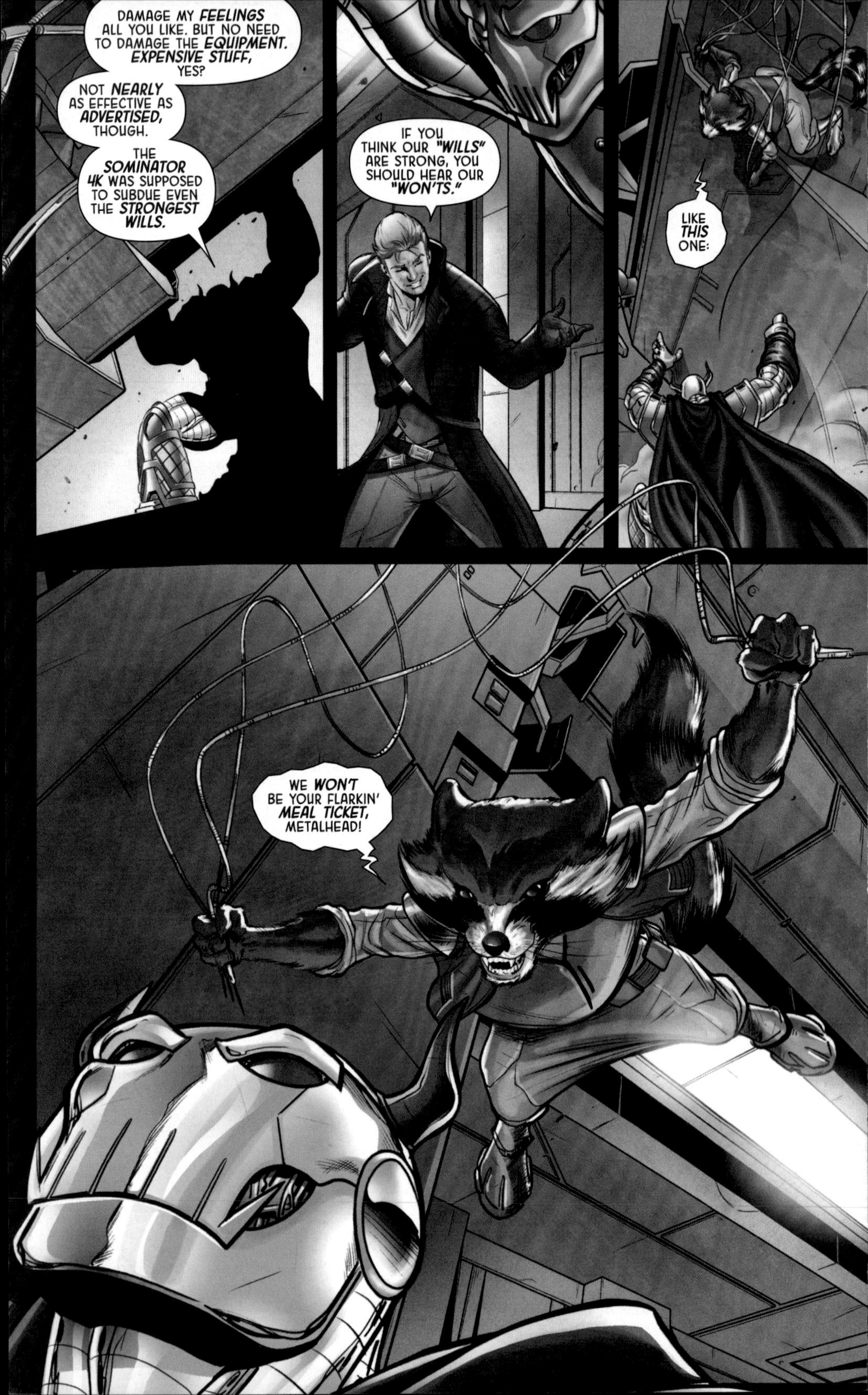
DAMAGE MY FEELINGS ALL YOU LIKE. BUT NO NEED TO DAMAGE THE EQUIPMENT. EXPENSIVE STUFF, YES?
NOT NEARLY AS EFFECTIVE AS ADVERTISED, THOUGH.
THE SOMINATOR 4K WAS SUPPOSED TO SUBDUE EVEN THE STRONGEST WILLS.
IF YOU THINK OUR "WILLS" ARE STRONG, YOU SHOULD HEAR OUR "WON'TS."
LIKE THIS ONE:
WE WON'T BE YOUR FLARKIN' MEAL TICKET, METALHEAD!

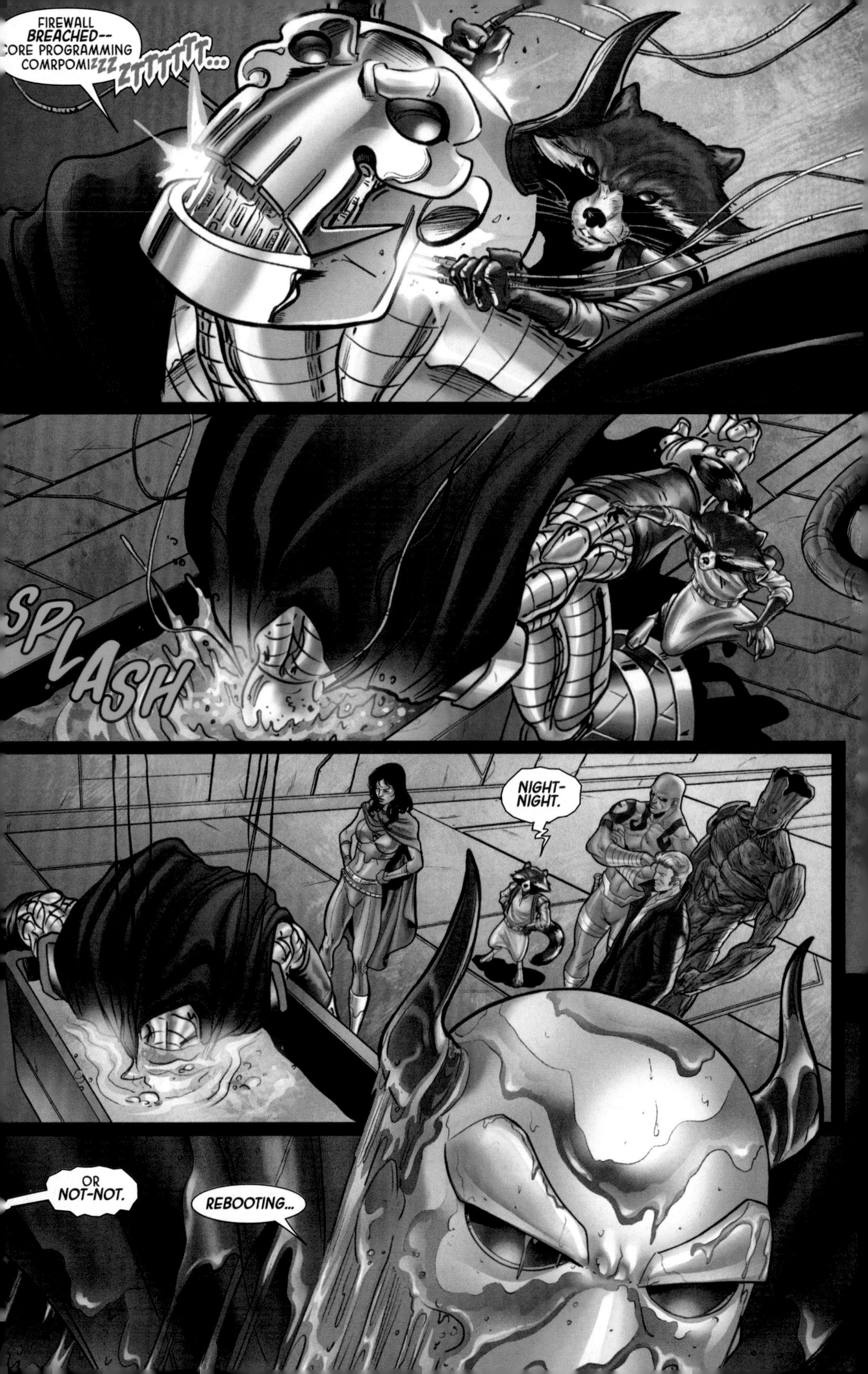
FIREWALL BREACHED-- CORE PROGRAMMING COMRPOMIZZZ ZTTTTTTT...
SPLASH
NIGHT-NIGHT.
OR NOT-NOT.
REBOOTING...

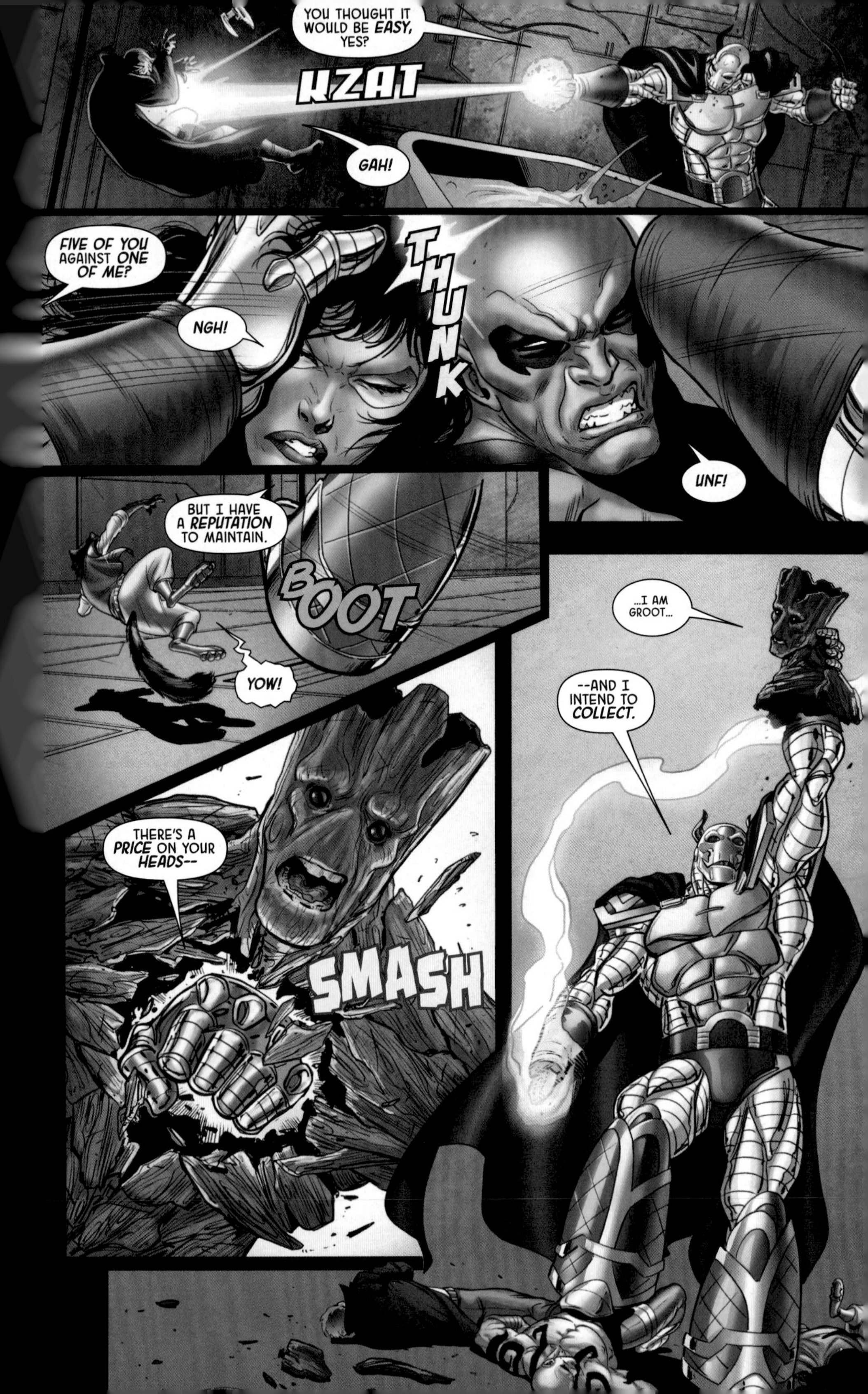
YOU THOUGHT IT WOULD BE EASY, YES?
KZAT
GAH!
FIVE OF YOU AGAINST ONE OF ME?
THUNK
NGH!
UNF!
BUT I HAVE A REPUTATION TO MAINTAIN.
BOOT
YOW!
THERE'S A PRICE ON YOUR HEADS--
SMASH
...I AM GROOT...
--AND I INTEND TO COLLECT.

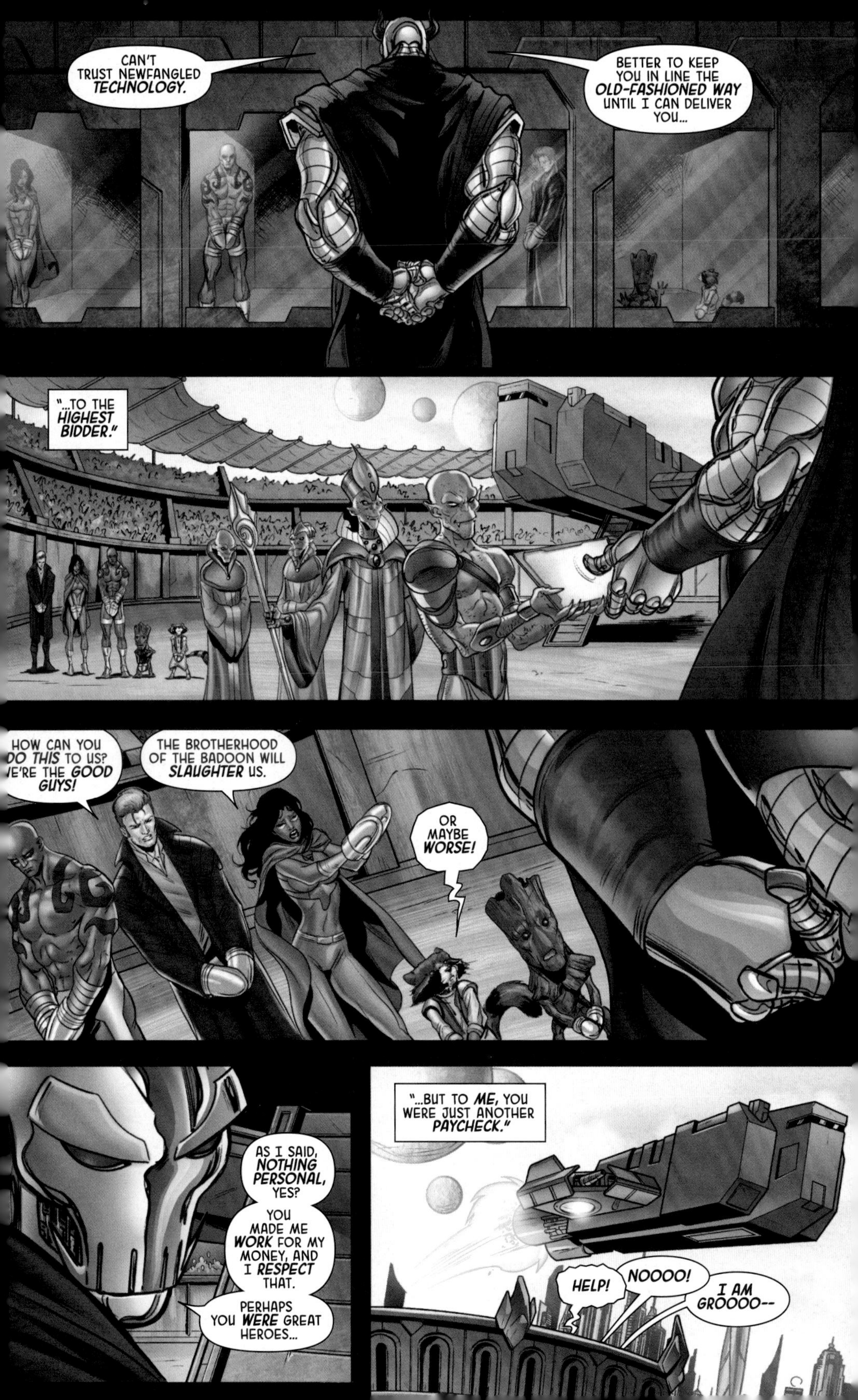
CAN'T TRUST NEWFANGLED TECHNOLOGY.
BETTER TO KEEP YOU IN LINE THE OLD-FASHIONED WAY UNTIL I CAN DELIVER YOU...
"...TO THE HIGHEST BIDDER."
HOW CAN YOU DO THIS TO US? E'RE THE GOOD GUYS!
THE BROTHERHOOD OF THE BADOON WILL SLAUGHTER US.
OR MAYBE WORSE!
AS I SAID, NOTHING PERSONAL, YES?
YOU MADE ME WORK FOR MY MONEY, AND I RESPECT THAT.
PERHAPS YOU WERE GREAT HEROES...
"...BUT TO ME, YOU WERE JUST ANOTHER PAYCHECK."
HELP!
NOOOO!
I AM GROOOO--

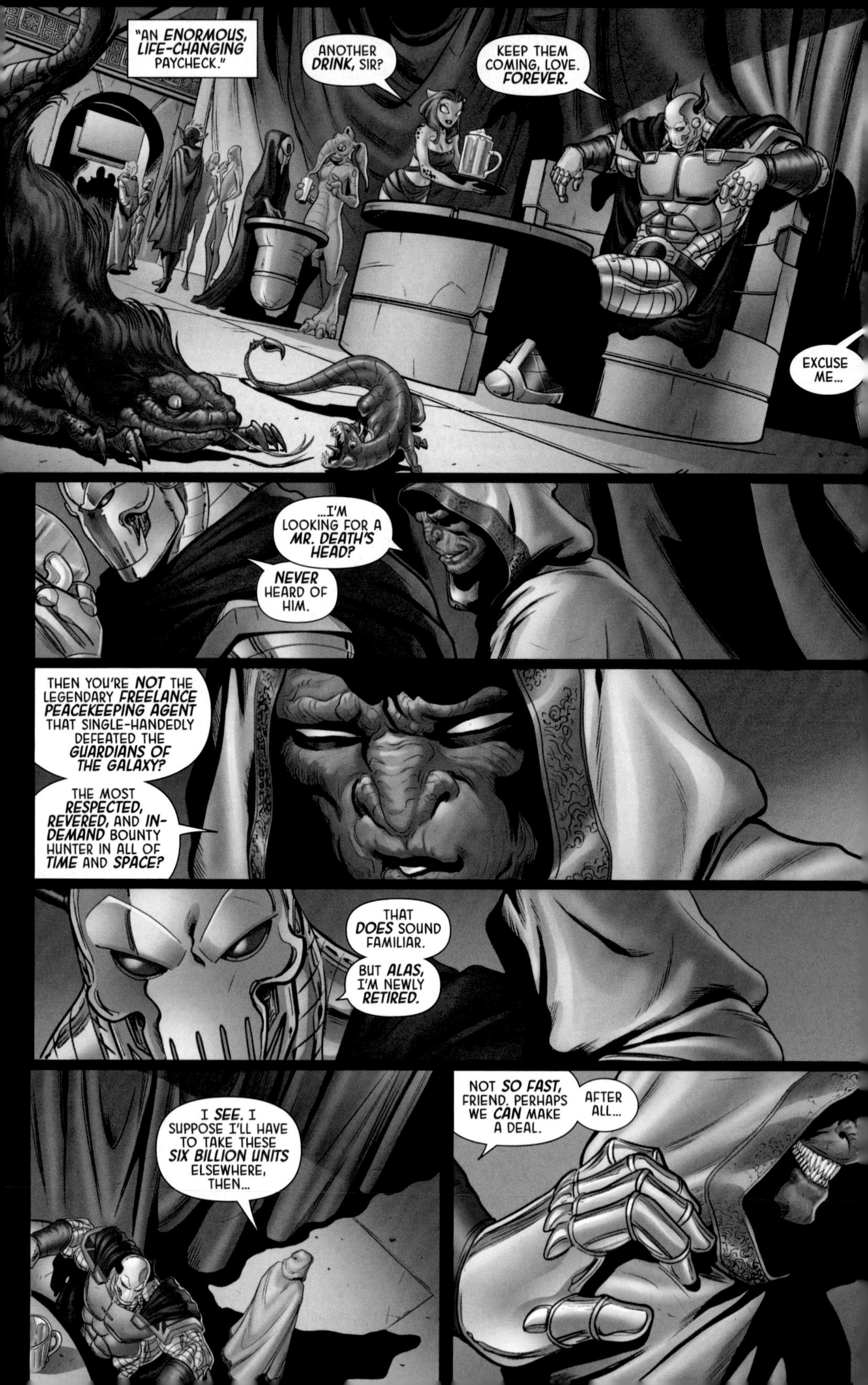

"AN ENORMOUS, LIFE-CHANGING PAYCHECK."
ANOTHER DRINK, SIR?
KEEP THEM COMING, LOVE. FOREVER.
EXCUSE ME...
...I'M LOOKING FOR A MR. DEATH'S HEAD?
NEVER HEARD OF HIM.
THEN YOU'RE NOT THE LEGENDARY FREELANCE PEACEKEEPING AGENT THAT SINGLE-HANDEDLY DEFEATED THE GUARDIANS OF THE GALAXY?
THE MOST RESPECTED, REVERED, AND IN-DEMAND BOUNTY HUNTER IN ALL OF TIME AND SPACE?
THAT DOES SOUND FAMILIAR.
BUT ALAS, I'M NEWLY RETIRED.
I SEE. I SUPPOSE I'LL HAVE TO TAKE THESE SIX BILLION UNITS ELSEWHERE, THEN...
NOT SO FAST, FRIEND. PERHAPS WE CAN MAKE A DEAL.
AFTER ALL...

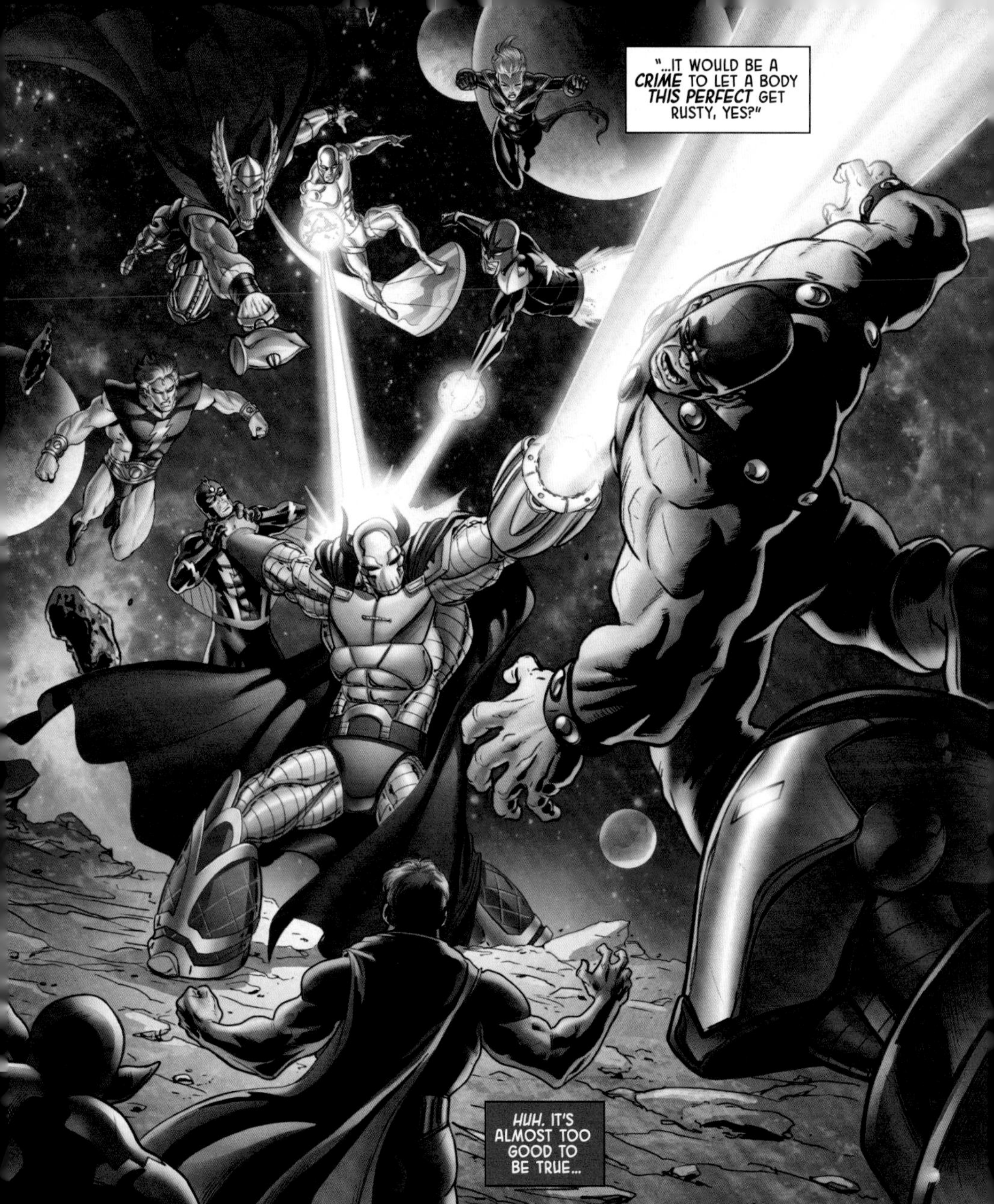
"...IT WOULD BE A CRIME TO LET A BODY THIS PERFECT GET RUSTY, YES?"
HUH. IT'S ALMOST TOO GOOD TO BE TRUE...

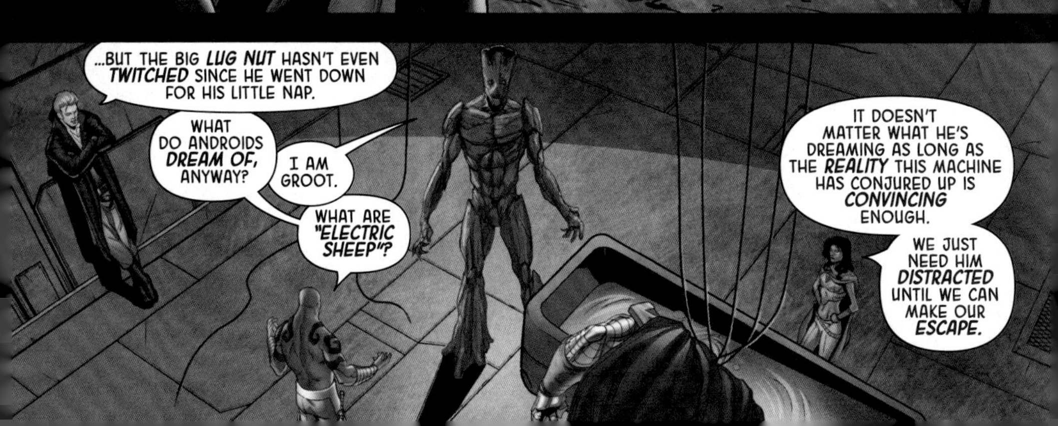
...BUT THE BIG LUG NUT HASN'T EVEN TWITCHED SINCE HE WENT DOWN FOR HIS LITTLE NAP.
WHAT DO ANDROIDS DREAM OF, ANYWAY?
I AM GROOT.
WHAT ARE "ELECTRIC SHEEP"?
IT DOESN'T MATTER WHAT HE'S DREAMING AS LONG AS THE REALITY THIS MACHINE HAS CONJURED UP IS CONVINCING ENOUGH.
WE JUST NEED HIM DISTRACTED UNTIL WE CAN MAKE OUR ESCAPE.

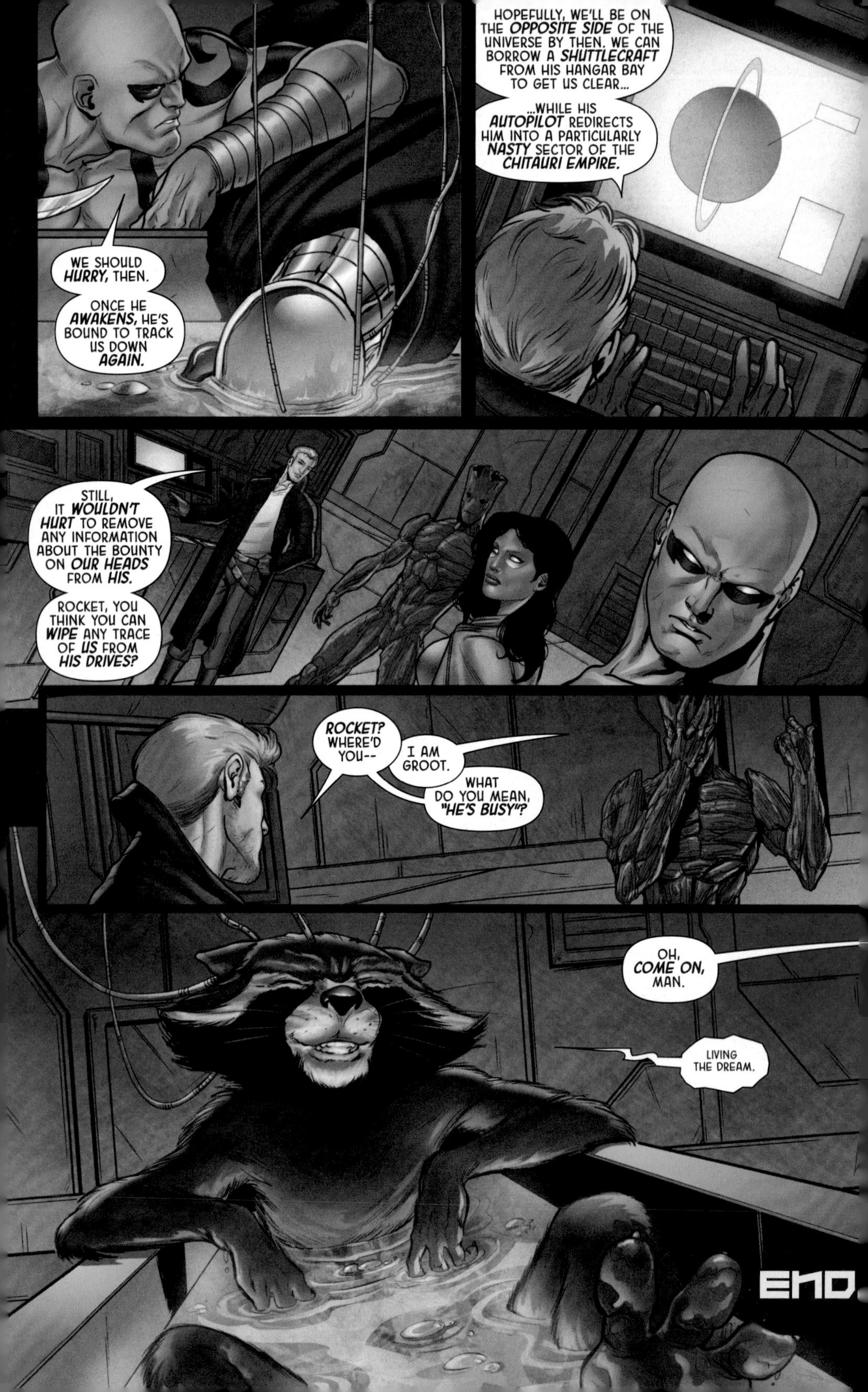
HOPEFULLY, WE'LL BE ON THE OPPOSITE SIDE OF THE UNIVERSE BY THEN. WE CAN BORROW A SHUTTLECRAFT FROM HIS HANGAR BAY TO GET US CLEAR...
...WHILE HIS AUTOPILOT REDIRECTS HIM INTO A PARTICULARLY NASTY SECTOR OF THE CHITAURI EMPIRE.
WE SHOULD HURRY, THEN.
ONCE HE AWAKENS, HE'S BOUND TO TRACK US DOWN AGAIN.
STILL, IT WOULDN'T HURT TO REMOVE ANY INFORMATION ABOUT THE BOUNTY ON OUR HEADS FROM HIS.
ROCKET, YOU THINK YOU CAN WIPE ANY TRACE OF US FROM HIS DRIVES?
ROCKET? WHERE'D YOU--
I AM GROOT.
WHAT DO YOU MEAN, "HE'S BUSY"?
OH, COME ON, MAN.
LIVING THE DREAM.
END.

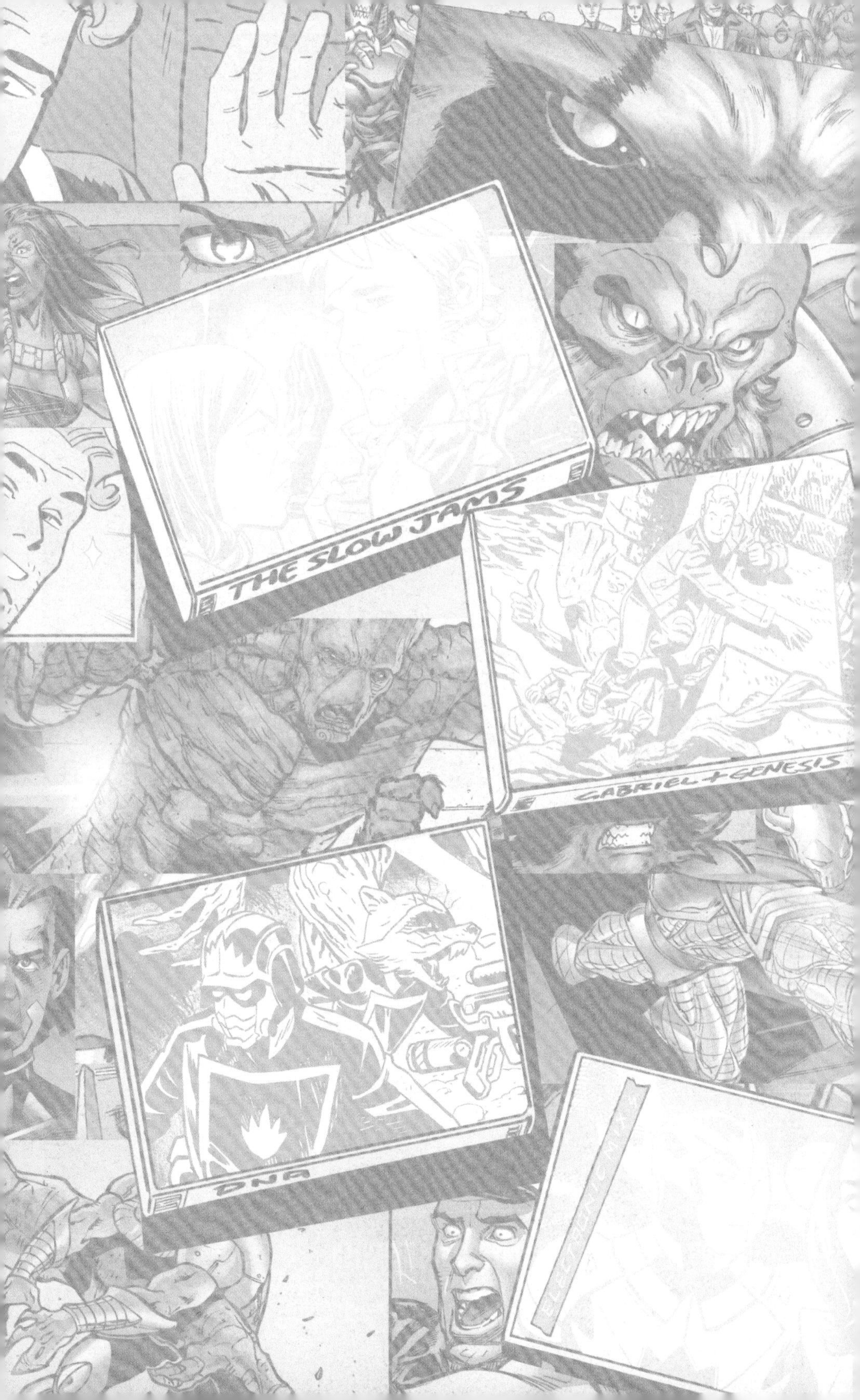
THE SLOW JAMS
GABRIEL + GENESIS
DNA
ELECTRONIC MIX

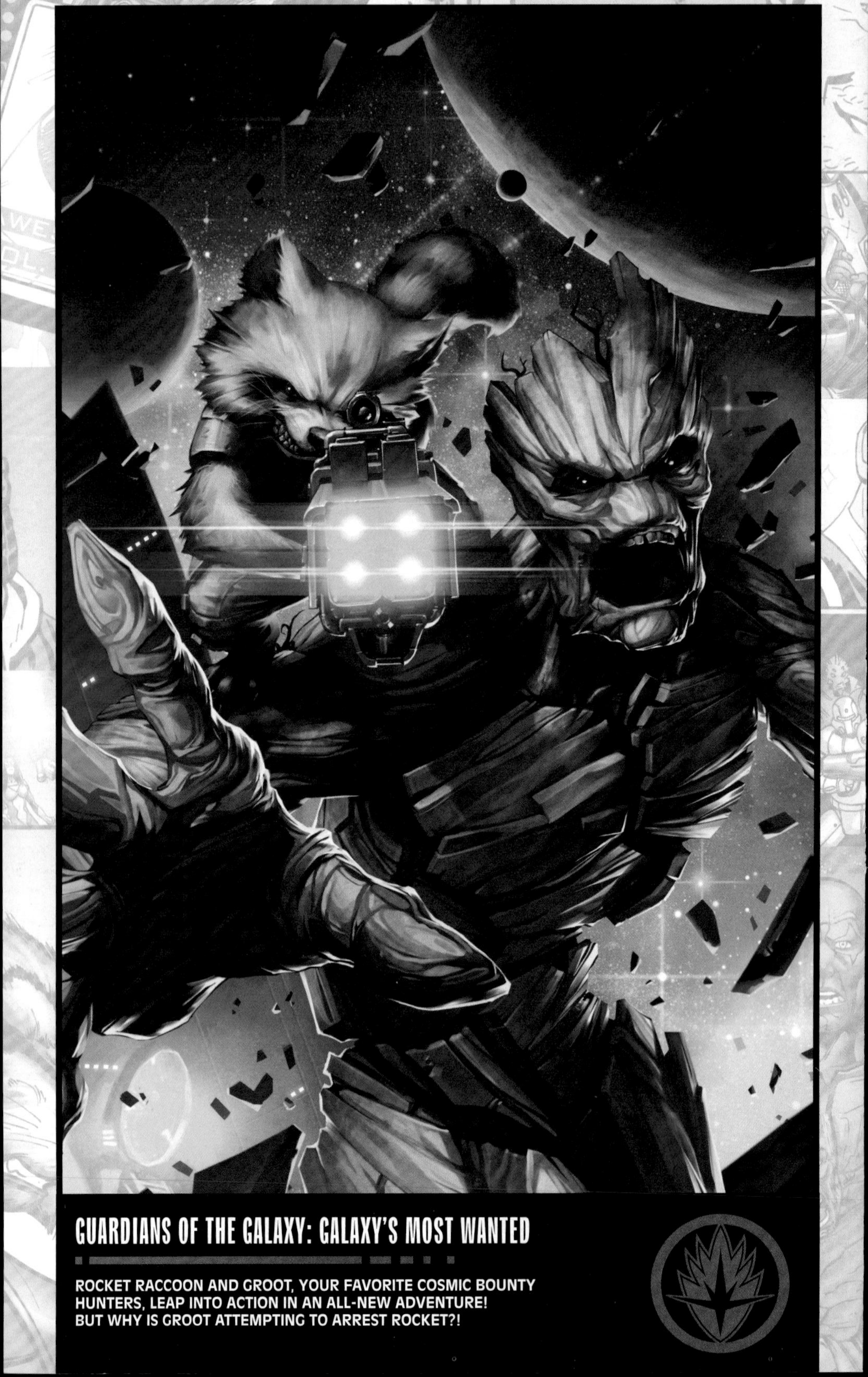

GUARDIANS OF THE GALAXY: GALAXY'S MOST WANTED

ROCKET RACCOON AND GROOT, YOUR FAVORITE COSMIC BOUNTY HUNTERS, LEAP INTO ACTION IN AN ALL-NEW ADVENTURE! BUT WHY IS GROOT ATTEMPTING TO ARREST ROCKET?!

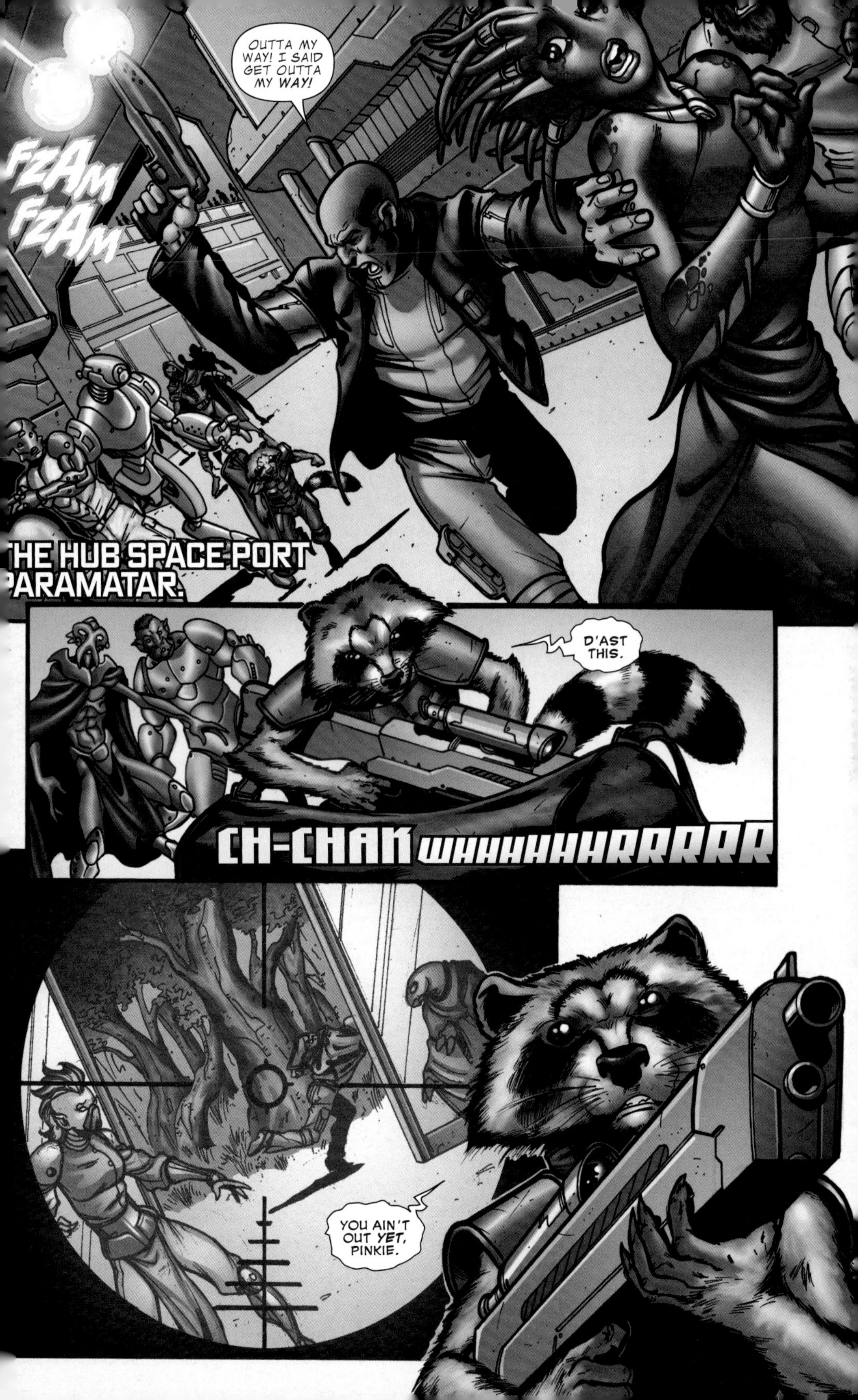
OUTTA MY WAY! I SAID GET OUTTA MY WAY!
FZAM FZAM
THE HUB SPACE PORT PARAMATAR.
D'AST THIS.
CH-CHAK WHHHHHHRRRRR
YOU AIN'T OUT YET, PINKIE.

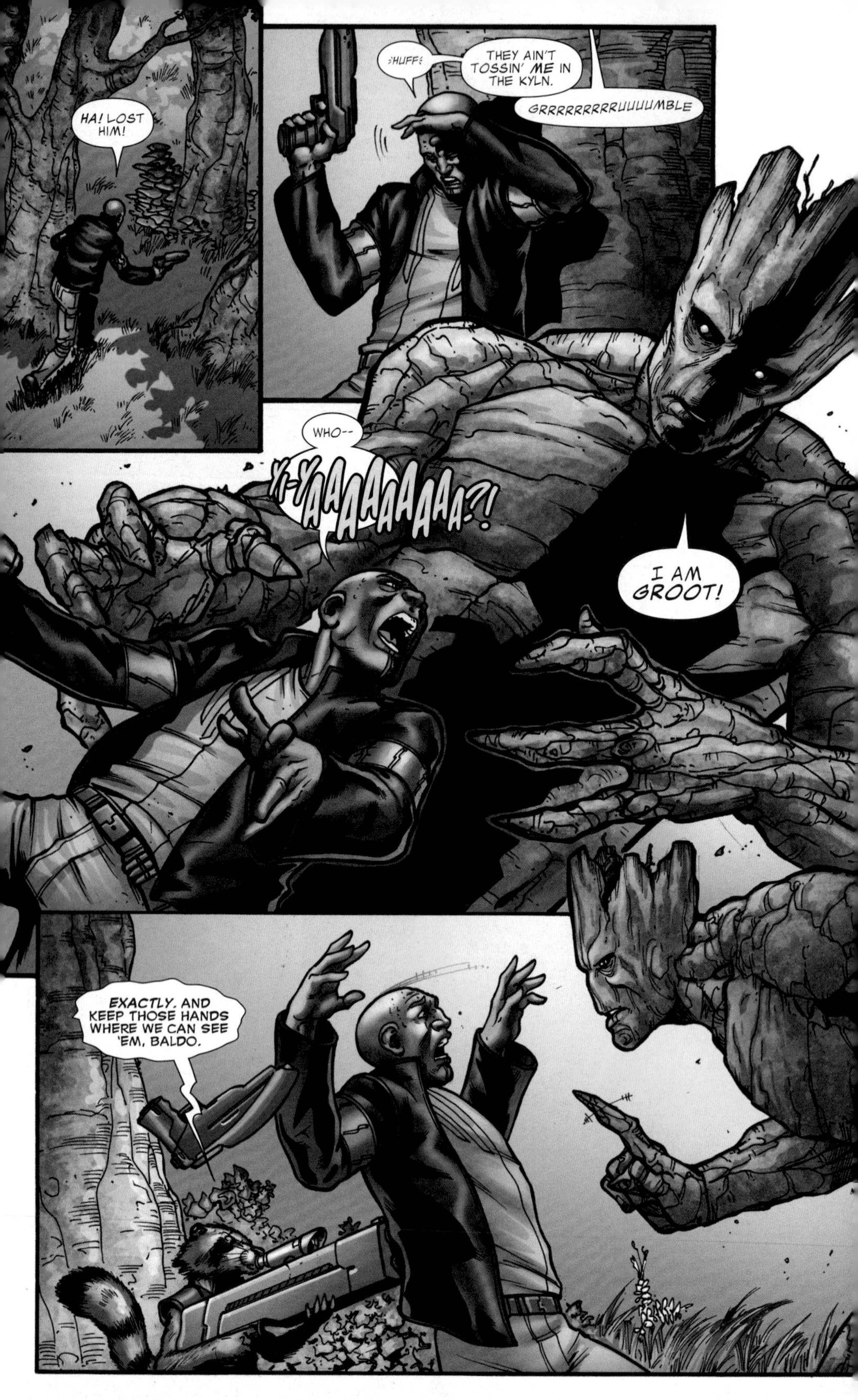
HA! LOST HIM!
HUFF
THEY AIN'T TOSSIN' ME IN THE KYLN.
GRRRRRRRRRUUUUMBLE
WHO--
Y-YAAAAAAAA?!
I AM GROOT!
EXACTLY. AND KEEP THOSE HANDS WHERE WE CAN SEE 'EM, BALDO.

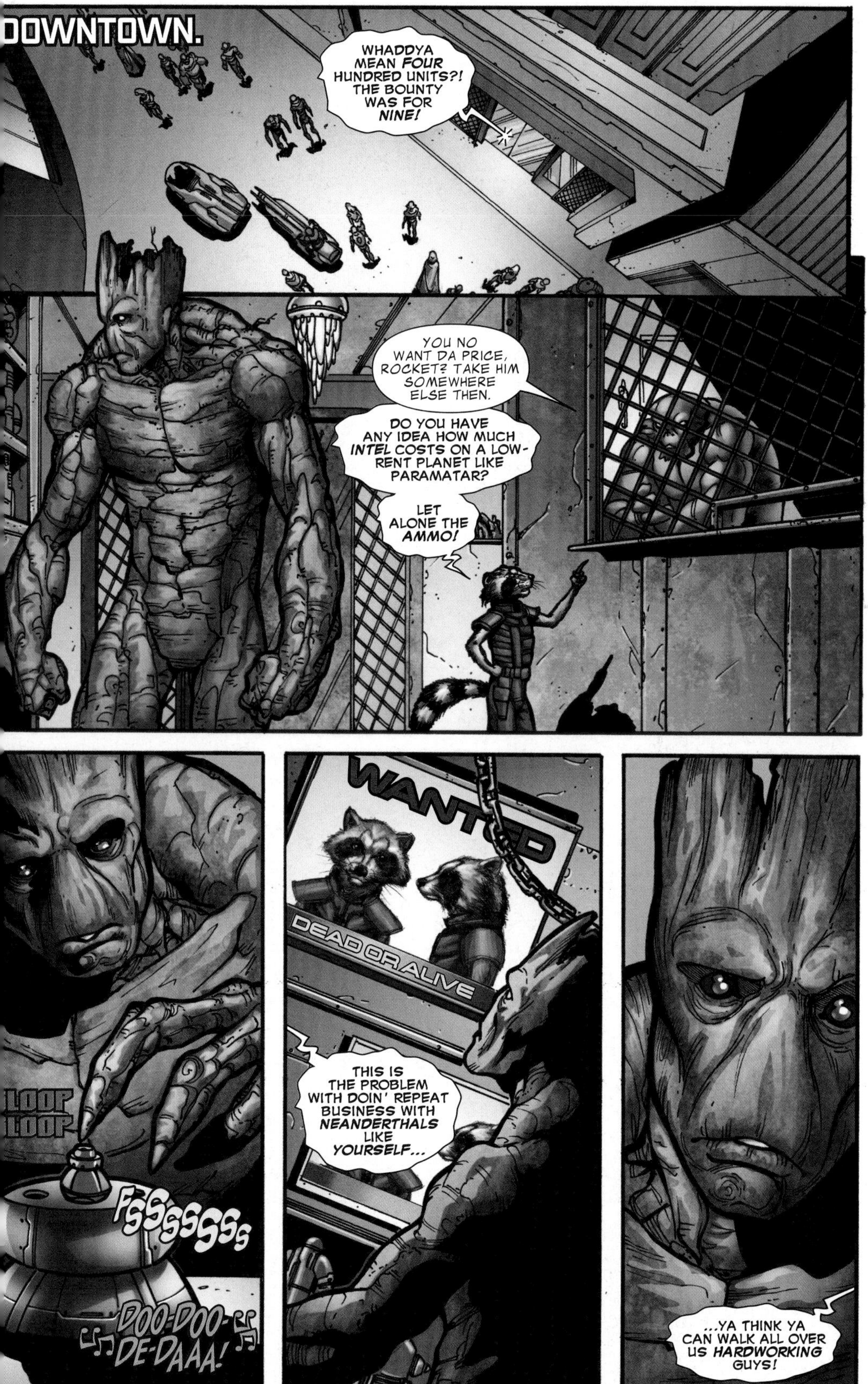
DOWNTOWN.
WHADDYA MEAN FOUR HUNDRED UNITS?! THE BOUNTY WAS FOR NINE!
YOU NO WANT DA PRICE, ROCKET? TAKE HIM SOMEWHERE ELSE THEN.
DO YOU HAVE ANY IDEA HOW MUCH INTEL COSTS ON A LOW-RENT PLANET LIKE PARAMATAR?
LET ALONE THE AMMO!
BLOOP BLOOP
FSSSSSSSs
DOO-DOO-DE-DAAA!
WANTED
DEAD OR ALIVE
THIS IS THE PROBLEM WITH DOIN' REPEAT BUSINESS WITH NEANDERTHALS LIKE YOURSELF...
...YA THINK YA CAN WALK ALL OVER US HARDWORKING GUYS!

IF THIS PLACE WASN'T ALREADY CRAWLIN' WITH *LOWLIFES*, I'D TELL YA YOU OWED US *ANOTHER JOB*!

I AM GROOT.

FINE! FINE!

JUST SYNC THE MONEY UP IN OUR USUAL ACCOUNT, D'XTAR.

I'M SICK OF GUYS LIKE THAT NICKEL-AND-DIMIN' US, GROOT.

IT AIN'T LIKE WE'RE *NEW* TO THIS GAME.

BUT THEY KEEP PUSHIN' BACK ON THE ALREADY AGREED UPON FINANCIALITIES.

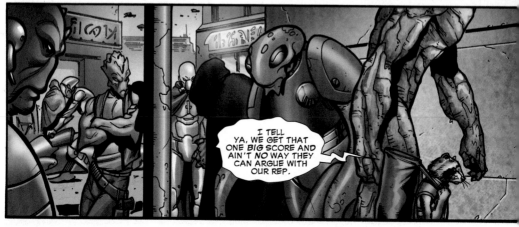

I TELL YA, WE GET THAT ONE *BIG* SCORE AND AIN'T *NO* WAY THEY CAN ARGUE WITH OUR REP.

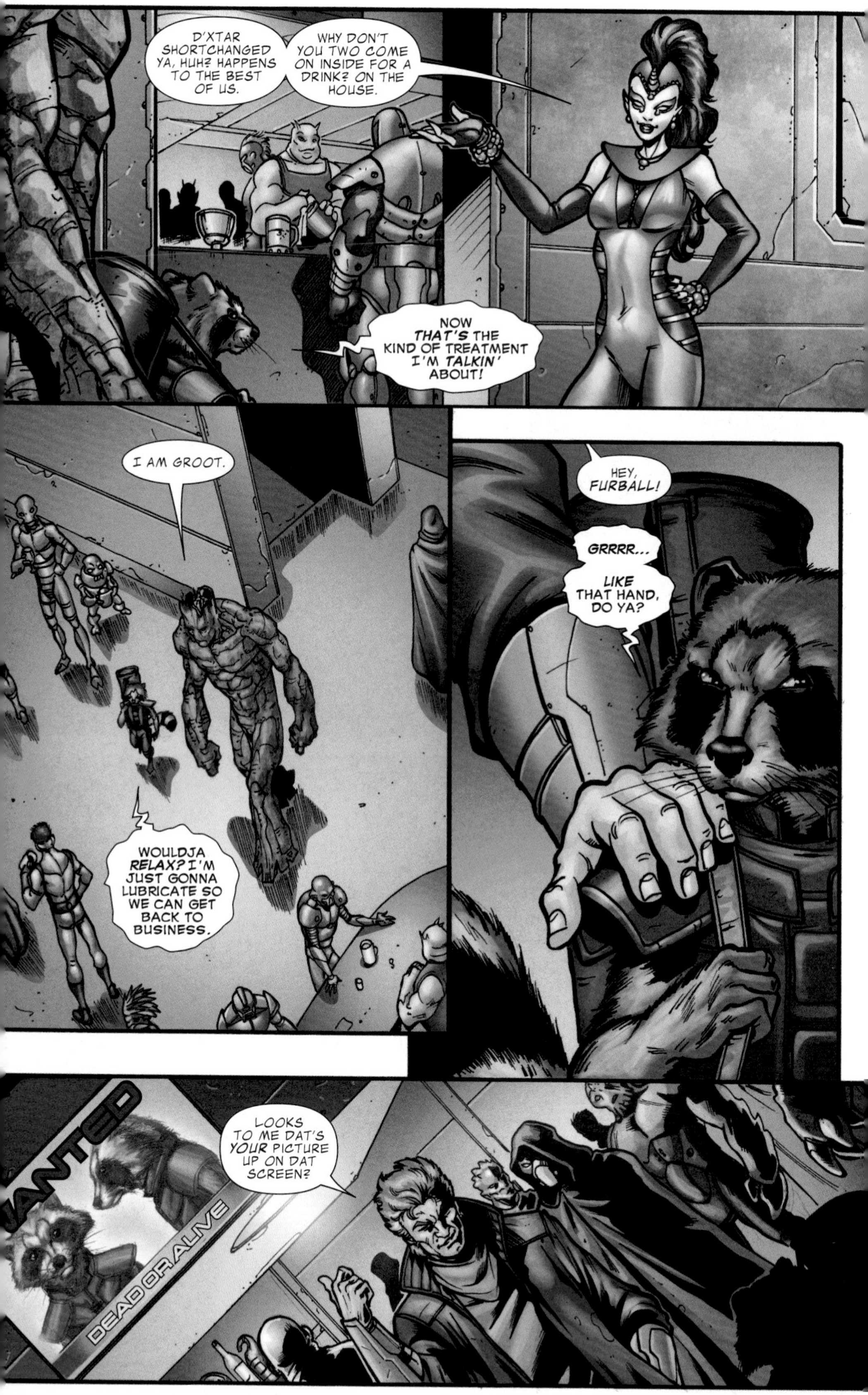
D'XTAR SHORTCHANGED YA, HUH? HAPPENS TO THE BEST OF US.
WHY DON'T YOU TWO COME ON INSIDE FOR A DRINK? ON THE HOUSE.
NOW THAT'S THE KIND OF TREATMENT I'M TALKIN' ABOUT!
I AM GROOT.
WOULDJA RELAX? I'M JUST GONNA LUBRICATE SO WE CAN GET BACK TO BUSINESS.
HEY, FURBALL!
GRRRR...
LIKE THAT HAND, DO YA?
WANTED
DEAD OR ALIVE
LOOKS TO ME DAT'S YOUR PICTURE UP ON DAT SCREEN?

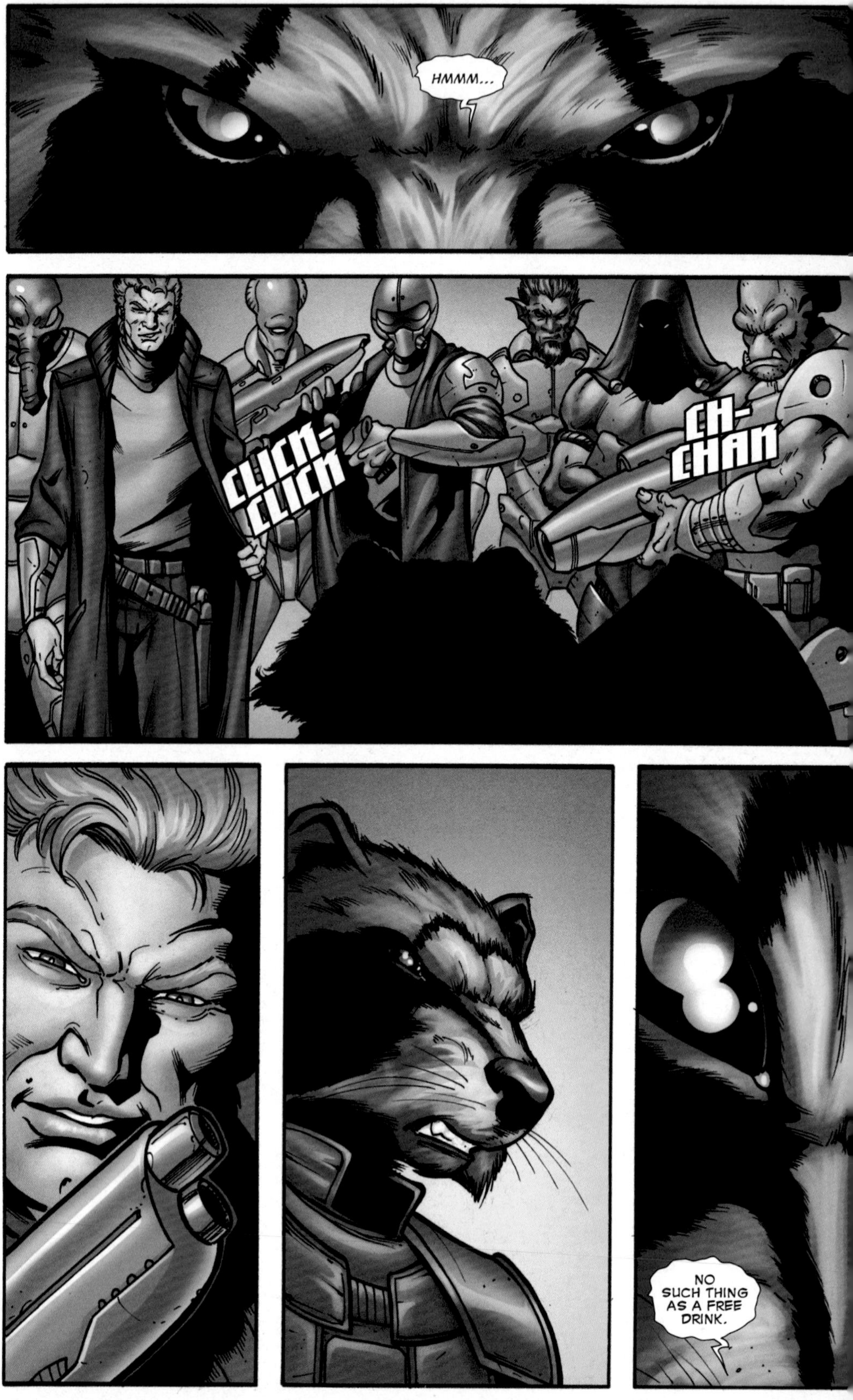
HMMM...
CLICK-CLICK
CH-CHAK
NO SUCH THING AS A FREE DRINK.

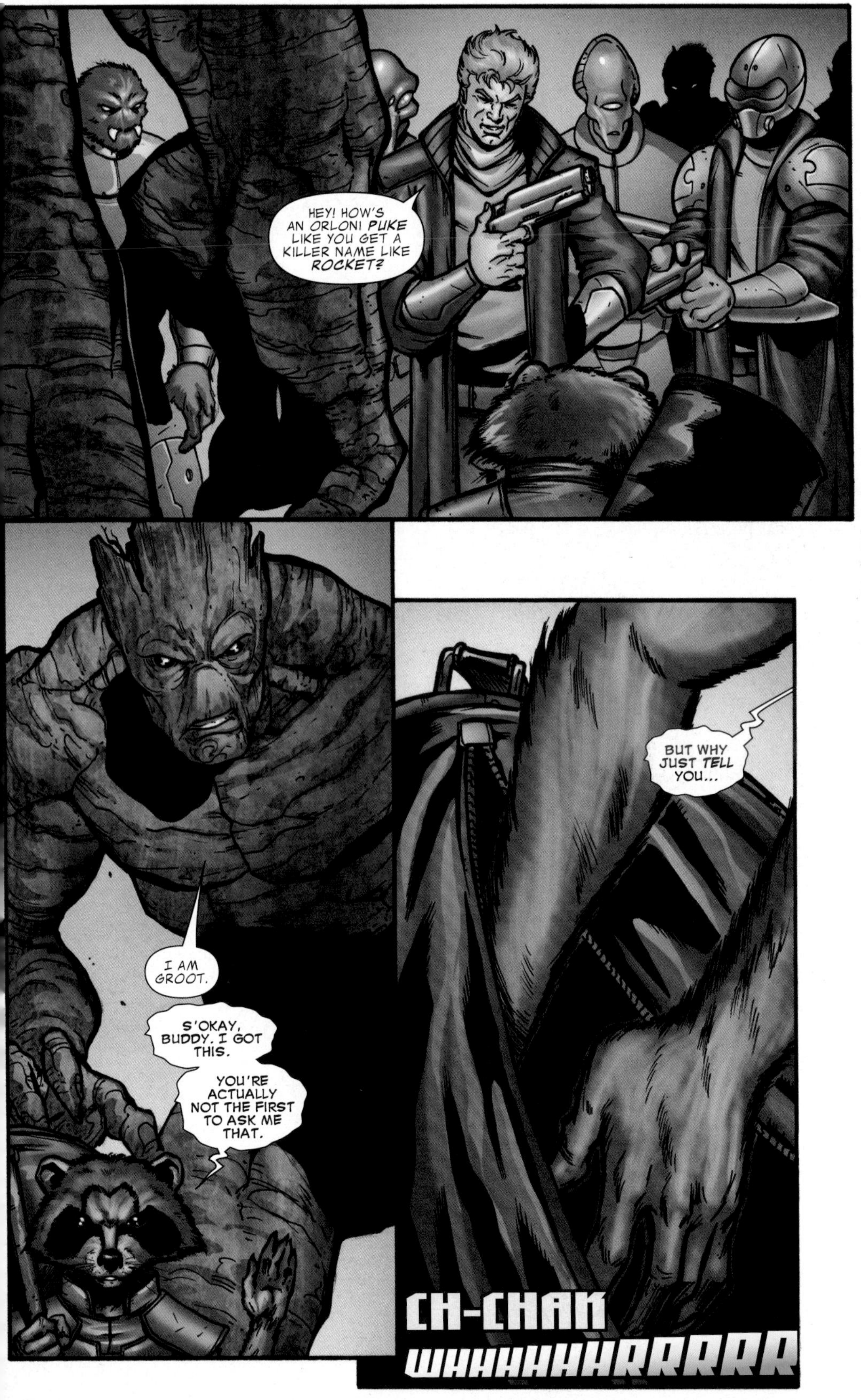
HEY! HOW'S AN ORLONI PUKE LIKE YOU GET A KILLER NAME LIKE ROCKET?
I AM GROOT.
S'OKAY, BUDDY. I GOT THIS.
YOU'RE ACTUALLY NOT THE FIRST TO ASK ME THAT.
BUT WHY JUST TELL YOU...
CH-CHAK
WHHHHHHRRRRR

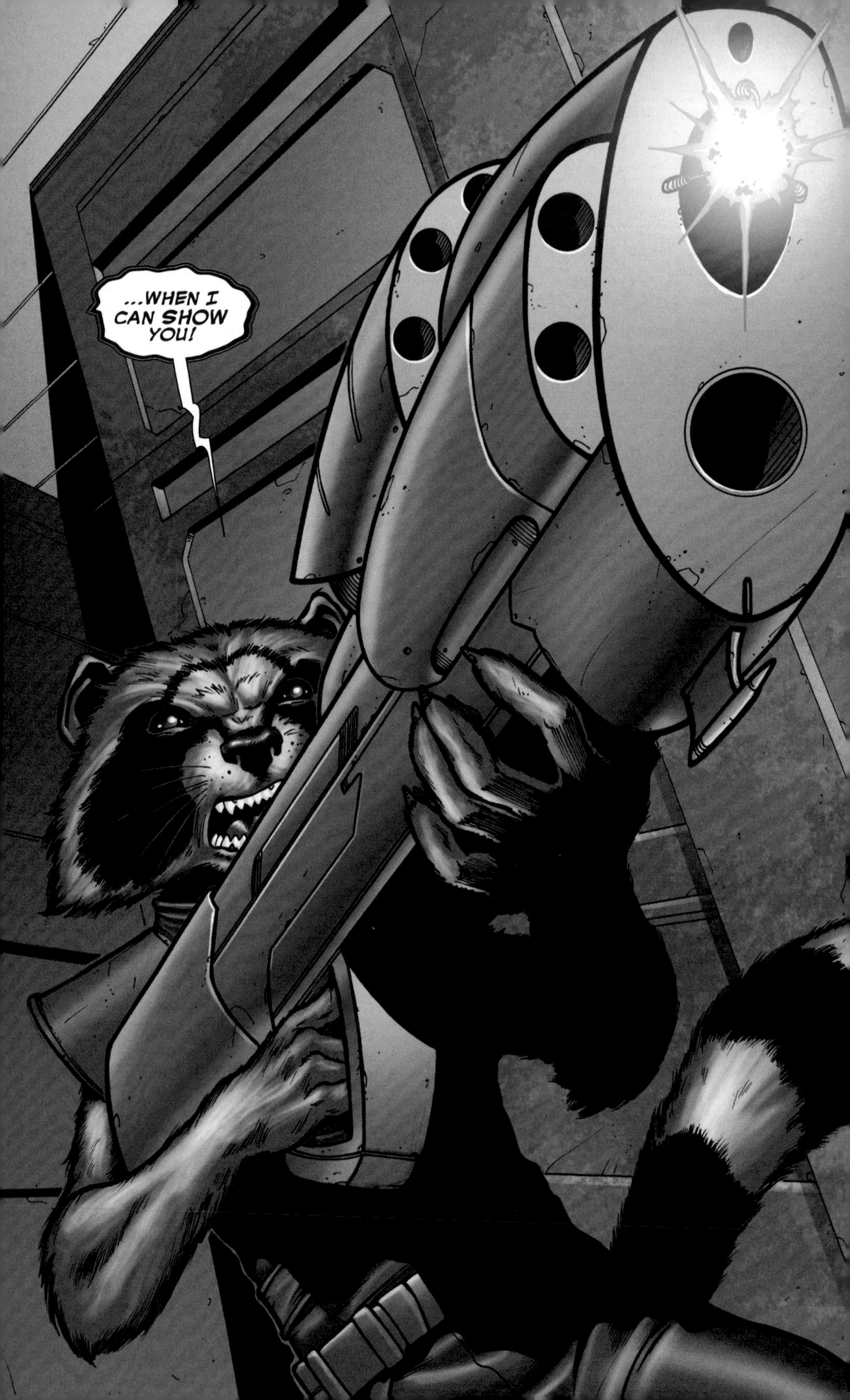
...WHEN I CAN SHOW YOU!

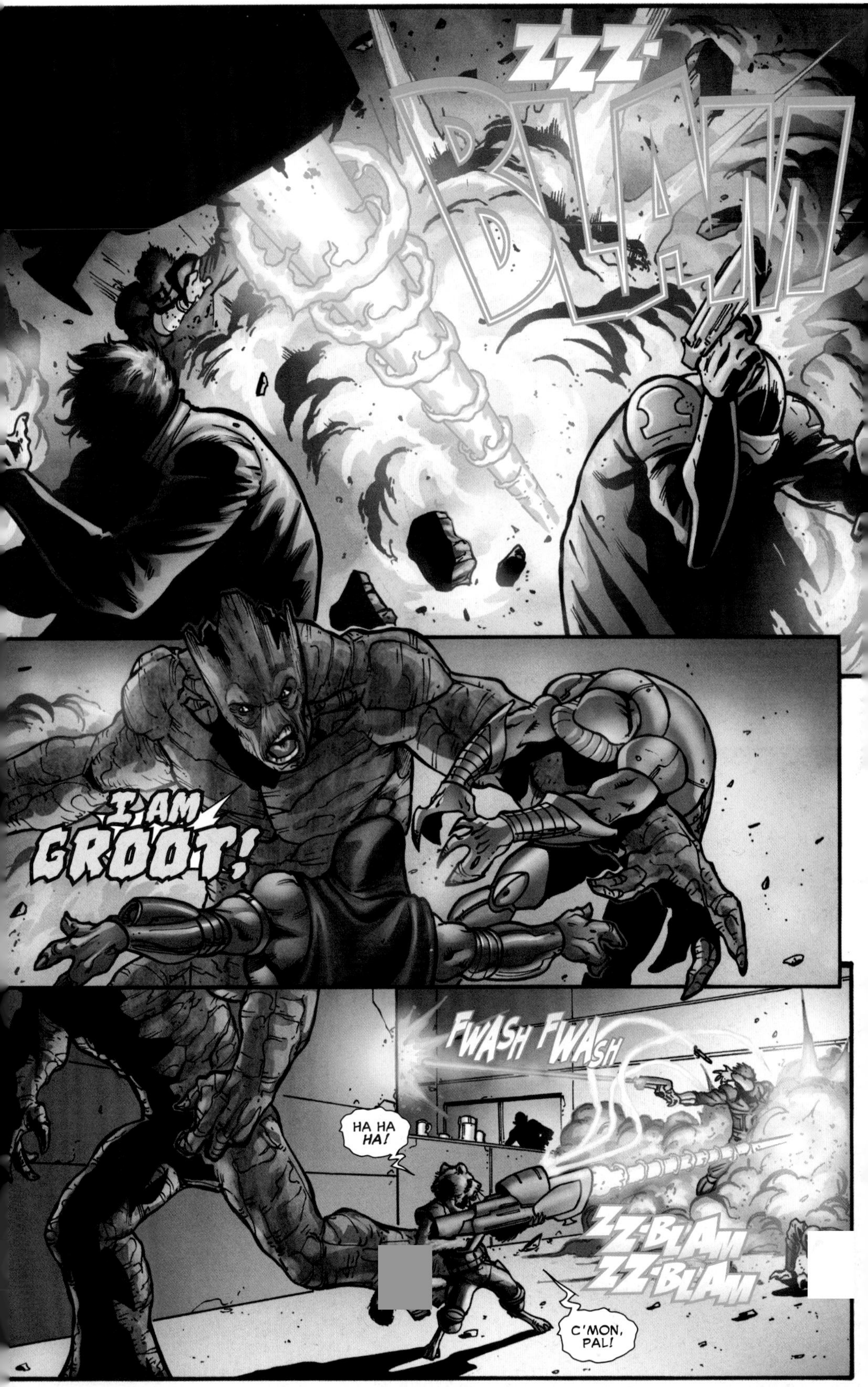

ZZZ-BLAM
I AM GROOT!
FWASH FWASH
HA HA HA!
ZZ-BLAM ZZ-BLAM
C'MON, PAL!

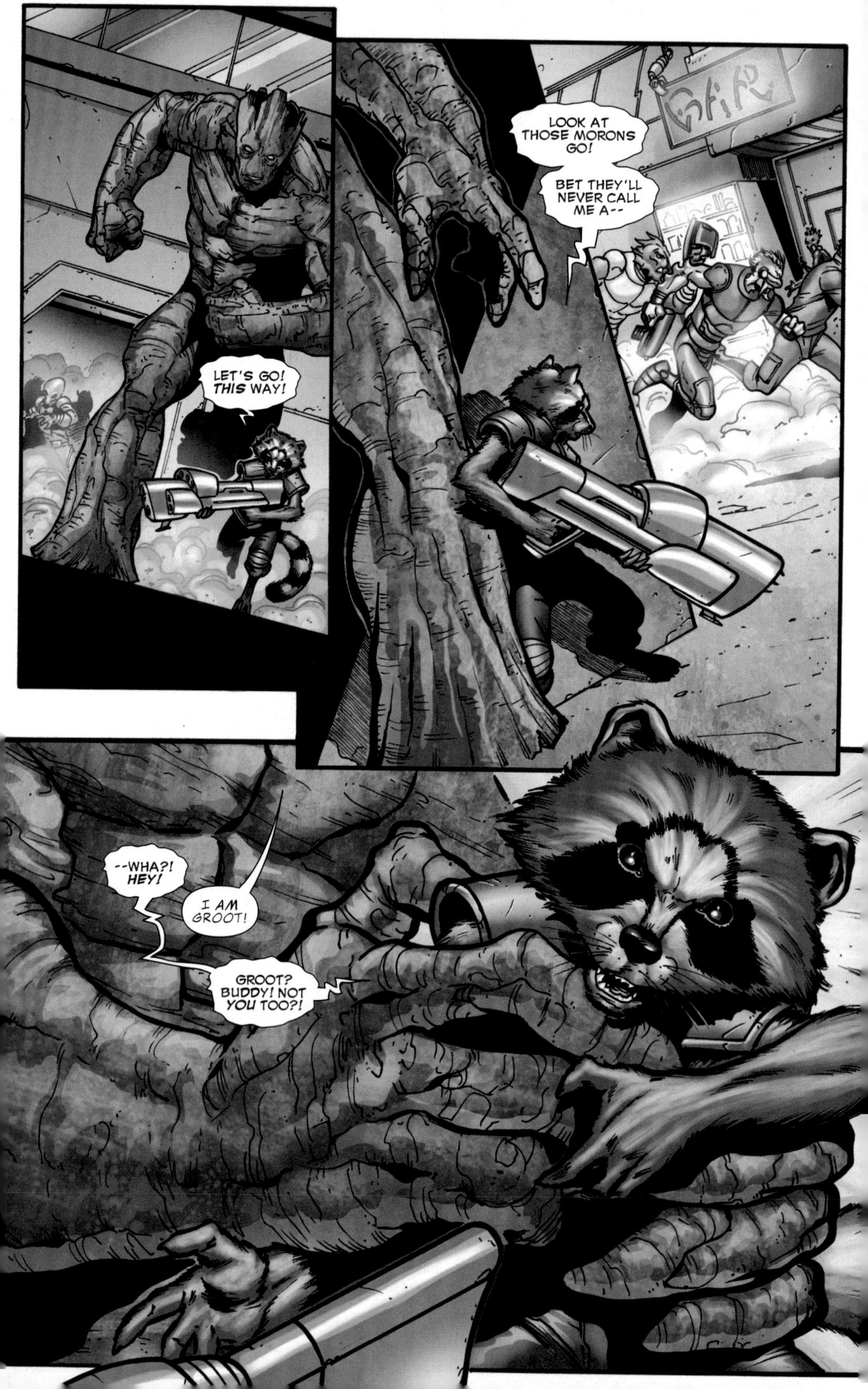
LET'S GO! THIS WAY!
LOOK AT THOSE MORONS GO!
BET THEY'LL NEVER CALL ME A--
--WHA?! HEY!
I AM GROOT!
GROOT? BUDDY! NOT YOU TOO?!

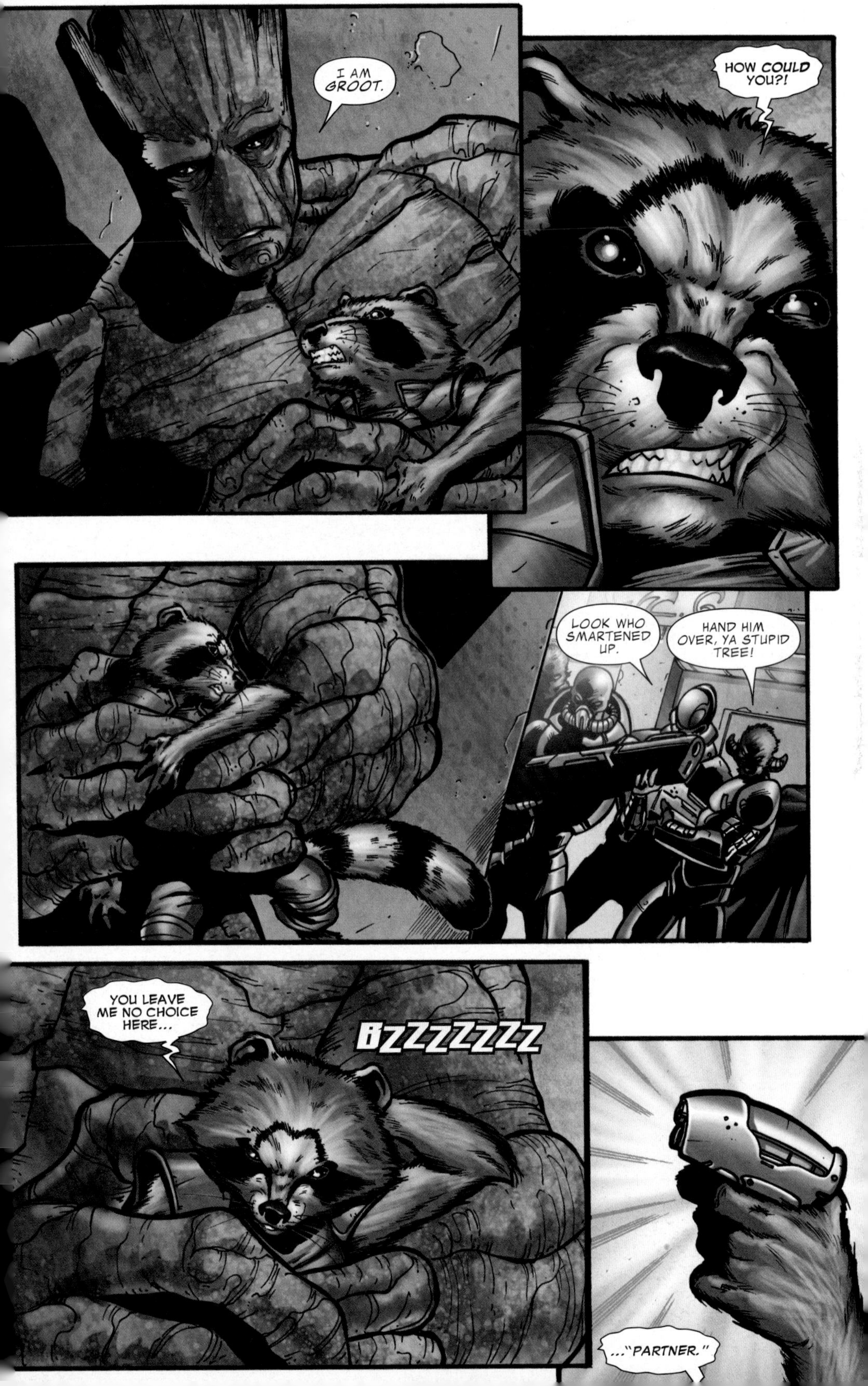
I AM GROOT.
HOW COULD YOU?!
LOOK WHO SMARTENED UP.
HAND HIM OVER, YA STUPID TREE!
YOU LEAVE ME NO CHOICE HERE...
BZZZZZZZ
..."PARTNER."

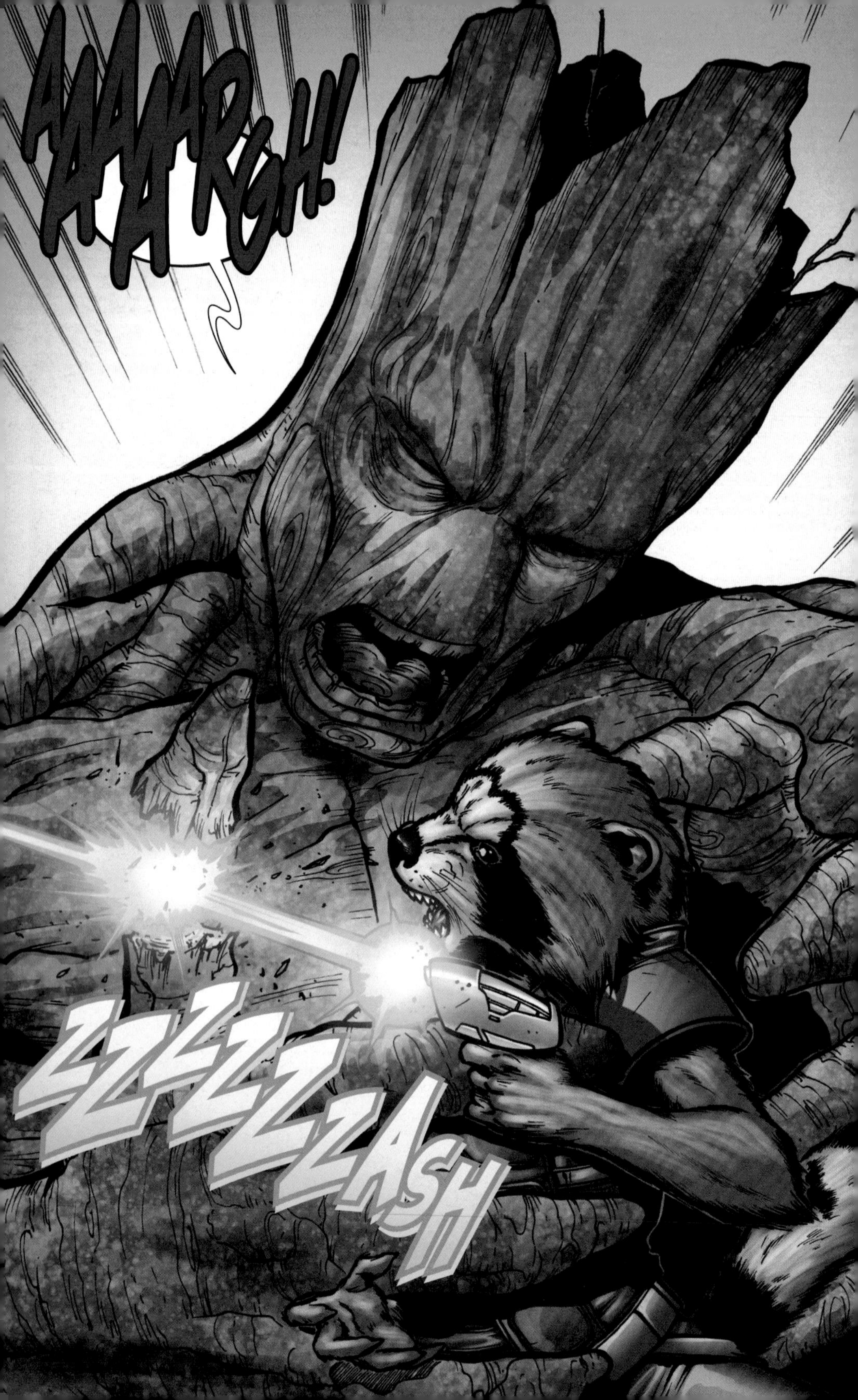
AAAARRGH!
ZZZZZZASH

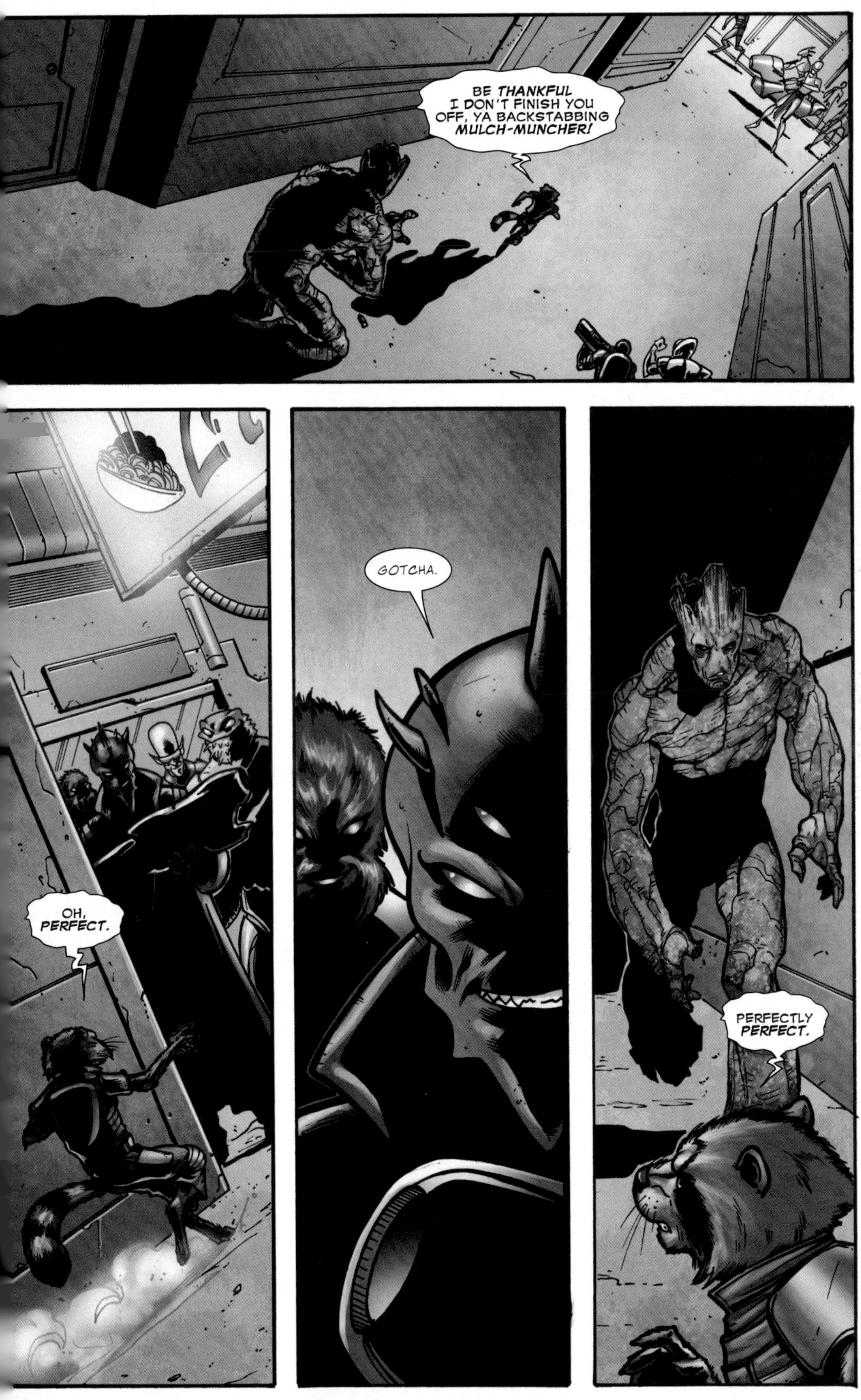
BE THANKFUL I DON'T FINISH YOU OFF, YA BACKSTABBING MULCH-MUNCHER!
OH, PERFECT.
GOTCHA.
PERFECTLY PERFECT.

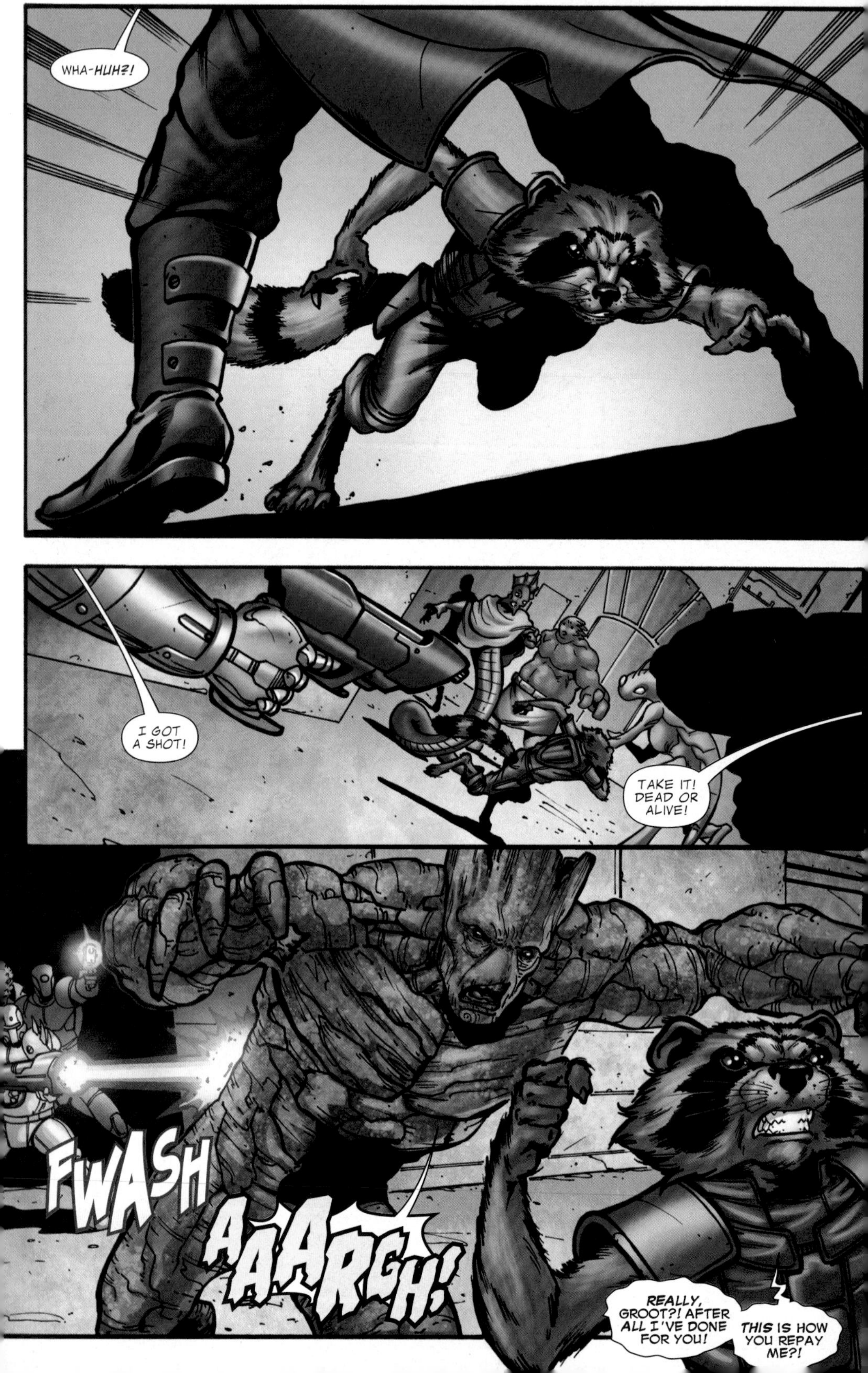

WHA-HUH?!
I GOT A SHOT!
TAKE IT! DEAD OR ALIVE!
FWASH
AAARGH!
REALLY, GROOT?! AFTER ALL I'VE DONE FOR YOU!
THIS IS HOW YOU REPAY ME?!

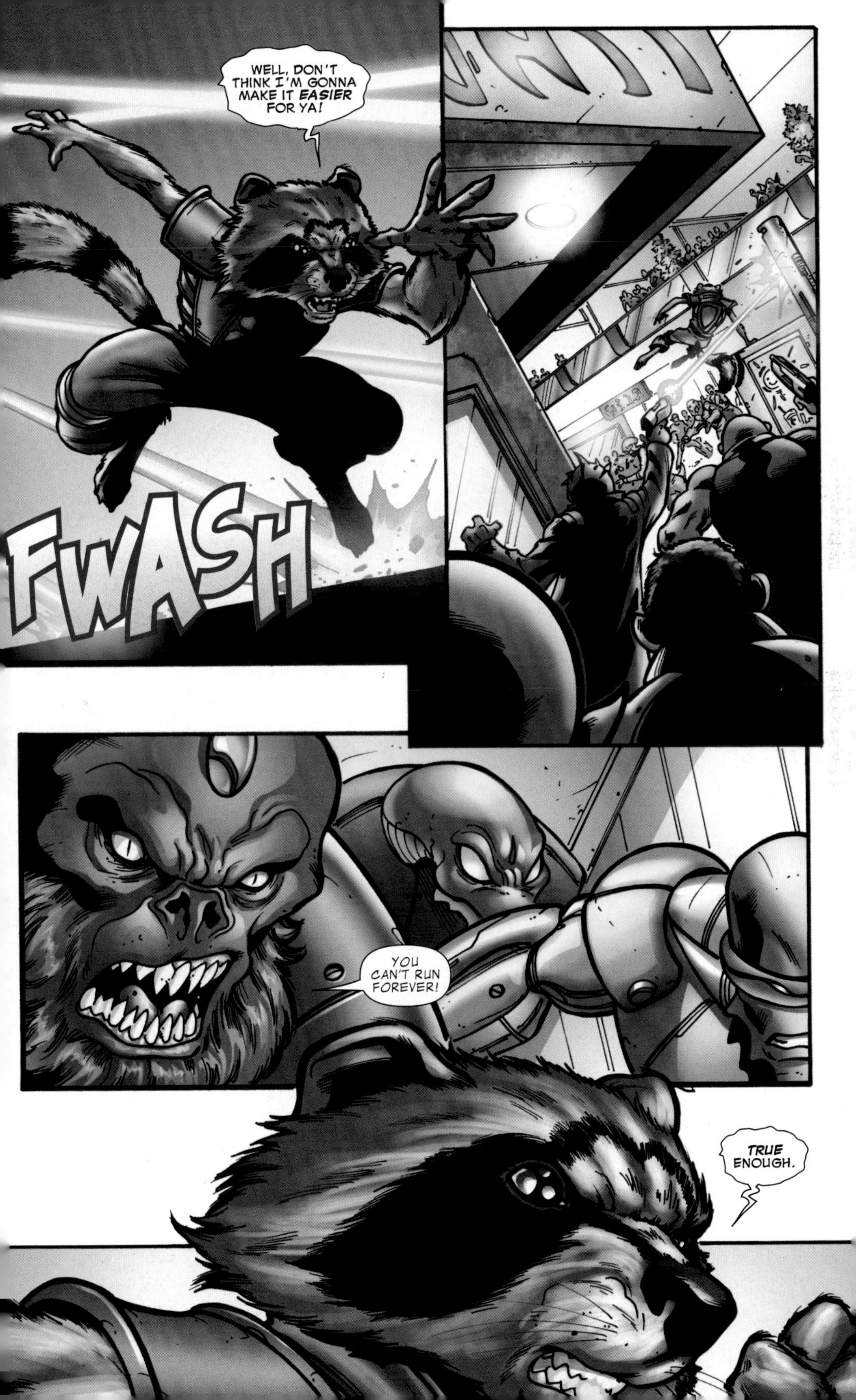
WELL, DON'T THINK I'M GONNA MAKE IT *EASIER* FOR YA!
FWASH
YOU CAN'T RUN FOREVER!
TRUE ENOUGH.

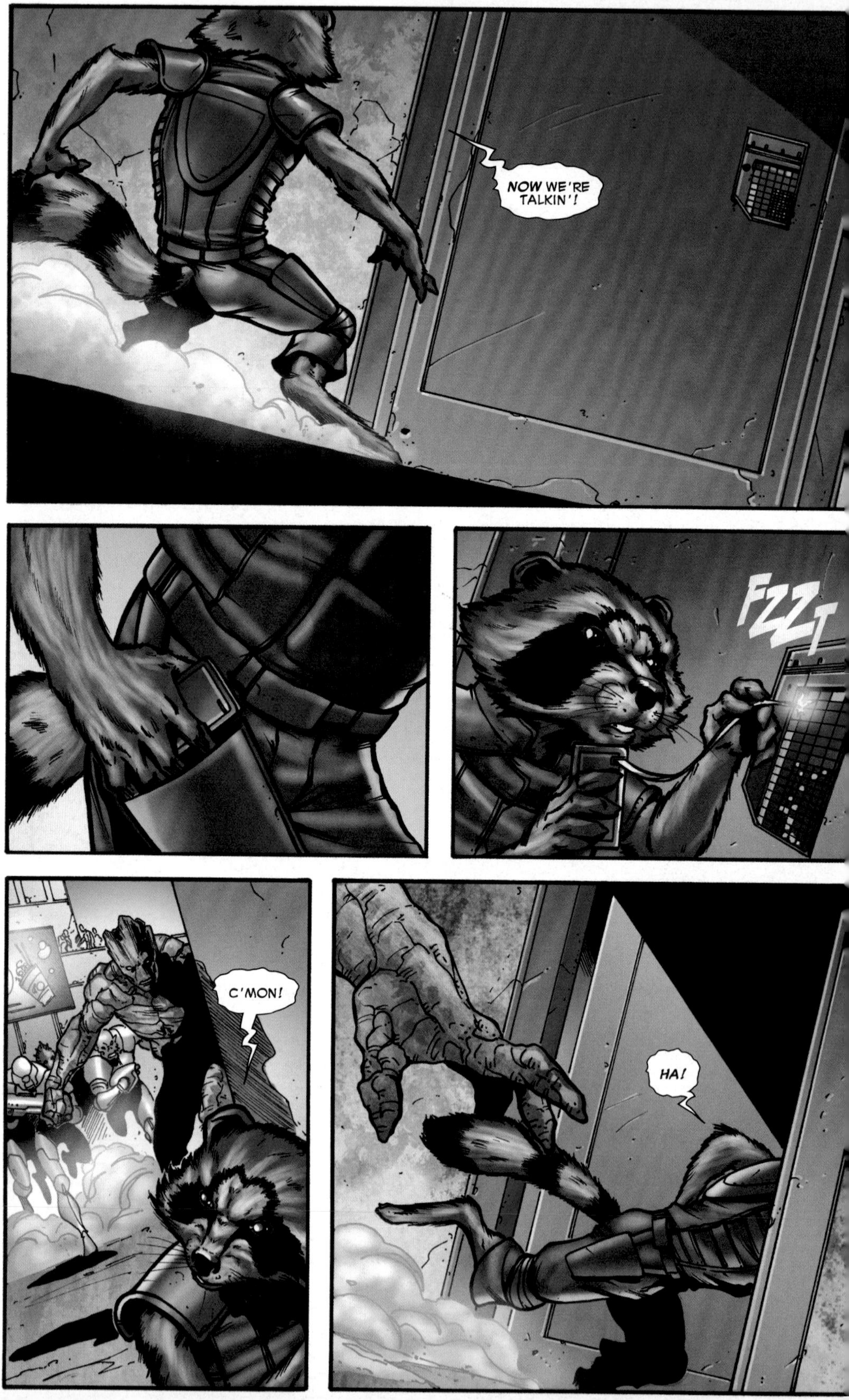
NOW WE'RE TALKIN'!
FZZT
C'MON!
HA!

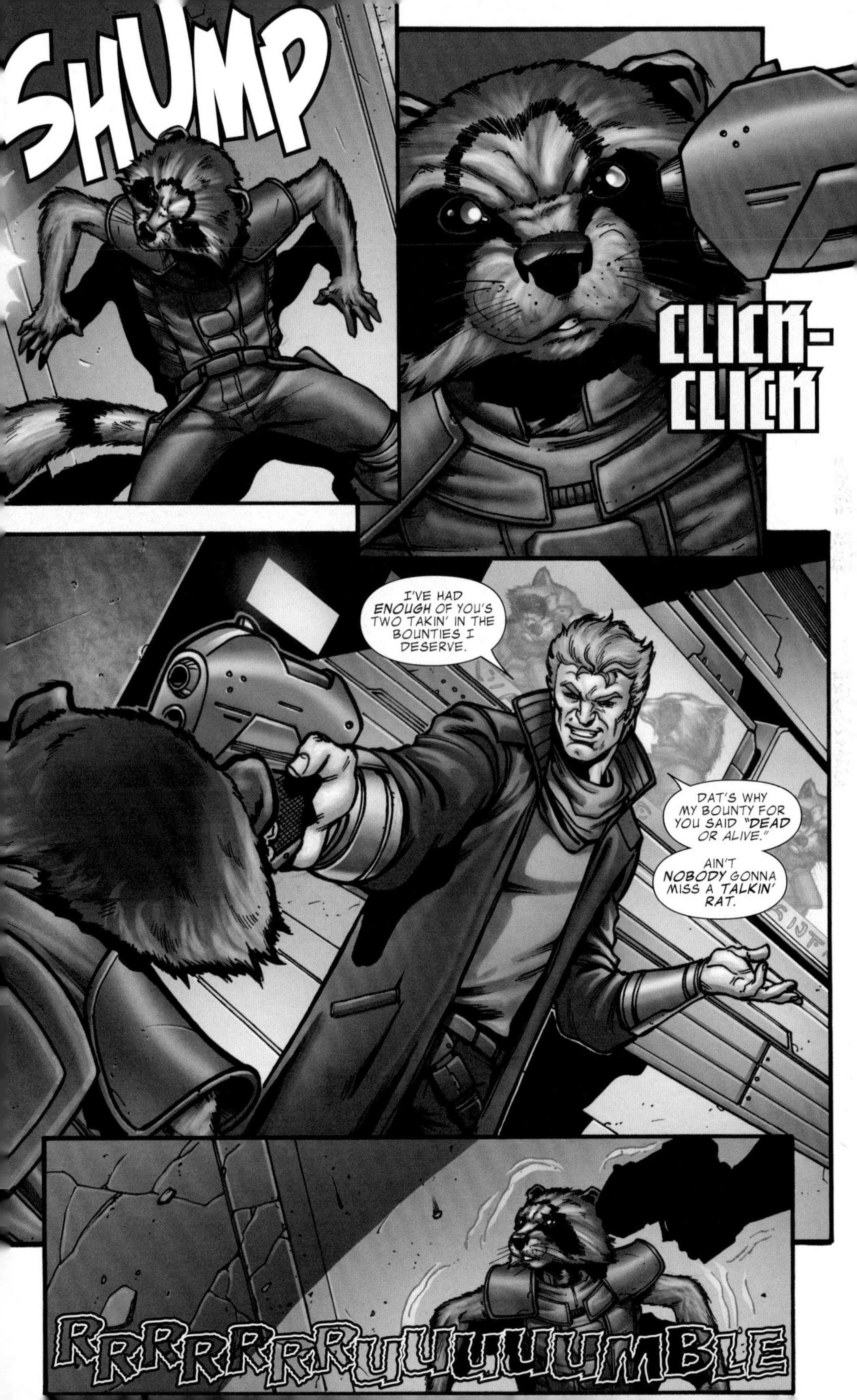
SHUMP
CLICK-CLICK
I'VE HAD ENOUGH OF YOU'S TWO TAKIN' IN THE BOUNTIES I DESERVE.
DAT'S WHY MY BOUNTY FOR YOU SAID "DEAD OR ALIVE."
AIN'T NOBODY GONNA MISS A TALKIN' RAT.
RRRRRRRRUUUUUUMBLE

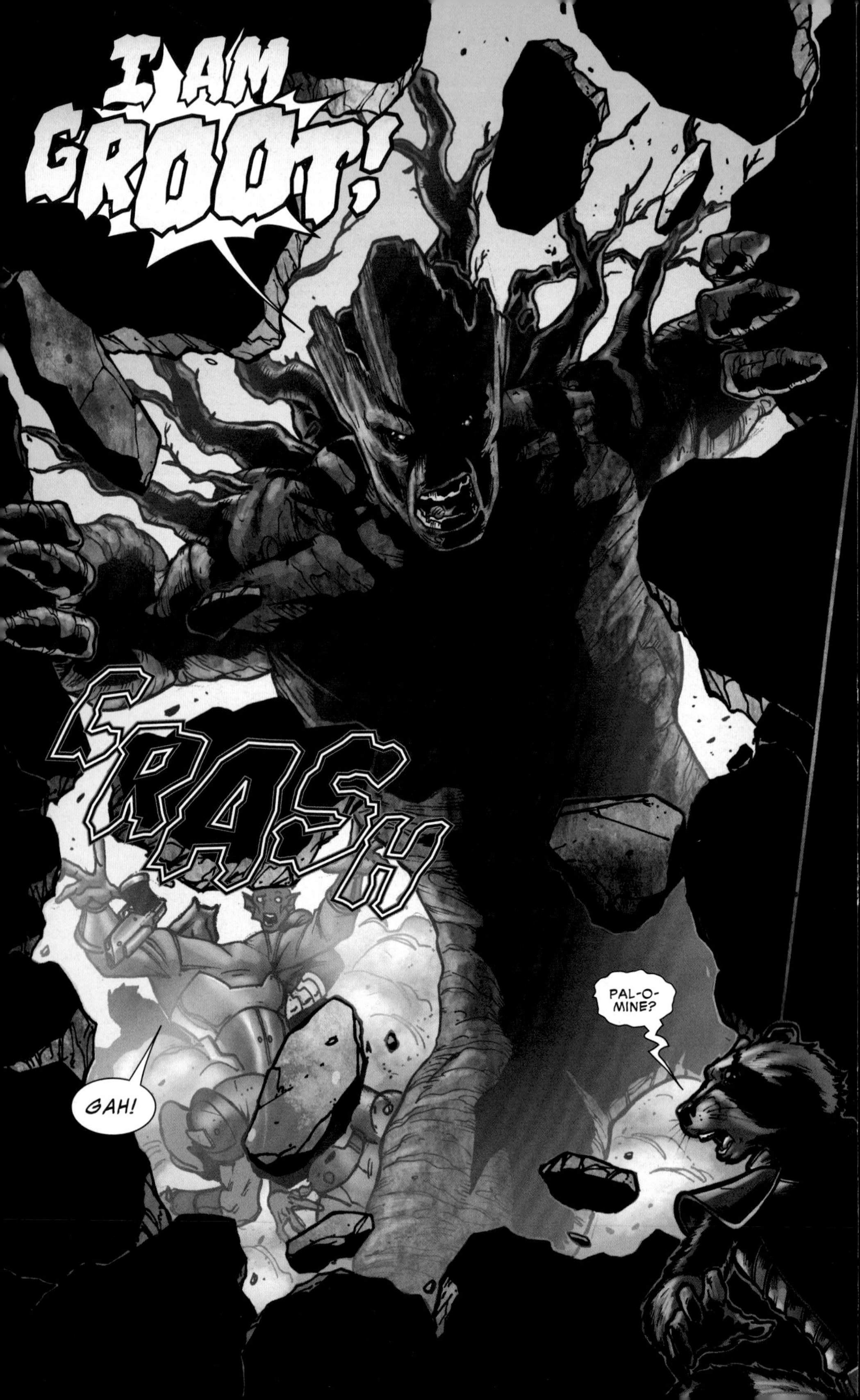
I AM GROOT!
CRASH
PAL-O-MINE?
GAH!

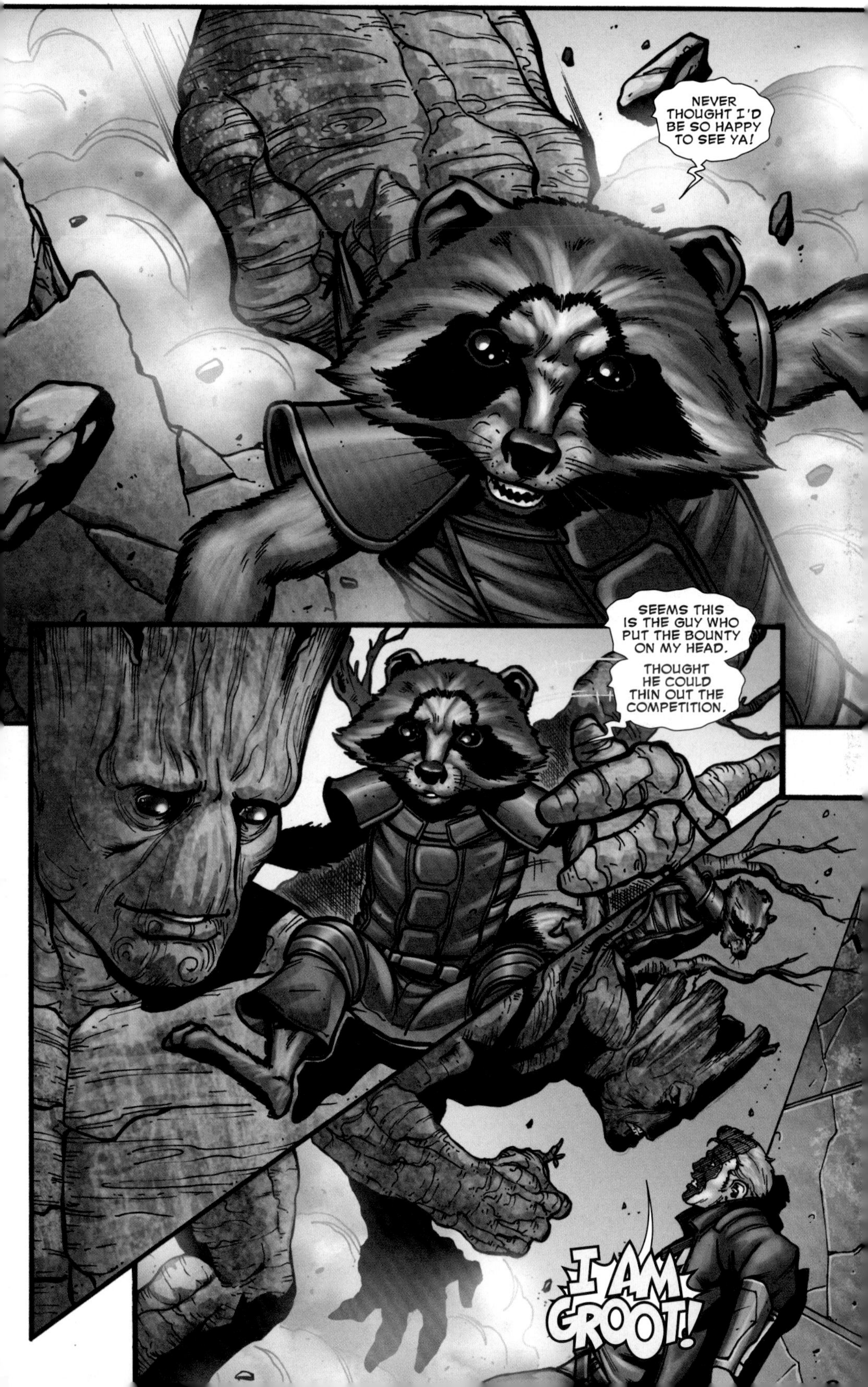
NEVER THOUGHT I'D BE SO HAPPY TO SEE YA!
SEEMS THIS IS THE GUY WHO PUT THE BOUNTY ON MY HEAD.
THOUGHT HE COULD THIN OUT THE COMPETITION.
I AM GROOT!

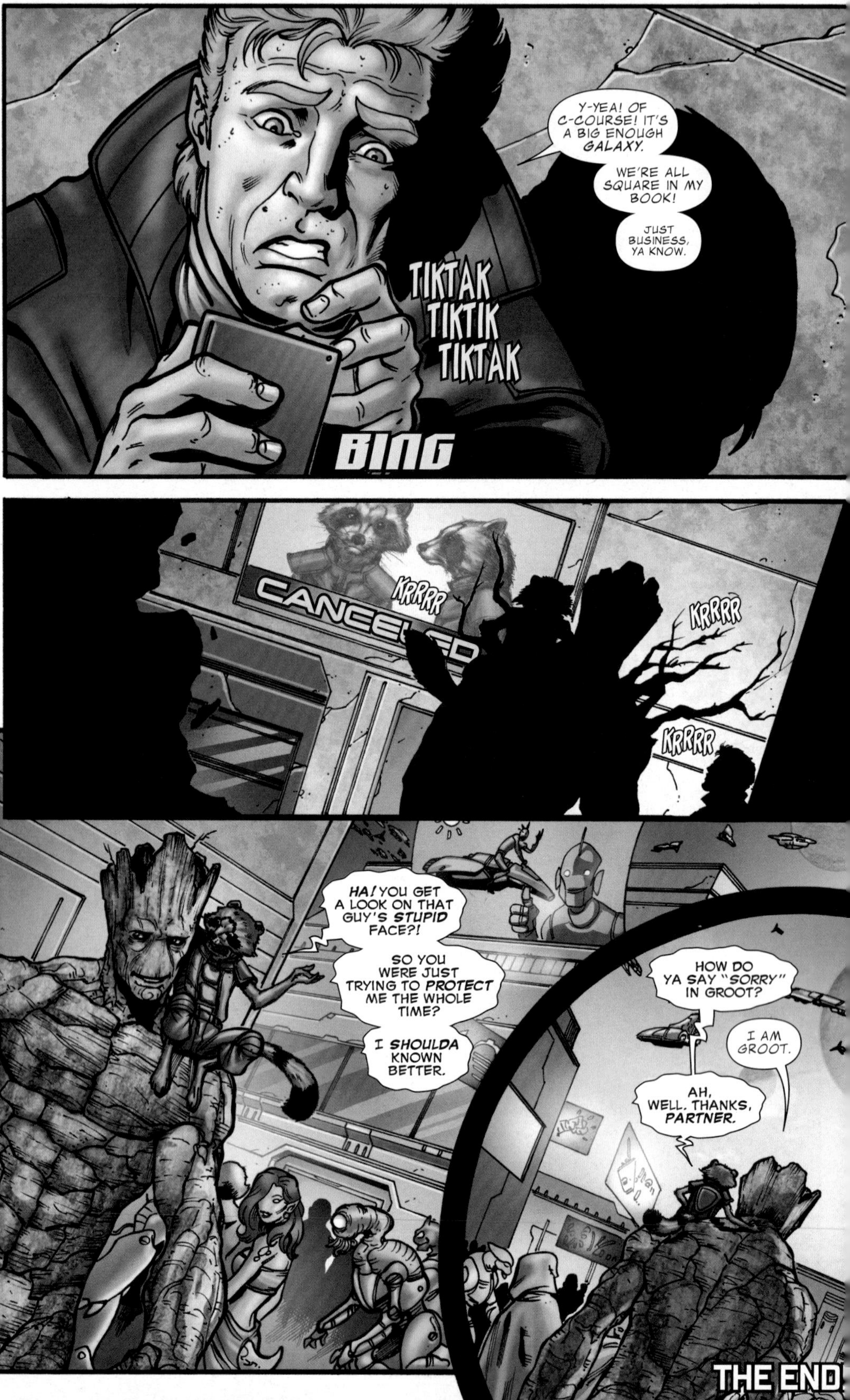
Y-YEA! OF C-COURSE! IT'S A BIG ENOUGH *GALAXY.*
WE'RE ALL SQUARE IN MY BOOK!
JUST BUSINESS, YA KNOW.
TIKTAK
TIKTIK
TIKTAK
BING
KRRRR
KRRRR
KRRRR
HA! YOU GET A LOOK ON THAT GUY'S ***STUPID*** FACE?!
SO YOU WERE JUST TRYING TO ***PROTECT*** ME THE WHOLE TIME?
I ***SHOULDA*** KNOWN BETTER.
HOW DO YA ***SAY*** "***SORRY***" IN GROOT?
I AM GROOT.
AH, WELL. THANKS, ***PARTNER.***
THE END

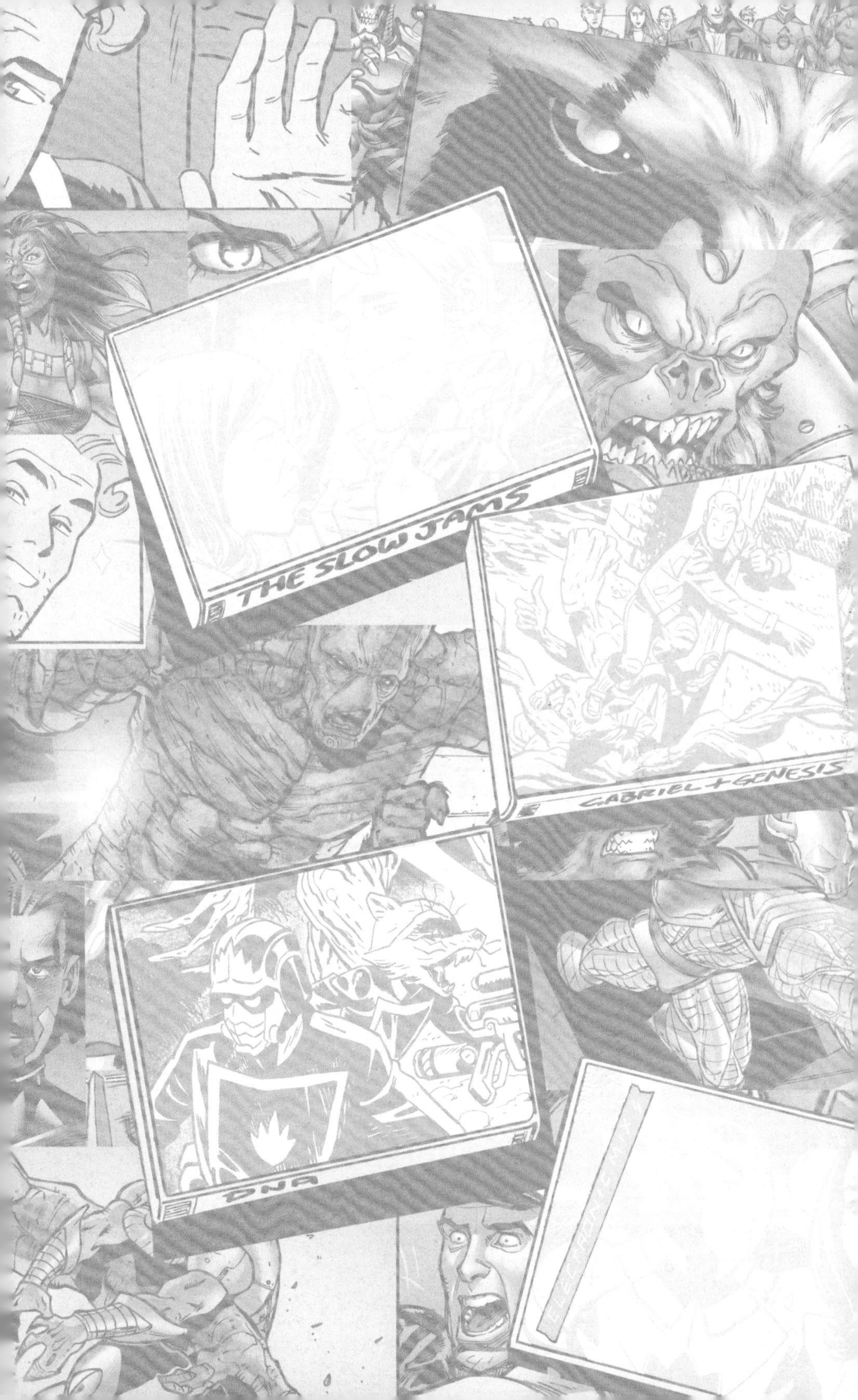
THE SLOW JAMS
GABRIEL + GENESIS
DNA
ELECTRONIC MIX

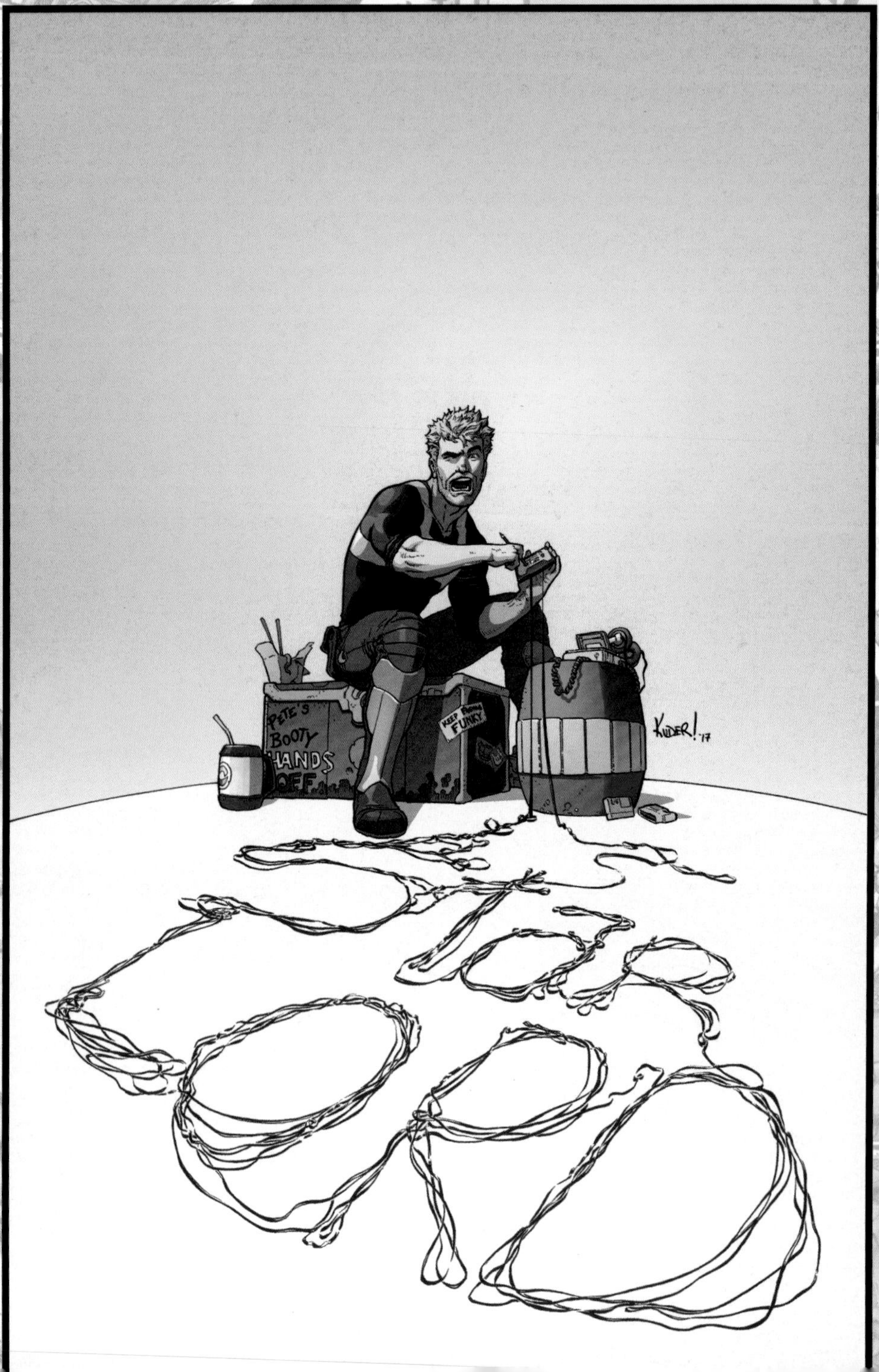

PETE'S BOOTY
HANDS OFF
KEEP
FUNKY
KUDER! '17

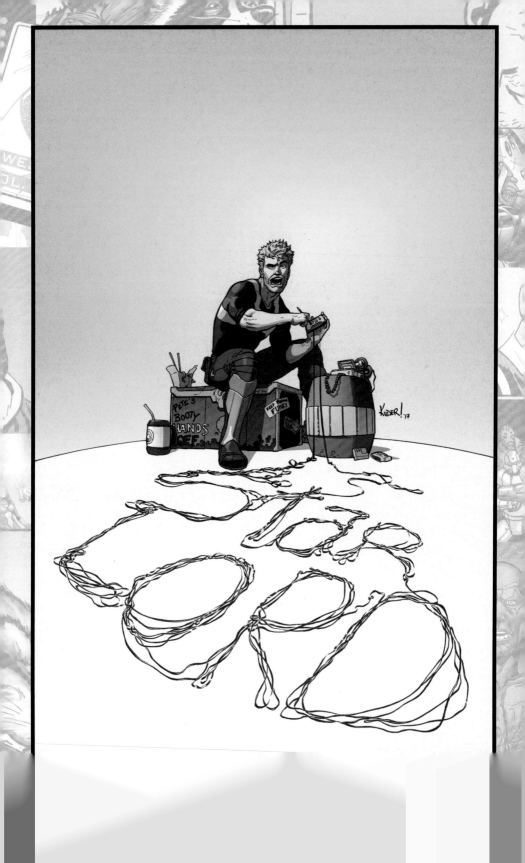

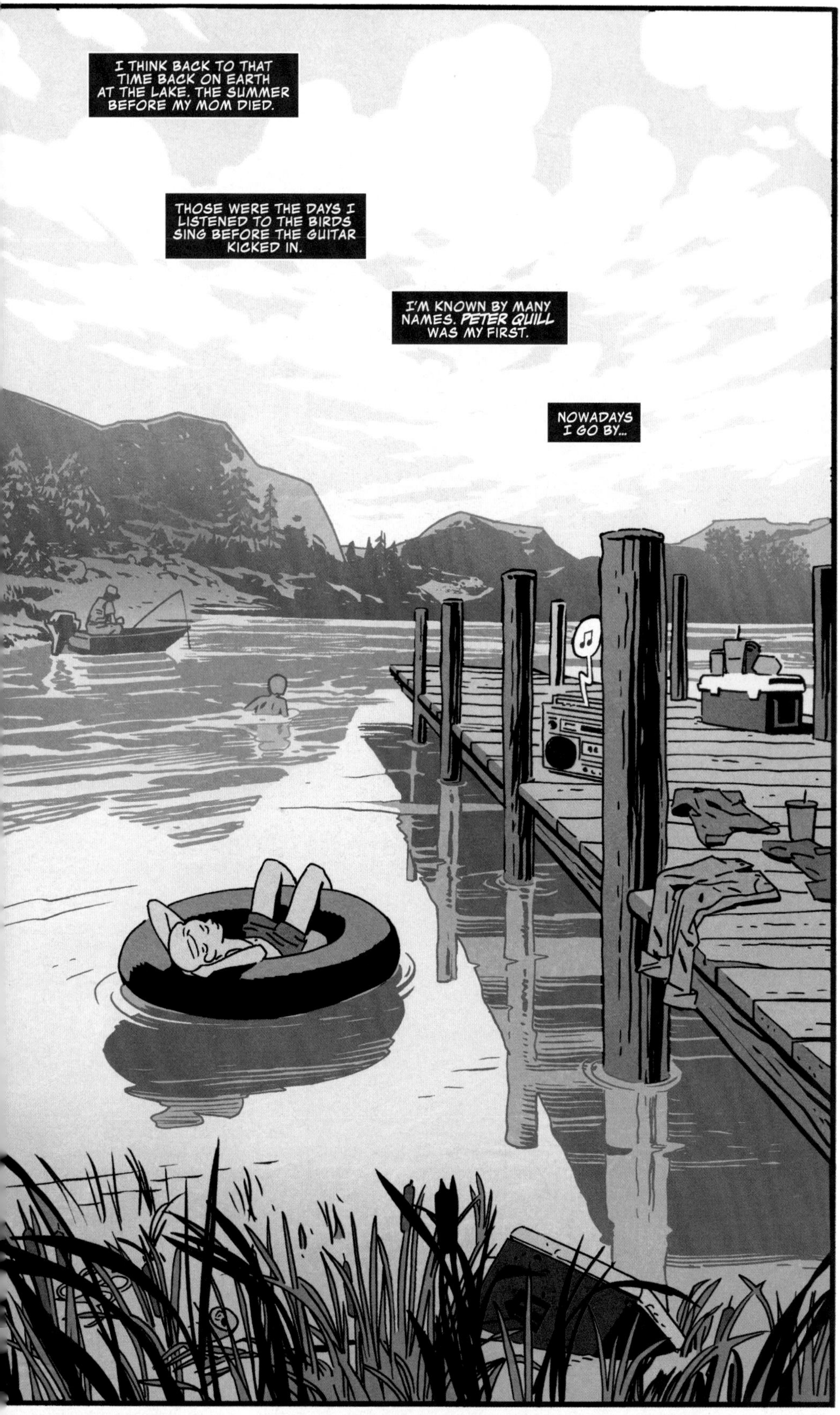
I THINK BACK TO THAT TIME BACK ON EARTH AT THE LAKE. THE SUMMER BEFORE MY MOM DIED.
THOSE WERE THE DAYS I LISTENED TO THE BIRDS SING BEFORE THE GUITAR KICKED IN.
I'M KNOWN BY MANY NAMES. PETER QUILL WAS MY FIRST.
NOWADAYS I GO BY...

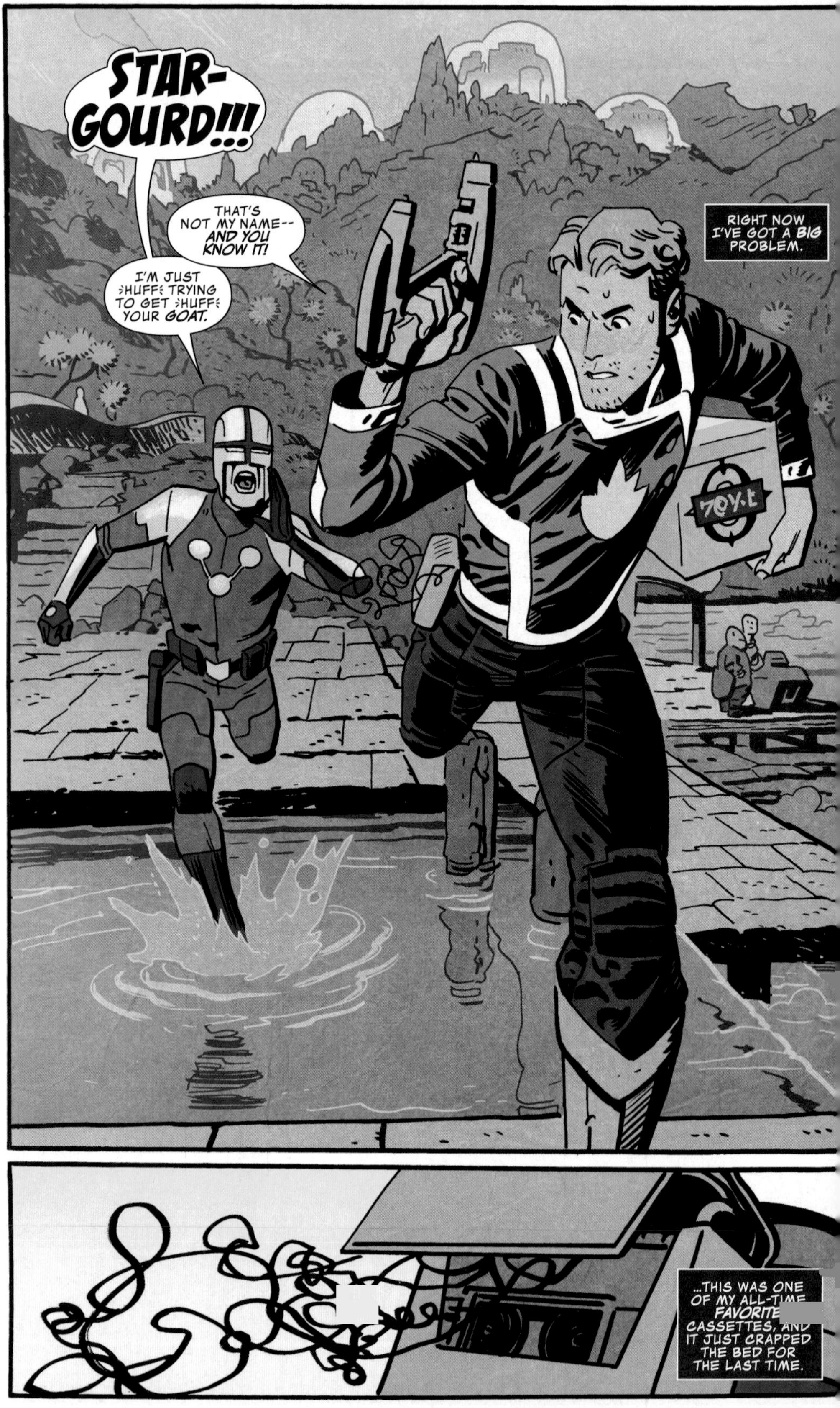
STAR-GOURD!!!
THAT'S NOT MY NAME-- AND YOU KNOW IT!
I'M JUST ≻HUFF≺ TRYING TO GET ≻HUFF≺ YOUR GOAT.
RIGHT NOW I'VE GOT A BIG PROBLEM.
...THIS WAS ONE OF MY ALL-TIME FAVORITE CASSETTES, AND IT JUST CRAPPED THE BED FOR THE LAST TIME.

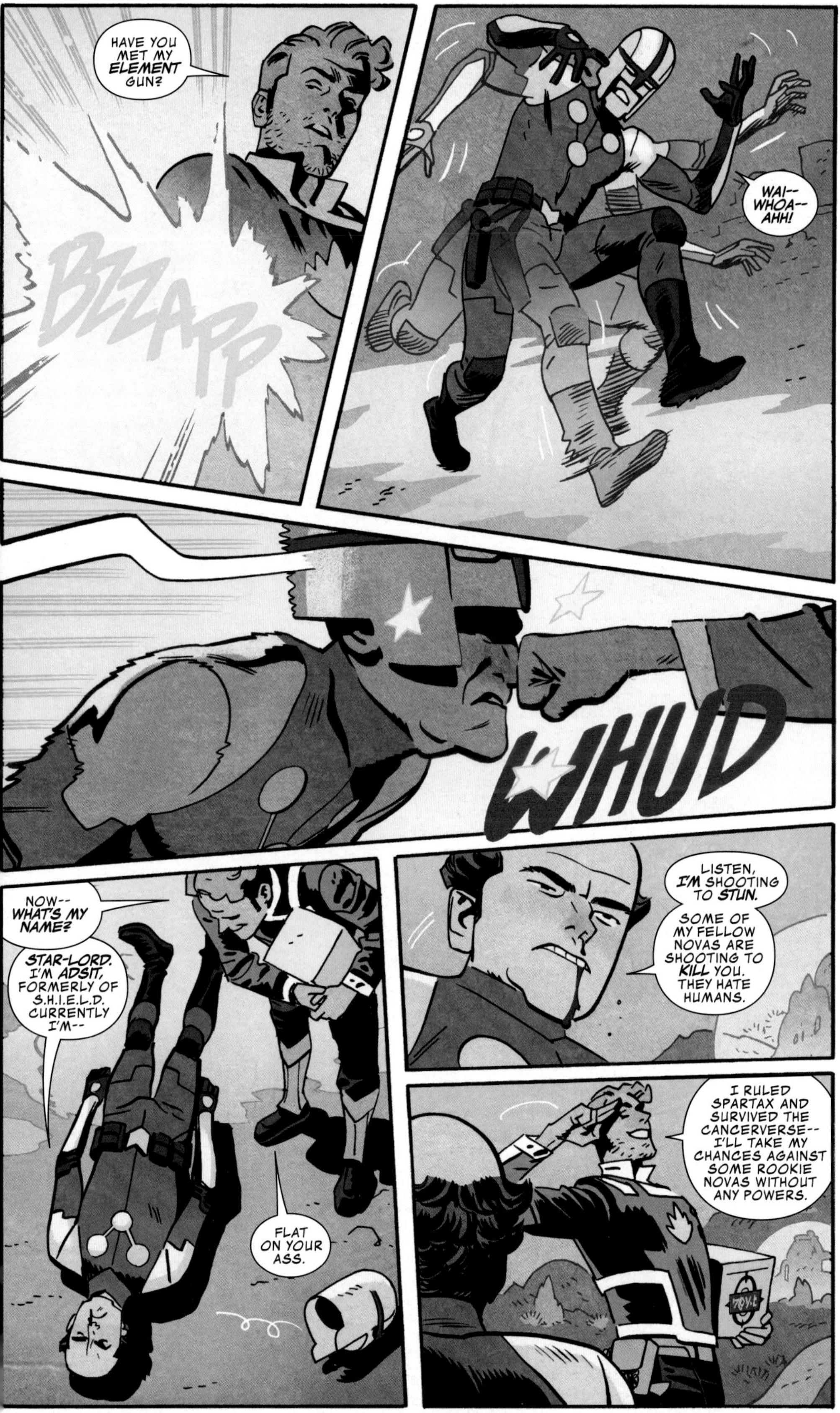
HAVE YOU MET MY ELEMENT GUN?
BZZAPP
WAI-- WHOA-- AHH!
WHUD
NOW-- WHAT'S MY NAME?
STAR-LORD. I'M ADSIT, FORMERLY OF S.H.I.E.L.D. CURRENTLY I'M--
FLAT ON YOUR ASS.
LISTEN, I'M SHOOTING TO STUN.
SOME OF MY FELLOW NOVAS ARE SHOOTING TO KILL YOU. THEY HATE HUMANS.
I RULED SPARTAX AND SURVIVED THE CANCERVERSE-- I'LL TAKE MY CHANCES AGAINST SOME ROOKIE NOVAS WITHOUT ANY POWERS.

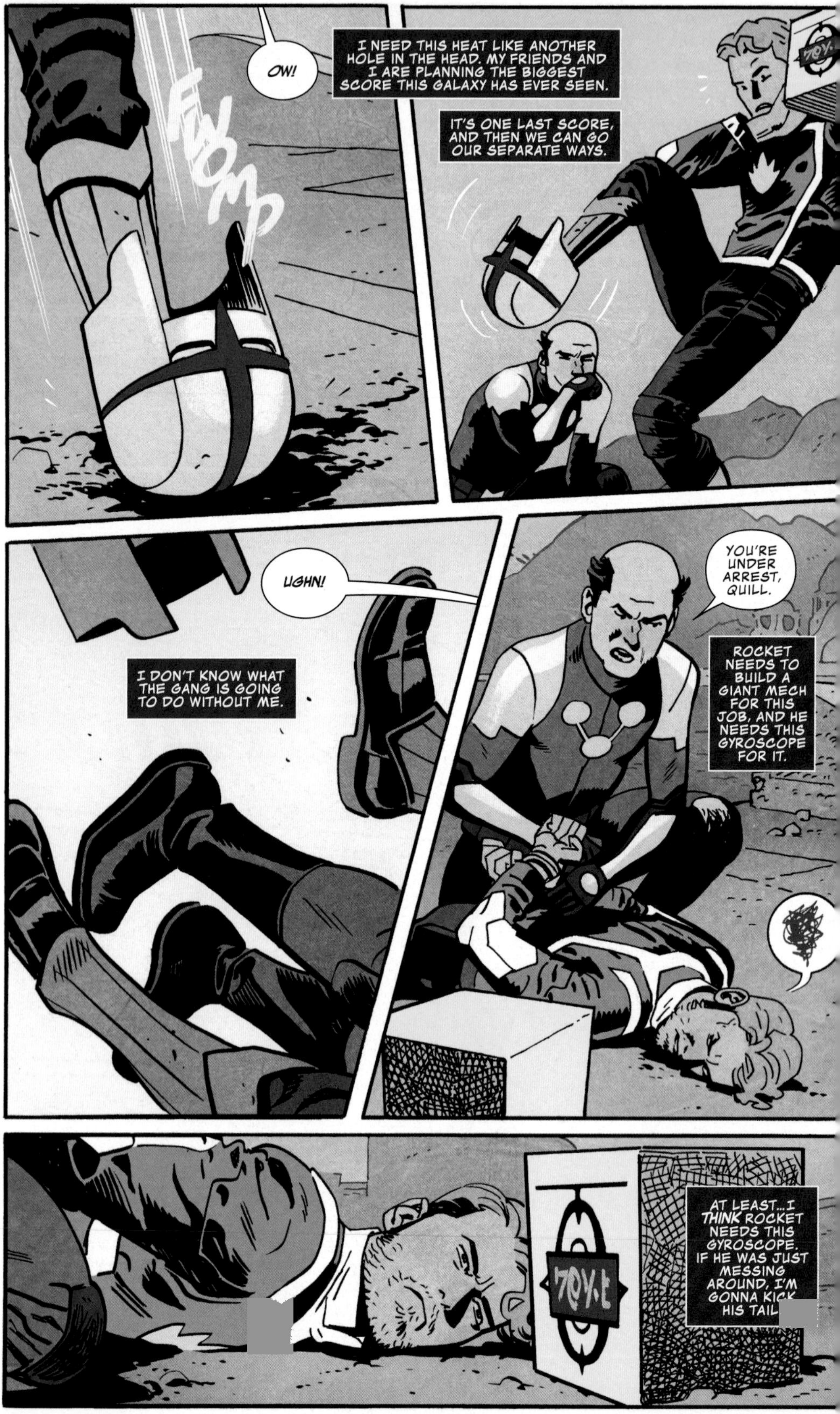
OW!
FWOMP
I NEED THIS HEAT LIKE ANOTHER HOLE IN THE HEAD. MY FRIENDS AND I ARE PLANNING THE BIGGEST SCORE THIS GALAXY HAS EVER SEEN.
IT'S ONE LAST SCORE, AND THEN WE CAN GO OUR SEPARATE WAYS.
UGHN!
I DON'T KNOW WHAT THE GANG IS GOING TO DO WITHOUT ME.
YOU'RE UNDER ARREST, QUILL.
ROCKET NEEDS TO BUILD A GIANT MECH FOR THIS JOB, AND HE NEEDS THIS GYROSCOPE FOR IT.
AT LEAST...I THINK ROCKET NEEDS THIS GYROSCOPE. IF HE WAS JUST MESSING AROUND, I'M GONNA KICK HIS TAIL.

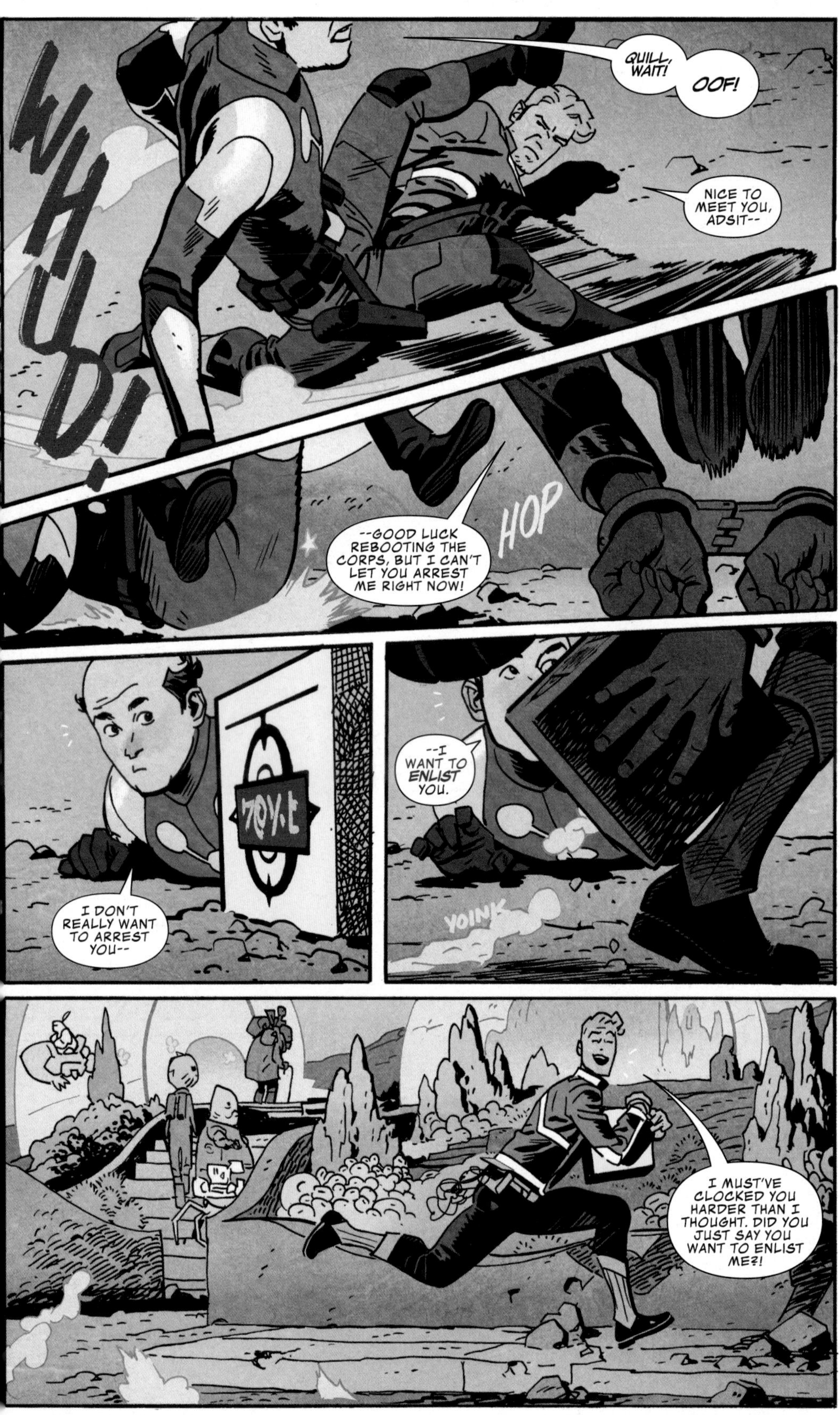
WHUD!
QUILL, WAIT!
OOF!
NICE TO MEET YOU, ADSIT--
HOP
--GOOD LUCK REBOOTING THE CORPS, BUT I CAN'T LET YOU ARREST ME RIGHT NOW!
I DON'T REALLY WANT TO ARREST YOU--
--I WANT TO ENLIST YOU.
YOINK
I MUST'VE CLOCKED YOU HARDER THAN I THOUGHT. DID YOU JUST SAY YOU WANT TO ENLIST ME?!

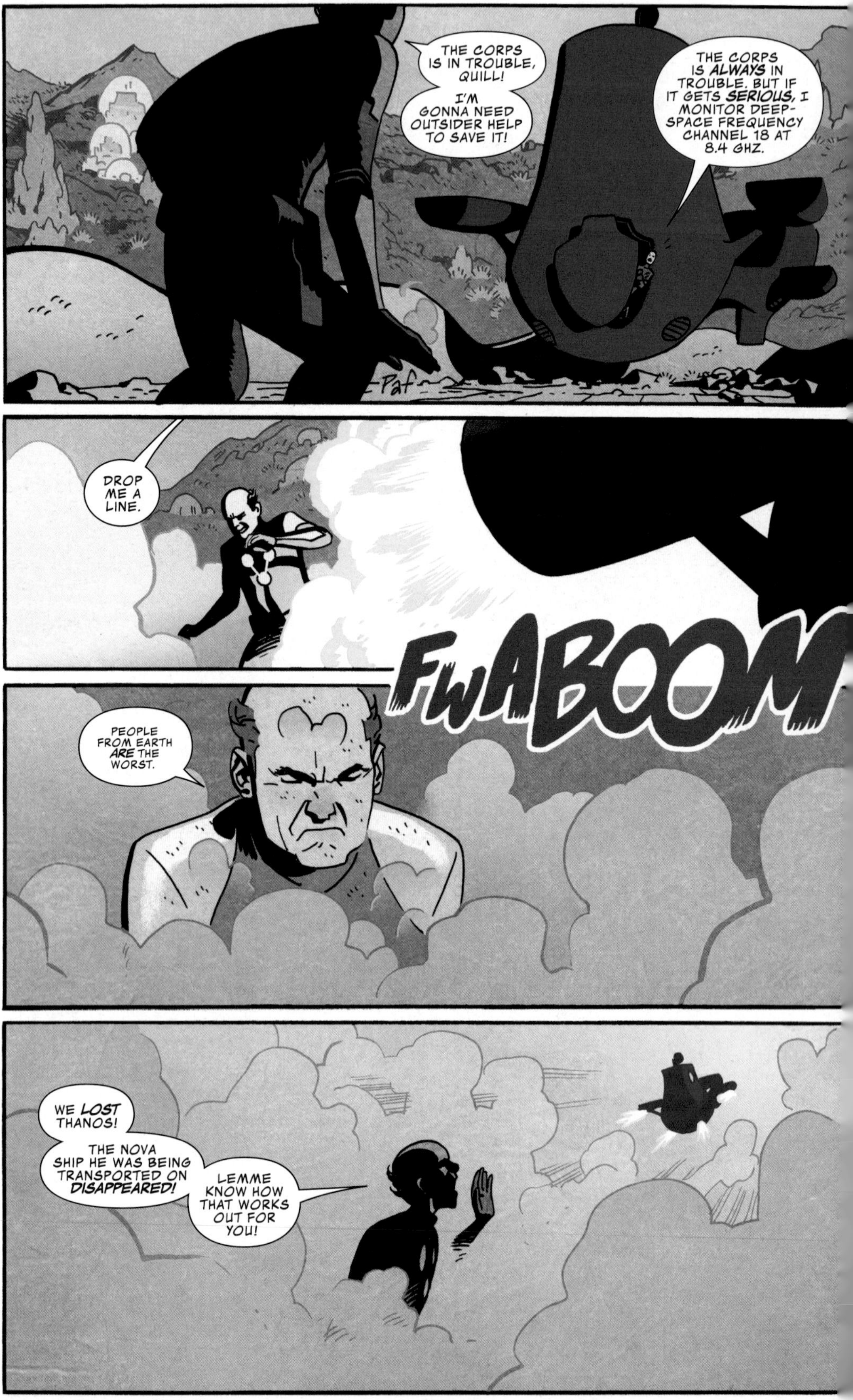
THE CORPS IS IN TROUBLE, QUILL!
I'M GONNA NEED OUTSIDER HELP TO SAVE IT!
THE CORPS IS ALWAYS IN TROUBLE. BUT IF IT GETS SERIOUS, I MONITOR DEEP-SPACE FREQUENCY CHANNEL 18 AT 8.4 GHZ.
DROP ME A LINE.
FWABOOM
PEOPLE FROM EARTH ARE THE WORST.
WE LOST THANOS!
THE NOVA SHIP HE WAS BEING TRANSPORTED ON DISAPPEARED!
LEMME KNOW HOW THAT WORKS OUT FOR YOU!

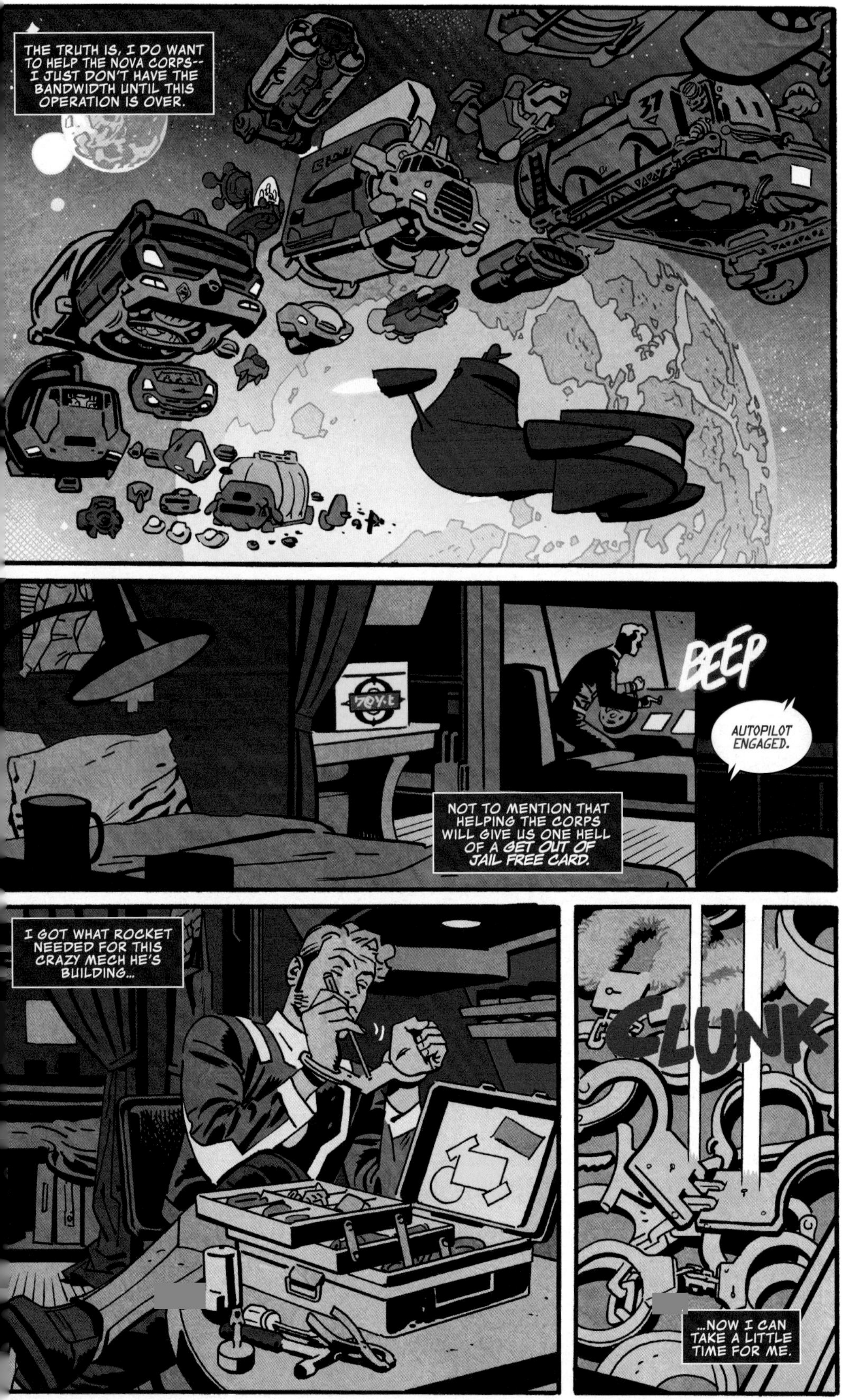
THE TRUTH IS, I DO WANT TO HELP THE NOVA CORPS--I JUST DON'T HAVE THE BANDWIDTH UNTIL THIS OPERATION IS OVER.
BEEP
AUTOPILOT ENGAGED.
NOT TO MENTION THAT HELPING THE CORPS WILL GIVE US ONE HELL OF A GET OUT OF JAIL FREE CARD.
I GOT WHAT ROCKET NEEDED FOR THIS CRAZY MECH HE'S BUILDING...
CLUNK
...NOW I CAN TAKE A LITTLE TIME FOR ME.

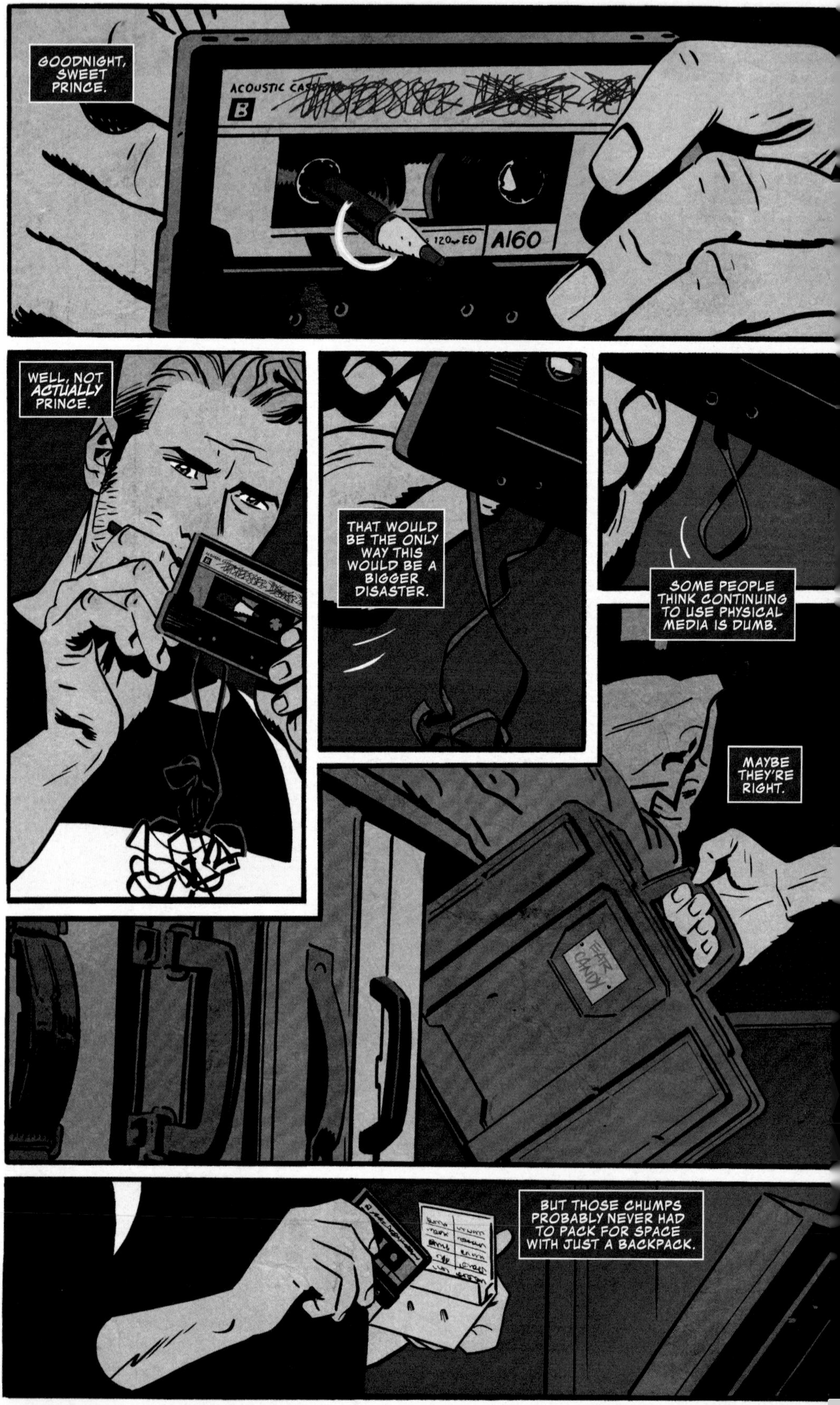
GOODNIGHT, SWEET PRINCE.
ACOUSTIC CA
B
A160
WELL, NOT ACTUALLY PRINCE.
THAT WOULD BE THE ONLY WAY THIS WOULD BE A BIGGER DISASTER.
SOME PEOPLE THINK CONTINUING TO USE PHYSICAL MEDIA IS DUMB.
MAYBE THEY'RE RIGHT.
EAT CANDY
BUT THOSE CHUMPS PROBABLY NEVER HAD TO PACK FOR SPACE WITH JUST A BACKPACK.

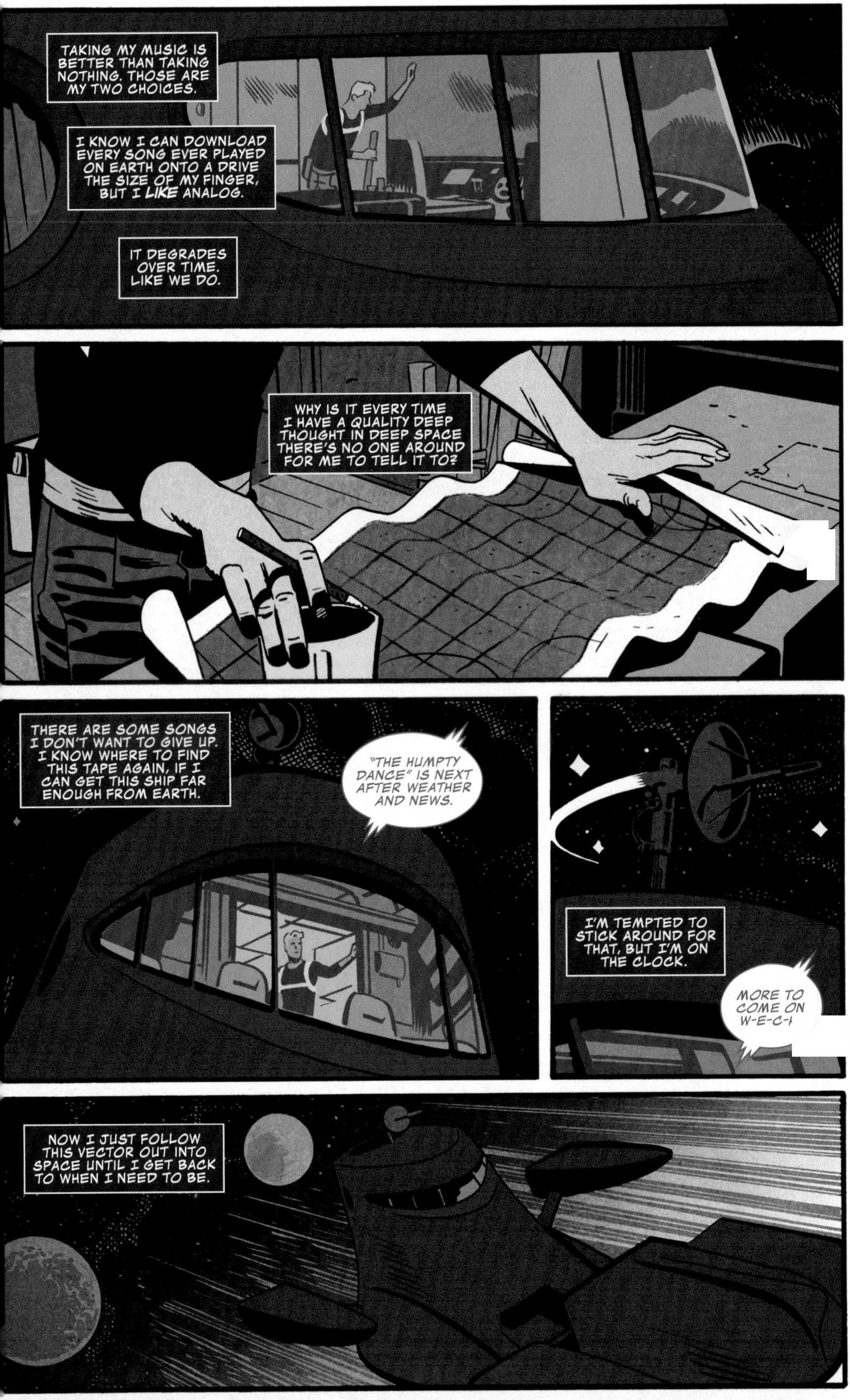
TAKING MY MUSIC IS BETTER THAN TAKING NOTHING. THOSE ARE MY TWO CHOICES.
I KNOW I CAN DOWNLOAD EVERY SONG EVER PLAYED ON EARTH ONTO A DRIVE THE SIZE OF MY FINGER, BUT I LIKE ANALOG.
IT DEGRADES OVER TIME. LIKE WE DO.
WHY IS IT EVERY TIME I HAVE A QUALITY DEEP THOUGHT IN DEEP SPACE THERE'S NO ONE AROUND FOR ME TO TELL IT TO?
THERE ARE SOME SONGS I DON'T WANT TO GIVE UP. I KNOW WHERE TO FIND THIS TAPE AGAIN, IF I CAN GET THIS SHIP FAR ENOUGH FROM EARTH.
"THE HUMPTY DANCE" IS NEXT AFTER WEATHER AND NEWS.
I'M TEMPTED TO STICK AROUND FOR THAT, BUT I'M ON THE CLOCK.
MORE TO COME ON
NOW I JUST FOLLOW THIS VECTOR OUT INTO SPACE UNTIL I GET BACK TO WHEN I NEED TO BE.

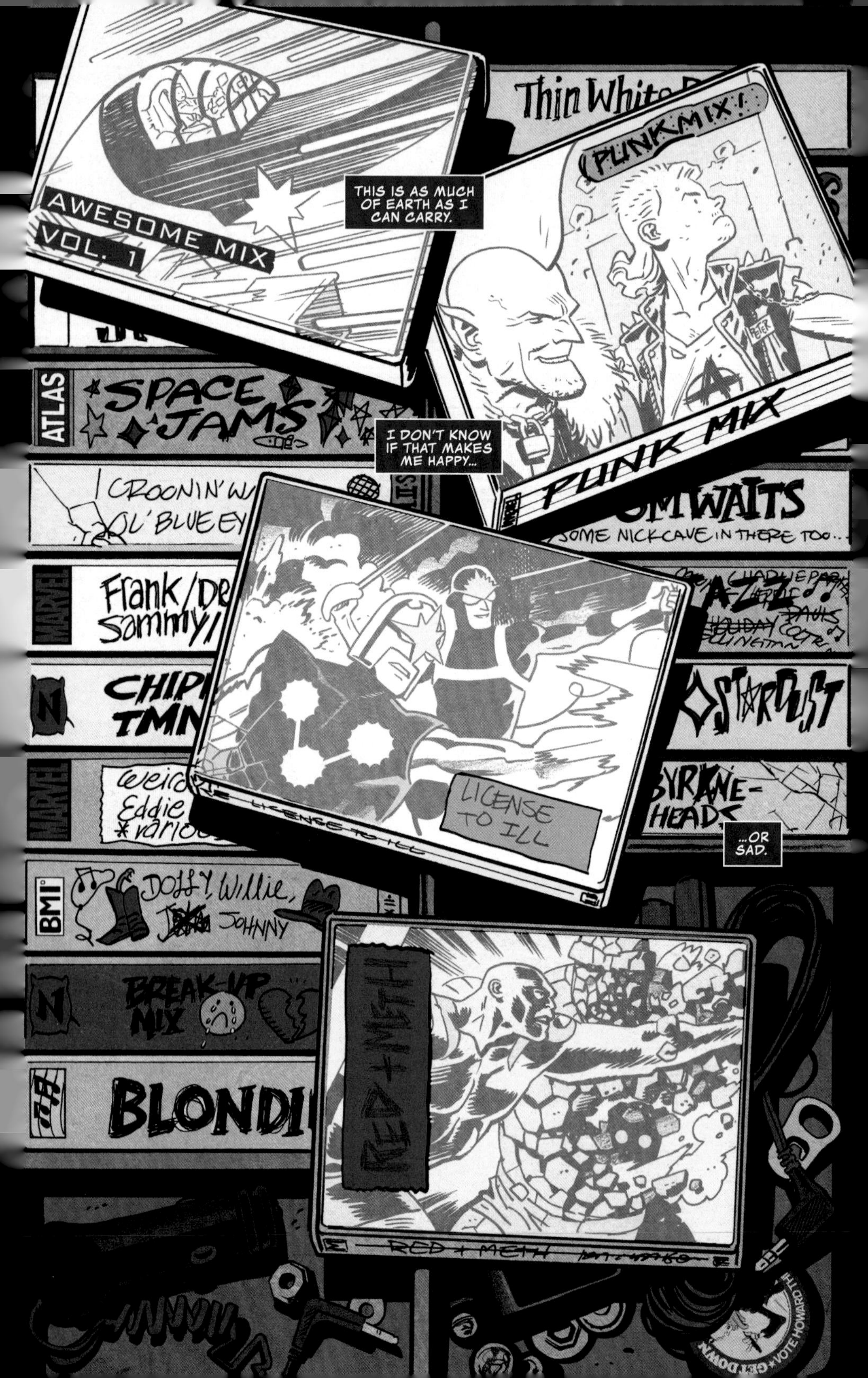
THIS IS AS MUCH OF EARTH AS I CAN CARRY.
I DON'T KNOW IF THAT MAKES ME HAPPY...
...OR SAD.
AWESOME MIX VOL. 1
PUNK MIX!
PUNK MIX
Thin White
SPACE JAMS
ATLAS
CROONIN' W/ OL' BLUE EY
TOM WAITS
SOME NICK CAVE IN THERE TOO...
Frank/De Sammy/
CHIP TMN
STARDUST
LICENSE TO ILL
BYRNE-HEADS
DOLLY, Willie, JOHNNY
BMI
BREAK-UP MIX
BLONDI
RED + METH
VOTE HOWARD TH

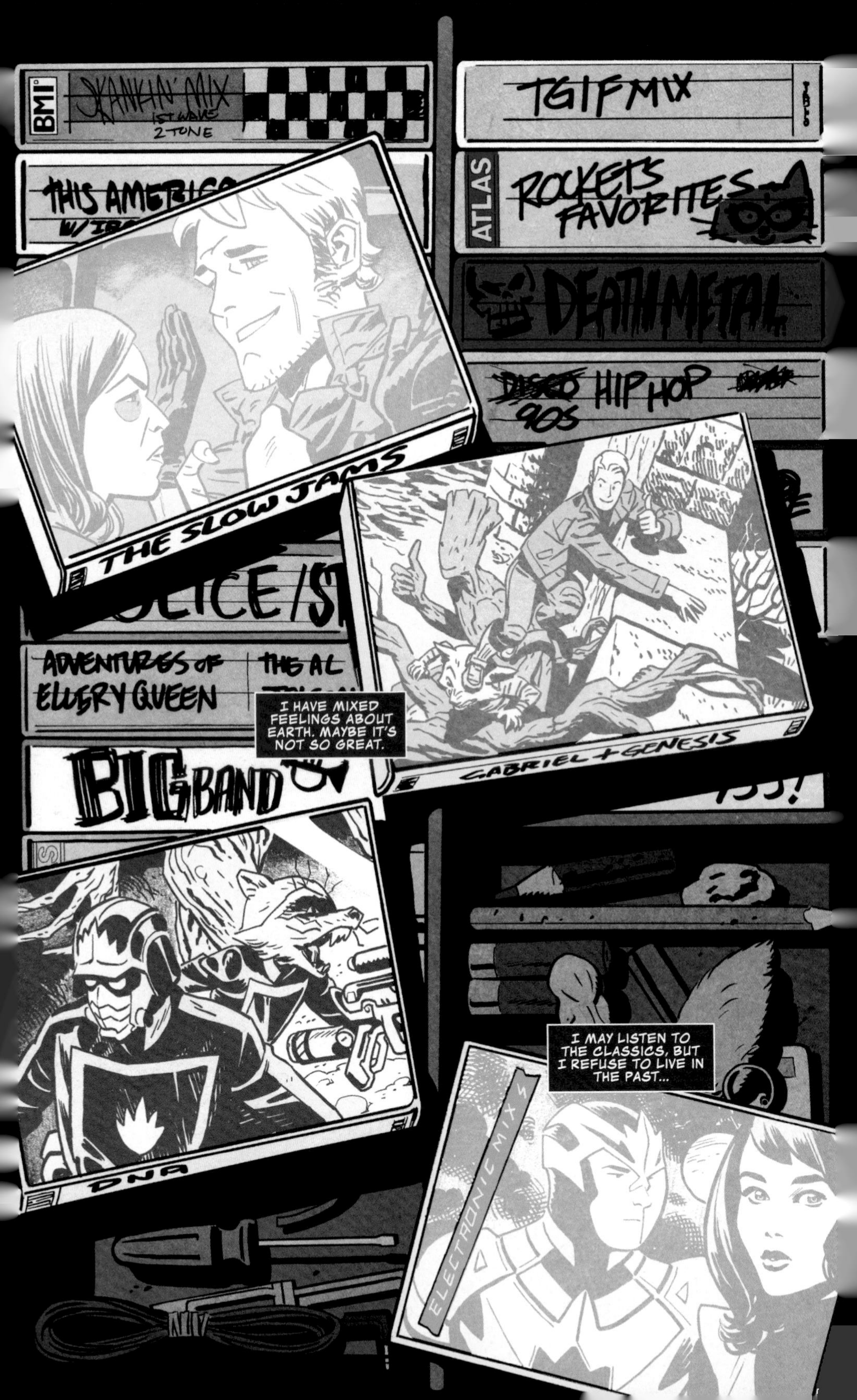
SKANKIN' MIX
1ST WAVE
2 TONE
TGIF MIX
ATLAS
ROCKET'S FAVORITES
DEATH METAL
HIP HOP
90S
THE SLOW JAMS
ADVENTURES OF ELLERY QUEEN
I HAVE MIXED FEELINGS ABOUT EARTH. MAYBE IT'S NOT SO GREAT.
GABRIEL + GENESIS
BIG BAND
DNA
I MAY LISTEN TO THE CLASSICS, BUT I REFUSE TO LIVE IN THE PAST...
ELECTRONIC MIX 5

...EVEN THOUGH I'M BASICALLY TIME-TRAVELING.
SAY WHAT YOU WILL ABOUT THAT VIOLENT MUD BALL I WAS BORN ON, BUT--THE MUSIC IS UNQUESTIONABLY *THE BEST.*
FOR OVER A CENTURY EARTH HAS PUMPED OUT RADIO AND TV SIGNALS. IF YOU POINT YOUR ANTENNA BACK TO OUR PLANET, YOU'LL VENTUALLY HEAR WHAT OU'RE LOOKING FOR.
YOU JUST HAVE TO CATCH UP TO THE WAVE YOU'RE LOOKING FOR.
THE ONLY TRICK TO AUDIO SURFING IS AVOIDING BLACK HOLES AND NEBULAE AND ANYTHING ELSE THAT WILL BLOCK TRANSMISSIONS.

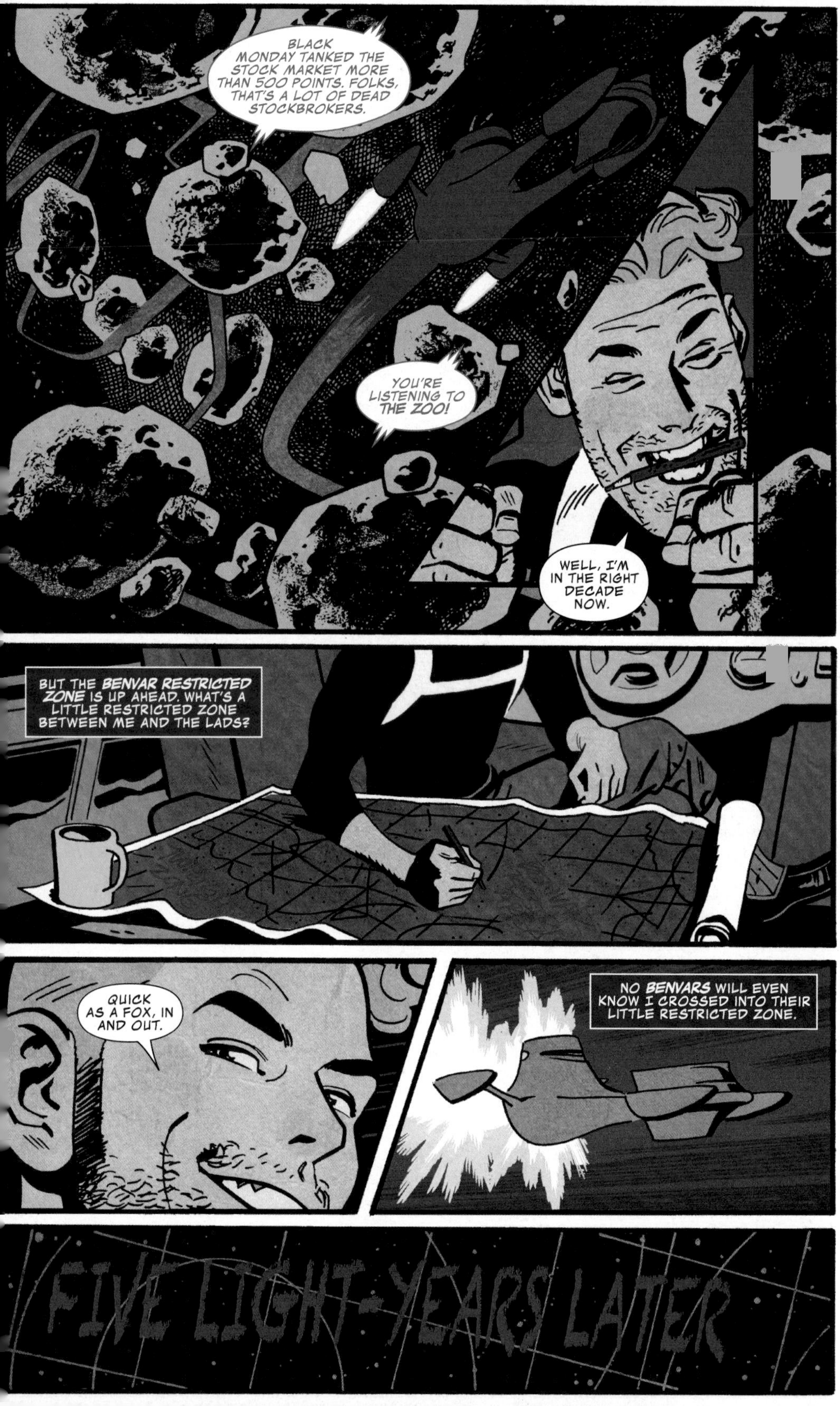
BLACK MONDAY TANKED THE STOCK MARKET MORE THAN 500 POINTS. FOLKS, THAT'S A LOT OF DEAD STOCKBROKERS.
YOU'RE LISTENING TO THE ZOO!
WELL, I'M IN THE RIGHT DECADE NOW.
BUT THE BENVAR RESTRICTED ZONE IS UP AHEAD. WHAT'S A LITTLE RESTRICTED ZONE BETWEEN ME AND THE LADS?
QUICK AS A FOX, IN AND OUT.
NO BENVARS WILL EVEN KNOW I CROSSED INTO THEIR LITTLE RESTRICTED ZONE.
FIVE LIGHT-YEARS LATER

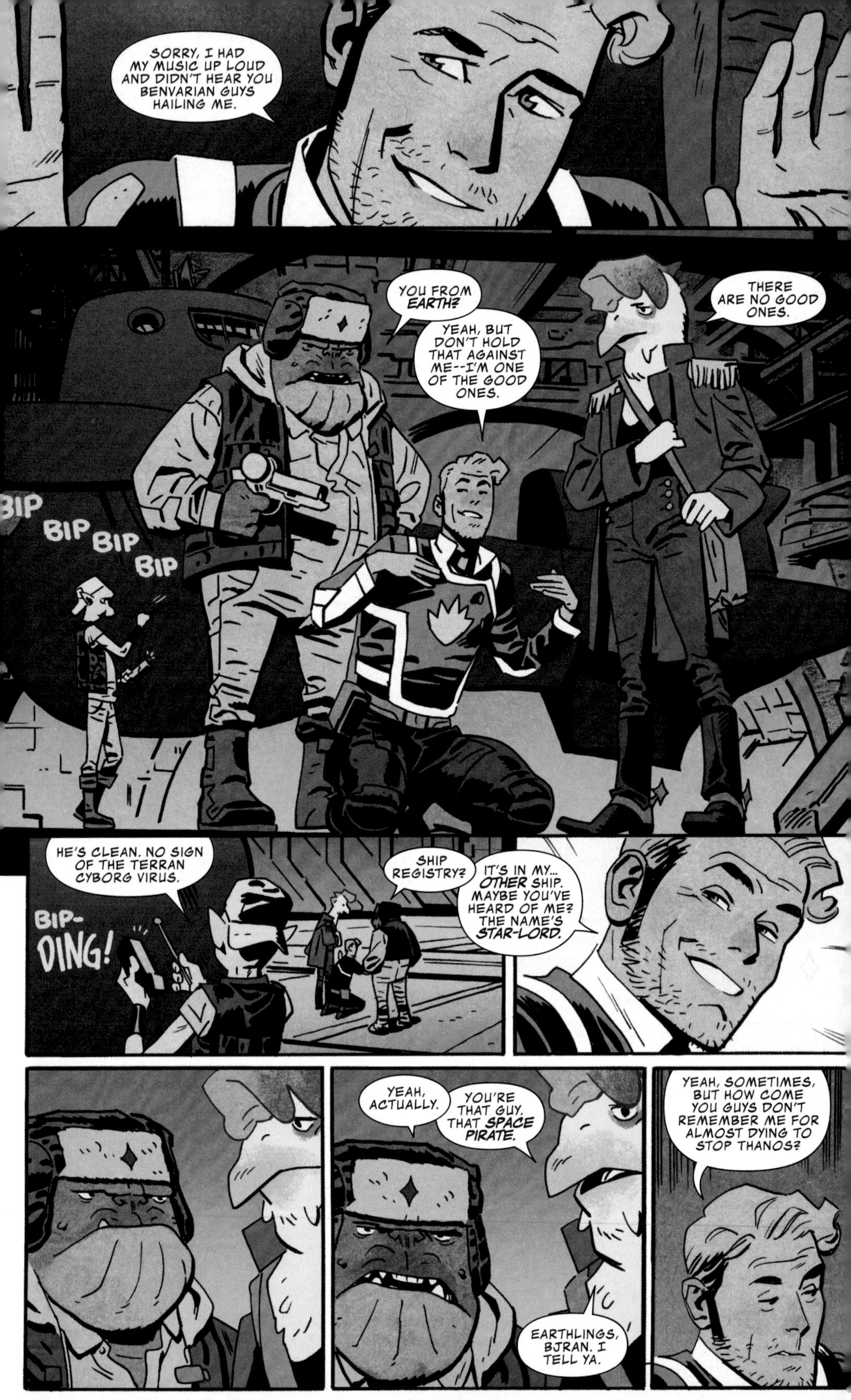

SORRY, I HAD MY MUSIC UP LOUD AND DIDN'T HEAR YOU BENVARIAN GUYS HAILING ME.
YOU FROM EARTH?
YEAH, BUT DON'T HOLD THAT AGAINST ME--I'M ONE OF THE GOOD ONES.
THERE ARE NO GOOD ONES.
BIP BIP BIP BIP
HE'S CLEAN. NO SIGN OF THE TERRAN CYBORG VIRUS.
BIP-DING!
SHIP REGISTRY?
IT'S IN MY... OTHER SHIP. MAYBE YOU'VE HEARD OF ME? THE NAME'S STAR-LORD.
YEAH, ACTUALLY.
YOU'RE THAT GUY. THAT SPACE PIRATE.
EARTHLINGS, BJRAN. I TELL YA.
YEAH, SOMETIMES, BUT HOW COME YOU GUYS DON'T REMEMBER ME FOR ALMOST DYING TO STOP THANOS?

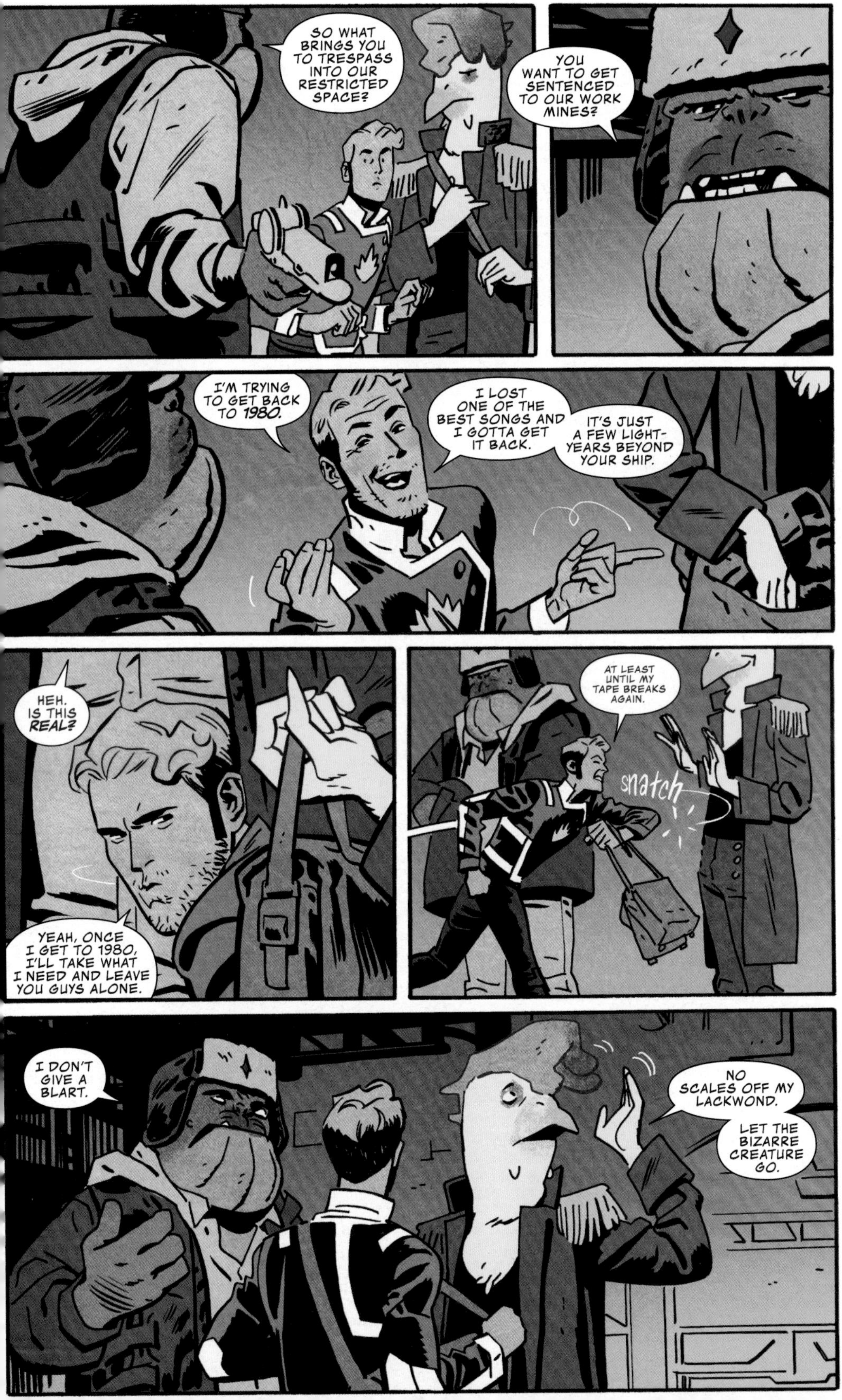
SO WHAT BRINGS YOU TO TRESPASS INTO OUR RESTRICTED SPACE?
YOU WANT TO GET SENTENCED TO OUR WORK MINES?
I'M TRYING TO GET BACK TO *1980*.
I LOST ONE OF THE BEST SONGS AND I GOTTA GET IT BACK.
IT'S JUST A FEW LIGHT-YEARS BEYOND YOUR SHIP.
HEH. IS THIS *REAL?*
YEAH, ONCE I GET TO 1980, I'LL TAKE WHAT I NEED AND LEAVE YOU GUYS ALONE.
AT LEAST UNTIL MY TAPE BREAKS AGAIN.
snatch
I DON'T GIVE A BLART.
NO SCALES OFF MY LACKWOND.
LET THE BIZARRE CREATURE GO.

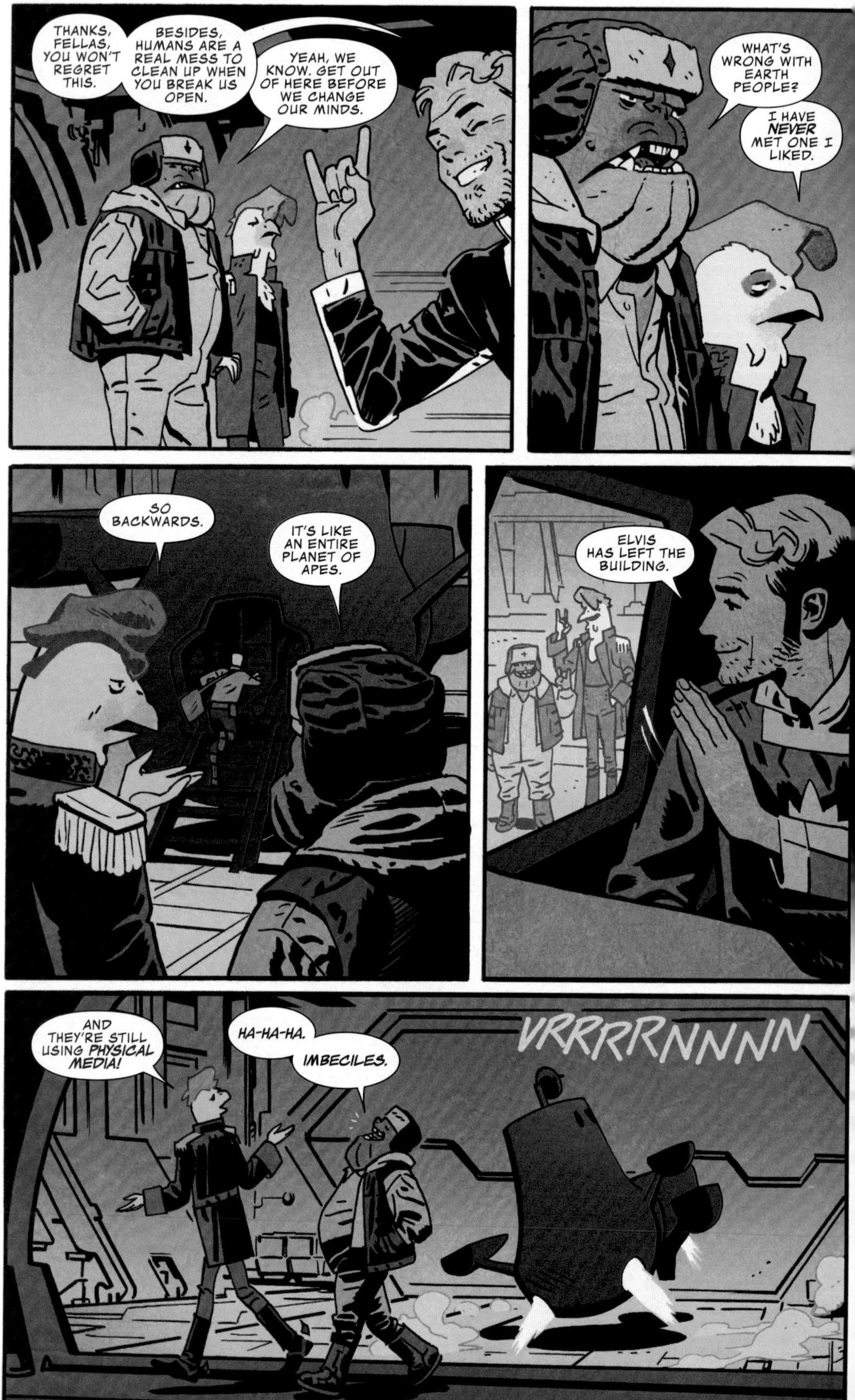
THANKS, FELLAS, YOU WON'T REGRET THIS.
BESIDES, HUMANS ARE A REAL MESS TO CLEAN UP WHEN YOU BREAK US OPEN.
YEAH, WE KNOW. GET OUT OF HERE BEFORE WE CHANGE OUR MINDS.
WHAT'S WRONG WITH EARTH PEOPLE?
I HAVE NEVER MET ONE I LIKED.
SO BACKWARDS.
IT'S LIKE AN ENTIRE PLANET OF APES.
ELVIS HAS LEFT THE BUILDING.
AND THEY'RE STILL USING PHYSICAL MEDIA!
HA-HA-HA.
IMBECILES.
VRRRRNNNNN

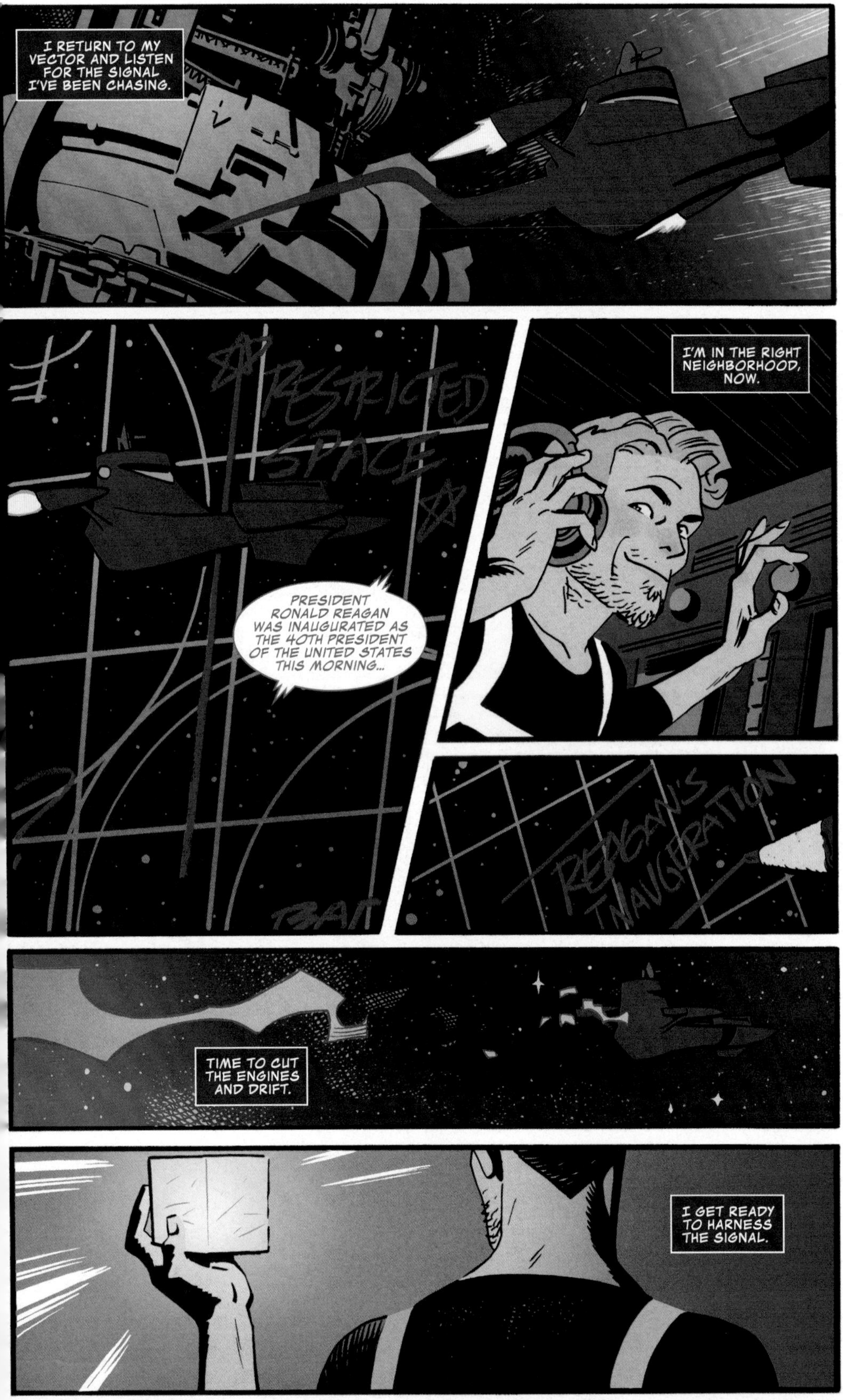
I RETURN TO MY VECTOR AND LISTEN FOR THE SIGNAL I'VE BEEN CHASING.
RESTRICTED SPACE
I'M IN THE RIGHT NEIGHBORHOOD, NOW.
PRESIDENT RONALD REAGAN WAS INAUGURATED AS THE 40TH PRESIDENT OF THE UNITED STATES THIS MORNING...
REAGAN'S INAUGURATION
TIME TO CUT THE ENGINES AND DRIFT.
I GET READY TO HARNESS THE SIGNAL.

JUST A COUPLE OF LIGHT-YEARS OUT.

SHRPPt

GOTTA BE READY.

ATLAS

AUDIO CASSETTE

NORMAL BIAS
UR

SUPER SIZE

KLAKT

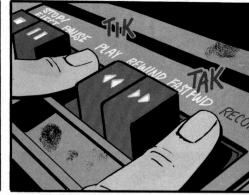

STOP/PAUSE
PLAY REWIND FASTFWD RECO

TIIK

TAK

TZZT

LUNA

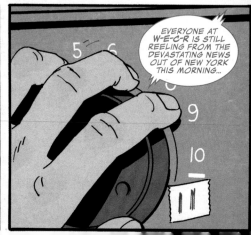

EVERYONE AT W-E-C-R IS STILL REELING FROM THE DEVASTATING NEWS OUT OF NEW YORK THIS MORNING...

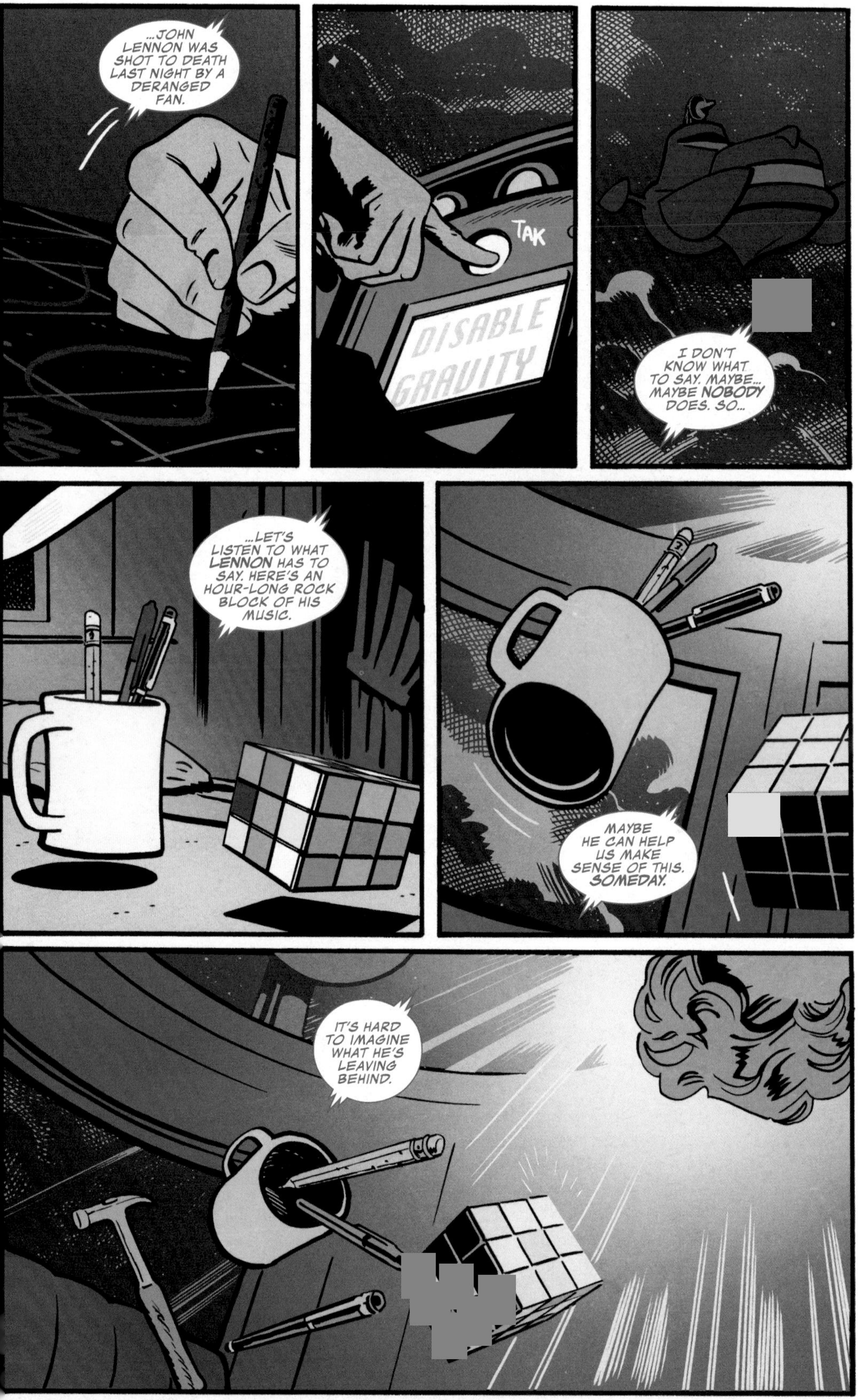
...JOHN LENNON WAS SHOT TO DEATH LAST NIGHT BY A DERANGED FAN.
TAK
DISABLE GRAVITY
I DON'T KNOW WHAT TO SAY. MAYBE... MAYBE NOBODY DOES. SO...
...LET'S LISTEN TO WHAT LENNON HAS TO SAY. HERE'S AN HOUR-LONG ROCK BLOCK OF HIS MUSIC.
MAYBE HE CAN HELP US MAKE SENSE OF THIS. SOMEDAY.
IT'S HARD TO IMAGINE WHAT HE'S LEAVING BEHIND.

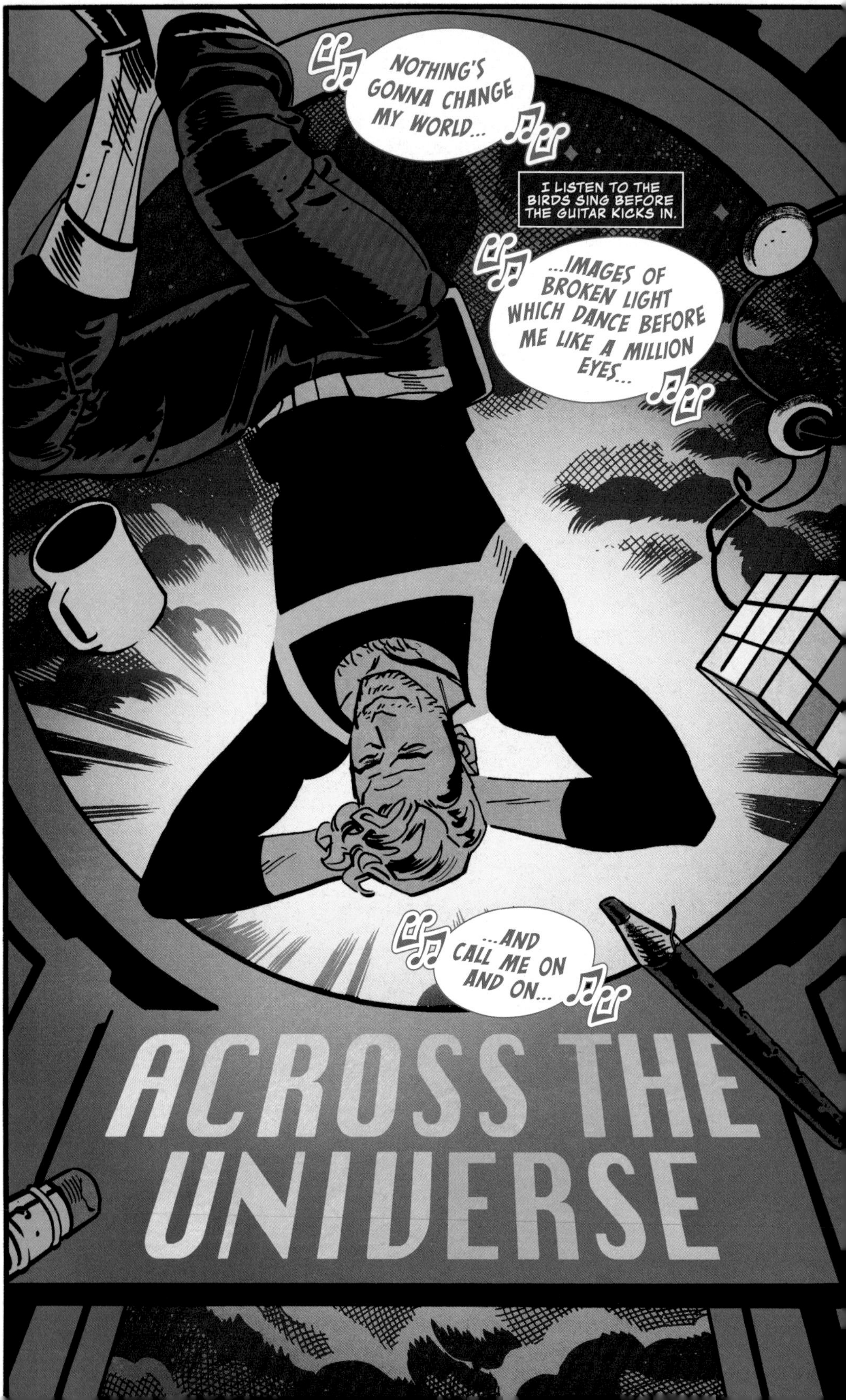
NOTHING'S GONNA CHANGE MY WORLD...
I LISTEN TO THE BIRDS SING BEFORE THE GUITAR KICKS IN.
...IMAGES OF BROKEN LIGHT WHICH DANCE BEFORE ME LIKE A MILLION EYES...
...AND CALL ME ON AND ON...
ACROSS THE UNIVERSE

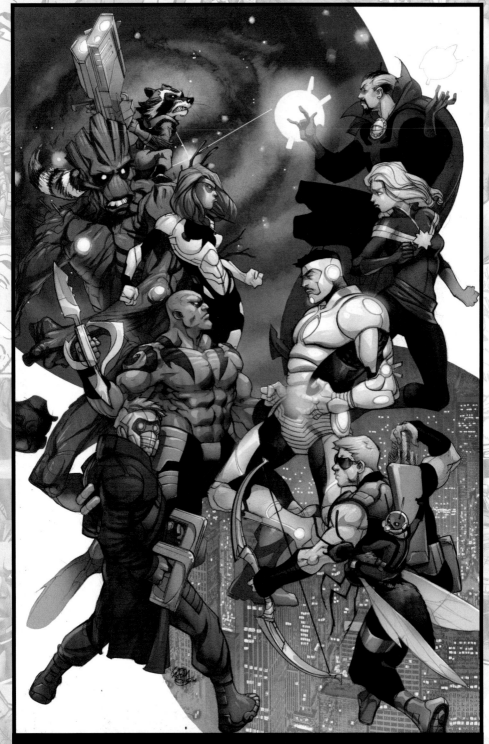

GUARDIANS TEAM-UP #1

VARIANT BY PASQUAL FERRY

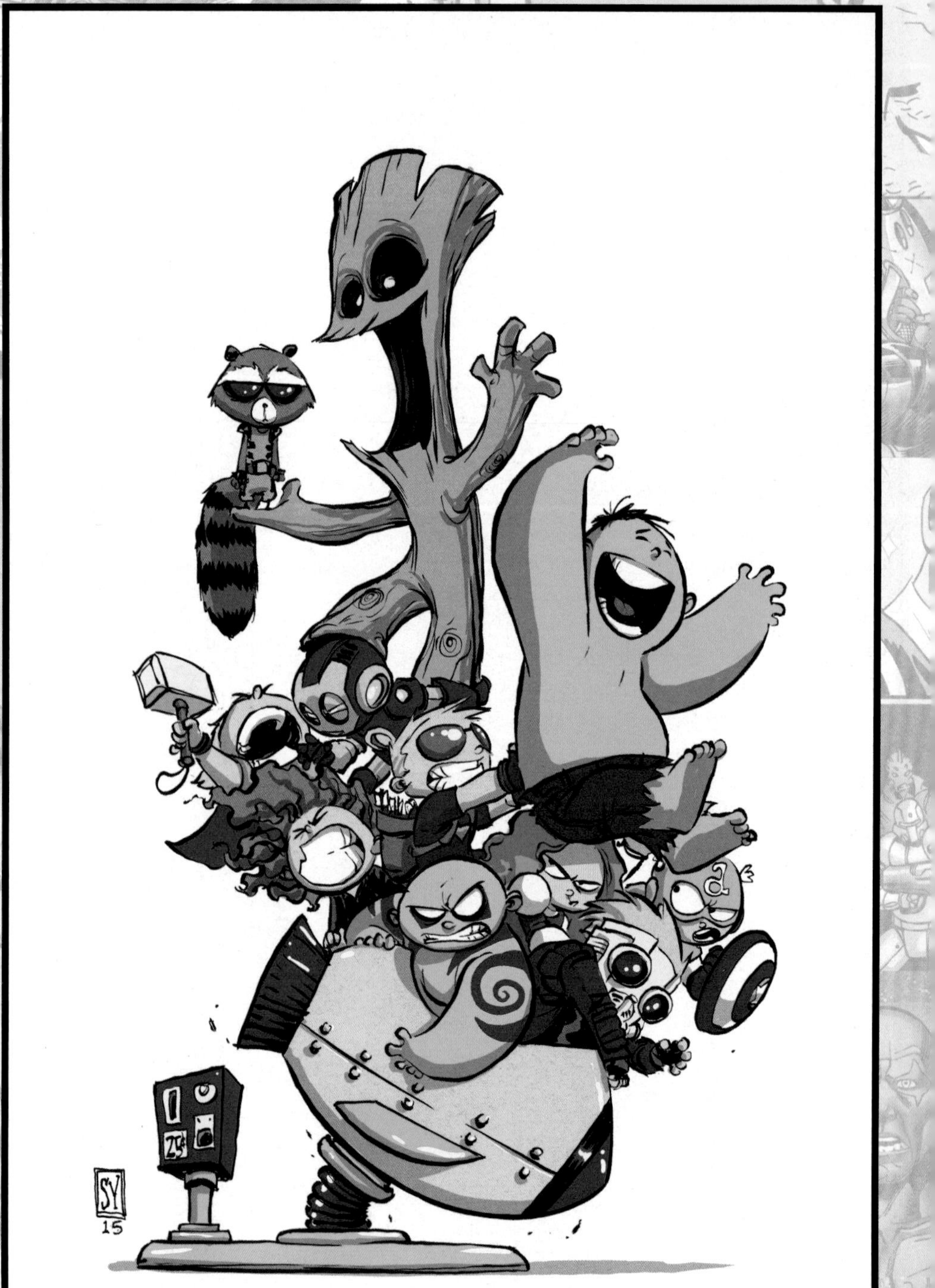
SY
15

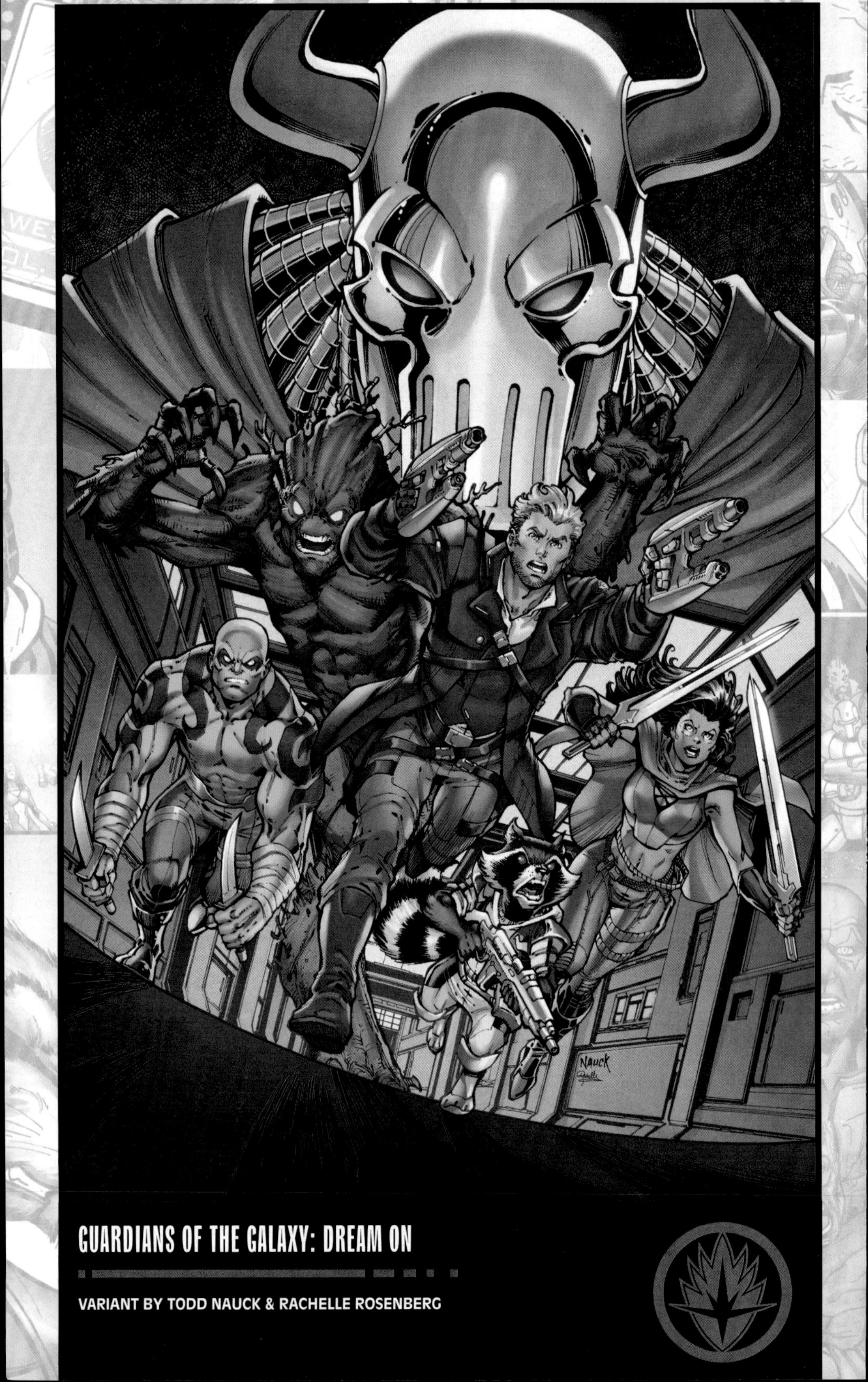
NAUCK

GUARDIANS OF THE GALAXY: DREAM ON

VARIANT BY TODD NAUCK & RACHELLE ROSENBERG

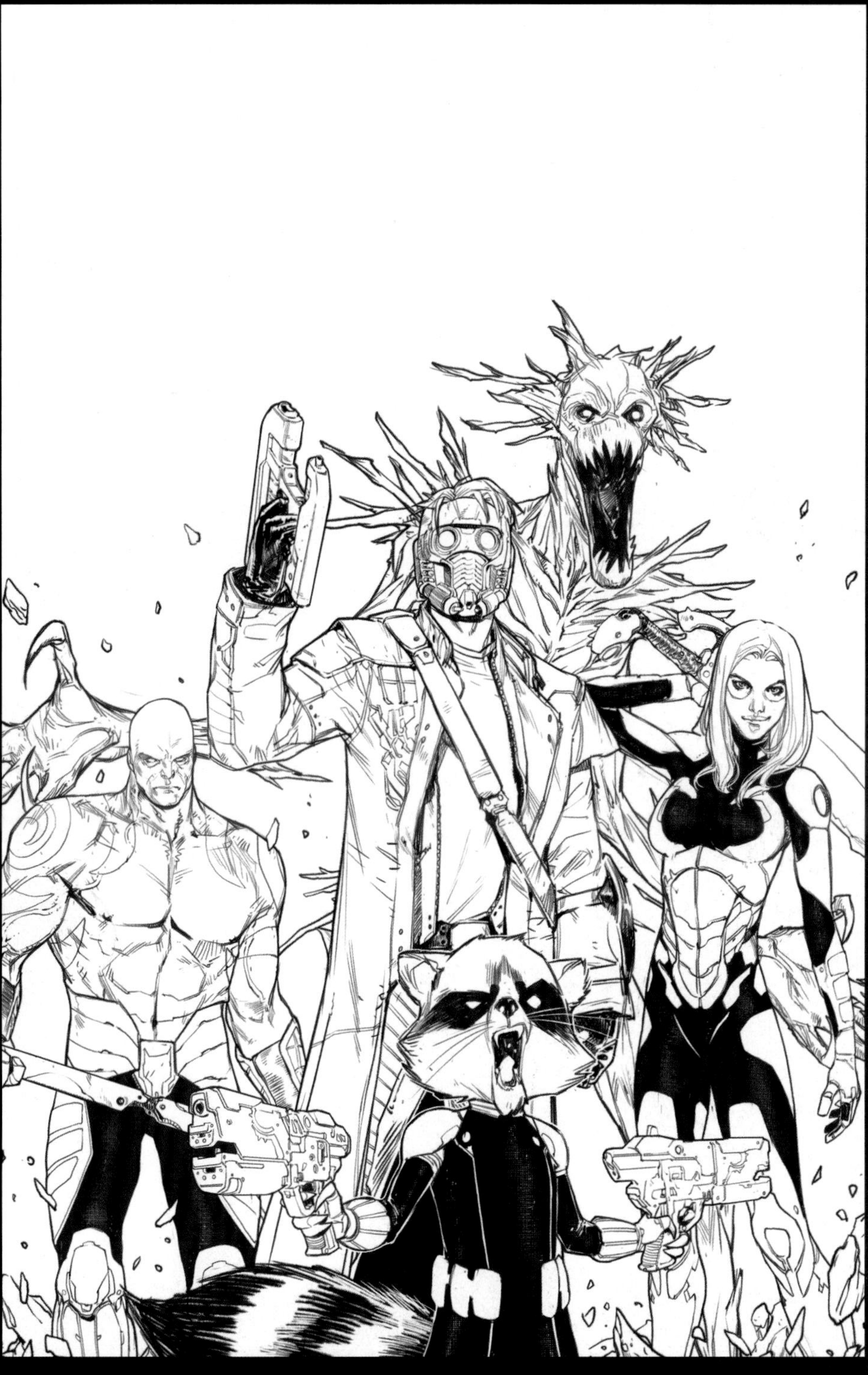

GUARDIANS OF THE GALAXY: GALAXY'S MOST WANTED

SKETCH VARIANT BY SARA PICHELLI

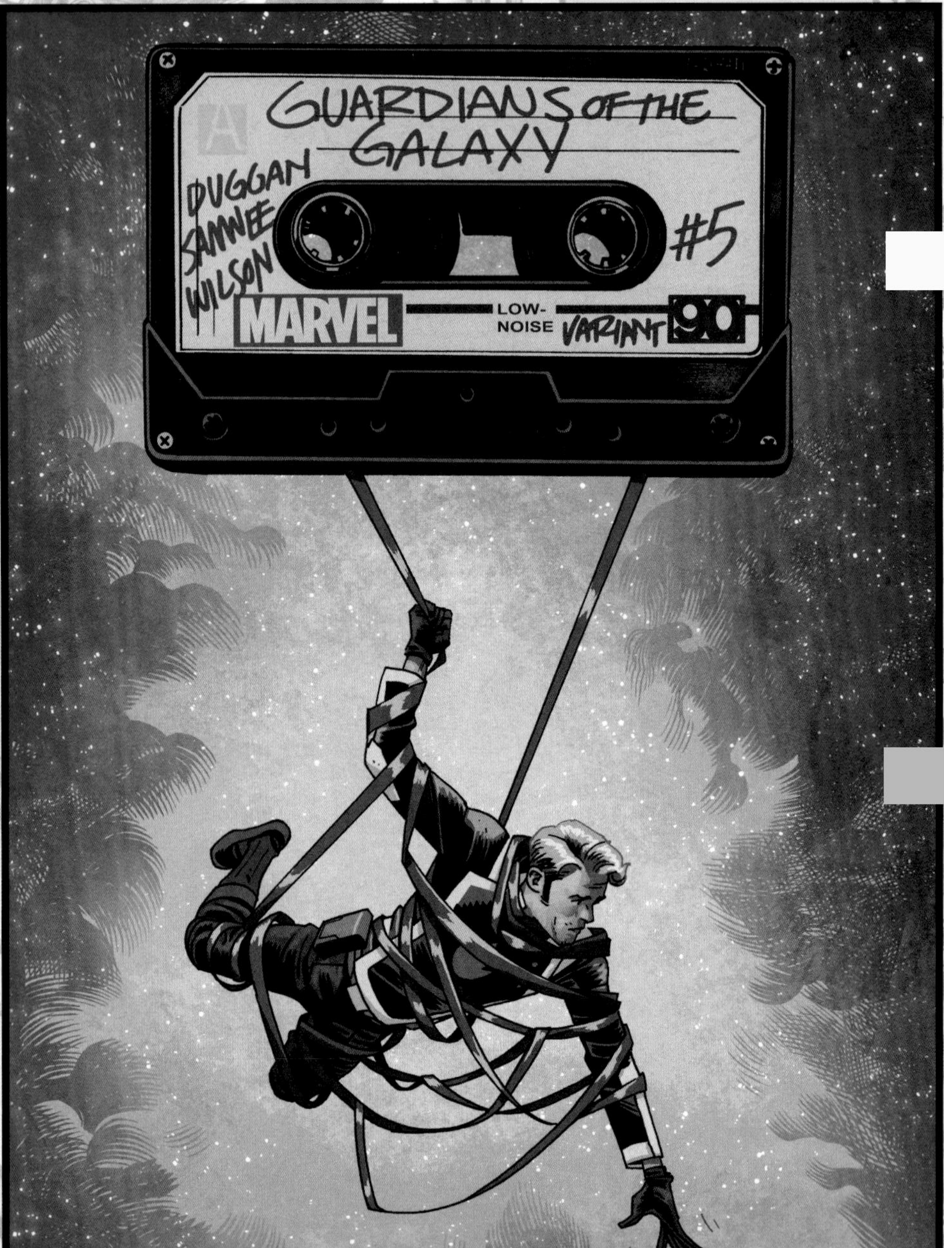
GUARDIANS OF THE GALAXY
DUGGAN
SAMNEE
WILSON
#5
MARVEL
LOW-NOISE
VARIANT
90
SAMNEE '17
MW

ALL-NEW GUARDIANS OF THE GALAXY #5

VARIANT BY CHRIS SAMNEE & MATTHEW WILSON